Fate Will Bring You Home

DANIELLE LYNN

Fate will bring you Home

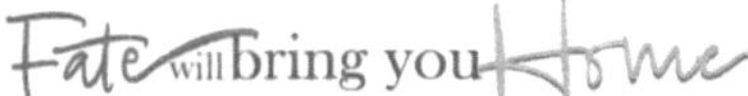

Cover Design - K.B. Barrett Designs
Formatting - DJ Krimmer
Editing- E.F. Watson
ISBN: 979-8-9894147-0-3 (Paperback)
979-8-9894147-1-0 (e-book)
www.Daniellelynnwrites.com

Content Warnings

Anxiety/Panic Attacks
Sexually Explicit Content
Talk of Sexual Assault (Side character in the past)
Talk of Child Abuse (Lightly talked about in the past tense)
Drug use (Lightly talked about in the past tense)
Talk of cancer in the past.

Dedication

To all the people who are finding themselves again through their love of reading and writing. I see you. You got this. This one is for you.

Playlist

Here are some songs that I listened to while writing this book.
They either stuck out or inspired me.
(NO particular order but I would love to hear which songs you
thought inspired what parts.)

Check it out on Spotify.

https://open.spotify.com/playlist/0oYy4QJriGpUDjYuwjpjXp?
si=LvPoTQfGTgatpaZy83ne_w&pi=u-e45PDJWuT7-P

Like My Father- Jax
P. G. N. L.- Conor Maynard
Medicine- James Arthur
Avalanche- James Arthur
This City- Sam Fischer
Just friends- Tim Gallager
Someone You Loved- Lewis Capaldi
Before You Go- Lewis Capaldi
Don't Give Up On Me- Amber Leigh Irish
Empty Space- James Arthur

It's You- Ali Gatie
Blames On Me- Alexander Stewart
You Proof- Morgan Wallen
Amnesia- Camylio
Let Em GO- Matt Hansen
Like This- Jake Scott
Hold Me While You Wait- Lewis Capaldi
Crowded Room- Conor Maynard
You Are the Reason- Calum Scott
Love Someone- Lukas Graham
Wreckage- Nate Smith
My Person- Spencer Crandall
Falling Like the Stars- Cole Norton
Yours- Russell Dickerson
Forever and Ever and Always- Ryan Mack
Hopeless- Clinton Kane
Fingers Crossed- Lauren Spencer Smith
Be Your Everything- Boys Like Girls
Walked Through Hell- Anson Seabra
Hopeless Romantics- James TW
Take My Name- Parmalee
Soulmate- Chanin

Contents

Aubrey 1

1. Aubrey 11
2. Lincoln 17
3. Aubrey 21
4. Lincoln 31
5. Aubrey 35
6. Aubrey 43
7. Lincoln 51
8. Aubrey 57
9. Lincoln 67
10. Aubrey 77
11. Lincoln 85
12. Aubrey 91
13. Lincoln 103
14. Aubrey 115
15. Lincoln 127
16. Lincoln 139
17. Aubrey 147
18. Aubrey 157
19. Lincoln 165
20. Lincoln 177
21. Aubrey 185
22. Aubrey 197
23. Lincoln 207
24. Lincoln 217
25. Aubrey 225
26. Lincoln 235
27. Lincoln 245
28. Lincoln 257
29. Aubrey 263
30. Aubrey 271

31. Lincoln 277

32. Lincoln 285

33. Aubrey 293

34. Aubrey 299

35. Lincoln 309

36. Aubrey 317

37. Lincoln 325

38. Aubrey 339

39. Aubrey 345

40. Lincoln 351

41. Lincoln 357

42. Lincoln 365

Aubrey 373

Song Lyrics 381

Acknowledgments 383

About the Author 387

PROLOGUE

"Guys...I...I can't...breathe."

I'm unsure if what I just tried to say was said aloud or only in my head. I don't know what is happening to me. We are on our way to Nashville and have just made our last stop for gas in a town called White Mountain. I was getting into the music and enjoying the view out the back window of Nick's car when my chest started to feel tight. It feels like someone is sucking the air out of my lungs. My heart feels like it will pound out of my chest, and my skin is feeling flushed.

I must have said it out loud because I opened my eyes and saw my friends and boyfriend looking at me with concern. My boyfriend Max seemed to realize what I said first, and he moved closer to me.

"Guys, something is wrong with Aubrey. Nick, pull over...Now!"

"What? What's wrong?" Callie asked while turning toward the backseat.

"Aubs, do you need me to pull over?" Nick asked.

"Babe, are you okay?" Max asked.

All of their voices at the same time overwhelmed me even more. Max tried to put his hands around my shoulders to pull me into a hug, but the last thing I wanted right now was to be touched, so I pushed him away.

I started talking even louder. "Don't...touch...me," I said between gasps for air. "I... I can't—"

My eyes were filled with tears, and despite my best efforts to hold them in, they began falling down my face. I could hear my friends talking, but nothing was registering in my brain until Callie opened the back door and pulled me out of the car and the fresh air hit my face.

Callie placed a cold bottle of water on the back of my neck and pushed me down into a sitting position on the curb. Max must be holding the bottle because she is now squatting in front of me with both hands on my cheeks.

"Aubrey...Aubs, Look around and tell me five things you can see."

"What—"

"Aubrey, just do it," Callie said sternly.

"Sky...you...Max...ground...car," I said, still gasping.

"Okay, good. Name four things you can touch."

I put my hands down and then touched her hands on my cheeks. I was reaching out to feel anything within my immediate surroundings. "Grass...pavement...your hand, and my jeans." Speaking was a little easier, and there was less gasping.

"Good, you're doing great. Okay, now tell me three things you can hear."

I sat for a moment and closed my eyes.

"Um.. cars...your voice and Nick chewing."

I opened my eyes and gave Nick a look. He was constantly chewing with his mouth open. His face went a little pink. It made me smile because I realized I was starting to calm down.

Callie laughed and gave Nick the stink eye. "Of course, you can hear his dumbass chewing," she scoffed. "So gross. Okay, now name two things you smell."

I stared at her, realizing I was almost completely calmed down, but I kept going. "My perfume and the Smarties on your breath." I almost laughed because this girl is forever eating those stupid candies.

"Fuck," she said as she laughed and covered her mouth. "Sorry. Okay, last one. Name one thing you can taste."

I took a deep breath before answering. "I can taste the chips Max and I were sharing."

She smiled at me. "Perfect." She removed her hands from my cheeks. "Are you feeling better now?"

I looked around for a moment, and Nick and Callie were focused on me while Max was texting someone. That man is always so focused on his phone. I looked back at Callie, "Yes, I think so."

Callie helped me to my feet. I could feel the embarrassment flooding my cheeks. "Sorry guys. I don't know what that was. It came out of nowhere."

"It was a panic attack," Callie said confidently.

"A panic attack? I don't have a panic problem." It came out sounding more defensive than I intended. I really just meant I don't have anything like that wrong with me.

"Sometimes shit like that just happens. It was probably a one-and-done thing. Maybe you're just nervous about being away from your family. It's the first time, right?" Nick asked.

I nodded my head yes. This is the first time out of state for Callie and Me. Max and Nick both lived in different states before moving to Connecticut.

This trip is the first college spring break for most of us, and we are meeting up with a few more classmates in Nashville, where we rented a huge house and are room-sharing to save money. The plan is to explore the music scene because most of us are music nerds in some way or another. Callie is a piano major, Nick majors in musical theater, and I plan to major in songwriting and voice. I want to be a singer-songwriter one day. Writing songs has always been my passion, but I could definitely improve my voice a little.

Max is a few years older than all of us and is on a hockey scholarship. He has hopes of getting drafted to play professionally. He supports my music obsession for the most part, but lately it feels like it has only been half-heartedly. Max finally got his face out of his phone and came over.

"Baby, I'm glad you are okay." He wrapped his arms around me. "I'm glad Cal knew how to do that weird breathing thing. I was clueless on how to help."

I rolled my eyes and pushed him off me.

"Let's just go; the others are probably waiting for us," I seethed. "I'm fine now."

As much as I was trying to be okay, I wasn't.

I took my phone out and started Googling panic attacks. I'm known for having no chill or patience; some might even call me neurotic. Some of these answers are just outrageous. I'm getting more and more uncomfortable as I read the search results.

Callie reached back and grabbed my phone. "No Googling."

I tried to protest, but she turned back toward the front of the car. She turned my favorite song on the radio just loud enough so she couldn't hear me protest. As much as I wanted to grab it from her, I knew it was the right thing. I'm just praying it won't happen again and I can move past this.

I was so anxious and stuck in my head the first few days that I could not bring myself to leave the house. I was rude to everyone whenever they tried to entice me to go with them. I'm surprised no one tried to off me with how irritable I've been. I haven't been able to get out of my head long enough to enjoy doing anything with my friends, so I keep making them go out without me.

Max and I have been doing exactly what we do at home: staying in, watching movies, and having mediocre sex. He doesn't ever plan anything outside of our dorms. He never wants to do anything new. Technically, he is on his phone when we're watching the movies. I always catch him smiling when he's talking to his friends, but when I ask who he is talking to he always tells me not to worry about it. He's been so busy lately. Max has canceled our last three date nights because of school-work and hockey practices. He told me he would be spending his time helping prepare his new teammates for upcoming games. He told me I couldn't attend his practice games anymore since looking at me was so distracting. I thought it was sweet, I guess.

I honestly didn't care much since I knew we were going on this trip together. I thought we would spend some quality time together and connect on this trip, and he might give the phone a rest, but I guess I was wrong.

Logically, I knew not going out and seeing Nashville was

ridiculous. Finally this morning, I was able to muster up enough courage and go out. It's been a long day of music, fun, and food. We also took Callie to the airport before returning to the rental house. She is flying home to spend time with her boyfriend, Jake, for the remainder of the break. Tomorrow is our last day here, but Nick, Max, and I have a few stops planned for the way home.

The Next Day

We were driving to our next stop today, and Nick said it was a surprise as to where. We had the windows down, and I heard some fantastic music that instantly drew me in. I looked around to find the source, and then I spotted it.

"Nick, stop!" I shouted as I reached out and grabbed his arm. "Look at that coffee shop, it's music-themed. It's so stinking cute." I gave my best attempt at puppy dog eyes. I know I'm acting pathetic, but they love me and won't judge. "Can we go?"

"Aubs, everything here is music-themed," he said with a chuckle.

"Nick, please. There is something about it that's calling me."

Nick looked at Max, and he shrugged. I felt discouragingly sad that his response was so nonchalant, but I'm learning I shouldn't be surprised by his lack of enthusiasm.. His interest in anything related to spending time with me has been going downhill for months.

As we walked up to the shop, the music stopped, and one of the men who had been playing welcomed us.

"Welcome to Brew Beats."

"Thank you!" I said in an excited voice. "This is such a cute shop; I just had to stop. Is it yours?"

"Oh no, no. Just one of the many places we meet up when we're all free." He gestured to the three other men who were sitting with him. They were eccentric-looking, and I loved it.

We all grabbed a coffee and got settled at one of the tables outside to continue talking to the band. They were all so welcoming and sweet. The one who had greeted us initially was a hippy-dippy type who talked about auras, fate, and the planets aligning. I ignored most of that stuff because I don't believe in it, but I would never stop someone from talking about what they love.

We started telling them about ourselves. Nick was chatting with one of the guys sitting a little farther away from the door while I chatted with our hippy friend.

"I love playing guitar and—" He cut me off and tried handing me his guitar.

"Here, play me something." He tilted it toward me.

"Oh no, I couldn't. That guitar looks special," I said nervously.

"Please, it would be a pleasure to hear you play it," he insisted.

I was hesitant, but I obliged. The guitar was a vibrant shade of green, almost like the color of fresh grass in the summer, with darker green striations throughout. The sleek and glossy finish of the body made it even more enchanting to look at. The fretboard was adorned with intricate inlays that added a touch of elegance to it. The sound that emanated from this guitar was just as beautiful as its appearance, producing clear and crisp notes that seemed to resonate with my soul. It was a truly breathtaking instrument that any musician would be lucky to own. It's not something you see every day. The moment I played it, I felt a release of stress.

After playing a few songs, I handed it back to him. "Thank you, I needed that. I'm saving up to buy a new guitar. Someone stole mine from my dorm a few weeks ago, so it felt really good to play again."

"No problem; it was a pleasure to hear you play."

He started telling us about his touring days and how his band had opened for some of the greats like Journey, Def Leppard, and even Rascal Flatts. I was blown away by how many pictures he had. He ultimately shared that he stopped touring because his health was declining.

"Oh, I'm so sorry to hear that."

"Oh, sweetheart, I'm not. I have a beautiful wife and people who miss me when I'm on the road. Spending time with them is more important than being a rock star. My wife is my once-in-a-lifetime love, and I will take advantage of the time I have left with her." He seemed a little sad at that admission, but he continued. "She and I both help at my best friend's shop a few towns over. We play and listen to music all day, which is good enough for me. As long as she is there, that is all I need."

His story was breaking my heart. I didn't ask exactly what was wrong with him because it was none of my business, and he was a stranger, but my heart goes out to him.

Max was bored, so he went off and found an arcade down the road. Nick and I ended up talking to them for three hours. We got up to leave, and my hippy friend pulled me aside.

"Here, I want you to have this."

My eyes went wide. I was so surprised that I blushed and laughed. Blushing is my telltale sign that I'm uncomfortable.

"What?" I asked.

He stood there with his arm outstretched, holding the guitar towards me. I put my hands up in protest. "Oh no, I can't. Thank you so much for the offer. It's very kind."

He continued looking at me but pulled the guitar back and set it down. "Please, I insist. It sounds like you have an amazing music career ahead of you, plus it's filled with good juju. I got it from my best friend. You actually remind me of him."

This man. This is the sweetest thing someone has ever offered me. I don't know how else to politely decline. I could never take something so precious. I declined his offer once more, insisting again that I couldn't accept it, and he dropped the subject.

I walked around and said goodbye to everyone else we had met. Finally, I said goodbye to my new hippie friend. He told us to look him up if we ever returned to Nashville.

I couldn't shut up about them after we left. They were so cool. They almost felt like old friends; it was weirdly calming.

We stopped at our first gas station about two hours into the trip home. Max ran inside to pay for the gas, while Nick and I got out to stretch quickly.

"Hey, Aubs," Nick grabbed my arm. He looked a bit nervous. "There's...um, something for you in the trunk." I gave him a puzzled look and followed him to the back of the car as he popped open the trunk.

"What...I can't...How?" I was almost speechless; I couldn't believe what I was seeing. There, lying in the trunk, was the beautiful green guitar. I looked at Nick with tears in my eyes.

He shrugged. "He told me not to tell you until we were far enough away so you wouldn't make me turn back," Nick said hesitantly. "Maybe it was just one of those serendipitous things, and you were meant to meet. He said to contact him if we ever return, so maybe we can do that."

I looked back at the guitar as the tears wet my cheeks. I looked at Nick as a surge of regret struck me. "Nick...we didn't get his name."

CHAPTER ONE

Aubrey

November Five Years Later

I stood in the attic silently for what felt like forever. It was as if time was standing still or I was having an out-of-body experience. I wasn't quite sure what I was looking at, but I got the feeling that this paper was about to change everything.

I've seen this document a few times throughout my life, like when I needed it for important things such as obtaining my driver's license or signing up for college. I would remember if it looked like this. Now that I think about it, I'm pretty sure I packed it already. Even if this is a duplicate, why would they be different? I definitely would've noticed...*right?*

My name on this birth certificate was different. I had my mom's maiden name. But the weirdest part is where my father's name should be...is blank.

I had to sit down because I was starting to have a panic attack. The walls felt like they were caving in around me, and I couldn't steady my breath. I don't know the cause of these panic attacks, but I do remember when they started.

Lately, I've been panicking more often whenever I think about moving out. I'm leaving my parents' house to move in with my best friend Callie and her boyfriend Jake. She and I have been discussing and planning this day since we were ten. We have scrapbooks full of ideas. We have always said that we were each other's soulmates, although we are opposite in every way. It seems to be a theme in my life because no one is ever like me.

Callie and I have always been close. We were roomies during college and planned to live together, or at least very close to each other, forever, no matter what. Even though she was in a relationship, she made it clear to her boyfriend that we would come as a package deal from the moment they met.

I insisted she and Jake take the house without me and start their life together. I was fine living at home with my family for now, while I'm still getting my music classes up and going. She was offended, saying she would never leave me high and dry. Luckily, he and I can tolerate each other. However, I've always felt as if something was off with him, but if she was happy, I was happy.

Now, here we are, planning our move for next week. The move is the reason I'm even up here in my parent's attic. I was looking for Christmas decorations to decorate the new place because Christmas is only a few weeks away. I want to be prepared, but nothing could have prepared me for this.

When I realized how badly I was panicking, I didn't know what else to do other than pick up the phone and call my sister.

My younger sister Brielle is my opposite in every way imaginable, but we are closer than any sisters I know. I've always been known as the girl with the hot, skinny younger sister. She's thin, like our parents, never having to watch what she eats. She's got dark hair and piercing green eyes that have those little gold specks in them. She also has the cutest freckles that spread across her cheeks, just like our dad. People are always drawn to her beauty. She wears glasses which adds to her hotness factor.

Besides our looks, we're also opposite in personalities. I'm extroverted, and she's introverted. I'm loud, and she's soft-spoken. Unless, of course, she's defending friends or family, then she is not someone you want to mess with. We have so many differences I can't even name them all.

I pressed on her contact in my phone. It rang once and went to voicemail, so I knew she was avoiding me on purpose. She's in the backyard, probably ignoring me to get me to go out there, but I tried again.

"What do you want?" She picked up on the second ring this time. I know she was trying to be funny because she laughed a little. She probably thought I was just being lazy.

I didn't speak right away. She got the hint and said, "I'm on my way."

I heard a thud before she hung up. I imagine she threw her book. Seconds later I heard the back door open and slam shut followed by her bare footsteps in the kitchen. She knew imme-diately that something was wrong and came running. This is one of the reasons she's my favorite person in the world. She just knows me. Luckily, she flew to the attic in just a few seconds.

"What's wrong?" She bent down and grabbed my shoul-ders to get me to look at her. I dropped the paper and stared at her. I couldn't get any words out. Tears were running down my face. I tried to hug her, but she had me at arm's length, checking for injuries to ensure I had no blood or anything on me. I tried pushing her off, but she grabbed me harder and asked again, saying the words slower and louder this time.

"What. Is. Wrong. Are you hurt?"

She finally let me go. All I could do was reach down to where I had dropped the paper and hand it to her. She stared at it for a few seconds, then leaned back off her knees and sat cross-legged with a look of confusion on her face. She looked back up at me. "Okay, what am I looking at? This looks like your birth certificate."

I nodded. "It is. Look at the names on it," I said through my tears.

She took another look, and I knew the moment she saw it. Her mouth dropped open and she covered it with her hand.

"What the...Why the hell is your name different?" Her brows went up in surprise. When she looked back at me, I just shrugged. "Did you know you were born with a different last name?" Now that she was with me and I had calmed slightly, I could finally speak more than a few words.

"Do you think I'd be freaking out like this, giving myself a panic attack, if I did?" I rolled my eyes at her.

I reached into the box where I found the birth certificate. The next thing I pulled out was a certificate of the name change for me, changing my last name from Maturo to Miller. After I finished gawking at it, I handed it to Brielle.

"What am I going to do? What does this mean?" I hung my head.

She put her hands on my cheeks and glared at me with her green eyes.

"We're going to go confront them," she said calmly. "We will figure this out. I'm not leaving your side until we get answers. There has to be an explanation for this."

After calming down, I found what I was initially looking

for while Brie grabbed all the remaining papers that were in the box. I wanted them in case they could help us figure this out. I frantically searched the entire attic for clues as to what all this could mean, but I found nothing.

There were a few other things, like pictures from the day I was born, a little bracelet they put on my ankle, and a damn picture of me in a god-awful dress at my parents' wedding. I stopped and stared at a picture of my dad holding me in the hospital; he was crying. Looking at this only made me more confused. How could he be there the day I was born but not be on the birth certificate?

My parents and I have always had open lines of communication between us. From a young age I knew that no matter my situation, where I was or how I got there, I could call my parents for help with no questions asked. God knows I've used and abused that. You could say their parenting style helped me grow the confidence I have today. I have never questioned being able to trust them, but this paper...this paper could change everything.

CHAPTER TWO

Lincoln

"Hey, Pops. Where do you want this stack of records?"

"Just make them look nice, Link," Pops yelled from the back room.

My family owns a music shop, and today we closed a little early to rearrange things. At the start of the new year we will be starting a local band program where different artists can perform for the patrons in the store. Not only do they get to practice, but they also get some exposure. Instead of having the radio or our phone playing songs, we will have live music, which may bring in more people.

I am trying to get all this moving stuff done as quickly as possible because I have a date tonight with someone I met online. I can't remember her name without looking, but I remember she had pretty eyes. We're going to dinner and then back to my place. I haven't asked her yet, but I know she will come. I don't usually have difficulty finding a companion for the night.

I'm hoping my parents don't catch me again. Not that there is anything wrong with enjoying some female company in my own home, but they have been giving me shit every time they see a new girl come by. I live in the guest house on their property. I moved out of the main house for more privacy after high school. It might as well be a bedroom and a place to watch TV since I don't use the kitchen often because my parents usually leave food for me in their kitchen. They really are the best parents anyone could have.

Living there saves me so much money because they don't charge me rent. I help my pops at the music shop on the weekends when I'm not teaching drama at the local high school in town. It allows the regular employees to rotate their weekends off, and I work for free, so my parents save money. I don't mind doing it for free because it's the least I can do.

Mom and Pops are the only people that have ever cared for me without neglecting me or beating the shit out of me. I was a foster kid and moved around a lot from the age of four until I was placed with them at fourteen.

My biological father was nonexistent in my life, I'm not even sure my biological mother knew who he was. She loved drugs and her string of boyfriends more than she ever loved me. The state took me away when they found me wandering the streets alone one night when I was only four years old. I was roaming the neighborhood looking for my mom, who hadn't come home for two days.

I vaguely remember the first home I was ever placed in, but the woman fostering me was diagnosed with an illness soon after I got placed with her, so she had to send me back. After ten years of moving around, I was so happy when I was finally placed with someone who didn't beat the shit out of me and even happier when I realized they planned on adopting me.

My bio mom never tried to regain custody of me. She

attended some visits, but was never consistent in showing up. I was fifteen or sixteen the last time I saw her. Mom and Pops reached out when we started to talk about them adopting me. By the time my birth mom finally signed her rights over, I was seventeen, so there was no need to go through spending money on adoption. Mom and Pops treated me like their son from the moment they got me anyway.

Their names are Liza and August. It took me a while to start calling them Mom and Pops, although it's so natural now. With the life I've had it's hard to trust that anyone will stay...but they did. I still try my best not to get close enough to care about people. I will never let someone hurt me by leaving me again.

My parents used the money they saved for adopting me to pay for college so I could get my teaching degree. I love being a drama teacher. I fully believe Pops is the reason why I love music so much. Although I don't play well, I do my best.

This girl is sexy. She is in town visiting her friend or cousin or something like that. I honestly don't remember what she said because I've been thinking about what her mouth tastes like the whole time she has been sitting across from me. She is brunette and skinny, which isn't my typical type, but who am I to judge?

"What do you think?" I heard her say. I can't even pretend I heard what she said because I have no idea.

"I'm sorry, I heard none of that. I was too busy thinking about kissing you." I smirked.

Her cheeks went pink and she started to slide her foot up my jeans. Then she said the magic words, "Wanna get out of here?"

I did...I really fucking did. I had to run to the bathroom to look at the dating app because I still can't remember her fucking name.

It's Lauren...Her name is Lauren.

CHAPTER THREE

I decided not to ambush my parents through a call or text. This was the kind of conversation you had in person, and they would be home in a few hours. Brie and I took everything to my room until they got home so we could try to piece it all together ourselves, but we had zero luck. Nothing made sense.

I wanted to bombard them with all the questions swirling around in my brain the moment they walked inside. Instead, I chose to let them settle in before asking them to sit down so we could talk. This was not anything new for me, so I'm sure they thought nothing of it. I have always asked them to sit when I would admit something to them or when I wanted to discuss something serious. My dad usually rolled his eyes and joked about me being pregnant. This time I knew he could tell something was off because he didn't even try to joke. I started to get everyone's food, but my dad stopped me.

"Aubs, don't worry about food. What's going on? Talk to us...what's got you frowning?" My parents and Brie were staring at me, but I wasn't sure where to start, so my eyes darted back and forth between them.

Brie grabbed my hand and whispered in my ear, "You got this. I'm with you every step."

I finally got the courage to open my mouth. "When I was upstairs in the attic earlier to grab some things to take to the new apartment...I found this."

I placed the box on the table, and my mom froze. Her eyes immediately went to my father, who was staring at the box, not saying a word. After a few seconds, he finally looked at me.

"Did you go through it?"

I looked at him in disbelief wondering why that was his first question.

"Of course I went through it," I said curtly.

"What did you find?"

"Are you serious? What do you think I found Dad? I found a birth certificate, and it doesn't have you listed as my father. God, it doesn't even have me listed as me. It has mom's maiden name as my last name."

I didn't mean to yell, but his question caught me off guard. My brain can't decide which emotion to act on first. My anger at the fact that he asked that or the feeling of betrayal that I could tell he knew exactly what this box was.

My dad grabbed my mom's hand because her eyes were filled with tears. She was doing her best to hold them in.

I didn't even realize that I had stood up when speaking to my dad, but now I was feeling a little uneasy, so I sat back down. As I did, my mom spoke.

"We were going to tell you, Aubs," she choked out.

"Tell me what, Mom?" I asked in a hushed voice as I fiddled with my fingers, not even looking at her.

My dad got up and knelt in front of me grabbing my hands

into his. I lifted my head to look at him with tears in my eyes. Then he said the words I'd dreaded for the last few hours...It was the only possibility I could remotely conclude, although I didn't know how it could be true.

"Aubrey...I'm not your biological father."

I pulled my hands away to cover my face. I started to sob uncontrollably. I felt another panic attack coming, and I didn't want to be near them anymore. I started to get up but Brie grabbed me and sat me back down.

"Just take a sec. Breathe. You can't run away from this." Her voice was shaking but I could tell she was trying to stay strong for me. "We need to let them explain."

Brielle has always been more level-headed than me, but she's not the one who just found out her whole life was a lie. I sat back down as my mom tried to reach for me, but I crossed my arms to keep myself at a distance. She looked defeated.

"I'm so sorry, Aubs... I'm so, so sorry."

I looked her right in the eyes and asked another question that I had been dreading.

"If he isn't my father, then who is?"

She looked at me with regret. "I don't know. I never saw him again after our one night together."

I saw Brie's eyes go wide. "Excuse me? What do you mean you don't know?" Brie asked, annoyed.

I looked at her with an almost pleading thanks because my brain couldn't form thoughts. "How could you not know, and why did you lie about it all these years?"

Brie was getting louder with every question she asked. Although she is level-headed, when she gets mad, she gets really mad.

My mom looked at my dad like she wasn't sure what else

to say. Dad took over again. "Before you start yelling, let us explain."

I nodded at him and looked over at my mom. She looked so embarrassed I almost felt bad. I guess that's the Pisces in me, constantly feeling bad for others no matter what they did to me.

"Almost everything we've told you is the truth. Your mother had you a few months before we got married, which you knew."

He smiled and looked at my mom as if he was recalling a thought. It was sweet. I felt a smile forming, but I tried hard to keep it at bay. Now was not the time for it, and I didn't want them to think any of this was okay.

"We met when I walked into her salon needing a haircut. That's all true, but she was already about four months pregnant then. We talked about how far along she was, and I asked if her husband was excited. She regretfully told me she didn't know the father and never got the chance to tell him. She told me it was a one-night stand from a party. She didn't know how to find him." He looked at her and smiled. "I'm not sure why she felt so comfortable sharing such a private thing with me, but I'm grateful because that's what started it all."

Brie and I just looked at each other in shock. I couldn't believe he was talking about my mom. She has always been a little bit of a prude. She never really talked about herself as a teen or young adult, and now I understand why.

Dad continued, "I offered to help her. We spent the next few months just as friends trying to find out if anyone that attended the party knew him."

My mom cut in. "I didn't remember much about him, only what he looked like, but since it was a summer party and off campus, it was a mix of people from different towns. Honestly, we were all a little too drunk to remember many details. I was new in Connecticut, living with Aunt Mary after Grandma and Grandpa died. By the time I realized I was pregnant, I couldn't even remember who invited me to the party. It was someone I met in passing that day. We clicked, so she invited me. I just went to the party to have fun and try to make some friends. I was a bit of a party girl, like someone else I know." She gave me a halfhearted smirk.

I tried to smile back, but I couldn't.

"He and I hit it off as soon as I got there. He was suave and charming and we had an instant connection. One thing led to another, and we ended up in a bedroom. We used protection that night, but I guess God had other plans."

She leaned over and grabbed my hand as if to comfort me. "I couldn't be more thankful for that either, because it gave me you."

I didn't know how to continue this conversation without crying, but luckily my mom kept talking.

"Your dad and I were just friends when you were born. I opted not to put anything on the father portion of the birth certificate and gave you my last name. Although I had a big crush on your dad, I didn't think he and I would date, let alone get married. I didn't think he would want to be romantically involved with a woman with a baby at such a young age."

My father looked at her, grabbed her hand, and smiled. "I was in love with her. She just didn't know it yet. I was in love with her openness and determination to raise you on her own with little to no help if she had to. I especially admired her willingness to let me help her find him."

Dad looked back at me.

"Aubrey, the day you were born was the best day of my life. Although mom and I were only friends, she had no other support here except for Aunt Mary, and what retired 70-year-old woman would want to help a young girl raise a baby, so I stepped up. We were very close for almost five months at the time of your birth. She was with me when she went into labor. I offered to be in the delivery room with her, and she accepted if I promised that I would stay by her head and hold her hand. I had no issues with that because I wanted no part of what was happening down there." We all gave a light chuckle. "I was doing my best to be strong for her and you." Brie and I laughed at the same time. "I knew the moment I held you that you were my daughter. I also knew your mother would be my wife. I promised myself at that moment that I would do anything and everything to protect my girls."

I paused and thought for a moment. Although that story was sweet, my anger settled back in. "Why did you stop looking? Was it not important for me to know where I come from or know who I am? Didn't you think I deserved to know? Didn't he deserve a choice? Didn't he deserve to know about me?"

My mom looked at me. "Of course you deserve it, sweetie. I just had nothing to go on. Internet and social media were no help, so I had nowhere to turn."

"Were you guys ever going to tell her, or would you have kept this secret forever?" Brie asked.

"We were selfish; I'll admit that. I wanted you and your mother all to myself. You are *my* daughter, and I would never let anything change that. I didn't want anyone taking you away."

I was quiet as I stood up and stared at them. I never raised my voice to them...ever, but this was different. I wasn't just hurt... I was broken. I was scared of what this meant. I couldn't believe the people I trusted the most lied to me about something so important.

"You should have tried harder! I could've had an entirely different life. I could have an entire other family who knows nothing about me. What if I have more siblings?"

Brielle gasped and Mom interrupted me, "Was your life so bad? Did you suffer living in this beautiful home, getting anything and everything you asked for?"

My tone threw her off. I could tell by the look in her eyes that she was surprised and almost horrified when I started yelling even louder. "NO! Don't you dare! How could you even say that? You know damn well I'm not talking about material things, Mom. I'm talking about the fact that I've never fit in with this family and you knew exactly why all along. The three of you are like carbon copies of each other, and then there's little ol' me—different hair, different eyes, even down to our body types. You blatantly lied to me about it every time I asked why or when someone commented on it. I deserved the truth. I deserved the choice of knowing him, and you stole that from me! Even if you had told me when I was a little older, and we had more options to look for him, I could have searched for him."

I turned away, and I was crying again. Being different was never easy for me. It was always the thing people pointed out and noticed the most about our family. My mom stands at exactly five feet, and Brielle is only two inches taller than her. My dad is a little taller than both of them but he is only five-foot-six. I'm taller than all of them at five-foot-seven. I have olive-toned skin compared to theirs, which is pasty white. I have piercing baby blue eyes that get bluer depending on my clothes and mood. My eyes are probably my favorite thing about myself. Their green eyes are probably the only thing I've never been jealous of. My hair is blonde with a few natural lowlights. People always comment how women pay hundreds of dollars to get my natural hair color. I'm sure they mean it as a compliment, but it's always just another reminder of how I look different.

Unlike my family who are thinner than rails, I have to run almost daily to keep my body fit, but I have also been on a "diet" and watching what I eat for as long as I can remember. If I eat a freaking M&M, it goes straight to my ass. I have hips for days and an ass and chest that turn heads. Society would call me "curvy in all the right places." I accept that now, but I used to think I was fat. I can only wish I still looked like I did in high school.

None of those things are terrible, but I've always been self-conscious because, just once, I'd like to look like my family. I'd like to fit into a picture and not stick out like a sore thumb.

My family has always done a great job of helping me feel less sad about it, and they never comment on my weight, except when I talk about it by calling myself fat or when I'm complaining. Mom's famous response is, "Oh honey, you are beautiful just as you are." I always roll my eyes.

I've always hated when she says stuff like that, but let's be honest; everyone does it. Everyone assumes that when you call yourself fat, you are calling yourself ugly or you hate yourself in some way. I always respond by saying, "I know I'm pretty. I didn't say I was ugly; I said I was fat." I think some of the most beautiful women in the world are plus-size.

People were constantly commenting on how I looked nothing like my parents. Nine out of ten times, they always asked who else in the family had blonde hair. My parents always laughed it off and said how beautiful it was and how it would darken with age. News flash: I'm 23 and still have a full head of beautiful blonde hair.

I was getting increasingly more upset as this conversation went on. I just don't understand why my parents didn't try to help me find what I've been missing all my life.

"We could have done one of those DNA tests online. Maybe I could have matched with him or something. What if he's dead? What if I never get the chance to know him?"

Brie walked over and took my hand. "Why don't you take a second and cool off? We can continue this once we've all relaxed a little. Being this upset while trying to talk will not get us anywhere. Let's go chill in your room and put on some music."

Mom and Dad nodded in agreement and stood up to head into their room. Before they made it too far, my mom grabbed my hand. "I love you and was only trying to protect you from pain. Please don't forget that."

I nodded and walked down the hall and up the stairs to my room. Brielle started to walk in but I stopped her. "I need a minute alone, okay?"

She grabbed my hand. "Of course you do. I'll be in my room, okay?" She hugged me harder than before and whispered in my ear. "Nothing changes for you and me. We are sisters and best friends no matter what. I will help you find him or do whatever you need me to do to support whatever you choose to do; I'm in."

She leaned back, and I could see some tears welling in her eyes, but she was trying hard to hide it. I gave her a half-hearted smile. "Yeah, okay."

I sat on my bed, grabbed my headphones, and grabbed my

favorite green guitar. I started playing the song by Tim McGraw called "My Little Girl." That was the song my dad dedicated to me when I was little. He always tried to sing it to me, but no one in my family other than me is musically inclined. Still, it always made me feel safe, and right now... I needed to feel safe.

CHAPTER FOUR

Lincoln

I let Lauren into the house. Before I could even shut the door entirely, she pushed me into it and put her body onto mine. Her kiss was a bit sloppy, but I'm sure that was the wine's fault. I dropped my keys and lifted her by her ass. I brought her over to the couch so she could straddle me while we made out.

"Wanna head to the bedroom?" Not sure why I bothered asking. I could already tell she wanted to do more than kiss me.

"Do you have a condom?" she whispered as she bit my earlobe and made my cock twitch.

I groaned and whispered into her ear as I stood up with her still in my arms. "I have multiple."

She smiled and then kissed me again. "How about we start in the shower?" she suggested.

"I like the way you think."

We showered with an orgasm for her included. I took her to bed and made her scream all over again.

"This. Is. So. Good. Fuck me harder, Lincoln," she screamed as I was pumping in and out of her. She was so tight that it was hard to fuck her properly. She was a screamer, and it was hurting my ears a little. It wasn't that sexy kind of scream that she did in the shower when she came on my fingers. This one was a bit like nails on a chalkboard. I switched to eating her out to get her off faster, and she finished me off with a mediocre blow job. I'll give her a few points for that.

She went to the bathroom to clean up, and I expected her to get dressed and go, but she came out wearing one of the shirts I had hanging in the bathroom. I realized at that moment that we didn't have the conversation I usually have before getting into bed with a woman.

I'm not afraid to use them and let them use me as long as they know it upfront. That's not something I should be proud of, but I am. That's how I like it. I don't sleep with women more than once because I don't want attachments. Attachments cause feelings, and feelings cause hurt. My motto is to give each other a good time and move on. No feelings are needed.

I started getting dressed as I talked. "Hey, did you need me to call you a rideshare?" I asked without any emotion hoping she would get the hint.

Her face dropped. "Oh, you don't want me to stay? We could have some good morning sex." She smiled and looked hopeful. Now I feel like a complete asshole.

I rubbed the back of my neck, uncertain how to let her down nicely. "I have an early morning, I'm sorry. I need to go to bed. Plus, I'm not a cuddler. I like my space."

She walked up to me seductively, trying to entice me and change my mind, but it wouldn't work. I held my hand up to stop her.

"Lauren, I'm sorry. I thought this was just a quick

hookup, and I'm sorry I didn't clarify it. I thought you just wanted some fun because you were just here for a few days."

She looked embarrassed. She picked up her clothes and went into the bathroom to change. When she returned, I asked again if she wanted me to call a rideshare for her.

"No, I can handle it," she answered angrily.

She gathered her things, and I walked her to the door. Before she left, she turned around again.

"I know I'm probably double embarrassing myself here, but don't you even want my number?"

I rubbed the back of my head again. "Lauren, I'm sorry I wasn't clear. I—"

She held up her hand. "No worries." She opened the door. "Thanks for the orgasms. Have a nice life."

She shut the door behind her and I felt the tension leave my body as soon as the lock clicked. That was probably the most awkward encounter I've had in a while.

I picked up all the blankets and crap I left everywhere this morning and headed to bed.

The following day I woke up and went for a run. Before going to my house to get ready for the day, I stopped at the main house to grab something. Pops was at the table drinking his coffee.

"Momma leave already?" I asked.

"Yep, I was just about to leave too. Are you good? I was just about to come to check on you."

I gave him a weird look because he's not typically asking me if I'm good before he leaves for work. I usually don't even see him.

"Uh, yeah, why wouldn't I be?"

He gave a sly smile. "I don't know. Just checking in."

A smile grew on my face. "Fuck. You heard her?" I was immediately embarrassed. "Shit. Did mom?"

We both started laughing uncontrollably.

"I don't think so. Mom is a heavy sleeper, you know that. I was in the kitchen getting water when I heard her... but seriously, Link, the neighborhood heard her; what the fuck was that?"

"No idea... sorry you were subjected to that," I said as both of us continued laughing.

I grabbed some breakfast once he left. Sitting alone always makes me think deeply, so I started thinking about the events of last night more seriously. I'm starting to wonder if I even have the capacity to let anyone try to get close to me. Although I hated being alone, it's all I've ever known. I just don't have the space in my heart to get hurt.

Sitting there drinking my coffee, I wondered if this would always be what my mornings looked like...tired and alone. Sadly...I think they will.

CHAPTER FIVE

Aubrey

I spent about two hours playing guitar and crying... mostly crying. I can't stop thinking about my parents and how they have dealt with keeping this from me for so long. Did they ever talk about it? Did they fight about it?

They have that kind of marriage everyone talks about. They've always been head over heels in love and never even considered divorce as far as I know. They have never fought in front of Brielle and me. My favorite memory of them is when I caught them dancing in the kitchen to no music. Dad was humming their wedding song. They are the definition of finding your soulmate and forever love.

It's a beautiful story, but as their daughter, it can sometimes get nauseating. Maybe I'm just jealous because I'm scared no one will ever look at me, treat me, or even love me the way my dad does my mom. I've always wanted a love story that reflects theirs. I want simple moments like dancing in the kitchen and kissing under the stars. Sadly, I've only dealt with heartbreak. I know I'm still young, but it feels like a love like that will never come for me. At least I have my love songs. I lit my favorite candle, honeysuckle pear scent, to try to help me focus. I had to finish writing a piece for Nick to use in the spring musical next June. Sadly I was getting nowhere.

I heard a knock at my door.

"Come in," I called out.

My dad pushed the door open. He had water, apples, and peanut butter in his hand, my go-to snack.

"Are you ready to talk? Can I sit with you?"

He placed the snacks on my side table and I just shrugged.

"I don't know what to say. I'm so angry at you both. I don't want to say something I don't mean. I don't want to hurt you just because I'm hurting."

He sat down anyway. "Aubrey, you deserve to get it all out. I will be here to listen; nothing you say could make me disappear. Especially because this is mostly my fault, and I deserve whatever you have to say to me."

I looked over at him as I picked up a piece of apple. That admission surprised me, and I was trying to figure out how this situation could be his fault. He must have seen the questions on my face because he started explaining himself.

"Mom wanted to keep looking but I asked her not to. I asked her to let me be your dad and told her that you not being biologically mine didn't make me love you any less. I told her that nothing would ever change that. She was vulnerable. She wanted to make me happy and went along with it. We were young and dumb, and I should have considered how this would affect your future. I am so sorry Aubrey. You were completely right earlier. You deserved to know the truth sooner."

We sat in silence as I rubbed my hands together. I was nervous about the answer to the question I was about to ask. I swallowed the lump in my throat. "Who else knows you're not my real...I mean biological, Dad?"

He smiled at my slip up. Just because we're not blood doesn't mean he is any less my dad. "Just Aunt Mary. Since neither of our parents were alive and your mother didn't keep in touch with any friends back then, no one even knew she was pregnant. Everyone else we knew here assumed you were mine. They thought having you made our love happen and, honestly, that was a big part of it."

I was relieved knowing that no one else had lied to me. I don't remember meeting Aunt Mary, so she didn't have the chance to lie. She died when I was only two.

My dad leaned in to hug me. I didn't think I had any more tears left, but once I opened my arms and hugged him back the tears came back with a vengeance.

We sat there for about fifteen minutes and he just held me and let me cry. He may have even cried a little too, but I didn't look up to find out. That would have made me feel worse. I've only seen my dad cry a handful of times.

A little while later, my mom came in and sat with us. She placed her hand on my leg. "Aubrey, I will do whatever I can to help you find him if that's what you want."

I looked up at her and saw the regret in her eyes. I know my parents would never do something to hurt me on purpose. I also know this hurt them just as much as it hurt me.

"I will spend whatever money it will take to help you get information about him," Dad added.

I looked down at my hands in my lap then back up at them. "I think I need to find him, or at least try. Maybe finding out about me will ruin his life, but I will regret not trying for the rest of mine if I don't."

A voice came from the hallway. "You should do a DNA test; that's a good start. If he's done it or anyone that he's related to has, then it will come up as a partial match. That's probably the easiest thing, right?" Brie asked as she walked into the room.

I looked at my dad. I wasn't sure how to start the next part of what I wanted to say. We sat silently, and then I found the courage.

"I will always love you. You will always be my dad. I hope you understand."

I'm not quite sure why I was trying to comfort him, but I am who I am, and I'm always trying to make other people feel okay no matter the situation, even when they are in the wrong or when I'm hurt in the process.

"Of course, Aubs. We understand completely. As we said, we will do whatever we can to make this happen for you."

The next day my best friends Callie and Nick were sitting on my bed as I told them what had transpired over the last twenty-four hours. I ordered a DNA kit, and it was on its way. I did priority shipping because I couldn't wait.

Everyone who meets the three of us can't believe we are friends. We are all so different it's unbelievable—mostly because of our looks but our personalities too. Callie is a few inches shorter than me and is a beautiful brunette with caramel-colored eyes and skin. She's got a feisty attitude and she's confident as hell. She couldn't give a shit about what anyone has to say. One thing we have in common is that we are both fiercely protective and loyal to each other and everyone we love.

Nick, on the other hand, has beautiful blue eyes and

blondish hair just like me. He wears glasses sometimes, usually only for work or reading. He's around six-foot-four so he towers over most people he meets and is built like a strong beanpole. He's got muscles and a toned stomach since he works out but nothing super defined. I would call it skinny athletic, I guess. He is a people pleaser like me but confident as hell like Callie. Next to Callie and I, and our curvy bodies, he looks like a piece of thin meat between two sexy, curvy rolls. We are a good mix, I think.

"So were they just never going to tell you? What if you got sick and needed medical info or something?" Callie asked.

I gave her an annoyed look. "Girl, I don't know; they would've had to tell me at that point, I guess. I'm over this consuming my brain when I can't do anything about it right now. It will only upset me more if I think about the what-ifs. I need to wait for this test, take it, and then see where it gets me. Let's keep packing."

I am the queen of subject changes. I don't know how to deal with the hard stuff. Callie usually calls me out, but this time, she nodded and stopped talking about it. We continued folding my clothes and placing them into their perspective-moving boxes.

Nick tried to break the tension and make me laugh by wearing one of my bras and walking around like a super-model. I rolled my eyes and threw my tissue box at him. Then we all broke out into laughter. This fun is just what I needed; my best friends just being here acting like everything is normal.

"Jake said the house is coming along great. He's done with almost all the painting and put up some shelves like we asked. He wants to know what color to make the music room and your room. He said he texted you yesterday, and you didn't answer; now I know why," she smirked.

I saw Nick roll his eyes. "What was the eye roll for?"

He looked at me, and I could swear I saw a blush creep up his neck like he didn't mean for it to be seen. "Nothing. I just can't believe you guys are moving in with him. He is such a tool bag."

Callie started to speak, probably about to yell at him. Nick has always had an issue with Jake. He never liked him but dealt with him because of Callie. Before this conversation got out of hand, I cut her off.

"Tell Jake maybe a muted pink for my room and a light blue for the music room? I trust his judgment. You know I'm not picky. What do you think?"

Luckily for us, Jake builds houses, so he knows all about home improvements. We are saving a lot of money in that department. When looking for houses, we made sure the one we picked had an extra room to make a music studio. Now we both can give lessons for money, me on the guitar and Callie on the piano.

"Okay, I'll text him. I like the blue idea. It will feel homey."

She seemed to forget about what Nick said, thank God. She started to go back to what she was doing but paused for a moment, clutching a pair of my shorts, then looking back up at me. "Aubs, are you sure you'll be ready for this move? Do you want to stay home since you don't know what's going on yet? Either way, it's fine. You know we can handle the rent without you, and your room is there when you are ready."

"Thanks, but I think I need this. Almost like a fresh start all around. My parents aren't my favorite people right now, so some space might be just what we need."

"Okay then, let's put these boxes in my car, and I'll drop

them off at the house for you. It will be one less trip for you since I'm going there anyway. Nick, get to it." She clapped her hands jokingly like he was a butler.

He scoffed at her and looked between us like he was appalled. "Why me?" he asked. "What's wrong with your hands, Sweets?"

Nick had nicknames for both of us. Hers was Sweets because she is obsessed with smarties, and mine is Buttercup because of the shade of my hair. My nickname lost traction over the years, only coming out every once in a while, but hers has stuck. She hates it and I think he likes to torture her.

She batted her thick eyelashes at him jokingly, "You're the big, strong man here, are you not?" She was trying to pump his ego by squeezing his arm muscles. He chuckled as he grabbed two boxes stacked on top of each other.

"Okay, but only because it's for Aubs. I don't like you anymore because you are so mean to me," he said to Callie.

He kissed my cheek as he left.

"You wish you hated me," Callie said as she winked.

They always had this banter about who loves who and who loves me more; it was pretty comical because I'm 99% sure they would choose each other over me without a second thought.

A few days later, the DNA kit arrived. Brie got the mail and left it on my bed with a note.

I will sit with you if you want. Let me know. I love you.
Love, Bean

That made me chuckle. That is a nickname I gave Brie when I was young because I couldn't say Brielle's name. She doesn't love when I call her that, but it's ingrained in my head and I still do it most days.

I did the test immediately and got it over with. I placed the swabs in the package and walked out to the blue mailbox at the end of our road. I contemplated not sending it at all, but I know it's something I need to do.

This could change everything.

CHAPTER SIX

Aubrey

A few weeks later.

I've been checking my email daily for weeks. Getting results can take up to six weeks so the results should be here any day now. I'm trying hard to keep my mind busy so I don't obsess over it.

Callie, Jake, and I moved into our house last week and we are finally getting settled enough to start our music lessons again. We are still decorating like crazy for Christmas. All three of our families are coming over including Nick. Callie and Jake's families haven't seen each other much since Jake's family is from California. She doesn't know this yet, but since all her favorite people will be here Jake is going to propose. I helped him pick out the perfect ring for her, and whether I liked him or not, he makes her happy and that's enough for me. I hope he can love my best friend the way she deserves. That bitch is my soulmate.

I will find that kind of happiness one day, but I'm okay with being alone for now. I feel like I have a lot of soul-searching to do at this point in my life, especially with how my last relationship ended. Also, with this new life development, let's just say I'm glad I'm not dragging anyone around with me.

I did have that kind of love at one point with Max...I think. We got together when I had just turned eighteen and we were together for almost three years. I thought he would propose. My world came crashing down one day when I took off work and went to his dorm to surprise him. My plan was to decorate his room since he had a hockey game and would be out until late on his birthday. Instead, he surprised me by being in bed with some redhead. She had no idea about me, either. She and I tried to become friends trying to bond over a common enemy but that didn't work out. She was a complete bitch and I'm one of those people who can't be fake. If I don't like you, then my face will tell you. It was also just too weird. Last I heard, Max was playing for the Pittsburgh Penguins, and the two of them were dating. Good for them, I guess.

It's Christmas Eve and we are hosting our first holiday in our new home. Our families were starting to arrive, and –big surprise– Nick was late. Callie's mom has been here since eight this morning. She owns a restaurant and is a fantastic chef, so she does most of the cooking for us anytime we have an event.

Brie and I sat in my room wrapping a few small things for my friends. We started talking about my old room and how she's making it into an office library. She's always wanted to own a cool sliding ladder for her bookcase.

"It's a great idea. I think that will look awesome."

She smiled but was looking down. "Have you got the results yet?" She was asking in a careful tone.

I grabbed her hand to reassure her. "You will know as soon as I do, Brie, I promise. I would never keep it from you."

I refreshed my email on my laptop sitting beside me—still nothing.

When it was time for dinner, I helped Callie's mom serve everyone. I loved being surrounded by everyone. Things with my parents were still tense, especially since I moved out. They've been trying not to hover. Instead they have been letting me come to them as I process everything without hovering. I was probably drinking too much to keep my nerves in check, but I wasn't driving anywhere, so BRING ON THE WINE!

Since I can remember I have always sat with Callie on my left and Nick on my right. If I didn't sit between them, they would bicker the entire time. They fight like a married couple.

Callie has been a part of our Christmas forever and Nick joined the crew when he was fifteen. He had just moved to town to live with his grandma after his parents died suddenly. Nick never speaks about it, and we don't ever push it. We became friends quickly, he's like an older brother to Brie, Callie, and me. Lucky for us, even though he was a year older, he was in the same grade because he was held back in elementary school. When he was ten he missed a ton of school because he was really sick. His parents chose to hold him back, which worked in our favor.

Everyone assumed Nick and I would end up together. We were always called "The blue-eyed twins". He is a very handsome man and we did try once. He was my prom date our junior year. We kissed that night, right outside the prom, and it sucked. It was awkward, like kissing a brother. I felt no sparks, and he said the same.

There is always someone joking about us making beautiful babies. We would laugh it off. We never really spoke of the prom incident again, except for the occasional joke when we were drunk. We are definitely better off as friends. I always thought he and Callie would end up together because they were always either flirting or fighting like they were married, but when Callie met Jake that idea faded fast.

We used to have Nick and his grandma over for the holidays since it was just the two of them. We liked giving his grandma a break by letting someone else cook for her. Nick was a horrible cook, but he tried.

We miss her so much; she passed away just last year. This Christmas will be hard for him, but so far he is the same ol' Nick. I am just glad he's here.

After dinner, we opened presents with the last present being Callie's engagement ring. Nick caught the entire proposal on video, and I took a ton of pictures. It was perfect. Callie couldn't believe I didn't tell her; I tell her everything, even when it's not my secret to tell. I'm downright horrible at secret-keeping and I also happen to be the worst liar on the planet.

About an hour after all the excitement ended everyone headed home except for Nick. He was staying the night at our house so that he didn't wake up alone on Christmas morning. Plus, I think he just wanted to drink a lot and not have to drive home. He also wanted some leftovers in the morning, I'm sure. The poor guy could barely make eggs without burning them. We have a pull-out couch in the music room for guests and that's where he sleeps when he stays over.

We all retired to our rooms so Callie and Jake could celebrate their engagement. Before heading to bed, Nick stopped in my room to say goodnight. I was sitting in the dark, using my book light to write.

"Hey, you doing all right?"

I looked up, smiled at him, and clicked on my lamp. "I'm good. My nerves are just getting to me waiting on these results. I'm kind of in a constant state of wanting to throw up."

He chuckled. "Well, if you need to talk about it, you know where I'll be."

"Thank you, Nick; I appreciate you."

I knew he could tell something else was wrong because he didn't leave and instead walked in.

"What's up, buttercup?" He sat down on my bed.

"I just hate being alone on nights like this. I'm so freaking happy for Callie and Jake but—" I didn't want to finish that sentence because I really am happy for them. "I'm just...a little jealous, I guess."

"I get it." He looked at me and I could see the hurt in his eyes. Part of me always believed Nick would someday admit that he had feelings for Cal, but he hasn't. He looked off into the room a little, and I cleared my throat, bringing him back to reality.

"Want me to stay with you until you fall asleep?" he asked.

"I'd love that." I hugged him.

He gave me some privacy and I changed into the ridiculous pajamas my parents had gotten me. The shirt had a huge light-up Rudolph on the front, but I love my parents, so I am willing to look like a goofball for them. I thought refusing it would cause more drama that I didn't need. I laid down and Nick snuggled up onto my pillow so I could put my head on his chest. He was mindlessly rubbing my hair.

"You sure you're, okay?" I asked him. I was really asking if he was okay with Callie being engaged and he understood.

He looked down like he knew what I was asking. "You know?" He looked so surprised.

I sat up a little still looking at him. "Of course I know, Nick. You're my best friend." I laid back down on his chest, and he was quiet again.

He leaned back and put his head against my headboard. "I guess it's too late now, huh? She will probably ask me to be a bridesman or something, and of course, I'll do it because I would do anything for her. I will have to watch her—" he cut himself off. "Am I absolutely pathetic?"

"You're not pathetic, Nick. You love her."

He was quiet again for a few moments. "I think I always will," he whispered.

We fell asleep lying like that, just comforting each other like we've done a million times.

A ding noise woke me up. I saw that my laptop screen was lit up. It was still open on my desk, so I walked over and started to close it, but hit refresh again, just in case.

My eyes widened. There it was—big, bold, black letters saying:

DNA RESULTS WITHIN

I wasn't sure whether to laugh or cry. It was a Christmas miracle. I hovered my finger over the mouse for a few seconds. I realized I didn't want to be alone for this, so I called for Nick to get up. He groggily came over and sat on one of the chairs. I clicked the link and held my breath. It only took seconds to load, but it felt like forever. When the screen finally opened I let out an audible gasp. There it was. The name that was going to potentially change my life forever. August Foster.

Foster? Does that mean my name should have been Aubrey Foster? If he knew about me, would I have even been named Aubrey, or would he have hated it and wanted to name me something different?

What if he hates me?

What if he never wanted kids?

What if he's dead?

All these questions were swirling around in my head. I wasn't sure if the death date was on a DNA test, but there was a link to a family tree. I scrambled to look at all his info. "No death date," I said aloud.

"That's rather morbid," Nick said as he laughed.

I shushed him. "I just meant, thank God, he's not dead."

He shook his head at me in disbelief. "He has a wife. No kids listed. That's almost refreshing, but what if he never wanted them? Am I going to search for this man and possibly uproot his life?" I honestly wasn't that sure I wanted to do this anymore. It was getting too real.

"Aubrey, you are spiraling. Relax." He stood and grabbed my shoulders.

I kept reading more about him, and then the coincidence of all coincidences smacked me in the face. The current town that was listed for him was White Mountain, Tennessee. I was shocked; I couldn't help but bring my hand to my mouth. "Nick," I whispered.

"What?" He looked at the screen and then me, clearly confused. "What is it? I don't get it."

"Remember when we were on our Nashville trip? We were in the car and I had that stupid panic attack." He nodded his head. "That's the town, Nick. That's...that's where we were when my panic attack hap—". My words caught in my throat.

Nick looked shocked. "Are you sure, Aubs?"

"I'm positive. That can't be connected, can it?" I put the laptop to the side and leaned onto my desk. Nick put his hand on my back but didn't say anything. I looked back up at him.

"I have to do this. I can't ignore it now, not with this huge sign smacking me in the face."

He smiled. "I think you do or you will always wonder."

I wasn't sure how I was getting there, whether I would fly or drive, go alone or if someone was going with me, or even how long I would stay, but I knew I was going.

CHAPTER SEVEN

Lincoln

December 26

Yesterday was Christmas and my parents and I stayed in and watched some old movies. My mom's favorite movie is *It's A Wonderful Life,* so of course we watched that one first. I think I cherish days like this the most because I missed so many before I found them.

I got my mom a new bookshelf for the guest room — my old bedroom— and a gift card to a local furniture store so she could furnish it a bit. She is planning a few room makeovers to make the guest rooms more inviting. My old room still has a peeling paint job and some old Playboy posters hanging all over the walls. No one has been in there for years other than me to grab things randomly.

My mom has been yelling at me for months about getting that room cleaned out, so that is my task today. I need to move everything I'm not keeping out into the shed or into the trash pile. Pops asked me to tape off the room to prep it for painting. He and I are going to tackle that in the next few days.

It's ridiculous, the stuff I've kept in here over the years. I just found some old merch from my friend Elijah's band before he was even in the band. I am starting to think I am a bit of a hoarder. I'm sure it stems from me having nothing as a child and wanting to hold onto everything.

Mom and Pops had to head off to work. I stayed behind to finish up before heading to work to meet up with Pops. I'm not sure why we are even open today, but Pops never closes except for holidays. The man never takes a vacation...it's annoying actually.

Today I am handling some of the paperwork and emails in the back since I was right, and the store is dead. A few hours passed when Pops finally said we should close early. He left me to lock up.

I was finally getting to emails because my dumbass thought I should tackle some of the end-of-year inventory while we were slow, but I definitely should have let the people here during the week do it, because I do not know what the hell I am doing.

One of the emails looked different from the usual order updates or inquiries, so I flagged it. The subject line said **NEW DNA MATCH AVAILABLE**. Looks like Pops might have matched with a new cousin or something. We don't have a huge family, which I surprisingly like, but it might be cool to meet someone new.

Pops still hasn't figured out how to change his personal emails from coming to the work email, so I get to filter through them. I've offered to change it for him, but he said he doesn't like checking one email let alone being bothered with two. I left a note so he would see it tomorrow when he comes in.

I walked into the main house to find luggage blocking the

entryway. Mom and Pops were in the kitchen, apparently meal-prepping, so I sat at the counter and waited for them to acknowledge me.

"Hey Link, how was work?" Mom asked.

"Where are you going?" I asked, without answering her question.

Mom's face lit up with a huge smile. "I am taking your father on a trip. We leave tonight. Oh, by the way, can you drive us to the airport?"

I was racking my brain, trying to remember her telling me about this, but I came up blank. "What about the store? Did you tell me this?"

Mom put her hand on my cheek. "Honey, I couldn't tell you. You would have opened that big mouth of yours. I've never been able to surprise him. I wasn't going to let you ruin that for me." Then she patted my cheek again and walked back to the food. She wasn't wrong. I am horrible with secrets.

"So I'm watching the store then? Am I doing all the painting and cleaning in the guest rooms alone too? Shouldn't that have been something you shared with me? What if I made plans while I'm off for Christmas break?" She smiled, knowing damn well I was planning on being at the store anyway so Pops would get a break.

"Do you have plans, Lincoln?" she asked condescendingly.

I rolled my eyes with a smirk. "Fine, you win."

"As far as the renovations, I hired someone to come a few days to do some of it for us and I knew you would be my favorite son and take care of the store for us." She placed some food in front of me and thanked me with a kiss on the cheek. "I also meal-prepped some stuff for you. The directions are on each meal."

"I am your only son," I smiled and rolled my eyes. Mom and Pops both laughed. "But thank you for the food."

I drove them to Nashville to make their eight o'clock flight. I hugged them, gave Mom a kiss on her cheek, and told them I would be back on Friday night to pick them up. Seeing them walk away gave me a weird feeling in my chest, but I tried to ignore it.

On the way home I called to see if Elijah and the guys wanted to come hangout, but they were busy practicing. They told me to come by but I decided to stop at a bar and grab a beer instead. The minute I sat at the bar two girls walked up to me, one on each side.

"Hello ladies," I smirked and sipped my beer.

"Hey handsome," the one on the right said. "Do you wanna play some pool or something?"

I looked over and saw a few people at the pool tables, but I was not in the mood for pleasantries.

"Nah, I think I'm okay ladies. I'm just having a beer and then heading home."

"Can we come with you?" the other one asked.

I looked between them and considered it. This could be a lot of fun, but I just wasn't in the mood. This wasn't the first time I've been propositioned for a threesome, and it won't be the last I'm sure.

They gave me shit about saying no, so in order to get them to leave me alone I just told them I had to get tested for STDs. It wasn't a total lie; I was going tomorrow. I go once a month or so to make sure I'm staying safe, even though I always use a condom. I couldn't get over that feeling of loneliness even though they were offering to help me do just that.

My parents will only be gone for five days, but for some

reason this trip is making me realize that if something were to happen to them, I wouldn't just be parentless, I would literally be alone in every sense of the word. No one else in this world would care about me if I didn't have them.

CHAPTER EIGHT

Aubrey

One week later

I have everything planned for my trip to meet my biological father. Callie offered to come along for the fifteen-hour drive and we're hoping my piece of shit car makes the trip with zero issues. We are also praying for no snow. Callie has been insanely supportive, and I am grateful I won't have to navigate this on my own.

Brie wanted to come but she's still in college. Although she was on a break until the end of the month, she already had a non-refundable trip planned with her friends. Nick was insistent on coming, but there was no reason for it. He didn't need to take off work when Callie was already going to be there. Callie and I had a lot easier time getting the time off. Luckily, the parents of our students understood. As for the restaurant shifts, Callie's mom told me not to come back until I was ready, so that was covered.

I can't believe I am really doing this. I am going to meet my biological father. When I looked him up on social media, there was only one August Foster living in Tennessee. It didn't matter anyway, I saw those eyes. Seeing him for the first time felt...weird.

Although it had been a long time since she'd seen him, my mom confirmed the photo I found was him. Despite his hair being mostly salt-and-pepper colored now she was sure nonetheless. His page listed him as the owner/operator of a place called The Music Bar. The thought that he might be even remotely musically inclined excited me. I couldn't wait to see if we had anything in common. I was too afraid to message him, though. I assumed he had gotten the email about having a DNA match, but I wanted to do this in person. What's the worst that could happen?

I stood there hugging my parents, who had come to see us off. It was harder to let them go than I thought it would be. It almost felt like I was doing something wrong or betraying them in some way or another, even though they were the ones who had betrayed me.

"Are you sure you don't want one of us to come with you? Maybe we could explain this to him once you meet him."

"Yes, Dad, I'm positive. You all need to work. I am sure he will have questions, and I'll answer what I can with what you've told me. Anything else I need to know, I will call. I love you. I will be back when my soul feels settled. I promise."

Brie was working, but she called to wish me luck. Callie and I packed up the car, hugged them goodbye, and went on our way. As we drove away, I saw my dad consoling my mom in the rearview mirror. I knew she was scared about what this meant, but I needed to do this. I can only hope that she understands. I need some time and space to find the missing pieces of me. Finding out about him has given me some answers, but I want them all. I need to find out who I really am and where I come from.

We were finally closing in on our destination after fifteen hours of driving and one sketchy hotel stay. I only had one mini panic attack, so I was doing pretty well. We got lost for about twenty minutes until I realized Callie was going north-east –toward home– instead of west, but we still managed to make good time.

White Mountain was a quaint little town, and by the looks of it, everyone knew everyone. There was nothing but smiles and waves all around. A few people even waved at us, which threw us off because we don't get that in Connecticut. New Englanders are built differently. If someone you don't know talks to you or waves at you, you ignore them or run the other way.

I was getting more nervous the closer we got to the music store, so we found a cute coffee shop to stop at where I could collect myself. The shop had outdoor seating with open umbrellas, and the building was covered in wood panels with adorable painted outlines of different coffee and breakfast items along the front. True to the small-town feel, it had that mom-and-pop vibe that instantly made me feel comfortable. After we entered and stood in line for a moment, I noticed the barista seemed to recognize everyone who walked in and she already knew their orders.

I was standing in front of The Music Bar, looking up at the sign. Callie came up beside me, interlaced our fingers, and leaned her head onto my arm.

"Want me to come in with you?" Callie asked.

I looked over at her, but she wasn't looking at me. She continued to look up at the sign.

I squeezed her hand and brought my gaze back to the sign again. "I don't think you should, honestly. I think this is something I need to handle alone."

We were both quiet for a few moments. I finally looked at her and let go of her hand. My eyes had already started filling with tears a little, but I've never been afraid to show her when I'm emotional.

"Why don't you take the car back and I will text you when I'm done? Or I can walk back. The hotel isn't far from here."

She laughed and shook her head, "You always want to walk everywhere. Are you sure? I could also just wait out here if you want."

"I'm sure. I love you. Thank you for doing this with me. Text me when you make it to the hotel."

She smiled and wiped away a tear that had fallen down my face, then pulled me into a tight hug. Without saying another word, she got into the car and left. Once she was out of sight, I wiped my face once more and checked my reflection in the window. I took a deep breath, and then pulled the door open.

As soon as I walked through the door I felt an instant comfort wash over me. It was like the shop was giving me a warm hug. I felt an instant sense of belonging. There were bells on the door that chimed as it shut behind me. At that moment someone spoke from the back room.

"Be right there." His voice was alluring and deep.

"No problem. Don't rush," I called out as I looked around.

I was in music heaven. Every kind of instrument imaginable hung on the walls in front of me. This was the prettiest music store I'd ever seen. There were bins and bins of records. I made a mental note to come back and look through them before I left town. I don't think I'd ever seen so many records in one place in my life. There was a band practicing and a handful of people looking around. Some were near the back checking out different instruments, while others were in the front browsing through the bins of records. The music the band was playing was a little out of tune, but I assumed that was why they were practicing.

I was wandering around and started to browse through the records myself.

"How can I help you?"

My stomach dropped at hearing the voice behind me. I tentatively turned around and my mouth went dry. The sexiest man I'd ever seen was staring right at me. The first things I noticed about him were his hands. They were massive. My eyes traveled up and landed on his smile. His teeth were perfectly straight and whiter than his T-shirt. His smile was almost contagious, but it was his full lips that were surrounded by that sexy ass five o'clock shadow that absolutely drew me in. I was starting to wonder what it would feel like to run my hands over his beard. I don't know what it is about beards, but I have a thing for them.

My gaze traveled up until our eyes finally met. Piercing blue orbs, like mine, stared back at me. *I could get lost in those eyes.* His hair was a dark dirty blond and he had that shaggy James Dean look about him, like just the top of his hair needed to be cut. He had that 'I didn't try' look, but in reality, he probably spent twenty minutes getting it to fall that way.

My eyes traveled down his body again, and I could tell he was fit, but his muscles weren't overwhelming. He had tanned skin and a few tattoos on each arm. One arm had a tattoo of musical notes on it, but I couldn't see it in detail from this distance. He didn't appear to be obnoxiously tall, but he still towered over my five-foot-seven-inch frame. If I had to guess, he was over six feet tall. My eyes traveled back to his just as I realized I was gawking, so I looked away for a moment to compose my thoughts, and when I finally looked back, he was smirking at me.

My first thoughts were, *Please don't be related to me. Please don't be related to me. If there is a god, please don't let this man be related to me.* I felt myself blushing, but I cleared my throat.

"Hey, I'm looking for August Foster. Is he here?"

He looked a little surprised. "Are you sure you're looking for August and not me?" he said smugly. I nodded because I was sure I couldn't speak right now if I tried.

"Are you a debt collector?" he asked.

I shook my head again. "No," I said with a snort.

"Is he in trouble?"

"No," I repeated. "I am just looking for him for personal reasons. Is he here or not?"

He thought for a moment. "Personal reasons, huh?" His eyebrows went up in curiosity. "You know he's married, right?"

I nodded once again.

"Well, he isn't here today. Can I leave a message and tell him who was looking for him and how to contact you?

"He doesn't know me yet. I can just come back when he is here. Will he be here tomorrow?"

His smile dropped a little like he was getting worried or something. He started eyeing me up and down like he was checking me out. He leaned in toward me, placing his elbows on the counter between us.

"You in trouble or something? Need some money?" he asked with genuine concern.

My eyebrows went up in surprise. "Why would I be asking someone who doesn't know me for money? Is that a normal occurrence for him?" I scoffed, almost like I was offended, and started to step away. "I will just come back tomorrow. Thanks for your time." As I was turning around, he spoke again.

"Wait. Is it really that important that you speak to him today? You seem anxious, like you're in trouble."

I tried acting like I didn't know what he was saying and turned fully away to calm my nerves. I pretended I was looking at some of the records in front of me. I gathered myself, then turned back around and looked at him again; my voice was calmer.

"I'm not in any trouble, and it's not life or death," I shrugged. "But yes, it's somewhat important. Maybe even life-changing." I raised my eyebrows and smiled.

"Life changing you say? Well then, let me get him on the phone for you and see if he can make some time to come down." His smile grew. It's like he got hotter the more he smiled.

He caught me staring at his mouth. God, I haven't been kissed in so long. *Calm down, girl. He still might be your cousin or something.* I rolled my eyes at myself and my sex-filled thoughts. I felt myself getting all hot and bothered, and I knew if I didn't stop soon, I would start to blush even more. If the heat crept up anymore there would be no controlling it.

He stepped away, but I could still hear his conversation a bit.

"Hey, Pops. I have a beautiful girl here looking for you." He looked out at me and chuckled. I assumed he added the beautiful part because he knew I could hear him and he was trying to flirt. "Yes, I'm sure she's here to see you; I've never seen her before; she must be from out of town. I don't know what she wants, but she only wants to speak to you."

He leaned his head out from behind the doorway and said, "Can you come back in the morning? He is about to have a meal with some friends. They just got back from a trip late last night, but he will come down here if it's really necessary."

I smiled. "Oh yes, tomorrow is perfect. I can be here at nine tomorrow morning if that's okay?"

He repeated what I said into the phone. "Okay, I'll tell her; Enjoy your dinner, don't forget to save me some."

That was not a good sign. He called him Pops and asked him about saving food. This man cannot be related to me. I will die. Hopefully, it's just a nickname he used or term of endearment. I resisted rolling my eyes at myself when he came back out front.

"He said nine is a bit early since tomorrow is Sunday, but he will be here when we open at ten."

"Perfect, no problem; I'll see him then. Thanks for your help." I waved and started to walk away as he leaned down on the counter.

"Anything else specific I can help you with, miss?"

I felt the slight sensation of a blush begin to creep up my neck because his words almost sounded like an innuendo. "It's Aubrey," I said with a smirk.

"Okay, anything else I can help you with, Miss Aubrey?" The way this man said my name, I was going to need a cold shower. It still felt like he was propositioning me...maybe he was. He had a sexy grin that I wanted to lick off his beautiful face.

I smiled, "Nope, guess I'll see you again if you're here tomorrow. Have a good one."

As I turned around, he yelled after me. "Oh, I will make sure I'm here, darlin'. Bright and early. By the way, my name is Lincoln, but my friends call me Link."

"Nice to meet you, Lincoln" I smiled again, but I didn't turn around this time because I could feel his eyes checking out my ass. These leggings make my ass look bomb; that's why I bought them in almost every color.

He called out to me, "By the way Miss Aubrey, how old are you?"

I turned and smirked. "Why do you ask?"

"I wanna know if I'm being a dirty old man or if you are available for dinner tonight," he said with a grin.

I raised my eyebrows in surprise and looked down at myself. "You think I look like I'm under eighteen? Really?"

He laughed. "No, I would guess around twenty-two, but you never know these days. I'm praying that I'm right. Will you go to dinner with me?"

I was stunned at the determination of this man. If I'm being honest though, it's actually quite sexy.

"Well, how old are you, old man?" I asked with a chuckle.

"Twenty-nine years young," he said proudly.

"Got it. Thank you for the invite, but I'm busy tonight."

I turned and started walking toward the door again.

"Tomorrow night then." It was a statement, not a question this time. I smiled and kept walking. "Bye, Miss Aubrey." I heard him give a low chuckle as the door closed behind me.

Lincoln

"Who the hell was that and how do I get her in my bed?" I accidentally said that aloud, but luckily no one was around to hear me. She was beautiful in the most natural way. She had the most perfect smile I've ever seen, and those eyes...*damn.* They were a pretty light blue. She had curves that I wanted to explore, and don't get me started on that ass— I shook my head to get my brain out of the gutter. At least I get to look forward to seeing her in the morning.

I knew she wasn't local. I absolutely would have fucked her already. There aren't many girls my age around here that haven't already been in my bed. I couldn't help but to wonder what the hell she wanted with my Pops that was so important. She seemed a little desperate towards the end.

I closed up the shop and headed home. I stopped in to see Mom and Pops and grabbed the leftovers I knew they had left for me. They were sitting in the den in their chairs doing some reading and online shopping. I sat down on the couch across from them.

"I think I want to paint the bathroom this color, what do you think? It's like a mauve." Mom said, showing Dad a picture on her computer.

Dad looked over his glasses at her screen and squinted. He does that all the time, and then wonders why he can't see. I motioned for him to push his glasses up and he rolled his eyes at me. Then he pushed them up and looked back at what Mom was showing him.

"How do you even know if that's what the real color will be? Those computers distort everything, don't they?" Pops replied.

I smiled at their banter. She is always trying to get him to care about what the house looks like, but in reality he doesn't give a rat's ass what she does as long as she's happy. He's stopped asking her how much things cost because he knows he's just going to go along with it either way.

"I don't care, I like it. It will give the room character. We can go shopping tomorrow when you get out of work," Mom said.

"It's a bathroom, Mom. What kind of character do you want it to have?" I asked.

She waved me off. "Oh, you hush. You don't even live here." She smiled and I knew she was trying to be funny.

"How was your day, son?" Pops asked.

I looked over at him and he was looking at me over the rim of his glasses again. The man will never change. "It was pretty boring until that girl came in, honestly. I was just doing some paperwork in the back while the band was practicing in the back of the store. We had a few people come in today, but Miss Aubrey was definitely the highlight of my day. She was hot; I hope she's looking for a job so I can stare at her every weekend."

Mom looked over at me in disgust. I smiled as I stuffed the bread from my plate into my mouth.

"Want me to heat that pasta up for you?" Mom asked.

"No need. The plate will be empty in a second," I said with my mouth full. Mom rolled her eyes. She hates it when I do that. She always comments that I'm going to die from choking.

Pops cleared his throat to get me to look at him. "Link, if she's looking for a job, you better not bring her back here. I can't have you monopolizing my employees again."

He is referring to when I was nineteen. I hooked up with one of the girls who worked with us. When I didn't want to continue seeing her, she started causing all sorts of issues for me, including recruiting her brother into trying to kick my ass inside the store. Her brother and I had to pay for quite a few broken instruments.

Pops looked up from his book and grinned at me over his glasses. I just shrugged and smiled big like I was an innocent angel.

"I'm serious, Link. No more monopolizing the women in this town. You need to settle down. You're a catch. Why aren't you dating a nice girl instead of just fuckin' around?"

"August, please! Watch your language!" Mom said.

She was a saint for dealing with us all these years. She hates it when we swear, and I swear a lot. I think I rubbed off on Pops. It has always been her biggest pet peeve; we were like a pair of sailors swearing up a storm.

"He is right, though, Link; we are ready for cute, little, blue-eyed grandbabies."

I choked on my bread. "I don't think I'm the having babies' kind of guy, momma. Maybe when I'm older." I honestly didn't mean it, because I do not want kids. Kids deserve to have a father who loves their mother fully, and I just don't see that ever happening for me. I won't ever get close enough to someone to fall in love like that. Falling in love can lead to people hurting you and I'm not letting that happen.

"Lincoln, you're not a spring chicken, you know. It's time, dear."

"Mom, I'm only twenty-nine. That's not exactly checking into a retirement home age." I laughed and stood up. "I'm heading out. I'm going to hang with the band, so I'll be home late tonight. Don't wait up," I said with a smirk.

Mom pointed at me and gave me the stink eye. "Behave and be the gentleman I know you are...and I don't wanna hear it this time."

She did hear me last time...shit. I laughed and put up three fingers.

"Scouts honor, mom." I walked over and kissed her on her cheek. She poked me in the ribs, and I winced.

"I'm serious, Lincoln Matthew, behave."

"I will Momma, I love you guys. See you in the morning after my run."

I went straight to my house and got ready. It was fifty-five degrees, which was warm for January in Tennessee. Just in case the weather changed while I was out tonight, I wore jeans, a tight black long-sleeve sweater, and a tee underneath in case I got hot. I brought my brown leather jacket in case whoever I was bringing home with me tonight needed it to cover her short-ass dress. I went into my bedroom to grab a few condoms. You never know when you are going to need them, right? If she doesn't want to come back here, the car or her house are fine choices too, in my opinion.

AUBREY

"That was fast," Callie called out.

"Hey," I walked over and plopped myself onto the bed with her. "It was...something, that's for sure." I was in a daze and I couldn't really even remember the walk here.

She nudged my shoulder.

"So, how was it? Was he nice? Tall? Was he super weirded out? It couldn't have gone too well. That wasn't even an hour. Tell me about–"

She kept rattling off questions as I tuned her out and sat there looking at the ceiling. I could feel that I was still quite flushed. She leaned over me putting her head directly above mine about an inch away. She was so close; I could smell the candy on her breath.

"Why are you so flushed? Did something happen?" she asked with caution.

"He was...hot," I blurted out.

She sat back with a disgusted look on her face. "You think your dad was hot? Aubs, I know this is a new thing for you, but you really shouldn't be thinking that way ab–"

"God, Callie. No. Not my dad. The guy working there. He was absolutely gorgeous. He was unlike anyone I've ever met.

I haven't had those types of flutters in my stomach in a long time." I felt myself getting flushed all over again, just thinking about him. "I need to shower," I professed.

I got up and headed to the bathroom. In true Callie fashion, she followed right along with me not caring for one second about privacy.

"Oh no you don't," she said as she sat on the toilet. "You are telling me right now about this mysterious hot man. Who was it? Was your dad not there?"

I stripped down and got into the shower, turning it on. I made the water cooler than normal to try to calm all the heat running through my body.

"He was just some guy working there, but Cal...he was so fucking hot. I wanted to lick his smirk right off his face. He was playful, a little bit snarky, and you could just tell he was one of those suave types." Now that I thought about it, he acted just like my ex, Max. God that's upsetting. That ruins the image a little bit for me.

"Wait so hot-man was there but no Dad?" Callie asked.

I chuckled, I loved that she was trying to keep me on task by making sure I answered all the questions asked.

"Yes, Callie. I will meet my dad tomorrow. He was just settling in from vacation, or something, so he was home.

"Okay then. Now about this hot man..." She wagged her eyebrows.

I chuckled. "Well, I basically told you everything. I was only there for a little while. Oh, but his eyes were this perfect shade of blue, and the scruff on his– ugh, I need to stop."

Callie and I both laughed.

"Okay, well do I need to–" She stopped talking abruptly, so I peered around the shower curtain with shampoo dripping down my forehead, nearly missing my eye.

"What?" I asked, annoyed.

"Well, I was going to ask if I needed to make myself scarce tonight so you could bring him back here, but then I realized he is probably your cousin."

Shit. I had that thought, too. I really need to stop thinking about him until I know for sure. I let the shower curtain go and went back to showering.

"Well you just ruined my lady boner, thank you very much." I laughed. "Kidding, but I had the same thoughts when I was there, thanks for the reminder. I need to chill a little."

She smirked. "Want me to change the subject?" she asked jokingly.

"Yes, please." I breathed out, dragging the please.

"We should go out and get drunk tonight, and maybe get some food, too."

I smiled at her words. That is the perfect subject change for me because I could use a good drink. We didn't usually go out much, just the two of us, since Jake was always with Callie. I try not to complain about it, but we don't get much alone time anymore, so this would be a nice change.

"There is a karaoke bar not too far from here, Want to try going there?" Callie asked, looking at her phone.

"Yeah, that's perfect. Oh, by the way, dinner is on me. Well technically, on my mom and dad because I'm using their money," I laughed.

"You don't have to tell me twice."

My parents transferred some money to me so I wouldn't have to worry about any expenses while on this trip. I'm thankful because I'm tapped out from moving and Christmas on top of that. They felt guilty and wanted to take care of most of the expenses. I didn't argue; I wouldn't have been able to come otherwise.

I heard her get up off the toilet. "Okay, I'm going to let you take care of that lady boner. I'll be out there with headphones on."

"I hate you," I said with a smile as I rolled my eyes.

"No you don't," she said as she shut the bathroom door.

She wasn't wrong. I really did need to take care of it.

It was time to figure out what to wear and get ready. The way Callie and I dress is another one of our differences. Callie wore a red bodycon dress that was shorter than her temper. She paired it with a cropped leather jacket and some heels. I, on the other hand, went with a more comfortable approach. A tight gray top with a cut-out on the chest that showed off the girls, and hip huggers with some cute ankle boots. I chose boots because when I wear heels, I look like a baby giraffe trying to walk after just being born.

My hair was down, which I didn't normally do, so I had Callie curl it for me. Although I'm a girly girl, I don't know anything about doing my hair, so it's always in a bun.

The bar was only a twenty-minute walk away from the hotel. We waited fifteen minutes for a table, which wasn't horrible because this was clearly the place to be tonight. I could definitely see myself hanging out here if I lived closer.

We walked to the bar to grab drinks while we waited. The bartender tried flirting with Callie, but she shut him down with a wave of her ring. We both opted to start with a glass of wine, mine white and hers red.

"How are you feeling about this?" Callie asked.

I took a sip of my wine. "Honestly, like I'm gonna shit my pants at any moment." We both laughed.

"It is going to be great. There is no possible scenario where he wouldn't love you."

"I wish you were right Cal, but what if he wants nothing to do with me? Do I just leave and pretend it didn't happen, forget I even found out? I don't think I can do that."

She thought for a moment. "Just don't put that into the world. Just know he's going to love you and that's it."

"Whatever you say, Cal."

Our hostess came to seat us and we ordered dinner. We got grilled chicken salads and split a plate of sweet potato fries. We call it our best friend dinner.

The music playing was great, and the people singing weren't half bad.I just wanted to chill and take in the scenery. I might dance a little, but I probably won't sing tonight because I have no confidence to sing without my guitar. Callie was okay with that because she would rather play music on the piano, not sing it.

We finished our meals but we weren't ready to go, so we ordered another appetizer. Wings are the perfect drunk food.

Jake called, so Callie stepped away. "I will be right back; I'm going to go take this call outside on the patio where it's quiet."

"Okay, I'll go get us more drinks," I said as we both got up.

"Margarita, please!" Callie chimed.

I watched her walk outside as I walked over to the bar and ordered both of us watermelon margaritas, mine with sugar and hers with salt.

It suddenly felt like someone was staring at me but I looked around and didn't immediately see anyone paying attention to me. I figured it was just my anxiety kicking in a little. I turned back towards the bar to throw a five-dollar bill into the tip jar and that's when I felt someone touch my arm, causing me to jump.

"Hey Miss Aubrey, didn't think I would see you here tonight. What are you up to?"

Those blue eyes I thought about while in the shower stared back at me. He leaned onto the bar next to me.

"I'm sorry. Do I know you?" I smirked.

"Oh, you wound me." He clutched his chest jokingly like I hurt his ego or something. The bartender placed my drinks down and I was relieved I had a reason to walk away. He was making me nervous already and all he did was say hello.

My laugh was apprehensive, "Okay, I will see you tomorrow Lincoln. I've gotta get these drinks back to my friend."

"Let me carry those for you, darlin'." He stepped in front of me and grabbed them both off the bar. "Lead the way."

I rolled my eyes but turned and led him toward the table anyway because I didn't want him to see my cheeks flush or the shit-eating grin on my face.

CHAPTER TEN

Aubrey

Callie was already back at the table giving me the look. She was silently asking if she needed to intervene. I pointed at the drinks and gave her a wink so she relaxed a little.

"Who's the sex god?" she mouthed. I'm almost positive he saw it. She is just about the least subtle person ever. I pointed to my eyes while mouthing "music store" to get her to understand I was talking about the guy from earlier. He placed them down on the table, nodded his head, and left. I thought he was gone for good, but he came back not even ten seconds later with his beer and slid into my side of the booth.

"Hey, I'm Lincoln, but friends call me Link. Nice to meet you." He reached across the table and shook Callie's hand. She shook his hand with her left hand to show off her ring, and he didn't miss the gesture.

"Nice to meet you, Lincoln," she said.

"You ladies are sassy. I like it." He put his arm over the back of the booth behind me, which made me shiver a little. "What are you ladies getting into tonight? Are you getting up there to sing?" I sipped my drink so Callie would answer.

"Nope. I suck, and she's too chicken to sing without her guitar."

I practically spit out my drink. I was so embarrassed. I swallowed hard. "Callie!"

"What? That's why you won't get up there, isn't it?" she challenged.

He smiled and turned his head. "You scared? Or do you suck too?" I caught the innuendo.

I cleared my throat. "I just don't want to sing tonight, that's all. I'm enjoying the music and food."

He kept that sexy ass smirk on his face, and I was sure he knew I was lying, but he didn't push any further. "What are you up to tonight?" I asked, trying to get the subject off me.

"I'm just here with some buddies, blowing off steam." He used his beer bottle to motion over to the bar where they were sitting. "We usually sit at the bar, but I like this seat a lot better. I think I may want to sit here all night."

"Is that so?" Callie questioned.

He just smiled and sipped his beer. "So, what are you ladies doing in town? Here for business or pleasure?"

"How do you know we don't live here?" I asked.

"I would know if a pretty girl like you lived here, darlin'." I blushed. This man is making me do that a lot today. Luckily it's dark in here, so he probably can't see it.

"How could you possibly know every girl in this town?"

"I would just know." He smiled again. I had to look away and sip my drink. I looked over and Callie was smiling from ear to ear.

"Maybe you should get back to your friends," I said without looking at him.

"They are fine. I see them all the time." He waved to his friends at the bar, and they nodded back. His friend gave him a look kind of like the one Callie gave me, Lincoln gave a thumbs up back, then turned his attention back to me. "Plus, wouldn't you miss me too much if I left?"

He is trying hard to get his flirt on, but I still don't know if this man is related to me, so I need to do some recon. I ignored the question and changed the subject again.

"How is it that you know August?" He looked surprised that I didn't respond to the flirty banter. He sat up a little straighter and removed his arm from behind me.

"He's my dad." My heart sank. "Not biologically, but he's the closest thing. He and my mom became my foster parents when I was fourteen, and I just never left. I guess you could say I'm their son without the paper to say so."

Oh, thank you, Jesus, there is a god.

"That's awesome," Callie said. Her smile was getting even more prominent. She gave me a nudge under the table and then stood. "I'm going to head to the bathroom."

"Oh, Cal, I can come with you." I tried to get up, but she pushed my shoulder down.

"It's all right. I'll be fine."

I know damn well she doesn't have to use the bathroom.

He moved to the other side of the booth as soon as we could no longer see Callie. He leaned in looking me up and down with his gaze lingering on my lips.

"So, clearly, she's taken. What about you?"

At that moment, a beautiful redhead stopped at our table. I immediately started having a flashback to when I caught Max cheating. This girl was beautiful, but also knew it, which was annoying already.

"Linky poo! I didn't know you would be here tonight." She leaned down and gave him a two-cheek kiss. I tried my hardest not to react with an eye roll, but I'm one of those people whose face tells you what I'm thinking. "Come sit with us outside. Some of us are going to sit by the bonfire for a while. You can warm me up a little."

She winked at him, and I raised my eyebrows. Could she be more desperately obvious? She was acting like she didn't even see me. Not that I'm anything to him, but still.

Lincoln turned toward me. "Kayla, this is Aubrey; we met today at the music shop. She's staying in town for a bit."

She gave me this disgusted look like I was moving in on her turf or something. I stuck out my hand to shake hers. "Nice to meet you."

She returned the shake with a limp hand. "Likewise." She looked back at him, and I was invisible once again. "So, will you come to sit with us, Linky?"

"Maybe in a bit; I'm quite enjoying the company here right now." He looked back at me, and I swear he made my panties wet just by smiling.

"Suit yourself," she said as she rolled her eyes and walked away.

I smiled at him. "Friend of yours?"

"More like a casual sex acquaintance," he shrugged. "We slept together once, and she teaches at the same school I do. She's interested, I'm not." He ran the lip of his beer bottle over his smile and took a sip.

I leaned in a little toward the table. "Got it; seeing her daily must be awkward, no?"

"Nah, it takes a lot to make me uncomfortable. I don't let my emotions get involved. Luckily we work on opposite sides of the building. She always finds reasons to see me though. It's a crush. Nothing crazy. I just don't want to hurt her feelings so I just brush her off. We hang with the same people sometimes so I don't want to make it awkward."

I took the comment about making him feel uncomfortable as a challenge. "Good to know you care so much."

We sat silently for a moment as I sipped the rest of my drink. Callie came back, grabbed my hand, and pulled me up onto my feet. "Let's go dance."

I set my empty drink down and let her pull me along. I mouthed *sorry,* and he motioned to say go ahead. I could feel him watching me. I tried my hardest not to look over to see if he was still at our table, but every time I managed to sneak a look, he was. He sat there with a huge grin on his face, elbow on the table, and his finger tracing his lips. He stared at me like he was assessing me.

"He's staring," Callie whispered.

I pinched her side. "I see that. Just ignore it. Maybe he will go back to his friends."

"Ow," she laughed. "You should ask him to dance. He would be a lot more fun to rub up against than me. Maybe even get him to take you for a ride," she winked.

I gave her a knowing grin. "No one's better than you," I winked back at her.

"You told me he was a hottie, but damn girl. He's like the fucking sun, he's so hot. Are you going for it? Maybe you can call him Daddy." Then she made a vulgar humping motion that I'm sure he saw.

"Callie," I dragged her name out. "Down girl." We were both giggling uncontrollably now. That is our sign that we've had enough to drink for now, but I didn't say no to the idea of going for it.

A few moments later, she leaned in and said, "Okay, don't freak, but he's walking this way." I turned, and there he was.

"May I have this dance m'lady?" He did a dorky bow and

put his hand out for me. It's as if he knew the song was changing, the music soon faded into a slow song.

"Of course, you can," Callie said as she pushed me into his arms. He caught me. "I have to call my mom anyway. I forgot to tell her we made it here okay." I gave her the 'I'm going to kill you look'.

He leaned his head toward my ear. "She really isn't subtle," He chuckled. He slid one of his hands down my lower back, instantly sending tingles down my spine. I couldn't help the goosebumps that formed over my body from his touch.

"Nope, but that's why she's the perfect best friend. I never have to wonder what she's thinking or if she's lying."

"That's a good way to look at it." He leaned down and whispered, "You look beautiful tonight, by the way. I don't think I've said that yet."

"No, you haven't." I smiled and tentatively placed my head on his shoulder. We danced for about a minute or so.

"You never answered my question before."

"What question would that be?" I looked him right in the eyes, knowing exactly what he was talking about.

He smiled. "Are you single, or is some poor guy missing his perfect girl back home?"

I was so turned on that I could barely speak. I gulped. "Yeah," I choked out.

"Yeah, to which one?" he asked as he raised one eyebrow in question.

"I'm single. You think I would have let you this close to me if I had a boyfriend?"

"I don't know, maybe. I know nothing about you." He paused and made sure he had my attention. "I'd like to get to know you. You're quite the mystery, Miss Aubrey."

"Does that work on all the girls?" I tried to pull away a

little, but he held me tightly. He leaned in so I could feel his breath again.

"Not all of them." He said with smugness. I practically melted. It was clear it was working on me. I had to find a way to leave this situation before I went home with this man and made him do dirty things to me. I spotted Callie coming back in. I pulled away, and this time he let me.

"We've got to head out. You should probably go find your friends and that beautiful sex friend of yours. She looked like a good time."

He caught the snark in my voice, I'm sure of it. I walked back to the table. I wasn't sure if he was following me until he grabbed my arm lightly and I turned around into him.

"Are you sure you have to leave? I can buy you another drink, and we can do the getting-to-know-each-other thing." His fingers were tenderly rubbing over my knuckles.

I quirked my head to the side. "People don't say no to you often, do they?"

"Honestly, not usually," he smiled shyly.

I leaned in like I was going to kiss him and whispered. "I'll see you tomorrow morning, Mr. Lincoln."

I pulled away, and he visibly shook as if he was removing the chill I had just given him. I turned and linked my arm with Callie's and walked out the door.

CHAPTER ELEVEN

Lincoln

How the hell does she do that? I've never had a woman turn me on and fuck my head up so much without trying. Usually, that's my job. I shook myself out of my stupor and realized she was walking out the door. I know I will see her tomorrow, but I have to try again.

What the hell is wrong with me? I don't chase girls. I don't *have* to chase girls. She's got me wrapped around her pinky and I need to flip the script. I rushed to the door and stepped out just before it closed behind her.

"You guys need a ride?" I asked.

"I think we will manage; we called a ride share. It will be here in a minute. Plus, I wouldn't want to take you away from all the fun you're about to have."

"Well, I was going to head home since you're leaving me. No reason to stay now."

She started laughing uncontrollably. It was adorable. She thanked me for the dance. Then the ride share car pulled up. I stepped forward and opened the door for them. Callie slid in first.

"Thank you, you are such a gentleman," Aubrey said as she rested her hand on my bicep.

I pulled her toward me a little. "I wish I weren't right at this moment. I wish there was something I could do to make you stay."

My smugness was getting gross; even I have to admit that. I'm trying way too hard. I've never wanted to be in someone's presence this bad before; again, what is wrong with me?

She kept smiling at me. "Have an amazing night, Lincoln."

She pulled away and got into the car. I shut the door and watched them pull away. I can't believe she left without even trying to kiss me. I could still smell her shampoo. It smelled like sweet strawberries mixed with something else.

I headed back into the bar to catch up with my friends, Connor and Elijah. They were trashed, so I knew I would be driving both of their drunk asses home. Although the way Connor was flirting with Kayla, he was probably going home with her. Elijah though, I'd definitely be worried about him getting home safe. He's the closest thing I have to a best friend if you can call it that.

Elijah is an up-and-coming rockstar. He is the lead vocalist in his brother's band, Reckless Riders, and they're home on break from touring.

Elijah doesn't drink when he's on tour because he is a mess after just two drinks, so he always tries to keep his wits about him, which I guess is somewhat responsible. When he is home though, he gets like this. It probably could be seen as a problem, but he says he is safe. He doesn't drive, and he clearly abstains when needed.

Elijah started tripping over himself so I decided it was time to go. I paid my tab and helped him out of the bar's back door and into my car. He continued singing and playing air guitar with the windows down. I offered to walk him into his apartment because it has a shit ton of stairs, but he declined. I waited to leave until I saw the light pop on through his window. Despite my calloused image, I can be nice sometimes.

On the drive home, I found myself smiling like a dork. I knew exactly what and who I would be dreaming about tonight.

I woke up with the biggest erection I've ever had, coupled with a pounding headache. I made my way into the kitchen and made myself a cup of coffee. My mind was swirling with the events of last night as I stood at the counter looking out the window. I still couldn't believe she didn't come home with me; I guess there was a first time for everything.

All I could think about before I fell asleep last night was fucking Aubrey. I was dying to know what it would feel like to be inside her. I needed to know what she would sound like when she—*Fuck*!

I subconsciously began pleasuring myself. Somehow this girl has taken over my every thought. If the mere idea of her did this, I think she may be the death of me. Seeing Aubrey again seemed to be my only focus. I am so ready to make my dreams a reality.

I returned to my bedroom and finished what I had started in the kitchen. I needed to take care of this erection, or I wouldn't be able to run otherwise. I chugged my coffee and protein shake, and then I was out of the house by seven in the morning to start my morning run. Although I feel like complete trash, I know I'll feel worse if I go back to sleep.

Running has always helped me clear my head, and right now I need it to clear up fast before I see her again. I haven't thought about a girl like this...well...ever. I still can't fathom how after only one dance and a few fleeting touches she seems to occupy my brain more than anyone I've ever met. I was about half a mile away from home when I heard her breathless voice.

"Hey, fancy seeing you here."

I stopped short and turned around. "Aubrey? What are you doing on this side of town so early?"

My eyes roamed over her body. Why did she have to look so sexy in her tight top and leggings? She was wearing a long-sleeve top with a zipper that was only zipped halfway up so the tops of her breasts were showing. Her leggings were hugging her curves perfectly. My dick enjoyed the view, for sure. I had to look away from her for a moment to keep my body from reacting so I bent down to tie my shoe.

"Early? This isn't early," she chuckled. "I've been up since six this morning, which is late for me. During the week at home, I get up closer to five."

She smiled at me, and I realized she didn't have makeup on like the other times I'd seen her. She had her hair up. It looked like it may have been a bun, but some strands were loose and falling out. Having her hair away from her face showed off her features. She was genuinely and naturally pretty. Her eyes were darker today, more of a deep blue. I liked this Aubrey better, honestly.

"I like running when no one else will see me; I don't enjoy people staring at me. Most people don't understand how a big girl like me runs, so I just avoid others as much as possible. I feel like I look crazy when I run anyway."

"Number one, there is absolutely nothing wrong with your body. You're fucking perfect. Anyone who thinks differently needs their fucking eyes checked." I saw her cheeks blush a little. "Number two, I'm only about a half mile into my run if you care to join me but, be warned, I will be staring at you, and you will enjoy it. So will I, for that matter." She slapped my shoulder with the back of her hand and took off running. "Hey, wait up. I can't ogle you if you run away from me."

"Such a charmer, Lincoln," she called out.

We ran for another two miles. I kept letting her run in front of me so that I could check out her ass. We ended up in front of her hotel. I didn't realize it, but she had her maps app telling her where to go in her headphones. I was wondering why she wasn't asking me which way to go.

She laughed as she leaned down and put her hands on her knees to catch her breath. As she was leaning down, her boobs almost fell out of her top. At that moment, I swear all the blood in my body went straight to my dick. My mouth went completely dry, and I had to take a sip of my water just to help myself breathe.

"That was fun, thanks; I love a good challenge," she said smugly

After a moment, she stood up straight, wiped the sweat from her forehead, and then looked me in the eye like she was looking right through me. "I'll see you at The Music Bar in a bit, right?"

"I wouldn't miss it."

She smiled, put her hand on my bicep to say goodbye, then turned and walked inside. Now, I have to go home and beat off for the second time today.

CHAPTER TWELVE

Aubrey

Today is the day I'd been waiting for. I had a panic attack in the shower and had to sit down and do my breathing exercises. I wore jeans and a nice sweater because it seemed colder today than it was yesterday. I put my hair up in my signature bun, and I put on some light makeup. I had a feeling that I may cry a lot in the next few hours.

Callie finally woke up at nine-thirty when I was getting ready to go out the door. She slept through the entirety of my leaving, coming back, and even showering and drying my hair. That girl can sleep through anything. She is the furthest thing from a morning person. God help her if she ever has kids.

"I'm heading there early so I can stop and grab some coffee. Do you need anything before I go?" She stood up from the bed and hugged me tightly.

"Do *you* need anything before you go?" she repeated back to me.

"No. I just need to go. I already broke down in the shower after my run with Lincoln." I smiled really big because I knew that would set her off.

"Your what? With who?" she asked as her eyes bulged out of her head. She pulled back but still had her hands on my shoulders. "Explain!"

I kissed her cheek. "Okay, love you. Byeeee. I'm walking so you can have the car," I said as I walked out the door.

She hated it when I did shit like that, which I did often and on purpose because I love pushing her buttons. I heard her yell something else, but I wasn't sure what since the door had already shut. Probably just that I would have to tell her later or something.

I stopped at the coffee shop and ordered a mocha for myself and two black coffees for them. Then I remembered this barista knew everyone's order.

"Hey, do you know what August and Lincoln from the music shop get when they come here?"

Her smile was sweet. "Of course, darlin'. Is that who these other two are for?"

"Yes, I'll take my light and sweet mocha and then whatever they get. Forget the black coffee please."

"You got it, darlin'." She turned and started making our drinks. "Are you working there or something? You're new around here." The last part wasn't a question, more like an observation.

"No, I am just passing through for now. I have some personal business to take care of in town. I'm just grabbing coffee to thank them for welcoming me yesterday."

It was a half-truth, but I think she bought it. She handed me the tray of coffee.

"You give them my best, will you? And you tell them to stop by and see me more often. I miss seeing those beautiful blue eyes they both have. That handsome young stud Link sure is nice to look at." That made my stomach jump; I'm not sure why. She stuck her hand out to shake mine. "My name is Mable, but most people call me Miss Mable because I'm the old lady around here." I laughed a little and shook her hand.

"I'm Aubrey. Nice to meet you, Miss Mable. I will let them know to show their faces more." She smiled as I turned and headed out the door.

I started shaking as I walked by the table, so I sat down and called my parents. I just wanted to hear their voices and say good morning; I hoped hearing them would calm my nerves. We spoke for a few minutes, and it did help a little. I was just about to get up to leave the coffee shop when someone sat down beside me.

"Audrey, right?" Kayla said as she sat down. Her red hair was all mangled into a bun, and her makeup was a bit smudged. She was wearing the same outfit from last night.

"No, actually. It's Aubrey." I smiled, knowing she was trying to be facetious. "How are you today?"

"Oh, I'm great; I was just going to head over to see if Linky Poo wanted to get dinner tonight. We spend time together quite often. He's a very busy man if you know what I mean. He's always out with someone new, so you gotta tie down plans when you can."

"Oh really? He told me you guys hooked up once. He said you were interested, unlike him." I gave her a knowing smile.

She rolled her eyes and stood up almost as if she were offended. "Have a nice day, Audrey."

"Again, it's Aubrey. And Kayla, you may want to check a mirror babe." She gave me a dirty look. "You're welcome. I hope you have the day you deserve." I smiled, as she scoffed and walked away. I sat there for a few more minutes in case she really was going the same way. I didn't want her to think I was following her.

I walked over to The Music Bar and looked up at the sign. *I'm really doing this.* Good or bad, I will be happy with the outcome; I got this. I grabbed the handle to the door and walked in.

Link was at the counter and, for some reason, that comforted me. I saw him talking to Kayla. The girl moves fast. He looked pretty uncomfortable, so I walked over and handed him the coffee with his name on it.

"Good morning again!" I said, a bit too chipper, to both of them.

Link looked at the cup I offered him and took a sip. "Mmm, this is the exact coffee I drink." He looked at me with a wicked grin. "I knew it wouldn't take you long to start stalking me."

I rolled my eyes and snorted. "Hardly."

He laughed. "Thanks. How did you know what I drink?"

"You can thank Miss Mable for stalking you for me. Maybe you could try your luck with her. She seems to think you're quite the catch." I smiled.

He smirked. "Ah, yes, that woman remembers everything. Even the things I wish she would forget," he chuckled. "Miss Mable has saved me many mornings when I drank too much the night before. She never did rat on me," he smiled.

"I was grateful. I was going to bring you black coffee. It looks like you got some frilly drink there. What is it exactly?"

"Honestly, I don't even think it has a name. She just made it for me one day when I asked for something with a ton of sugar, and now that's all I get when I go there."

"Well, I'm gonna head out." We both turned to look at Kayla. I had forgotten she was standing there. "Linky, let me know about dinner. You have my number."

Link smiled as she walked out. "Sorry about her. She's getting worse, if that's even possible."

"Oh, so she didn't go home with you?" I asked. I'm not really sure if I honestly wanted to know.

He leaned toward me. "Why? Are you jealous?"

I was about to respond when August came out. He had a massive smile on his face. I felt my own smile drop, and then I went numb. He was handsome for an older man. I could tell he originally had light hair, but it was now very salt-and-pepper.

My eyes.

He has my eyes, or rather, I have his. I've never seen someone with my eyes before. He interrupted my thoughts by speaking.

"Hello. Are you Aubrey? Nice to meet you. What can I help you with today? Link over here said you had something life-changing for me." He chuckled, almost as if he was being sarcastic or thought Link was just being dramatic.

"Um, I do, actually. I mean, yes, I'm Aubrey. Sorry, I'm a bit nervous. Can we talk somewhere privately?" I handed him the coffee, and I could tell he was getting weary. He looked at it, almost scared because it was his exact order.

"Miss Mable," I said. He looked at me with recognition.

"Ah, okay, and sure. Would you like to talk here or outside?" I bit my lip because I honestly wasn't sure.

"Um, wherever we will have the most privacy, please." August looked at Link, and one eyebrow arched.

"Okay, dear. We can talk in my office if you're comfortable with that?"

"Yes, that works for me." I started walking toward the back, all the while fidgeting with my fingers. Link gave me a concerned look, but I just ignored it and went on back.

August came in behind me and closed the door. He looked at me as if to ask if the closed door was okay. He could tell I was extremely uncomfortable. I nodded yes. He pulled up an extra chair across from his desk for me and then went to the other side to sit in his own chair.

"Okay. So how can I help you?" he asked. The concern was evident in his tone.

I had to swallow the lump that had formed in my throat. "Well, I'm not quite sure how to start this or even attempt to say this with any type of finesse, so I'm just going to come out and say it." I paused and took a breath. I started fidgeting with my hands again.

"I'm...um...I'm actually your daughter."

His eyebrows went up, and he looked at me like I had two heads. He sat up a bit straighter and cleared his throat. "Okay, I'll play. What gave you that conclusion?"

I handed him the DNA test that showed our results.

"We have a fifty percent match for DNA. That makes you my parent. You actually should have received an email that you had a new match. We were matched almost two weeks ago now." I couldn't tell if he was just stunned or stopped breathing altogether. He looked at the results for a few minutes longer.

"What? How? Wait a second, I didn't get anything. I did this years ago when my whole family did it for fun at Christmas. We thought it would be interesting to trace our heritage back." He was shuffling papers around on his desk. "Sorry, I just got back from vacation a few minutes ago. Well, I got back Friday night, but today was my first day back here."

"I ramble too," I blurted out, trying to break the tension.

He reached for his phone. I assumed to check his email. He

kept rubbing his eyebrow, just like I do when I'm about to panic. He had a few beads of sweat forming on his forehead.

I didn't say anything. I was sitting quietly letting him process the news.

"Oh wow! It looks like I missed it. I'm so sorry. I usually don't check my own email." He thought for another moment. "How did you come across this? Why are you just now finding me? How old are you? I have never cheated on my wife. We have been together for over twenty years. This is impossible."

I let him catch his breath from all the questions, and I started to share the whole story. "I found a birth certificate that was blank in the father portion, which was weird because I grew up with a dad. I found a few other things that led me to confront my parents, and I'm twenty-three."

"Who's your mom?" he asked abruptly.

"Her name is Michelle. She was nineteen when you met at a party at someone's apartment who went to Southern Connecticut State University."

He seemed to be doing some math in his head, trying to figure out where he was or how this happened. I showed him a picture of her, and his face suddenly went white.

"That's your mother?" he said with disbelief.

His voice was shaky. He looked like he was trying to recall some memories. "This can't be. It's just about impossible. I was always careful when I was young. I always used—" He stopped talking; I think for my benefit.

"She did mention that you took precautions that night. She said, 'God had other plans.' When she found out she was pregnant, she tried to reach out to people there to find out who you were. She tried for her whole pregnancy to find you, but she had no luck." I could tell his mind was reeling.

"No one there really knew me. I was only there for a few

days and, if I remember correctly, I was visiting my cousin. I forced him to take me out because I was bored. He told me he had friends who went to the local college, and we all met up for a house party. He didn't even stay long at that party; I only did because I met your mom. I didn't even get her name that night. I also looked for her for a while, but no one knew her from how I described her. I gave up because I wasn't from there, and figured she would have asked for my information if she had wanted anything more. When I woke up the morning after…she was gone." He blushed a little. "Sorry, this conversation is a bit awkward." He was rubbing the back of his head. It was like he read my mind. "Why didn't she keep looking until she found me?"

I swallowed the lump in my throat. "Well, she kind of hit a dead end. As I said, she didn't really know anyone. She was new in town and barely knew the person who invited her, plus," I paused. "My dad also asked her not to. They met after you two, obviously, but they were in love, and he didn't care that I wasn't his biologically, so they raised me like I was and never told me. They legally changed my name and had my birth certificate 'fixed,' if you will."

I paused for a moment to get him to look at me. He didn't, so I looked at my hands.

"I know you probably still have a million and one questions, which I still do, too. I've even had time to process it somewhat. I want you to know I don't want anything from you. I'm not looking for handouts or anything like that. I have now—and have always had— a great life." He was still looking down. "I just wanted you to know I existed and to meet you once. You don't have to get to know me if you don't want to."

We looked at each other, but his gaze was too intense, so I lowered my eyes down again.

"If my showing up here ruins or derails your life, it doesn't have to leave this room. I can leave right now and never contact you again. I know this is crazy weird, and I—"

I heard a sniff. I looked at him, and tears were running down his face. He was holding my DNA results paper. "I can't believe this; I can't believe I have a daughter."

I was stunned at his reaction.

"Can I hug you?" he whispered.

I stood up way too eagerly. "Yes, please!"

I started crying the moment we touched. He smelled like wood and Carvin. It's a lacquer that goes on guitars. Which smells like vanilla to me. I felt a massive wave of relief when his arms wrapped around me. My chest filled with warmth. I can't even explain how good it felt to hug him. He held me for a few minutes until he pushed me back to look at my face up close.

"You have my eyes."

I nodded, and the tears just kept coming. August rubbed my cheeks and looked at me like he was studying me.

"My daughter. I–I can't believe this. You are an absolute gift from God; do you know that?"

I laughed through my tears. August let me go as he went to grab me some tissues to clean my face. I was thanking God that I went with light makeup today.

He moved my chair to the other side of his desk, right next to his so we were a bit closer when we were talking. He leaned onto his knees and held both my hands in his as we spoke.

"I can't wait to learn everything there is to know about you and your family."

"You aren't angry?" I asked. I was still kind of stunned and was trying to tread lightly.

"I know I will probably have some different feelings once the shock and happiness wears off, but right now, gratitude is the only thing I can feel." He paused so he could take a breath. He was speaking so fast, just like I do. "So, tell me everything."

This excitement was not the reaction I was expecting. I was shocked he was taking this so well. Could he really be this nice?

I went on to share everything I could. I shared how I always felt out of place growing up. I told him how I always knew something was missing, and we talked about my love of music. He found that quite ironic. I found out that he also plays guitar from time to time. He took a class on instrument making and made something once, but it wasn't his thing. We decided we would jam together at some point. I couldn't stop word-vomiting about my life once I realized how similar we were. About an hour later, we were interrupted when there was a knock at the door.

"Hey, sorry to interrupt, but someone out there needs to talk to you about a tuba," Link said.

August looked at me with worry. "I'll be right back. Don't go anywhere. I want to take you to lunch." He said with hope in his voice. He put his hand on my shoulder before he walked away.

I put my hand on his. "I wouldn't dream of it. I'd love to get lunch with you."

Link stepped out of the way and let him go by. He stepped into the office. "You guys have been back here for a while; you good?" He had a grin on his face like he could tell whatever was going on was good news.

"I'm great." I smiled.

"You gonna let me in on the secret as to why you're here?"

I shook my head. "I will leave it to August to share that information with you." I was still smiling ear to ear. "Do you have a bathroom here? I would love to freshen up a little bit."

He pointed to a door to my left.

"Thanks."

Lincoln looked as confused as ever. Understandably so.

CHAPTER THIRTEEN

Lincoln

I had no idea what was happening, but she was smiling, which, if I had to guess, seemed like a good sign. I've seen her smile a few times since yesterday in several different settings, but not like this. This smile was reaching her eyes, making them sparkle. It was a new kind of beauty. Somehow, they were a brighter blue than yesterday.

Her eyes were brighter than yesterday. What the fuck? I don't think about girls' eyes like that.

I shook off my thoughts and went back out front to see if anyone else needed help. I really just needed to get out of Aubrey's space and get a grip on myself. I barely know this girl. I don't call women beautiful or think about the different shades of their eyes. What the hell kind of shit is that? Something is seriously wrong with me.

"Hey, are you going to be able to join us for lunch?" Aubrey asked as she walked out from the back. I didn't even realize she had come out. She startled me, but I don't think she noticed— otherwise, she would have made fun of me. She seems to be very sassy like she's not afraid to break your balls...it's fucking hot.

I kept myself from saying what I really wanted to say; what I really wanted for lunch was Aubrey. I cleared my throat. "Unfortunately, someone has to slum it and stay here for all these customers." I gestured to the empty store. I smiled to let her know I was sort of joking. "But feel free to bring me something delicious. I'll gladly take anything you're willing to give me." I said with a wink. I meant it exactly how it sounded.

Her head went back, and she laughed loudly. Her laugh was contagious. I started to smile as soon as I heard it.

"Is that so? I'll have to think about it a little." She winked right back. She had some sexy sass, I'll give her that.

Pops was making his way back to the front where we were standing.

"Sorry about that," he said, putting his arm around Aubrey's shoulder. For some reason, I felt a flutter in my chest, almost like I was jealous or something. "Did you tell Link the news?" he asked.

My eyebrows went up in confusion, and I gave them a questioning look. Aubrey looked up at Pops, and she was beaming.

"Oh, no. I figured that was your news to share."

"It's our news," he said excitedly.

I don't think I've ever seen him this happy before. Pops looked at me as he pulled her in even closer to himself and spoke. He looked right at me as if he was about to drop some serious news.

"You have a sister," he said with a huge grin.

A what? "What?" Aubrey and I both said simultaneously. We were both looking at him like he was crazy. I saw her stiffen in his arms, and her cheeks became flushed.

"Link, this is my daughter. She came all the way here to

find me from Connecticut." He was beaming at her once again. "Can you believe this? I have a beautiful daughter." He pulled her in and hugged her tighter.

"That doesn't make her my sister," I said curtly. Then I looked at her and could tell by her face that she was having the same thoughts. At least, I hoped she was.

"Well, no, not biologically but theoretically. You are my son, are you not?"

"Yeah, I guess, but that still doesn't make Aubrey my sister. She can't be my sister. She's too—"

He started to understand what I was talking about because he held her tighter and gave me a look like I was doing something wrong.

"Don't even think about it, Lincoln Matthew. This perfect girl is off-limits. She will not succumb to your bullshit charm."

She chuckled and tried to cover her laugh with her hand, but I saw it. I'm going to get her for that one day soon. Her genuine smile was showing through again. It was the kind of beauty that not everyone noticed right away. It wasn't that 'oh my god, she's fucking hot' look. She is pretty and doesn't know it, making her even more attractive.

Pops cut off my thoughts, "Let's talk about this later; she and I have some catching up to do and lunch to eat. We will bring you back something, okay Link?"

Then I looked over at Aubrey. Although she was still smiling, she looked just as uncomfortable with being called my sister as I felt.

"Uh yeah, let's go eat, I guess. See you later, Lincoln Matthew." She smiled again when she enunciated my middle name.

Pops laughed his hearty laugh.

"That's my girl. You fit in already," he said.

I'll get Aubrey for that later, too.

AUBREY

August and I walked to a cute sandwich shop just down the road from the music store. The town had all kinds of shops and quaint little places to stop and hang out. I even spotted the cutest little bookstore on our walk. I would have to tell Brie about it. It was totally up her alley, mine too, depending on what they had in stock. I like reading music theory and romance novels. I have quite a few book boyfriends since I'm not having any luck finding a real one. I'm obsessed with the happily ever after I will probably never get.

On the walk over, I texted Callie to tell her everything was going well. She asked again about the run with Link, and I sent my signature kissy-face emoji, then silenced my phone. I knew that would piss her off.

August and I ordered burgers, but I got mine with no tomatoes; those things are my worst enemy.

"So, where are you staying?" he asked.

"My best friend Callie and I got a room at the Mountain Inn. We booked it for a few days and figured we would plan it out as we go."

"Oh no, no, no. You must come to stay with us." Then he sat back and thought. "I need to talk to Liza first and explain everything, of course, but there is no reason you should spend money on a hotel. We have perfectly good bedrooms that were just painted and refurbished. Only one is ready, but if you give us a day or two, we will get the other one ready for you. Also, Liza is an amazing cook." I smiled because the thought of getting to know him and his wife on a deeper level made my heart happy.

"That's so generous, but I wouldn't want to leave her alone in a hotel."

"She's just as welcome to stay as you are," he added.

I looked at him in awe. I couldn't believe he was taking this news with such ease. "Can I ask you something?" He nodded. "You barely know me. Why would you let complete strangers stay with you?"

He grabbed my hand. "You aren't a stranger. You are my daughter. We are family."

I smiled a little. "Sorry if I'm acting like I'm not grateful. Believe me, I really am. I just can't believe you don't want more proof or something. I mean, you have known me for all of two hours. Maybe you want to research me? I would totally understand, of course. It's just...how do you know I'm not a crazy serial killer?"

He chuckled. His laugh was just like mine but more profound. He took a sip of his water.

"I can tell by looking at you that we are related. I thought it before you even told me and...Are you a serial killer? Should I be worried?" he laughed again.

I smiled. "No, but what kind of murderer would I be if I told you?"

"Okay, you got me there. I'll still take the chance on you staying with us." He leaned forward. "Just do me a favor. If you are a killer, kill me first and let Liza go. She is too important for this world to lose her just yet."

My heart warmed with emotion at that statement.

"Got it," I grinned. "It is very kind of you to offer the rooms to us. Callie will most likely have to go home. She was only staying so I wasn't alone. Her mom, our boss, lost us both at her restaurant just so Callie could accompany me here. I want her to return to the restaurant and her piano students as quickly as possible." I paused for a moment. "As long as you guys aren't serial killers." We both burst out laughing.

He composed himself and said, "No problem, just know the offer is there. Also, please let your boss and your students know that I am forever grateful they allowed you the time to come find me." He paused and started to look a little uncomfortable. "I would love to talk to your mother and father, if possible. We have a lot to discuss." He smiled, even though it was a little forced.

The thought of him talking to my parents made my stomach turn. I prayed that the conversation would go well because I didn't want to lose this happiness. I'm sure it will be tense. I just hope they can get along. I hope he can be part of my life in some capacity now that we have found each other.

We finished eating and got lost in conversation while our food settled, and then August paid the bill.

"Okay, I've got to return to the shop. I need to give Link a break and get some work done. Sundays are usually my paperwork days. Although I don't know if I'll get much done today, this was life-changing." —he smiled like he was thinking of something funny— "Maybe I should just call today a wash and close early; I need to talk to Liza as soon as possible. I want her to know you. Once she gets over the initial shock, I'm sure she will be so excited."

He looked a little sad, "We couldn't have kids, even after years of trying. Liza got sick, so we started fostering. That's how we were blessed with Link." He was getting up but stopped abruptly. "Come to dinner tonight?"

I smiled. "I will ask if Callie is okay with that when I return to the hotel. Thank you for lunch. I really appreciate it. All of this, really. I had so much fun learning about you and Liza. I can't wait to meet her; she sounds charming."

He offered to walk me to my hotel, but I insisted he return to work. We exchanged cell numbers, and I headed to meet Callie.

When I entered the hotel room, I was assaulted by the smell of chlorine mixed with my body wash. Callie apparently took it upon herself to go through my stuff because my hairbrush was next to her, and she was sitting on the bed against the headboard in her towel with her legs up on my bag. She didn't even turn to acknowledge me.

"Comfy much?" I asked with a laugh. I pushed her feet off the bag when I walked by to get to my bed.

She laughed and stood up. "Yes, actually. I just got back from swimming in the pool and took a nice, hot shower. Jake called. He is acting super weird. It's like he needs to know exactly every detail of what we are doing and when. He asked me who I was with last night, can you believe that? Like I have the time to be with anyone but his stubborn ass, plus I called him like three times."

I laughed at her admission, and she continued.

"And I hung up on him because he thought he would get loud with me." She removed the towel leaving her in just her bra and underwear. She sat up staring into *my* bag, "I'm trying to decide what to wear, but I wasn't sure what we were doing today."

She laid back and acted like she was relaxing, but then her

eyes flew open like a light bulb went off, and it was clear she just remembered where I came back from.

"Oh my god, how was it? Was he nice? Was he tall like you? Did he have your eyes? Was he mean? Did he believe you? Did he blow you off? Wait, what about Lincoln? What happened with him?"

I put my hand up to stop her questions, "Bitch, really? First of all, why would Jake suddenly care so much about your whereabouts? That's new for him, No?"

She scoffed in mock offense.

"Cal, shut up, you know what I mean. Of course, he cares about you, but why so intently all of a sudden?" She just shrugged. She was about to speak again, but I stopped her.

"Sit down, crazy. Let me tell you everything. I told you over the phone it was going well. I promise I won't leave anything out. Starting with the run this morning."

I wagged my eyebrows which made her laugh. She gathered her blanket off her bed, wrapped it around herself, and then sat beside me while I told her everything.

A few hours later, I got a message from August. That warm feeling was consuming me again; I hadn't felt this content in a long time. He made sure we were okay with what they were having for dinner and double-checked that we didn't have any food allergies. I asked him what Liza's favorite wine was so I could bring her something. He sent me a picture because I had never heard of it. I really didn't want to mess this up. It was heartwarming how excited we all were. Hearing his excited tone made my heart swell with contentment. It felt like a piece of me was being healed by his voice.

LINCOLN

My mind is buzzing with questions. That beautiful, sassy, sexy girl cannot be my sister. I guess, technically, it doesn't matter because Pops and I aren't biologically related. He will fucking kill me if I try to get with her. Problem is...I *need* to. She intrigues me more than anyone I have ever met.

I saw Pops coming back through the window. My stomach dropped in anticipation of seeing her, but within a few seconds, I realized she wasn't following. Pops walked in, waved at me, and went right to the back. A few minutes later, he came out with a piece of paper.

"After these last few people leave, close up for me, okay? We're closing early today."

I looked at him with complete disbelief. He *never* closes early. The only other time was when we were rearranging the store last month. Even when he's sick and can't come in, he ensures someone is here to keep the store open. This store is his baby. That vacation was the first time he wasn't here in years.

"I need you to come home so I can talk to you and Mom together."

"Is everything okay?" I asked with apparent hesitation.

"Yes, of course; I just need to explain what's happening, and it will be easier to tell the both of you together."

"Yeah, what is happening? You just dropped the bomb that she was your daughter and bounced. Where is she? Did she leave? Is she coming back?" I felt like I was running out of air. Why did I sound so desperate?

"Yeah, she is coming over later." I felt my stomach flip a little. "Link, I'm serious about leaving her alone. Do not run her off or mess with her."

"Pops. You can't ask me not to—" I cut myself off because I didn't want to fight with him about this, "I will close up as soon as I can." He left me the paper and went on his way. The paper just said we had to close early for a personal day. I guess that is true. I felt like it was taking forever for these last few customers to leave.

I couldn't wait to get home to talk about everything. My excitement died when I walked in and my mom was crying into her hands. She looked up at me, and I realized she was crying happy tears. I stepped forward and she pulled me into a tight hug.

"Did you hear? You have a sister."

I groaned in disgust. "Mom, she's not my sister, but I heard about her being his daughter, yes."

She gave me a knowing look. "How pretty is she? That's the only reason you would have said that. Don't you da—"

I cut her off because I was not having this conversation right now. "Are you okay, Momma? This was some big news for you guys."

"It's big news for all of us, Lincoln. I'm just overwhelmed. My brain can't decide if it's angry, excited, or sad. I guess it's all three, honestly. I wish we had known about her all this time. We missed out on so much, and I have so many questions."

So do I.

Pops started telling me everything he had told Mom, and I was dumbfounded. I honestly didn't know what to ask first.

"Aubrey will be coming over for dinner with her girlfriend tonight. Make yourself look like a respectable human please."

My stomach dropped.

"Wait, Is Aubrey gay?" I asked, way too interested, "And for the record, I always look good, old man."

"Lincoln Matthew!" Mom exclaimed. "There is nothing wrong with being gay."

"I didn't say there was. I love lesbians. She just doesn't seem gay to me," I said smugly. Mom slapped me playfully.

"Ouch," I said with a chuckle as I rubbed my head.

"I don't know if she's gay, which is fine either way," Pops gave me a look, "What I meant was she and her friend are coming over. She has a friend who traveled with her, so I invited them both for food and drinks," Pops corrected.

Oh, thank God he's talking about Callie. Crisis averted. Pops said she would be over in about two hours. I need to change so I can make another good impression. I need to get her into my bed, so it's time to up my game.

CHAPTER FOURTEEN

Aubrey

Callie and I got ready to head to dinner with the Fosters. I wanted to look nice but casual. I changed about five times. I settled on a knee-length sweater dress with skin-colored tights and cute ankle boots. I felt more nervous about meeting Liza than I had been about meeting August. I didn't think that being more nervous than that was even possible. I don't want her to hate me. I hope they aren't fighting because of me.

"I hope this goes well," I said to Callie.

She linked her arm to mine and put her head on my shoulder. "It will. He already loves you; she will too. You are too amazing not to love."

I looked at her with admiration. "How did I get so lucky to have you as a best friend?"

"No idea, but you're a lucky bitch, Aubs," she laughed and then got more serious. "We both are."

I nudged her and laughed as we grabbed our purses. I told her we should text Nick and let him know it was going well. She rolled her eyes at me. I stopped dead in my tracks.

"What could you possibly be mad at him for? How is that even possible? We aren't even home, Cal."

Callie was always mad at him for something. I think it's purely sexual tension.

"No, I just didn't wanna think about him while we were here."

She started walking again and stepped in front of the elevator door to press the button.

"What's that supposed to mean?"

Callie rolled her eyes again. She pulled me to get me moving. "Never mind, let's just go."

I let it go and made a mental note to ask her about it later. Something was off, but now was not the time to get into it with her. I sent Nick a quick text on the way over instead.

It was a gorgeous home with a cottage further back into the backyard. It was almost something you see in the movies. It was a white house that had blue shutters and a black door with perfectly cut grass and a white fence. It reminded me of the perfect life I had always wanted.

We approached the door, which flew open before I could knock. Liza was so pretty. She had pretty brown eyes and short, curly, auburn hair that was turning gray at the roots. She was tiny. If I had to guess, she was shorter than my mom.

"You ladies are beautiful!" she exclaimed, looking us up and down. She cradled my face in her warm palms as tears welled in her eyes.

"Oh my gosh, look at me keeping you in the cold; please, come on in." She opened the door wider and gestured for us to enter. "August will be right down. Come sit with me in the den while dinner finishes cooking."

I was so nervous. I was almost too scared to speak. Callie gave me a look, and I just shrugged.

"I'm Callie; nice to meet you, Mrs. Foster." She reached out to shake her hand, but Liza went in for a hug before she could sit.

She scoffed. "Oh please, call me Liza, and we hug in this family." Then she looked at me and grabbed my hand, "I could tell when I saw you that you must be our precious Aubrey." She pulled me into the tightest embrace. She smelled like cocoa and apple pie.

"Yes, I...Uh...It's great to meet you. August couldn't stop talking about you at lunch." I added. My brain had stopped working, and I was stuttering.

She couldn't stop smiling. She stared for a second, and then I think she realized she was gawking. She stood back up.

"Can I get you ladies anything while we wait? Water, wine, soda?"

I realized I was still holding the wine we brought.

"Wine would be great," Callie answered as she grabbed it from me.

I nodded my head in agreement. Liza headed into the kitchen. I let out a breath as soon as she left, but I quickly tensed back up when she returned; she was still smiling from ear to ear.

"Your home is so pretty. You pay such attention to detail. I love it." Callie said.

I agree. This house is beautiful. She even had those little wine charms so we could keep track of which wine glass was ours. Mine was a cute flower. Liza set the wine down, and I heard a grunt come from behind me; I turned and saw Lincoln standing there.

I was staring, and Callie had to knock my knee with her leg to get me to snap out of it. I could tell by the stupid grin on his face that he caught me. It was kind of sexy, which made me mad at the same time because he clearly knows exactly how hot he is. It's annoying. I wanted to hate him for it, but I didn't. He sat beside Liza and kissed her cheek. She waved him away from her cheek.

"Oh, stop it," she blushed a little. "Go in the kitchen and check on the food."

"Yes, ma'am," he said with a salute. When he entered the kitchen I heard him say, "Don't go in there. They are having girl talk." I can only assume he was talking to August.

Liza started talking again. "So, what have you ladies done since getting here?"

August came in to join us, so I stood and hugged him. He held me tight, making me laugh because I hugged him back just as tight. I still can't believe this is real.

"Hey, good to see you again. This is my best friend, Callie."

She stood and shook his hand.

"Nice to meet you, Callie; I've heard only good things about you. Thanks for caring for her on the ride down here and ensuring she wasn't alone. I really appreciate it."

Hearing him thank her for caring for me warmed my heart. It was very fatherly.

"Of course," she pulled him a little closer and dropped her voice, "Please make sure she's just as taken care of when I leave. That girl is my soulmate, and I would die without her."

I slapped her thigh playfully. She looked down at me and laughed before sitting back down beside me.

I looked back at Liza. "To answer your question, Liza, we have only been here for just over twenty-four hours. We went to a nice dinner last night and did some dancing. We saw Lincoln there and talked a little." She gave me a look like she was worried. "Then today...Well, I guess you already heard how I spent my morning," I laughed.

"And I just relaxed at the hotel," Callie added.

"That's great. Any plans for future days or are you not sure yet?"

Liza was so sweet and genuine, but I looked at her a little wearily because I wasn't sure what August told her about me staying here.

"Well, actually, Callie leaves tomorrow. She needs to get back to work as soon as possible. The less time her mom has to cover our shifts, the better. I didn't think this meeting would go so smoothly." I started to twist the hem of my sweater in my hands.

"I don't know if August has already spoken to you, but—"

"I did," August interrupted. I think he saw how uncomfortable I was.

"You did what?" Link came walking back in, chewing on something. He sat on the arm of the couch next to Callie.

"He offered me a room so that I could stay here for a bit while he and I get to know each other." I looked at Liza and August. "I can pay you some money, of course. I want to contribute."

She raised her hand to stop me. "You will do no such thing. Family stays here for free."

"I insist," I said. "I need to earn my keep. Maybe I can help Lincoln and August at the shop, then?" Link's eyes got wide.

August was beaming. "I would love that. Link isn't there during the week, but I'd be glad to have you come hang out with me. Maybe you can teach me a thing or two." He laughed.

"How long are you staying?" Link asked. He looked worried, or was it hopeful?

"Lincoln Matthew! Don't be so rude," Liza said.

"I wasn't being rude, Ma. I was just wondering." He looked at me, making sure I didn't think he was trying to be rude.

I laughed a little. "It's okay. I didn't take it as you being rude. I'm not sure yet, actually. I'll stay until it's necessary to go home. I don't want to overstay my welcome, so you can kick me out as soon as you're ready." I smiled like I was making a joke, but I honestly didn't know.

"I don't have much waiting back home except my family, who will come here if they miss me enough. Callie's mom told me to take as long as I needed. She is well aware of what's happening. I also set my students up with a friend to continue their guitar lessons so they won't fall behind in their workbooks."

Callie looked concerned. "Don't stay too long. I need you to help me plan a wedding," she joked.

I grabbed her hand. "I wouldn't miss it, babe. You and me, soulmates forever."

Liza stood up. "I'm so excited about this. Let's move this to the dining room to chat. I'm sure dinner is done by now."

We had a lovely dinner and conversation. We talked about my life, and I learned more about theirs. August's love of music comes from his dad. Mine does too, I guess. I learned all about Link as a teen and all the trouble he caused. It sounded like he was exactly like Max, which is annoying. I don't associate with fuck boys anymore. I'm surprised Liza put up with him. She's a literal saint from what I can see.

Callie took my car and returned to the hotel around seven o'clock P.M. She wanted to get to bed early and call Jake to finalize everything to go home tomorrow. Link offered to drive me back so I could stay until I was ready to go. I stayed for about two more hours. Understandably, we couldn't stop talking.

I finally worked up the nerve to leave them. I said my goodbyes and followed Link to his car.

"I don't mind walking. You can just go on with your night. I'm sure you're busy."

He gave me a weird look. "What's with you wanting to walk around a place you don't know?"

I felt a bit embarrassed. "I like seeing new places."

"Aren't you a little freaked out being alone in a place you've never been?"

I thought about it for a second. "No, which is new for me, honestly. I'm usually pretty anxious." I gave a polite smile. "Should I be scared of getting jumped or something?" I laughed.

"Maybe," he said with a sly grin. "I'll walk with you just in case."

I didn't say anything. I just smiled and started walking with him on my heels. I kept catching him sneaking looks at me, but I think he was just nervous.

"I hope me staying a while doesn't mess up your flow." I tried to break the awkwardness, but he didn't even look at me.

"Mess up my flow? How so?" He raised his eyebrows.

"You know what I mean. I hope you don't feel like I'm completely shoving you aside. If there is ever a moment you are sick of me and no longer want me here, say the word. This is your home."

He chuckled. "That's very considerate of you, but I don't think anyone around here will get sick of you."

A blush ran up my cheeks. "You just haven't spent enough time with me yet,"

"I plan to change that," he said without any hesitation. He smirked. It almost looked like he was blushing, but I couldn't see clearly since he was still looking down.

We got to the hotel, and I stopped at the door. I did a mock bow just like he did last night when he asked me to dance. "I thank you, kind sir. I'll see you tomorrow night at your house."

He looked a bit uncomfortable. "Do you run every day? I ask because I do most days, so we could do that again in the morning if you wanted to. It was fun." He was looking me in the eyes now.

"Yeah, I'd like that. What time are you thinking?"

"How about I text you when I get up, and we can decide then. I have to be at work at seven thirty in the morning for a meeting, so probably around five, maybe, but I won't know till I get up. Sometimes I drag my ass."

I laughed. "Yeah, that works. I'll be up." I took his phone, added my number, and handed it back. "Are you sure you're okay with this? I can stay at the hotel if that's better for you. Again, I don't want to make anyone uncomfortable. I feel like I make you nervous or something."

"Or something," he chuckled. "I'm good; seeing a beautiful woman in the kitchen every day isn't the worst thing that could happen to me," he shrugged. "I'll see you bright and early, sunshine."

I gave him a smile and walked inside.

I had just gotten back from a run with Link, and I realized Callie was still in bed sleeping. I woke her up before I left, but she clearly didn't budge.

"Wake up, sleepy head. It's already six o'clock. Your flight is soon, isn't it?" I nudged her.

"I don't wanna, Momma," she whined as she pulled the covers down and smirked at me. Ultimately I won the conversation because she shuffled out of bed and into the shower. After her shower she sat with me on the bed. "So what are ya thinking?"

I gave her a look. "About what?"

She gave me a knowing smile, and I rolled my eyes. "Bitch, your brother is fucking sexy as fuck. Even I'm a little affected by his charm."

I slapped her shoulder. "He's not my brother." Callie got a huge grin on her face. I think I just reacted the exact way she expected. I tried to cover up the outburst. "He's a player, so nothing will happen with us. You know I can't date someone like Max again. I need to be careful."

Her smile fell, giving me a sad look like she felt bad for me. I never really wanted to talk about Max and how much he hurt me when it happened. In the beginning, she made me, but I put up a fight for sure.

"Girl, he isn't like Max. Max hid shit from you. Lincoln seems to be pretty forward and truthful, don't you think?"

"I don't know. He seems the same to me. I got the player vibe from him."

"Aubrey, you don't even know him yet, don't count him out. It's been years since Max, and you haven't let anyone get near you because you always say they are like Max with zero evidence. If you don't let someone in soon, your lady cave will shrivel up and die. You will be an old, lonely, and decrepit bitch."

I looked at her, stunned. I didn't know whether to be

offended or annoyed. "Tell me how you really feel bitch." We both laughed and continued to get ready for the day.

A few minutes later, after Callie had made sure she had everything, she handed me a box. My eyes went wide when I realized it was full of my favorite things: a beautiful new pink planner and a sparkly green pen with musical notes on it. It sort of reminded me of my guitar. She also added a new guitar pick and some comfy socks. My favorite thing, of course, was a brand-new candle from my favorite small business back home. Honeysuckle Pear is the best scent on the planet. I go through about three of those candles a month because I light them so much. It will be nice to have that piece of home with me.

"I wanted to give you a piece of home for when I left." Her eyes were brimming with unshed tears.

I had no words; I just hugged her tight and held on to her for a while

When I dropped Callie off at the airport, I cried like a baby. Although I wanted this, I was still a bit scared to be doing this alone. She promised to call or text me every day.

I packed all of my things and checked out of the hotel before bringing her to the airport. I wanted to head right to the house and settle in afterward.

When I got there, it was like the room came straight out of a magazine. Everything in the room was new. I almost felt bad for being here, like I would mess it up or something. The room had baby pink walls with a floral design trimming the top. A private bathroom was off to the right, and everything in there was peach-colored. There was a four-poster bed to the left, with a big open space, with room to walk over to the balcony window just big enough for one person. A beautiful mauve chair sat in the corner opposite the bathroom.

I put my guitar in the closet because I didn't want anyone touching it. I unpacked my clothes and placed them into the vintage dresser, noting all the hand-painted flowers on the fronts of the drawers.

I basked in the view of my beautiful room for a bit then went downstairs to talk to Liza. I asked her if I could handle dinner tonight, and she was elated that someone was finally here who could cook other than her. She took me food shopping but didn't let me pay for it, even though I was trying to do it as a thanks for them taking me in. I've only been in White Mountain for a few days, but I really like being here. I can't explain it, but I feel like I belong here.

CHAPTER FIFTEEN
Lincoln

Aubrey and I went for a run around four thirty this morning. We had such a great time talking. I'm still replaying our conversation in my head. She told me all about her high school days. She was quite a music nerd, just like me.

"So you kissed your best friend; what was that like?"

She chuckled, "Yeah, it was like kissing my brother. We only went together to get everyone off our backs. Callie didn't speak to us for a week because she thought we were seriously dating, and she thought we would stop being friends with her."

"Damn, and what about after that? Did you date much?"

She gave me a sad look, "No comment," she muttered as she took off running again.

When we stopped, she apologized. "Sorry, I don't really talk about my ex much. It's been a few years, and it's still a super sore subject."

"I get it. No ex-talk," I reassured her.

"Thanks, Lincoln."

"Of course. I'm not the most open person either. I'm sure we will open up to each other eventually."

"You think so?"

I smiled at her. "I do."

She nodded her head, and we finished the rest of our run. When she walked into her hotel, I got a weird sense of loss. I know she will be at my house when I get home, but it was bizarre to feel this way about her. I barely knew her. I'm not sure if I hate it or love it. Talking to Aubrey felt like talking to someone I'd known forever. It was the most comfortable feeling I've ever felt.

I stopped by The Music Bar to see if Pops needed anything before I headed home after work, which was dumb because it was closing time, and he was going home soon. If I'm being honest, I think I just wanted to see if Aubrey was there. She had already gone home to get herself settled in. Pops told me she was cooking us dinner tonight. That made me even more excited to get home to her.

As soon as I entered the house, I was greeted by a smell that made it feel like I had walked into a fancy Italian restaurant. Curious, I made my way to the kitchen and opened the oven to find the source.

"Caught you!"

I turned and found Aubrey standing in the doorway. I chuckled and smiled as I closed the oven and put my hands up in defeat. "Just looking. It smells amazing; what is it?"

"I made stuffed shells with garlic bread. It's a little

different than my mom's because she makes the pasta herself, and I am just not that good." She laughed, making fun of herself.

God, her laugh was perfect. It seemed like everything about this girl was.

She shrugged like it was no big deal. "Something simple and easy that I love to make."

I smiled at her. "Well, it smells amazing."

I realized she had sauce on her nose when she looked at me again. I reached to wipe it off.

She let out a small gasp when my finger touched her skin. Her hand went to where I touched. "Uh, thanks." She turned back around. "That sauce would have been there all night knowing me. I'm so messy. I will be done in about twenty minutes if you want to freshen up and come back."

I leaned in like I was going to say something in her ear, but I veered at the last minute and sniffed the sauce. I heard her breath hitch again. "Yeah, I think I'll do that."

Dinner was phenomenal. All three of us were giving Aubrey compliment after compliment. She must not be used to being praised for things because she bit her lip while trying to keep her blush under control a few times. It was just about the sexiest fucking thing I've ever seen. It made my dick jump every time. This girl is doing shit to me...and I don't hate it.

We all went to the den after dinner to chat more. We even taught her how to play Canasta, which is Pops' favorite card game. She is just as competitive as him; it was really funny.

She wrapped herself in a blanket and sat on one of the chairs. She had pieces of hair falling down around her face.

She is beautiful. I can tell she doesn't realize how desirable she truly is. I kept stealing glances, and she caught me staring a few times.

My parents headed to bed around eight o'clock. They told her to leave the dishes for tomorrow. Pops pulled me aside before he went upstairs.

"Lincoln, give the sex eyes a rest, please. You're going to scare the girl. Don't fuck this up."

I chuckled, "I can't help it, she's fucking beautiful."

He gripped onto my bicep, "Try harder." He gave me that stern look like I was in trouble.

Aubrey said goodnight and went upstairs, or so I thought. I was cleaning up the den when I heard her in the kitchen. I heard the water in the sink turn on. I walked through the doorway to the kitchen, and she was startled when I spoke, "You don't follow directions very well, do you?" I crossed my arms over my chest.

She smiled over her shoulder at me. "I only take directions when I need to."

I don't know if she meant it to sound like an innuendo, but my dick sure thought she did. She bit her lip as she returned to the sink, which told me she was blushing.

My eyebrows went up in surprise, and a smile played at the corner of my mouth because I didn't know what to say for a second, and I don't get thrown off that often. She was being sassy and I really fucking liked it. I walked up behind her and whispered, "Need any help?"

She turned her head toward me. "With what? Directions? I think I can manage."

Her beautiful eyes caught mine. I was a bit surprised she

was being so bold. Then she turned back to the sink again and shook her head no. I smiled.

I leaned in a little closer so my lips would almost brush her earlobe. "Have a good night, beautiful girl."

I heard her breath hitch and watched her body tense. She cleared her throat, "You too, Lincoln."

It made me smile even more as I walked away because I knew I was having an effect on her. Then I called over my shoulder.

"Call me Link."

AUBREY

I fell asleep as soon as my head hit the pillow. At one o'clock A.M., I was startled awake by a noise. I am sure I will get used to the new noises around. Now that I was awake, I couldn't get my mind to relax to get back to sleep. I went downstairs, hoping I was quiet enough and didn't wake anyone. I figured a drink and maybe a small snack might help. Stress-eating champion over here.

I walked into the kitchen and opened the refrigerator. I heard a groan of some sort come from behind me. I grabbed the clean pan that I had left on the counter to dry and turned around, holding onto it for dear life. My heart was racing when I turned and saw it was just Lincoln sitting at the table.

"Christ!" I said rather loudly.

"No, just Link," he said with a smirk.

"You scared the living shit out of me. What are you doing in here this late?" I gripped my chest, trying to get my heart to stop racing.

"Sorry." He chuckled, and his smile made my stomach flutter with butterflies.

"I assume I'm in here for the same reason you are; the food is here. I couldn't sleep because I can't stop thinking about you."

His admission surprised me, but I tried my hardest not to react. His smile was shining in the moonlight. He gestured to me with his utensil.

"You can put that weapon of mass destruction down now. I won't bite you... unless you want me to." He shoved another bite of food in his mouth and chewed it with a big smile. It looked like he was eating some sort of brownie in a mug or something. It looked good, whatever it was.

I put the pan down and rolled my eyes. My stomach and heart were doing all kinds of flips trying to process what he was saying.

"Sorry, you just startled me."

I turned and went to the cabinet to grab a glass. Then I returned to the fridge, which was still open, and grabbed an apple and water from the door. I turned back towards him and leaned one hip against the counter.

I tipped my head toward him, "What are you eating over there?" I asked.

"It's a protein mug cake with chocolate chips. Chocolate helps me sleep." He said it with a mouth full of mug cake. It was cute that he wasn't trying to be super proper and polite around me. It was that sexy, I-don't-give-a-fuck attitude that was going to get me in some trouble.

"Want me to make you one?"

I held up my apple. "I'm good with this. That will make my ass bigger with one bite."

"Is that a bad thing?" His smile was devious.

I turned back to the sink to clean my hands, mostly to hide the blush on my face. A few seconds later, Lincoln came up behind me and placed his mug in the sink. I could smell him; his scent was intoxicating like a deep woodsy smell. He leaned over me, putting one hand on each side of me, allowing his chest to hit my back ever so slightly. He lowered his head and put his lips right at my ear lobe. His hot breath made my own breath hitch. I had to close my eyes to gain some composure.

"Lincoln, what are you—"

"Why won't you call me Link?" His voice was low and sultry.

My whole body tensed, shivers ran down my spine, and I felt flutters erupt in my stomach. This man was making me feel things I haven't allowed myself the freedom to feel in almost two and a half years. The last time I felt anything remotely like this was before Max ripped my life apart by cheating on me. I've kept all thoughts and feelings close to my heart, guarding them with all I have.

I placed my hands on the edge of the sink so I wouldn't be tempted to reach out and touch him. I turned my head so I was somewhat looking at him and cleared my throat. "You said that's what your friends call you; I wasn't aware we were friends yet, Mr. Lincoln." It came out much more whispered than I intended, making one side of his mouth turn up. He knew he was making me nervous.

"I hope to become more than that, Miss Aubrey."

I felt myself getting aroused. My mind was racing. I needed to get some space between us before I let him fuck me right here on the counter. I gained my bearings and tapped my lip like I was thinking about it. He seemed to back off a little, and then I successfully ducked under one of his arms to get out of his direct contact. I couldn't think while having him that close to me. I turned to look at him.

"Haven't thought about it, honestly," I said with a nervous smile. He knew I was lying.

I leaned against the island in the center of the room, keeping some distance between us. He was still standing there with both hands in the same place, head hanging low like I hurt his ego or something. He turned around to face me and crossed his arms. My breath stopped when I saw his erection tenting his pajama shorts. He was clearly not shy because he did nothing to hide it.

My eyes traveled up a bit. He had the nicest set of abs I think I'd ever seen in my life. The moonlight in the dark kitchen was hitting them perfectly. I wanted to run my hands, mouth, tongue, hell; I wanted to rub my entire body all over him. I shook my head and averted my eyes, hoping he didn't catch me staring, but the snicker I heard told me he had.

"What will it take for you to be my friend? What's stopping you?"

My brows went up in surprise and confusion, and I wasn't quite sure what he was asking. For some reason, I grew some balls and asked him straight out.

"If that is all you want, we can be friends." He was quiet and didn't respond. I sighed. "What is it exactly that you want from me, Lincoln?"

He took several steps forward, closing some of the space between us. "I want you to be honest with me."

My brows creased in confusion. "About what? I haven't lied to you."

He took a few more steps, and the space between us was

gone entirely. I tried to look away, but he placed his finger and thumb around my chin and lifted it so my eyes would meet his.

"I want you to admit you want me," he smirked.

He tried to keep his finger on my chin. I pulled his hand off my face and, this time, he let me. For whatever reason, I felt a little snarky.

"Not every girl wants you if you can believe that."

He just stared and didn't say anything at first. It felt like he was peering into my soul.

"Name one?" he said with a grin. I've never wanted to punch and kiss someone simultaneously before, but it's a bizarre feeling.

"Okay, fine," I rolled my eyes. "There's some attraction here." He smiled. "Seriously though, I can't give you what you want, Lincoln."

I shook my head and tried to push him away, but somehow, he moved his body closer to mine even though there was no space left, and his presence was becoming overwhelming. My nervousness increased.

He put his face right next to mine, and his lips were mere inches away when he said, "I think you want me just as bad as I want you."

His body engulfed mine. He started to speak again, but I was so caught up in the moment that I leaned forward and kissed him.

I immediately felt sparks. His mouth fit perfectly with mine. This was a feeling I would remember for a long time. When we both pulled back from the kiss, he groaned. He leaned back in, and his hands grabbed me by the ass and lifted me onto the counter. A small moan escaped me, and I tangled my fingers into his hair. My lips parted as he slipped his tongue into my mouth. It felt like his mouth and hands were trying to memorize every inch of me. His hands were on my thighs, slowly moving up to my hips. He started moving them up my nightshirt onto my stomach toward the bottom of my breasts. His hands felt like they were made to touch me. I arched my back, letting my hands rest on the counter behind me to give him better access as he kissed down my neck and collarbone.

"Lincoln," his name hitched in my throat and came out as a whisper. I leaned further back on the counter. My hand knocked into a metal spoon. It clanked so loud it snapped me out of whatever trance he had me in. I pushed him away and hopped off the counter, both of us gasping for air.

"Aubrey, where are you going?" He asked with a growl between breaths. He stepped toward me.

I covered my swollen lips with my fingers and looked up at him, then back down to the floor. I started to back away toward the stairs. I wasn't sure if I could meet his eyes.

"We can't do this," I said weakly, "I heard what August said to you."

I finally looked up at him, and he had a desperate, wanting hunger in his eyes. He stepped toward me again and tried to catch my hand, but I only backed away farther. "Aubrey?"

"Don't. Please don't. You're his son Lincoln, even without the paper, and I really am his daughter. We are in each other's lives forever now. I don't do flings, and I know you do. This isn't a one-time thing. If this goes wrong—"

My words caught in my throat. My eyes were getting a bit misty, but I did my best not to let any tears fall. I didn't understand why I was almost crying.

He ran his fingers through his hair. "Why is this so wrong

if we both want it? What if I don't want it to be a one-night thing?" he said as he tried to reach for me again.

"You don't mean that; you told me yourself you don't sleep with people more than once, and I'm sorry to say, but that's not me. Plus, you know nothing about me," I whispered.

His voice got a little more stern. "I know I've never wanted someone so badly in my life. I know I haven't been able to stop thinking about you. I know I've never had someone occupy my thoughts the way you do. I know I've never wanted to know someone the way I want to know you." He pulled me into his arms and looked me directly in the eyes. "Give me a chance."

He leaned down to kiss me again, but I pushed away and stepped out of his embrace. I bit my lip and looked at him.

"I'm sorry, we just can't do this. I can't ruin things with August and Liza, or with you for that matter, over some lust. We're going to be a family, right?"

That made him wince, but I took that moment as an opportunity, so I turned and ran back to my room. The tears finally started to pour down my cheeks. I don't know why, but this hurt more than my freaking breakup, and I barely know the guy.

CHAPTER SIXTEEN

Lincoln

I stood in the kitchen, staring at the stairs in disbelief. I struggled to comprehend what just happened, unsure whether I should go after Aubrey—and risk waking my parents up—or let her be. Ultimately, I chose to give her space for now.

I couldn't help but recall the taste of her as I touched my lips. It was a kiss unlike any other I had experienced before. Although I consider myself experienced in the art of kissing, that one undoubtedly ranked as the best, even though it didn't lead to anything more. The thought of how I would manage to sleep tonight was daunting. I returned to my house and sat on my bed. Glancing out the window, I noticed the light in her room was still on, prompting me to text her.

Me: Hey.

A few minutes passed, and I didn't think I would get an answer. But then my phone lit up.

Aubrey: Hi.

Me: Are you okay? Do you want to talk about it?

Aubrey: Yes, I'll be fine, but no. We don't need to talk. I'm sorry I kissed you. I shouldn't have done that. I meant what I said about not ruining things with August and Liza. They are important to me, and so are you.

I thought about how to respond for a second.

Me: I'm not. I'm glad it happened.

I smiled like an idiot when I saw the three dots pop up as she responded. My heart started to quicken, and I felt my cock stir. *Who the fuck am I? This girl is making me act like a stupid ass teenager.*

Aubrey: Goodnight Lincoln. Sweet dreams.

Me: I know what I will be dreaming about. Night, Aubrey

Then I saw her light go out. I sat there for a while and started idly scrolling through my phone. *I can't wait to kiss her again.*

Aubrey and I haven't returned to normal after our dream-inducing kiss. Although we've exchanged a few flirty texts, our conversations haven't progressed to where I want them to be. We've been on several runs together over the last few days but barely spoke during them. It's been driving me crazy that she's so close yet so out of reach, and I feel like she gets more beautiful every time I see her.

Aubrey has been catching up with Pops and working at The Music Bar, but she hasn't spent much time with us outside of that. She's been going straight to her room after dinner to write or play her guitar.

Earlier today I overheard her planning a visit for her parents to come here to Tennessee. Pops is eager to meet her parents, and I hope the conversation goes well for her sake. She has expressed how nervous she is about it.

As for me, today marks the end of my work week at the school since it's Friday, and I couldn't be more excited. Usually, I don't get this excited because I love my job and my students, but tomorrow I will be at The Music Bar with Aubrey all day. She's giving some of the younger kids in town guitar lessons to try to help promote kids joining the school's band. I helped her put up some flyers around town the last few days, and she has had a surprisingly big sign-up.

I am starting to wonder about how long she will stay. She must have to get back to her everyday life eventually, but I'm hoping the class means she's staying for a while. I know she misses her family and friends like crazy. She's always talking about them. She told me she's never really been away from them except for a college trip years ago. I can understand because when my parents went on that trip, it was the longest five days of my life.

Mom and Pops told me they were taking Aubrey to our favorite restaurant tonight to change it up a bit so no one had to cook. When I finally left work and walked into the main house, I froze when I saw a handsome man I didn't know sitting on the couch. I'm confident enough in my manhood to admit when a guy looks nice.

He looks familiar, but I can't quite place him. He was laughing with Aubrey. They sat there with their knees touching, looking at a book together. Then he put his hand on her knee, and I walked forward. My gut felt like it was going to fall out of my ass. *Is this jealousy? It can't be.* They're only laughing. Why do I even care? She has a right to do whatever she wants, but I don't have to fucking like it.

Aubrey stood up fast when she saw me come in, almost like she was caught doing something wrong.

"Lincoln, this is Dan; his dad owns the bookshop on Main St."

He stood. "Hey man, I think we met a few years ago when I was home from college," he said as he shook my hand. "Aubrey came into the bookshop every day this week to check it out and loved so many books; we just had to keep talking; we seem to have a lot in common."

Then he smiled at her. Fucking smiled. It was like looking at a little schoolboy with a crush. "She invited me over for some coffee so we could continue chatting, but I was just heading out to meet some friends. We are going to karaoke tonight if you care to join us?"

He seemed annoyingly calm, and I'm not sure why he was explaining what he was doing here to me, of all people, but whatever.

"Uh, yeah, sure. I guess that could be fun. I'll see what's on my schedule." I was trying not to sound rude.

She gave me a knowing smile and looked back at him. "Let me walk you out."

She nodded politely at me, excusing herself. When she

came back in and walked by me I could smell her shampoo again. I'm starting to really love strawberries. She passed me to pick up the coffee cups they had left and went into the kitchen without saying a word. I followed her and heard her snicker when she noticed my presence.

"So, you're going out with that tool instead of attending the dinner Pops and Liza planned for you?" I said rudely. It was none of my business, but I had to ask.

She didn't even turn to look at me when she laughed. "How do you figure he's a tool? You just met him."

I sighed rather loudly, "I just know. I can tell."

"Can you now?" She turned to me with an annoyed look, "Not that I owe you any explanation, Lincoln, but dinner with August and Liza is at six-thirty. I'm not meeting Dan at karaoke until around eight. Is that okay with you? As he said, you can come if you want."

The way this girl says my name. Ugh, it turns me on every time. "Do you want me to come?" I asked, almost hopeful.

"It's up to you, Lincoln; you are a big boy who makes his own decisions." She sounded condescending, but I let it slide. "It's just a bunch of his friends and me hanging out. If I'm going to be here for a while, I need to make friends, so that's what I'm doing. You are the one who told me you don't have many friends. If you don't want to—"

"I am a big boy, and I'll be there," I said curtly, cutting her off. Then I thought for a second. "Want me to drive you?"

"I thought you had to check your schedule?" she said smugly as she bit her lip. She returned to what she was doing but kept talking. "As far as a ride, no, I don't need one, but thanks for the offer. I'm going to walk from the restaurant to the karaoke bar since it's so close. I could use the exercise, plus if I'm early, I'll just sit and enjoy the music."

I scoffed. "You do not need exercise. You run almost daily, and your body is fucking perfect."

She blushed and bit her lip again. As she turned and walked away, she smirked. "See you later... if your schedule is free."

She knew damn well I wasn't checking my schedule. Why did it make me so mad, yet so intrigued, that she could already read me like a book? I feel like I just got played into going there tonight. Honestly, it doesn't matter. All I know is that I want to, and I will ruin their date if it's the last thing I do.

After dinner, I walked with her to the karaoke bar. That way, if we drank too much, we could just rideshare home. Plus, the thought of her walking alone at night worried me for some reason. She is anything but a delicate flower, and I'm 90% sure she could kick ass if she needed to. We walked in silence the whole way to the bar.

Dan was ready and waiting to hug her. He picked her up and twirled her around and commented about her ass and how good she looked. I can't believe she didn't punch him. Instead, she smiled and smacked his chest like she was flirting. Then he walked over to get us drinks.

I wasn't sure if it was jealousy before, but now I know it is exactly that. An image of me punching him for talking to her that way just flashed in my brain. I felt myself getting angrier with every smile and slight touch on the arm he gave her. I finally started calming down when he introduced us to everyone at the table. His friends were actually cool, which made my dislike for him suck even more.

Aubrey got up on stage and sang a few songs, which surprised me since she was the one who told me she doesn't usually do that without her guitar. Aubrey was good, like really fucking good. She even did a duet with one of Dan's friends.

Everything was going great, but then my mood went sour when Dan asked her to dance, and she accepted. She quickly looked back at me when she walked away, but I caught it. I watched them dance to a few songs. I never took my eyes off her; I literally couldn't. She looked phenomenal tonight. I saw her whisper in his ear, and then he walked my way.

"Hey, Aubrey told me to get you off your ass and go dance with her." He motioned over to where they had been dancing.

I looked at him, baffled. "I thought you were on a date with her. Why would you let her dance with me?"

His eyebrow quirked up, and a laugh billowed out of him. "I've only known Aubrey for a few days or so, and I could be totally off base here, but I don't think anyone 'lets' Aubrey do anything. You should ask her why I'm 'letting' you dance together; the answer might surprise you." He didn't even look back at her as he walked away.

CHAPTER SEVENTEEN

Aubrey

As Lincoln walked toward me, I couldn't help the smile that covered my face. He looked so confused and a bit mad. I saw him watching me the entire time I was dancing. I knew it was time to put him out of his misery. When he finally reached me, I started breaking his stones a little.

"Hey, Mr. Grumpy Butt, why do you look so upset? This is supposed to be a fun night." It was meant to be funny or sassy, but he didn't think so.

He pulled me close and put one of his hands on my lower back, almost touching my ass like he was being possessive. My breath caught in my throat when my body hit his. He hadn't touched me since the day we kissed, and I didn't realize how much I had missed and craved his touch until right now. He slid his other hand into mine, lacing our fingers together. He stared at our hands joined together for a moment. Then our eyes met. He looked...different. It felt like I was just now seeing the real him for the first time. I wasn't seeing the player who acts like he doesn't have a care in the world. I saw a man who was genuinely hurt and actually cared enough to have a reaction.

"I've been watching you dance with your new boyfriend. He had his hands all over you." My breath hitched again as his grip on me tightened. "What about that should be fun to me? I'm surprised he's letting you dance with me. He's a fucking idiot, but clearly he's not worried about me. I wonder why that is? Did you tell him not to worry about me?" he asked.

I pushed back a bit to really look at him. Now I knew it was hurt that I saw reflected in his eyes.

"You sound jealous, sir." I smiled, trying to break his anger, but it didn't work. "You could have gotten up and danced too, you know?"

"I didn't want to dance or spend time with anyone else, Aubrey," he said in a way that I couldn't misunderstand him if I tried.

"Link, I'm flattered by your jealousy, but..." I leaned into him and whispered, "You know Dan is gay, right?" I pointed over his shoulder. Dan was cuddled up next to his boyfriend, who had just walked in.

Link turned to look, and I saw the light blush creeping up his neck like he was embarrassed.

"Well, shit," Link said with a bashful smile.

This man's smile when he turned back to face me was something out of a movie. He was perfect. Why the hell does he have to be so close to August? Though I probably wouldn't know him if he wasn't. Why the hell do I have to be such a rule follower? I must be a glutton for punishment or something. Not that there is a rule for dating your dad's foster son, but I feel like I just made up some rules to protect everyone involved.

He leaned his head down so his lips were near my ear. "You called me Link."

He kissed the sweet spot behind my ear, and a shiver ran down my spine. He moved back a little to look into my eyes, but he didn't let me go far.

I thought about it for a second. "I guess I did." I smiled up at him. I placed my head on his shoulder as we kept dancing. I felt him gently rubbing one of his fingers up and down my spine. It was the sexiest and most intimate feeling I've ever had. It made my stomach flutter.

I pulled back a little to look at him.

"So, am I allowed to call you Mr. Grumpy Butt? I was thinking of putting that as your name in my phone; I thought it was fitting." I started laughing hard.

He tugged me in closer. The feel of his hard erection stopped my laughter. He leaned toward my ear. "Only if I can call you Songbird. You were great up there, you know. Now, I will always think of you as my personal Songbird. I am among the few to see you in your element and singing without your guitar. I feel special."

My breath hitched. I wasn't expecting that. *You are special.* I thought to myself. *Songbird.* A name just for me. I tried to compose myself.

"Songbird, huh?" I tried to act like my legs weren't about to give out from how turned on I was. I smiled and placed my head back onto his shoulder. We continued dancing until the music picked up a bit. We went back to the group and grabbed some food. He kept staring at me with that seductive smile.

I sang one more song, and then we were both ready to head back to the house. It was a cool night, but it was tolerable even though neither of us drank enough to warm ourselves up. We walked down the street in silence. I could tell

Link was hesitant in trying to hold my hand. I grabbed his hand and leaned in close to his arm with my head on his shoulder while we walked. I walk with Nick like this, but Nick doesn't make me tingle as Link does. This wasn't that awkward silence where we didn't know what to say, but the beautiful kind where we merely enjoyed being in each other's space.

He caught me looking around a little. I loved looking around at all the calm, dark shops that, just hours ago, were full of lights and people. He lightly nudged me with his hip.

"Sorry, I acted like a tool."

"You didn't," I said with a sly smile.

"I did, but thanks for trying to ease my embarrassment." His smile was genuine; it was beautiful. I looked down at the ground as we walked and couldn't help but bite my lip.

"I like that you cared so much, and you're welcome."

We continued to walk silently for a few minutes, and he spoke again. "So, what's your plan?" he looked down at me curiously.

"What do you mean? I asked. I wasn't sure what he was referring to.

"Well, you're not staying here forever, are you? You need to go home and live your life, right?"

I'm pretty sure he was asking out of curiosity and not being mean about it.

"Are you trying to get rid of me already?" I said it as a joke, and he just stared at me. He wasn't quite smiling, but his demeanor was friendly.

"Well, yeah, I do need to go back, but part of my life is here now, too. I need to figure out how I will have both in my world now that I found August and Liza." I paused momentarily, "And you."

We kept walking and stopped in front of an antique store. Link looked like he was thinking about something and then spoke up, "Why do you call him August and not Dad?"

I thought about it for a moment so that what I said didn't come out condescending or rude. "Well, I have a dad... and while August is my biological father, and maybe someday we will be at that point, he's not my dad in any way that matters yet. We just found out about each other and we're still kind of strangers. It's going to take time, don't you think?"

"Yeah, I guess you're right," he agreed. We stayed silent until we got home. I couldn't believe I was calling it home already. It felt like home –just different, but in a good way.

"Do you want to check out the cottage? You haven't seen it yet," he said.

"I don't think that's the best idea. I should let August and Liza know I made it home okay."

He chuckled. "They're knocked out. You don't have to, but the offer is there. I'm not asking you to sleep over," he smiled, "Just asking if you want to see it; you don't have to stay forever."

I smiled back. "I would love to see it."

The space had Lincoln written all over it. I could see some of his lesson plans spread out on the table; it looked like he was doing some research on Broadway plays. His kitchen was pristine because he didn't use it, or so I've heard. It was gorgeous, nonetheless. The cottage smelled just like him with that deep, woodsy scent. He had a beautiful guitar in the corner propped up on a stand.

"This is so nice. You are so lucky to have your own space like this." I pointed to the guitar. "Do you play a lot?"

"I'm not that great, but I can get by. I prefer the drums, but

I can't fit them in here. Wait, do you not have your own space at home?" he asked with curiosity written all over his face.

"Not really. I have my own space in the sense that I have my room, but I share a house with Callie and her fiancé for now. We moved in right before Christmas. Right before I came here, actually, about a month or so ago. I guess I would also consider the music room my space too. I get into a different world when I'm in there. Music is my sanctuary. When I move to a forever home it will have to have a music room and—" Oh god, I'm rambling. "Sorry, like I said, I travel to a different world when it comes to music." I put my head down so he didn't see me blush.

He stepped toward me and lifted my chin with one finger. He was smiling that sensual smile I've come to really look forward to.

"Don't ever be ashamed to talk about what you love. It's what makes you who you are. Anyone that meets you can see within minutes that you love music."

Link started to rub the inside of my left wrist. "When did you get this?"

I looked down at my tattoo. It is a G clef and bass clef that form a heart.

"I got that when I settled on becoming a music major. Sort of like a symbol for the next chapter of my life, if you will. Honestly, I forget I have it sometimes." I laughed a little. "Most people don't even realize I have it. I have another one on my leg."

"I know," he said as his lip curved up to one side. "For the record, I noticed," he said as he released my wrist.

I swallowed the lump that was forming in my throat. "Well, I guess I should go. Thanks for showing me your space. It's very you."

"Thanks, I'll take that as a compliment."

"I meant it as one." I turned towards the door, and he lightly clasped my wrist again to get my attention.

"Let me take you out, just the two of us."

I raised my eyebrows, and butterflies stirred in my stomach. I could feel my face getting pink. "Like on a date? What about August?"

He chuckled, probably at how surprised I sounded. "What about him? You can't exactly date him. He's your father, and he's mar— "

I slapped his shoulder with the back of my hand. "You know what I mean."

He caught my hand against his chest and kissed a few of my knuckles. "No, I don't, and yes, on a date." He was still smiling.

"What if us dating, or whatever, causes issues with him and me? Or worse, him and you? As I said before, we are stuck in each other's lives, even if you start to hate me or get bored."

He caressed my cheek with his thumb and then grabbed both of my hands. "I could never hate you; I don't think anyone could. Can we deal with whatever happens as it happens if we promise there's no hating each other?" He was rubbing my knuckles now, and it was making me melt. Ugh! I want to kiss that smug smile right off his face.

When I didn't immediately answer, he started to say something else, but I surprised him when I spoke up first, "Okay."

"Really...okay. How about—"

I cut him off and put one finger over his lips. "One condition though... You have to tell August before we go."

He licked my finger, and I pulled my hand away. "Done!

How about tomorrow when we are done with work?" he asked.

It made me happy that he was so excited about a simple date. "I'd like that. What should I wear?"

"You will look beautiful in anything you wear. Whatever you wear to work will be fine."

I blushed and bit my lip. "Thanks— uh, I mean okay... I'll see you in the morning for our run, right?"

"Yeah, text me when you're ready." I think he forgot he was holding my hand. I had forgotten, too. I craved his touch as soon as he let go.

"Sweet dreams, Songbird."

LINCOLN

It didn't even matter that I didn't sleep well; I woke up feeling excited. I wasn't quite sure what this date would lead to, but I was excited to find out. This wasn't going to be one of my 'go out for drinks and a fuck' dates. This one was going to be real. I'm not a date type of guy, but with her, I wanted to be different; I wanted to be someone worth knowing for her. Right then, I realized that I hadn't slept with or even spoken to anyone since I met her. Maybe I was changing for the better. We, of course, have a ton to figure out if this will ever be anything, but I think she's worth it.

After my run with Aubrey this morning I went to say goodbye to Mom and found Aubrey in the kitchen waiting for me. She held up her finger to signal that she was on the phone. It sounded like her sister was coming to visit soon.

I was staring at her and must have been smiling big because Mom caught me, and I immediately schooled my expression.

Aubrey hung up and then looked over at me. "Hey, I figured we could ride over together since we're going out later. Is that okay?"

"Uh, yeah. Good idea," I said.

Mom looked at me curiously. "Where might you two be off to later?"

"Oh, we're going—" Aubrey started to explain. I'm not sure what she was going to say, but I cut her off,

"I'm taking her on a date." Aubrey's eyes went wide, and her cheeks pinked a little. I love it when she does that.

"Is that so?" Mom said. I just smiled and nodded my head yes. "Does your father know?"

I shook my head no and laughed. "Not yet."

"Well, have fun and be safe." She kept eyeing me, and when Aubrey walked out of the kitchen before me, my mom mouthed, 'Be a gentleman, please.' I walked up and kissed the top of her head.

"Always am," I whispered.

A few hours later, I ran to the bookstore during lunch. I had a mission to complete, and this was the first part. Dan was the perfect man to help me plan the start of the perfect date.

CHAPTER EIGHTEEN

Aubrey

Link was gone during lunch, but The Music Bar was busy, so I just ate at the counter when I wasn't helping a customer. I helped a few people pick out and purchase some records and even got a few new signups for my class.

I went back to August's office when I had a lull in customers. The door was open. I politely knocked so I didn't just barge in. "Hey, you got a sec?"

He looked up from his papers. His glasses sat at the tip of his nose, just like my mom does when reading. "Of course, sweetie, come on in and have a seat. What's on your mind?"

I sat in the chair across from him, fidgeting with my fingers. "Well, I know it's only January, but I talked with my parents and told them I would be staying here for a while. I also let Callie know, so they will hire someone at the restaurant until I return. I feel like I need more time with you all. I love it here. Something feels unfinished, as funny as that sounds. I told my parents I would probably stay until at least my birthday if that's—"

He cut me off, and his eyes lit up. "Oh my god! When is your birthday? We need to do something fun."

I laughed. "Well, that's kind of why I'm telling you. My parents want to make the trip down here with my sister and friends to throw me a birthday party. I know you all want to meet and talk and all that jazz, so I figured this would be a good opportunity. The issue is that my birthday isn't till March second. Is it okay for me to stay that long? I can get out of your hair and sleep at—"

He cut me off again. He walked around his desk and embraced me. "You will do no such thing. Our home is yours, and please tell your parents we have a room for them if they want. Also, your friends and sister are welcome to stay in your room as well. We can get some air mattresses, and I'm sure Link can make room too. We can make it a whole reunion. We have the room."

I smiled up at him, and he let me go. "Thanks! I'll see what they say... Oh, and my sister will be flying from Canada to Nashville for a few days next week before returning to school. If it's okay that she stays, I will pick her up at the airport and bring her to the house."

"Aubrey, you do not need permission to have guests in our home, and you can come and go as you please. Just make us aware so that we make enough food."

"Thank you!" I smiled and hugged him again.

He looked nervous. "Aubrey, I hope you don't mind, but I've started telling people around town about you. I've kept it simple, just saying I didn't know about you, and now you're here. I hope that's okay."

I started to tear up a little. "That's perfect, actually. I was worried we were going to get questions."

"I've gotten a few questions, so I figured it was time to share."

I heard the jingle of the bells on the door. "Of course, I don't mind at all. I'll be back." Then I headed back to the front.

Ugh, just perfect.

"Oh hey. Kaylee, right?" I said as I walked up to the counter.

"Very funny," Kayla said as she rolled her eyes. "Is my Linky here? I wanted to give him this food that I made for him."

My brows went up as I snickered at her. "I don't know who your Linky is, but if you meant Link, then no. He's out on lunch already." I didn't bother telling her he was doing things for our date tonight. I'm sure I'd just be asking for trouble if I did. "If you want to leave it for him, I can make sure he gets it."

"Oh, no need. I will come back when Link gets out. I will just have him over for dinner, I guess."

She said it so nonchalantly, and I realized I had to tell her. If I didn't, she would come back.

"He's busy tonight."

She looked at me, almost stunned. "And how would you know? Aren't you like his sister or something? Does he clear all his plans with you?" She had a condescending smile, and I wanted to slap it off her damn face.

I remained calm and smiled though. I was not letting this girl take me out of character. "You know very well I'm not his sister Kayla. Probably the furthest thing from it at this point." I said it with a chuckle and stared right at her so she wouldn't misunderstand, "He and I have a date, so I'm sure he will be occupied well into tonight."

Of course, at that moment, he had to walk in. I blushed. I

didn't actually mean what I told her...or maybe I did. I don't know. "Link, you're back!" I exclaimed when I saw him.

"Thank you for the kind welcome, Songbird. Hey Kayla, what are you doing here?" She looked super pissed at me. She was giving me a look like I was her next murder victim. Then she turned and looked over at Link.

"Well, I was bringing you food, but I can see you don't need it. Unless you want to change your plans and come to my house when you get out, we can eat it then. Maybe we could catch a movie or something." She tried to lean into him, but he moved behind the counter next to me.

The audacity of this woman was like nothing I'd ever seen in my life. Link looked at me with his eyebrows raised, and I just shrugged. I'm pretty sure he was just as surprised as I was that she was being so forward. Then he looked back at her.

"No, I'm good, but thanks for the invite. Let me walk out with you. I need to grab something from my car anyway."

Then she gave me a condescending look like she had won his attention, as they walked away. I saw the look Link gave her as they neared the door. It was almost like pity, and I couldn't help the victorious smile that formed.

"Hey Kayla, I'm sorry if I ever gave you the impression that I wanted to be more than friends, but—"

The door shut and I couldn't hear the rest of that conversation. He seems like he's such a cocky, hard ass sometimes, and then he does something like that. I think he took Kayla away because he didn't want to embarrass her in front of me. How freaking sweet could this man be?

When he came back, my heart did this weird flip thing. I touched his arm to grab his attention. "That was nice of you to pull her away like that for that conversation."

"I don't know what you're talking about. I had to get

something out of my car." The look on his face told me he knew he was caught.

I knew he was lying, but I played along. "Where is it then? What did you have to grab?"

He pulled a pen out of his pocket and held it up. "Needed my favorite pen."

I held up the cup on the counter full of those exact pens.

He smiled. "You caught me; I was being nice for once."

"It's okay for people to know you're nice, Link. It's okay to let people know there is more to you than just a hot body and a pretty face."

He slid up next to me behind the counter. "You think my body is hot?" He wagged his eyebrows and smiled. I just rolled my eyes. Then he backed away a little. "It's okay. You don't have to admit it. I know you want this." He did some weird wiggle thing with his body. I think he was trying to be sexy, but it just looked silly. "You can't lie to me, Songbird. Oh, and don't think I forgot about what you were saying when I walked in.

Shit, he heard me. "You aren't going to let that go, are you?"

"Nope. I just hope you weren't kidding," he winked.

I slapped him on the shoulder with the back of my hand as I walked away rolling my eyes. All in good fun, of course. I honestly didn't know what was going to happen tonight, but I did know that it was getting more and more difficult not to kiss him. One of us is bound to get hurt, and I'm terrified it will be me.

I haven't been with anyone since Max cheated on me. I just haven't wanted to. Max was just like Link because he was always so suave; everyone loved him, and he knew he was hot. I knew Max was with a lot of girls before we met when he was in high school, but he always assured me that had ended when he met me. He wanted to be better for me. Even in college, he made it seem like he only had eyes for me. If girls hit on him, he seemed to brush them off immediately, and I never had the feeling I had to check his phone or anything like that, but I wish I had. Looking back I know how stupid I was for not seeing the signs, especially when he was pulling away. I probably would have saved myself a lot of heartache.

Link doesn't deserve the comparisons, but I'm afraid that even getting involved with him will be bad news for me. I can't have my heart broken like that again. He loves going out and meeting girls, so why should meeting me change that? You can't change a man like that. *Right?*

It was almost time to go out with Link, and I was getting nervous. All my thoughts about Max were making me rethink this. We also hadn't said anything to August about leaving early or at the same time, or at least I hadn't. I saw Link go into the backroom and I was hoping he was saying something. I heard raised voices but didn't hear exactly what was said. He came back out with a shit-eating grin on his face.

He put his arm over my shoulder and handed me my purse. "You ready to go, pretty girl?"

I looked back over his arm at the office. August was standing there with his arms crossed. He looked like he was worried about me or something. I looked back at Link because I wasn't sure whether to stay or go, which wasn't helping my anxiety.

"Uh. Yes. Is August okay with us leaving together? I can wait and meet you wherever we're going."

"He'll get over it." Then we started walking towards the door, and he called over his shoulder to August. "Love you, Pops."

"Behave, Lincoln. That's precious cargo you got there. Don't do anything stupid. I'll kill you if you do. Aubrey, call me when you get bored."

I looked back at him and nodded my head in agreement trying not to laugh. Link's arm went up, he raised his hand and gave him the finger. Luckily, no one was in the store because they may have taken him seriously if they didn't know them. August's concern warmed my heart; it felt like a real father-daughter moment.

Lincoln

I opened her car door and she saw the present I had left on the seat for her. Her eyes lit up as she started tearing it open before I even got into the driver's seat. Her mouth dropped when she saw it was one of the music books she wanted from the bookshop.

"I was going to get you flowers, but I thought this would be better."

"It is," she whispered.

I don't think she meant to say it out loud. She rubbed the cover and looked almost speechless. Her eyes were becoming misted. "Link, this is beautiful; thank you! How did you know I wanted this? This is a special edition, and I couldn't afford it, so I put it on hold. You have to let me pay you back; this is way too much."

I looked at her with an endearing smile. "Absolutely not. It's a gift, and you will accept it. I pay attention when you talk; that's how I knew."

She gave me a knowing look. "You are a horrible liar," she laughed.

She knows me too well already. I couldn't help but laugh. "Okay, maybe I asked Dan for some help."

She gave me the cutest smile and grasped the book against her chest like she was holding onto it for dear life. She bit her lip and shook her head like she was in disbelief. We put on our seat belts, and I started driving. I kept stealing glances at her, and I knew she caught me because the pink of her cheeks had deepened to a crimson as we drove. I really liked knowing I did that to her.

Nashville isn't too far away, so I planned a special date at one of the restaurants there. They have this really unique outside area where you can bring blankets and listen to live music. They have a ton of those tall outside heaters, thank God, but luckily, it's in the fifties again, so it's not super cold. Elijah's band is one of four acts playing there tonight, so I knew the mix of music would be good.

"Hey, you never told me where we are going?" she asked. She sounded so adorable and unsure. I remember her sharing her love of schedules and having to know everything going on during the first dinner we had together. I teased her about it.

I didn't look at her when I answered, "It's a surprise, but I know you'll love it."

I was trying to seem more confident than I felt. I reached for Aubrey's hand and placed our joined hands on her lap.

I caught her smile in the reflection as she looked out the window. "I'm sure I will love it too."

Her fingers fit into mine like a glove; I noticed it last night when we were walking home. Holding her hand makes me feel good. I've never felt this safe with someone, especially a woman. The one woman who was supposed to love me unconditionally threw me away like trash so she could get high. What did I do as I got older? I built up a wall so high. I used my looks and confidence to keep people just far enough away so that no one would ever hurt me again.

It's something I've never really gotten over, even though I remember nothing about her from back then. The one thing I do remember is feeling lost for a long time. Maybe getting placed with Mom and Pops was for a greater purpose. I'm not usually into that "everything happens for a reason" or "meant to be" bullshit, but this situation has me wondering. Maybe there was a reason we never went through with the adoption...Maybe it was her.

AUBREY

We pulled up to a beautiful restaurant. The parking lot seemed relatively empty for the amount of music playing and all the talking I heard, but from what I'd gathered, that was typical around here. People walk everywhere, enjoying the music on the streets instead of driving. I heard that bars around here were always full of life with loud country music playing. I was in heaven. He took me through the restaurant to the back door. I know I had to have looked confused as hell. He opened the door, and there was a beautiful stage with all kinds of lights flashing. To the left, there was a second bar with several tables in front of it and a few stand-up heaters throughout. People were relaxing on blankets, waiting for the bands to come out.

"Are we here for a picnic?" I asked excitedly. I grabbed his arm and jumped a little.

He chuckled and kissed my hand. "Yeah, I thought you might enjoy it. I had my friend Elijah set it up for me, so we got a good spot."

This man...he can't seriously be this perfect. Can he?

"Elijah's band is playing here tonight, along with a few others. It's a nice night to be outside. This area is heated, but we can go inside if it gets too cold. Just say the word."

I pulled his face to mine and kissed his cheek. "Thank you, Link, this is perfect."

He looked me right in the eye. "You're welcome, Songbird." He leaned in and gently kissed my forehead right back.

I brushed my fingers over his cheek. "I like the stubble; are you growing it out?"

He looked at me adoringly, "I'm glad you noticed."

I ruffled his hair with my fingers. "We need to do something about this mop on your head though." I was joking, but he pulled me in closer.

"Are you offering?" he asked.

"Sure," I smiled. We walked over to the grassy area and found our blanket. I sat down while Link went to the bar and ordered some appetizers and drinks. He remembered how I liked my margarita which made my heart ache a little, in a good way. It was a simple gesture, but it meant the world to me. Max always had to ask what I wanted to do, eat, drink, everything. He never just did something without me asking or because he remembered. Let's just say I planned many of my own gifts and surprises. I even planned the majority of our dates.

As the night went on, we chatted with a few of the people around us. I enjoyed the vibe here. His friend's band was getting ready on stage when they saw us and waved. His friend came over to introduce himself to me, which I thought was sweet.

He stuck out his hand. "Hey, I'm Elijah. I saw you at the bar last time I saw Link, right? We weren't properly introduced because you left my man hanging." He said it jokingly with a big laugh.

I smiled and shook his hand. "Hey, Nice to meet you. I'm Aubrey."

"Oh, I know." He winked at me, then smiled at Link. I think I saw Link's cheeks flush, and he wouldn't look directly at me, making me wonder what he'd been saying about me. I think it's cute that he talked to his friends about me.

Elijah stayed for a few minutes talking to Link about the Reckless Riders' upcoming tour. He was talking about his manager being a total dick, but I couldn't hear the extent of it because I was too into the music. Elijah got my attention and asked me where I was from. When I told him Connecticut, he told me they had a stop in Hartford in June. He told me he would get me some tickets and make sure my friends and I got into the VIP area so we could meet everyone and hang out afterward.

Link gave a sad look but tried to play it off. I think the talk of Connecticut made him think about me going home, and now I was thinking about it too. My heart sank a little.

Elijah didn't stay long because he had to finish the stage setup. When the music started, I was amazed. I didn't realize that anyone around here listened to anything but country music, but this was definitely not country music. I felt like an ass for stereotyping. The music was a mix between Journey and Fall Out Boy. I knew this would definitely be music I would continue to listen to once I got home.

Link was enjoying himself too. I caught him staring at me a few times. I grabbed his hand and leaned onto his shoulder. "I am having a great time. This is so fun. His band is so good; how are they not stupid-famous?"

"They will be, give them a few years."

He motioned his head, telling me to sit in front of him, so I moved over and sat between his legs with my back to him. I leaned back, and he put one of his arms around my neck and kissed that sweet spot below my ear. It sent tingles all the way down my back. The stubble on his chin against my skin was doing something to me.

I was singing my heart out; I even stood up for one song because I couldn't contain myself. He just let me be me and didn't comment on how crazy I was acting. He watched me like he was amazed.

I sat down again when the music changed to one of their slower songs. I felt him move a stray hair away from my ear and nuzzle his nose against my ear.

"I love watching you."

Holy fucking hell! That was hot as hell. I squeezed my thighs together to give myself some relief from the immediate arousal those four little words caused. My skin was covered in goosebumps. I swallowed the lump in my throat.

"What do you mean?" I whispered. I didn't turn my head to face him.

"I love watching you get into the music. It's amazing to watch you light up just hearing it. It's like you become part of it. It's beautiful to watch. You're beautiful."

I turned my head a little and talked over my shoulder. "Well, thank you, I like that you enjoy watching me." I looked into his eyes this time and bit my lip. "I usually don't let people see me geek out like this, but being with you makes me feel like I can be myself," I paused, unsure if I was ready to admit the next thought. "It makes me feel safe."

Then he turned my head so I was completely facing him. His smile dropped, and he became more serious. "Aubrey, you will always be safe with me. I promise."

He leaned in and kissed me softly at first, then it deepened. This kiss was nothing like the first; the first one in the kitchen was rough and rushed. This kiss was sensual. Slow. Teasing. Like he wanted me to feel just how much he wanted me. Like he wanted to take it slow and make it last. My body was humming with desire. I could feel the tingling traveling down my whole body, settling right where I wanted to feel him the most.

He pulled away and cupped my face. His hands were gentle like he was afraid to scare me away or something. He smoothed my bottom lip with his thumb as he studied my face. "I don't think you realize how beautiful you are."

I stared straight into his eyes. He leaned in and kissed me again. I felt his tongue slide into my mouth and tangle with mine. It was like everything around me went quiet, and it was only us outside. No one else mattered at that moment. I had never felt something that intense in my life.

He pulled back reluctantly. We were both breathing heavily, looking at each other like we were about to devour one another. He put his forehead against mine.

Trying to catch my breath, I smiled. "What was that for?"

He visibly swallowed like he was trying to clear his nerves. "I needed you to know I meant it."

He rubbed his finger over my bottom lip again, and I instinctively pushed my tongue out to lick it. He groaned when my tongue hit the tip of his finger.

I gave a coy smile. "That was the best kiss of my life."

"There is more where that came from."

He gave me a sexy grin and kissed me again. This one was quick. He seated me back against him. I was starting to love simply being in his space. I tried hard not to react to his bulging excitement that I was now feeling right at the top of my ass, where my body was nestled into his. Every once in a while, I would feel him move my hair away from my neck and lean in to kiss my shoulder or neck, and I couldn't help but smile. Being here in his arms was the safest I've felt in a long time...but that also scared the shit out of me.

I was getting so turned on. I got a little bold and gave him a taste of what he was doing to me. I moved my ass into him. I heard him groan and his hold on me tightened. He nipped at my shoulder. "Bad girl, don't start something you can't finish." I couldn't help but giggle.

After the live music ended, the DJ kicked back in. We said goodbye to Elijah and headed out to talk and get to know each other better. The rowdy bar wasn't exactly the best place for that. We headed to the car, and he ran ahead of me to open my door, but before I got in, I turned to him and grabbed his hand. "Thank you for this. I haven't been on a date in a long time."

Before he could say anything, I leaned into him and pushed him against the car to kiss him. His eyes widened, but he didn't give me even a second to take control. He immediately lifted me off my feet by my ass and moved me against the car so my legs wrapped around him. A quiet moan slipped out from between my lips, and I immediately felt the arousal building between my legs. My hands went to the back of his head and fisted his hair. I felt his erection push against me. I moved my hips to grind on it. He shuddered. I pulled away and looked him in the eye.

"Take me home, Link," I whispered.

He put me down but didn't immediately let me go. His head was still against mine. He was biting down on his lip and still holding onto my ass.

"Get in," he said, looking down at me. His chest was rising and falling like he couldn't catch his breath.

"I need you to let me go in order to get in," I chuckled.

I heard a groan come from the back of his throat as he squeezed tighter. "I don't want to; I don't want you to change your mind, and I don't want you to stop kissing me." The side of his mouth curved up as he kissed me again and then he promptly put me in the car.

Lincoln

"Hey, so I know you have been helping Pops during the week, but I have a proposition for you." I looked over at her in the passenger seat, and she seemed a bit intrigued.

"Is that so? Do tell," she grinned.

"I do. I am directing the school play this year and was thinking of having a few songs use the acoustic arrangement." Her eyes lit up. "I was wondering if you could help me with that. Maybe help out with some of the singers too and then —" she cut me off.

"I would love to." She smiled and grabbed my hand. "That will be so much fun."

"Really? Awesome, I'm glad you're so excited about it. Some of the other teachers will be helping periodically too." She smiled and looked back out the window.

We drove the rest of the way in silence, both of us with dumb grins on our faces, but hers was slowly fading. The closer we got to home, the more nervous she seemed.

She seemed reluctant to get out of the car when we got home like something terrible would happen if she did. I walked over to her door and reached my hand out to her. I was about to ask her to come in when she cut off my thought.

"Thank you for tonight. I really did have the best night ever." She was rubbing my fingers in hers, and then she spoke again. "Is it okay if I just head off to bed? I'm kind of tired from all the dancing."

She gave me a sweet smile, and I knew she was letting me know the night was over and anything that had happened before was simply an in-the-moment thing.

"Yeah, of course. Let me walk you in."

She kissed my cheek goodnight, and I watched her go up the stairs and shut her door. I walked out to my house, almost in a daze. She is always allowed to change her mind, of course, and I would never try to force her into it. I just couldn't help but wonder what had changed her mind.

I got into comfortable clothes and threw a movie on. I couldn't clear my mind from how abruptly tonight had ended. I definitely thought it was going to end differently. I didn't expect her to sleep with me, although I had hoped. I thought we would at least get a little hot and heavy. Lately, it's all I think about.

I tried just watching the movie, but something was persistently nagging at me about how that all went down, so I texted her.

AUBREY

I shut the bedroom door and leaned against it. "Why did I do that?" I said it out loud even though I was alone. I walked over and flopped onto the bed.

What am I doing? We can't really do this. I'm leaving, and he's staying here. That's the end of it.

Then why did it feel so wrong to walk away just now? I wanted to spend the night with him, and I just walked away like a damn coward. I haven't wanted to spend this much time with anyone since Max, let alone even thought about sleeping with someone.

I changed clothes and attempted to relax. I lay in bed trying to process how fantastic tonight was, all while trying to also figure out what was happening in my head. I know I'm just afraid to share myself with someone again.

Link is not Max, and I'm just being a chicken shit— my thought was cut short when I heard a text notification.

Mr. Grumpy Butt: Hey. I hope you are settled in okay. I didn't say it before, but I had a great time too. BEST DATE EVER in my book. I hope we can do it again soon. Maybe next time, a night in so it's not overwhelming, and we can talk more. Goodnight, Songbird. Sweet dreams.

I laughed at the excited tone I got from the capital letters. I started to type, 'Thanks, good night,' but then I got a rush of courage and knew I needed to go to the cottage and talk to him in person. I deleted the message I was writing and headed to the backyard. I have to share my feelings with him or my brain will never let me relax, let alone sleep.

I got outside and realized how cold it was with only thin pajamas on. I was praying he opened the door quickly. If I had to stand outside for long I would turn around. If that were the case, I wouldn't be coming back out. I got to the door and knocked. He answered the door quickly. His eyes went wide the moment he saw it was me. I looked down and saw that my nipples were pebbled against my top. I quickly put my arms around myself, and before I could say another word, he pulled me inside.

CHAPTER TWENTY

Lincoln

I felt my cock stir at the sight of her. She stood at my door in a strappy nightgown, covering almost nothing. I was trying my best not to stare at her nipples.

She wrapped her arms around herself. I immediately pulled her in. She walked over and sat down on the couch. She grabbed one of the blankets to cover herself like she was embarrassed.

I adjusted myself before walking over because I didn't want to make her even more uncomfortable with the huge bulge in my sweatpants. I grabbed another blanket in case one wasn't enough and sat beside her. I gave her some space, but I also didn't sit all the way over on the other side of the couch. I wanted to keep her within my reach.

"Hey, you okay?" She was quiet and didn't look at me at first. I pushed some of her hair behind her ear. "What's going on in that beautiful head of yours? You disappeared on me when we got home. Talk to me."

She looked up and smiled, then quickly looked down again. I didn't think she was going to answer, but then she whispered, "We need to talk."

I looked at her nervously. "Do you want a drink or anything to eat? I grabbed some snacks in case we came back here after the date."

"You did?" She gave me a small smile. She looked relieved. I think that made her more comfortable for some reason. She pulled her legs up under herself. "Do you have anything warm to drink?"

"I can grab you a tea bag or hot chocolate from the house. Does that work?"

"Yeah, either would be great, thank you."

When I came back, I tried to lighten the mood by joking a little. "So, will you tell me what's happening, or are you trying to keep me guessing?"

"I honestly don't know exactly what I want to say yet. I just wanted to sit with you for a minute." She looked up at me. Her eyes looked a little hurt. "I can go back to the main house if you want to head to bed."

I set the tea down on the table in front of her. I sat directly next to her this time. She smiled when I lifted her legs and put them across my lap. A few minutes passed, and she finally spoke.

"What are we doing? We can't really be doing this. We can't honestly believe we can date."

She leaned down to grab the cup.

"What do you mean? You are drinking tea, and I'm having water." I smiled, even though I knew what she meant.

"You know what I mean." She smiled and playfully kicked my leg, though the smile didn't quite reach her eyes. "I know this was only date one, and normally a first date doesn't get this deep, but this isn't exactly a conventional situation. We can't just never see each other again if things don't go well. You will still have to see me sometimes, especially on holidays and birthdays, or at least I hope so. Are we stupid for entertaining this? Like what are we going to do if—"

I grabbed a hold of the outside of her thigh, "Aubrey...what is it you're really worried about? I mean, I agree; yes, what you're saying is important, but that's not the only thing that's bothering you, is it?"

"No...it's not."

I pulled her closer. "Okay, spill."

AUBREY

I was nervous. Link grabbed ahold of my empty hand and started rubbing the backs of my fingers as he relaxed our hands on my knee.

"Aubrey, talk to me. What happened in the car before? Did I upset you or something?"

I shook my head and squeezed his hand tighter. "God, no. You were perfect; I meant it when I said I had a great time. Honestly, it was the best date I've ever been on. It's all me. I think I'm in my head about all of this. I am broken, and I ruined the night. I'm so sorry."

"You didn't ruin anything. You are allowed to change your mind, and you don't need to explain yourself if that's all it was. I do get the feeling that something else is happening though. Tell me, what's going on?"

I paused for a second, then lifted my pinky in front of him.

"Okay, but first, pinky swear there is no getting mad or offended and no judging."

He smiled and then interlinked his pinky with mine. "I pinky promise."

We intertwined the rest of our fingers, and the word vomit just started coming. "I'm scared you're going to hurt me like my ex did." I paused for a moment to see if I would get a reaction, and I didn't. He was listening intently. "I'm also scared I will somehow hurt you. I'm scared of a relationship again."

"Aubrey, so am I. I've never even been in one."

I gave him a weird look. "Never? You can't be serious."

He looked a little embarrassed. "Totally serious. I've had one-night stands and remained friends but never dated anyone. I've never trusted anyone enough to want more."

"That's not really what I mean." I took a breath and looked down at my hands. "Max was my first everything. Although I was a party girl and had quite a reputation for being a "fun" time. I never partied too hard or went home with anyone, and I especially never slept with anyone. I had the confidence and reputation of someone who did all that, but I was never really that person. Some may even say I was a bit of a tease."

His eyes widened like he was going to ask me a question, but I continued.

"I knew I didn't want to wait for marriage, but I did want to save myself for the person I thought I would marry. Max was my safe space, my person. He was my comfort. I thought I was with the person who would be my forever, and then that dream ended when I found him in bed with another woman."

"Oh, Aubrey."

He placed his palm on my cheek. I placed my hand on his and kept going; otherwise, I knew I would chicken out.

"He was a ladies' man like you are. He said I was the one to make him change. If I'm being honest, he had all the signs that one day he would cheat, but I ignored them all. Even when people told me he was trouble, I didn't believe them...He broke me, Link. He broke me so bad that I haven't been able to be with someone since. I'm 23 years old, and I've slept with one person, and the last time I even kissed someone besides you was over two and a half years ago. He made me feel worthless, and I've carried that with me all this time, and if I'm being totally honest, I'm scared you will be just like him."

He looked hurt. "Aubrey, I would never do that to you."

I continued without acknowledging his words.

"The issue is that I'm scared to want you. I am so scared of being hurt that I can't let myself give in to wanting you. It took me a long time to move out of the hurt phase, and I can't go back to that place."

He was looking at me with sympathy, like he was really understanding where I was coming from. The next thing I knew, he was hauling me onto his lap.

LINCOLN

I pushed the blanket off us and pulled her onto my lap so she was straddling me. I wanted to be face-to-face. I couldn't stand how far away she felt. I needed to look her in the eyes. I placed my hands back on her cheeks and rubbed my fingers over her features. She put her hands on my forearms.

She was silently crying, and her cheeks had turned a

darker shade of pink. I gently wiped some of her tears away. I started to kiss them away, but she pulled away. I didn't misunderstand anything she was saying. She's afraid to let me in.

My heart sank because I understood. I'm nothing to write home about in the relationship area, but knowing I ever made her doubt me hurt more than I care to admit. But really, why would she think differently? Nothing I've said could make her think anything different. If anything, I probably made it ten times worse by bragging about it like a dickhead. No matter how comfortable and safe she may have felt earlier on the date, my past reminds her of him. I finally broke our silence.

"I'm sorry, Aubrey. I'm sorry you had to go through that with your ex. I am sorry he was such a shitty human. I'm sorry that my past makes you uneasy. If that were something I could change or fix, I would." I paused, running my fingers through my hair. "I don't know why it's different with you, and I'm sure it sounds like a rehearsed line, but something changed when I met you. I can't explain why or how it happened, but since you walked into that store, I haven't been able to look at or even think about anyone else. You are consuming me, Aubrey, even though I barely know you."

She laughed and sniffled a little, then grabbed my hoodie strings and started twirling them around her fingers. Then she looked up at me with those baby blues. I felt a flutter in my chest. I brought one of my hands up to touch her face.

"You have this pull on me that I can't explain. All I know is that I like it, and I really like you." She tensed a bit, but I kept going.

"I know that this is a really complicated situation because you're right; it will be a big mess if things go bad. We're connected to the same people, and we can't just walk away without strings attached, but I do know that we can figure it out. I want to figure it out. I want to see where this goes, and I get the impression you do too. Otherwise, you wouldn't have agreed to a date. Am I right?"

I put my hands on her waist and pulled her closer to me. "I've never wanted someone like this before. As I said, I don't know what it is, but this isn't just some fling to me, which is new. I always said I never wanted anything but a hookup. To me, relationships mean giving myself to someone, and I never wanted to give someone that much power over me or give that much of myself to someone just to end up hurt. A relationship meant there was a potential for settling down and moving forward in life, and I've never had the feeling I wanted that before, but with you, I don't know. Is it weird if I say I can see this going somewhere? Will that scare you off completely?"

"Yes, Link, It scares me completely," she whispered.

"I just...I want to try. Please, let me show you how this can work. Let me show you what safe feels like again. I've never felt like this about anyone or poured out all my feelings like this before. I actually feel stupid to be honest, because I don't know what you're thinking. I was trying to keep my man card and show off by acting like I was some woman eater, but you have my man card in a vice grip. That shit expired the moment I met you."

She laughed again, and her smile took my breath away.

She moved her hands to my cheeks and stared at me like she was deciding something, and then her smile faded slightly.

"Link, what if—"

She started speaking, but I cut her off by putting my

fingers on her lips to stop her. I brought her face closer to mine. Our lips were almost touching.

"Aubrey, what if it works?"

She was quiet for a moment. She slid her fingers into my hair before she spoke against my lips. "Promise me something?"

It was a question, not a statement. I nodded my head yes.

"Promise me we will always be friends, and we will always put that friendship first. Even if romance isn't in the cards for us, and this is just a silly fleeting attraction."

"Aubrey, this isn't some fleeting attraction."

She put her fingers over my lips just as I had done to her.

"Just promise, and lastly, promise me that we will keep in touch no matter what. I want you in my life no matter what happens between us. Even if it's once a month phone calls to catch up when I'm back in Connecticut."

The thought of that turned my stomach. I didn't want to think of Aubrey not being here, but I nodded my head in agreement anyway. Then she leaned the rest of the way and kissed me. I dug my fingers into her thighs just below her ass to pull her in because she still wasn't close enough. I felt desperate, like I had to hold on for dear life and couldn't let her go, or she would change her mind again.

I can't believe I just said all that; it was like my brain exploded with all my thoughts from the moment I met her, but I meant every word. I felt things I hadn't ever felt before, and it scared me shitless.

CHAPTER TWENTY-ONE

Aubrey

He kissed me like he needed my breath to live. We both started to grind our hips, and I could feel what kissing me did to him right between my legs. When I finally pulled back a little bit, we were both breathing uncontrollably, just staring at each other. I put my forehead to his, "Okay, let's see where this goes."

He smiled and kissed me again. I pulled my face back to look at him. "Are you going to fuck me now?" I immediately covered my mouth and blushed. I couldn't believe I said that out loud.

He groaned, and I swear I felt his erection grow even more. He stood up with me in his arms. His hands were holding me right under my ass. I grabbed onto him because I thought I was going to fall, but he had a tight grip on the back of my thighs, so I wrapped my legs around him. Once I realized he wouldn't let me fall, I started kissing him from his neck down to his collarbone.

He pinned me against the wall and looked me in the eyes.

"If you don't stop kissing my neck like that, I will fuck you against this wall or cum in my pants. I've been thinking about this for weeks."

I bit my lip and laughed at how forward he was being. I loved it. I leaned in and whispered, "Yes, Sir."

"Fuuuck, don't do that either," he groaned with a smile. He walked us both to his bedroom. He placed me down gently and looked at me like he was going to devour me. He kneeled one leg onto the bed between mine and leaned over me. His hand touched my thigh and started traveling up my night-gown. Excitement coursed through my body as his hand reached my side. His finger brushed the underside of my breast. He cupped it and let out a satisfied groan.

"Perfect." Then he paused like he had done something wrong. "Is this okay?" he asked breathlessly.

"Take it off," I whispered as I nodded.

He smiled and lifted my nightgown over my head.

"Jesus Aubrey. You're—Fuck! You're perfect." He bit his lip at the sight of me, which turned me on. He cupped my breast again and slowly brought my nipple between his fingers. The feel of his fingers on my nipple sent shockwaves straight to my center. I couldn't help but moan when he touched me.

"Everything about you is perfect. You're breathtaking," he whispered against my ear. He took both my hands and gently pushed them over my head, holding me down.

"Is this okay?"

"This is more than okay," I said as I caught his lips with mine. He groaned at my response. I felt the warmth building in my core when he began kissing my collarbone. I hummed as he got closer to my breasts. His tongue slowly circled each nipple. I squirmed beneath him when he blew air where he had just licked. Keeping my arms up was hard because I wanted to grab him and pull him closer.

He pulled my nipple into his warm mouth. He was giving both breasts equal attention. I was like putty in his hands. Every time he kissed or touched me somewhere new, shockwaves went off in my body like I was being touched for the first time.

He let my hands go, and I laced my fingers into his hair as he kept getting lower and lower on my body, but I pulled him up a little to look him in the eye.

"You're too dressed,"

Without saying a word, he stood up. I helped him remove his shirt, and my mouth went dry as my eyes and hands roamed over his body. I stood up and traced my fingers along his abs before I pushed him down onto the bed and straddled him. I kissed his neck and chest and felt his muscles tightening under my tongue. He kept making the sexiest sounds as I moved lower and lower. I licked and kissed him, taking my time as I traveled down his washboard abs.

He was gripping the sheets like he was afraid to touch me. "Fuck Aubrey. You're so fucking sexy."

I smiled against his hip bone, then bit him a little. I started to slip my hand into the waistband of his sweatpants, and he lifted his head off the bed like he was about to sit up. Instead, he grasped my wrist.

"You don't have to do that. Let me take care of you," he whispered.

"I want to. Let me make you feel good."

"Fucking perfect," he said as he put his head back on the bed.

I leaned forward and kissed him again while my hands continued down further. My hand slipped past the top of his boxers, and I felt him twitch. I wrapped my fingers around him, and it sent a tingle of satisfaction down my body when I realized how thick he was.

I didn't know whether to be more turned on or scared for my vagina. Link hardened in my grasp as I stroked him. His dick was silky smooth, with the exception of only a few thick veins. He already had some moisture gathering at his tip, so I rubbed my thumb over it.

He lifted his head to talk but he couldn't, so he laid back and shut his eyes.

"Aubrey—"

He said it like he was losing his breath. He opened his eyes and lifted his head again to look at me. "I want you so bad I don't think I can last long like this."

He lifted his hips in an almost desperate request for me to go faster, but I had a better idea. I let go, and he let out a sigh. I leaned down and pulled his pants the rest of the way down. I put my tongue to the tip of his erection and tasted him. I ran my tongue down the underside of his dick.

"Fuck!" He moaned. His hands grasped my hair, but he let go immediately and looked at me. "Sorry, I didn't mean—"

I smiled and grabbed his hand to put it back in my hair. "I like it when you're rough."

He threw his head back again and gripped my hair even tighter. "God, baby..."

He gathered all the loose hair that had fallen out of my bun and held it away from my face so he could see me. It turned me on even more because he listened to me and pulled my hair harder while watching me.

I wrapped my lips around his erection and slowly moved up and down. I needed help from my hand because he was so long. He was hitting the back of my throat, and my eyes started watering a little. He was moaning louder now, which made me moan too, and then his hips shot off the bed choking me a little.

"Aubrey, you have to stop!" I looked up at him because I thought something was wrong. Then I realized he was getting close. I pulled my mouth away.

"I'm just getting started, Link."

He threw his head back once again. "My God—I—Holy fuck!"

That made me smile with pride. I was getting more turned on with every word coming from his mouth. After a few minutes, I hummed around his cock, knowing it would vibrate my throat and bring him that much closer to his release. That moan was the last straw.

He was holding my head. "Baby, If you don't—I'm going to—Fuck."

He let out a tantalizing groan as I sucked harder, giving him the answer to the question he couldn't quite ask. Moments later, I felt his release. I worked him through it, making sure none of it got wasted. When his grip on my hair loosened, I tried to sit up to look at him. Before I could fully right myself, he quickly pulled me up by my hair. *Good lord, that was hot.*

"Now it's my turn," he said with the most mischievous grin. He flipped our bodies, and now he was on top of me. He was staring down at me in my thong for a moment, and it made me feel so fucking sexy. I looked him in the eye and lifted my ass so he could slide my thong down my legs. Then he placed it on his nightstand. The gesture made me shiver.

He pulled one of my nipples into his mouth and sucked. He used his fingers to give the other one attention and then switched. He moved to kiss me on my belly button, then traveled down my body, biting my hip bone just as I had done to him. That made me grip the sheets in anticipation. His mouth went back to my breasts, and I felt him touch between my legs; he was teasing my inner thigh, rubbing up and down in soft strokes. He finally reached my center using one finger and started to rub the wetness that had formed.

"God baby, you are so ready for me."

It was a slow, sexy torture. All I could do was nod my head. Then one finger slid inside, then another, and he placed his thumb over my swollen clit. I couldn't believe my body was so close to climaxing. He had barely even started. I grabbed his shoulder as his mouth was still working on my breasts. I was riding his hand as he was bringing me toward the edge. My hips lifted from the bed seconds later, and I had the most intense orgasm ever.

I could barely speak, and it came out breathless when I did. "You're...I can't...That was amazing." I finally blurted out as I was still coming down from my high. I'd never experienced an orgasm so quickly before.

He licked his fingers and his eyes rolled to the back of his head with a groan, it was the hottest thing I think I have ever seen in my life. His mouth began moving down my body. His stubble was scratching my inner thighs in the sexiest way. He hovered his mouth over my center. I felt his breath on my wetness. It felt like he was waiting for permission. Before I could speak again, he licked slowly and expertly up my slit. I was gripping the sheets so hard my knuckles went white. My back was arching off the bed even further now. It was sensual. It felt like he was savoring every moment. He pulled back and looked at me.

"You taste amazing."

Then he said something I never thought I would hear during sex because Max wasn't into dirty talk...or any talk for that matter. I never even knew if he was enjoying it because he was so quiet.

"Don't scream baby," he said with a playful grin. He placed his hands under my thighs, lifting my lower half to get a better angle; then his tongue entered me, and it was like fireworks went off. I screamed from the intense orgasm that flooded my body after only a few minutes.

He pulled away and spread my legs further apart.

"Bad girl, I'm going to have to punish you." He bit his lip and slapped my inner thigh lightly. It sent a shockwave through me. It was a mix of pleasure and pain, and it was invigorating. I blushed because no one had ever talked to me like he did, and I really fucking liked it.

This type of pleasure was something I'd never experienced before. Max didn't go down on me. No matter how much I asked him to, he just didn't want to.

I pulled his hair as my back arched off the bed again.

"More...Please," I pleaded.

I was holding him to me. He hummed and bit my clit ever so slightly, making me scream his name because the vibration was about to send me over the edge again. Then he slipped two fingers inside me, and I began to grind harder and faster against his hand and face.

I was trying to formulate words.

"Link, I need you now." He lifted his head, and I pulled him up onto me.

He looked me right in the eyes. "You have me, baby; I'm yours."

My heart fluttered a little as he kissed down my neck. Then, he reached over to the nightstand to grab a condom.

"I love the rough side of you, Link."

He wasted no time as he put on the condom and lined

himself up with my entrance. "Baby, this is nothing." He leaned toward my face and whispered, "This is just the beginning."

He lifted my legs over his shoulder and slapped one of my ass cheeks. Hard. Then he inched in slowly; he was making sure my body could take him. I heard him whisper. "Fuuuck."

He was struggling to go slow, but I was grateful because I'm basically a virgin at this point since it's been so long, and Max was definitely not this big. I am not someone who spends a lot of time pleasuring myself, either.

He kept going slowly until he was at the hilt. It was a pleasurable ache. I let out a low whimper. I don't remember sex ever feeling this good. He stayed still so my body could fully acclimate to him. When he started moving, I gasped and gripped him tightly inside me. My back started to arch off the bed. He pushed on my stomach to hold me in place. The pressure from his hand made each thrust even more satisfying.

"God baby, you're so tight, just for me."

I was already so sensitive from the previous orgasms. After only a few minutes, I could feel my body ready to give in. I gripped my fingers onto his back to center myself; I knew I was leaving marks.

"Link, I'm—" I tried to say I was going to orgasm again, but my moans took over.

"Me too." He said breathlessly. He thrust into me a few more times. I was almost crying because it felt so good. "Let go, Aubrey."

At the sound of my name on his lips, I came undone. "Yes, Link! Yes!" I screamed.

He paused, leaning down toward my ear. He covered my mouth with his hand. He gave me that sexy grin.

"Shhh, baby. No one else is allowed to hear those screams but me."

He pushed himself to the hilt, and I saw stars as my legs physically shook. This one was even more intense. He let my legs down and pushed down on my hips to keep me still while he kept moving inside me to get me through my orgasm. Then I felt his release seconds later as he moaned my name.

God, this man is going to be dangerous for me. How will we ever stop?

He kissed my forehead before he got up and threw out the condom, but when he returned, he grabbed another. I tried to protest but I was too satiated lying there on the bed. I didn't think I could move another inch. Sex with Link was addicting already. I've definitely never had more than one orgasm in such little time. My vibrators are suitable, but this was leg-shaking good.

I smiled up at him. He leaned over me and ran his thumb across my lips like he was admiring me. I was about to pull his thumb into my mouth when I was caught off guard. He pulled me to my feet and he took my lips in a fierce kiss. I faltered a little because my legs hadn't started working correctly yet.

"We need to get cleaned up," he said with a knowing grin. He kissed me again as he walked me backward toward the bathroom, pausing against the door.

He was kissing down my neck again, and between kisses, he spoke. "You are so fucking beautiful. Do you know that? You are the most beautiful woman I've ever seen in my entire life."

His hands traveled over my body, warming every inch of me. His fingers traveled down and dipped inside me again. He lifted his head to look at me. I looked down, bringing my lips together to try to hold in the moans. My eyes began to roll back because his fingers felt so good. I never knew how to respond when people complimented me. He removed his fingers and cleaned them off with a lick. It was so fucking hot. He used his other hand to lift my chin and kissed me again. Then he spoke against my lips. "I will never stop telling you how beautiful and sexy you are." He grabbed me so I wouldn't fall right before he pushed the door open.

He leaned down, adjusting the water to make it the perfect temperature before we climbed into the shower. I don't know when he did it or how he still had stamina, but he was rock hard and ready with a condom on. He backed me into the shower wall, lifting both my hands with one of his. He lifted one of my legs around his waist as he slid into me. I let out another strained moan. Sex standing up was another first for me. It felt incredible.

"You are taking me so good baby," he whispered. I whimpered softly and bit my lip.

After pumping into me a few times, he let my hands go. They fell to his shoulders, and I leaned into him, moaning his name lightly. He used that hand to squeeze my neck lightly, running his thumb across my jawline while keeping his eyes on mine. His burning stare was causing my arousal to heighten even quicker.

His orgasm came fast, and I was screaming his name even louder this time. He covered my mouth while moaning through his own release right along with me.

"I told you I'm the only one who gets to hear those noises, baby."

I moaned again against his hand. He kept pumping into me while I rode out my orgasm to completion.

After showering and getting all cleaned up, he had to carry me to bed. My legs would not be working any time soon. He gave me a shirt to sleep in, and we snuggled up under his blankets. I had one leg draped over his, mindlessly tracing his abs with my fingers as I kissed his peck. He was rubbing my lower back just above the curve of my ass. It was turning me on, but I literally had nothing left to give, so I tried to push it out of my mind.

I placed my hand on his chest and my chin onto my hand to look at him when I spoke. He placed his hand into my wet hair, massaging the back of my neck as he focused his gaze on me.

"What's up, Songbird?" He looked concerned.

"That was incredible; you are incredible."

He pulled me closer and put his face next to mine. "No, Songbird. *You* are incredible."

Then he kissed me again. I've never felt so complete. We eventually fell asleep in each other's arms. It was the best night's sleep I'd ever had.

CHAPTER TWENTY-TWO

Aubrey

I woke up as the sun started to shine through the blinds. I was still in his arms, which surprised me because I usually sleep like a wild banshee, uncontrollably moving around all night. Whenever I fall asleep with anyone next to me, I end up rolling in the blanket or on top of them.

I didn't want to move, but I had to pee so badly, and since peeing in the bed would be pretty embarrassing, I had to get up. I slipped out of his arms, but luckily he stayed asleep. He looked so peaceful. His hair was in his eyes. I regret saying I would cut it now because I think I kind of like it as is.

I went to the bathroom and looked at myself in the mirror. I felt...new, almost like that had been my first time; I guess, in many ways, it was. A lot, if not all, of what went down last night was a new experience compared to what it was like being with Max. I looked at my breasts and stomach and saw some love bites where Link had sucked on my skin, and I couldn't help but smile as I ran my fingers over them. It made me feel sexy and desired.

Link stirred a little when I got back into bed, moving his face to my neck as he started to kiss me. His hand traveled down my side to my ass as he nipped at my collarbone. He was trying to turn me on all over again. I moved so I could kiss his lips.

"I need to go inside. August and Liza will be up soon, and I should get in before they know I stayed out here."

I whispered it, but I knew he heard me because he chuckled and grabbed my ass even harder with a low growl.

"Why? Is the perfect daughter scared of what they will say? We aren't in high school, baby; we're adults." His smile told me he didn't give two shits what they thought.

"If you must know, yes, I care a little." We both laughed at my admission.

He pulled me on top of him, so I was straddling him.

"Well, don't because you're stuck here. We can skip our run and just fuck all day." He gave me a hopeful look and pulled me in closer. "I really need to fuck you right now." He put my hand on his morning wood.

I gripped his erection tightly and rubbed him over his clothes. He gave a quiet groan. I leaned down and started kissing his neck. "I don't think that will work; we're both expected to be at the shop before ten A.M. I will, however, help you out with this."

His eyes rolled to the back of his head when my hands slipped into his boxers. "Fuck it! Tell him we're both sick."

I kissed down his body until my mouth covered his cock. He gripped my hair and had no problem showing me precisely how he wanted it. Pleasuring him was making me increasingly wet, but we had places to be.

He moaned. "Baby, I'm close."

I started moving faster up and down his shaft until I finally felt his release. I wiped my lips with my thumb when I was finished and smiled down at him. He was staring at me in awe. I let him catch his breath and whispered in his ear.

"Let's go, Grumpy Butt. Get your ass in your running gear, or I'll leave without you." I got off the bed and bent down to grab my nightgown.

"Can I borrow some of your clothes to get inside?"

He smiled and pointed to his dresser. "Bottom one."

As I bent down, I made sure he had a perfect view of my bare ass; I heard him groan, making me smile and bite my lip. I grabbed a pair of pants and started looking around for my underwear.

"Link, where is my thong? I saw you put it right here." I gestured to the empty nightstand. I looked back at him and saw he had a huge smile spread across that gorgeous face of his.

"Someone must have stolen them." He shrugged, then reached over pulling me back into the bed and started kissing my collarbone. "They are mine now, just like you."

His words turned my insides into mush. This man is going to be the death of me. He literally turns me on just by fucking breathing. He got on top of me and started making out with me. His hand slowly traveled down my body, but I grabbed his wrist to stop him.

"Okay, they are yours. Now get up, let's go; I'll even make you some coffee if you are a good boy."

I got out from under him and winked.

"You're no fun in the morning," he whined.

I just smiled at him. "Oh really? No more blow jobs then. Is that what you're telling me? That wasn't fun for you?"

He put up his hands in defeat. "Fine, you win," he chuckled.

We got dressed, then he walked with me into the main house. I froze when I walked through the door.

"Glad you guys got home okay."

Liza sat at the table with a cup of coffee and her book. She didn't even look up when she spoke. Link nudged me inside and shut the door. He walked around my frozen body, over to her, and kissed the top of her head. It made my heart twist with admiration.

"Hey, Momma. What are you doing up so early? It's not even seven yet."

He was acting completely normal like she hadn't just caught us doing the walk of shame.

My legs finally started to work, so I walked over to get coffee silently and made Link and me a cup, taking my time in order to avoid her for a little bit longer. I placed them on the table, and he pulled me into his lap before I could sit down.

"Link, stop it."

I blushed as I wiggled from him playfully to let me go to sit in my own chair. Liza smiled a little and gave a quiet chuckle.

"How was the concert?" She looked up this time, but there was no sign of judgment whatsoever in her eyes.

"It was wonderful. We had a great time," I said.

As I looked over at Link, I could feel my cheeks warming even more because I felt like we were caught doing something wrong. We sat there enjoying our coffee, and I looked at Link to keep the conversation going and make it less awkward, but he just kept smiling at me. I think he was enjoying my discomfort a little too much. Before I could say anything, Liza put her book down and placed her glasses on it.

"Link, go out and grab us some bagels and muffins. I think Aubrey and I could use some bonding time."

He raised his eyebrows as if to ask me if that was okay. I nodded slightly to answer his unspoken question.

"Okay, sounds good," he finally said.

He got up and walked over to me. "Guess we will have to skip our run this morning after all." He leaned down and whispered, "My reason for skipping would have been much more fun." He gave a smug smile and nipped the top of my ear lightly like he was proud he was getting his way. That single gesture was so damn sexy.

"I'll be right back; text me if you ladies think of anything else."

He kissed my forehead before leaving. It made my insides warm all over again. Once Link left the kitchen, I slowly turned my gaze to Liza's.

"I'm sorry," I wasn't sure what else to say. I put my head back down, realizing I couldn't look at her. I felt like a kid in high school all over again. I started fidgeting with my fingers, and she grabbed my hand.

"You have nothing to be sorry or embarrassed about. You are two consenting adults enjoying each other's company. You owe no one, especially me, an explanation for that. I just wanted to talk to you, check-in and see how you're doing; make sure everything is going well."

It felt like a weight was lifted off my shoulders. I think I even audibly let out the breath I was holding.

"I love it here. I wish I could stay forever. I can't thank you enough for allowing me to stay with you and for welcoming not only me but also my friends and family into your lives. When this all began, I was terrified I would be blowing up August's life."

"Oh. sweetheart," she leaned forward to grab my other hand, now holding them both. "You made his life so much better. He is so much happier now that he knows you. Many people in this town are better because they know you." I knew she was talking about Link. "You are helping so many kids learn how to play the guitar. You're getting kids excited about wanting to join the school band and even helping August in the shop. He seems to be a lot more organized, thanks to you."

"Thank you for saying all that. As I said, I really love it here. You guys have made my life more abundant than you even know. And yes, your husband needed organization. That man didn't even know half of what was happening in those books." We both sat there giggling together. It felt nice.

"Sweetie, you have no idea how much joy and faith you have brought this family."

I looked at her, confused.

"Did August tell you how we came to start fostering children?"

I shook my head no. She leaned back and let my hands go.

"We got married when we were both twenty five. We wanted to have children immediately. We tried for about eight months, but it never happened. We stopped putting pressure on it and just let it happen. We had been married for about a year before we sought help; we wanted to try IVF. When I went for an exam and some bloodwork to make sure I was a candidate, they discovered I had ovarian cancer."

My breath hitched. My eyes began to tear slightly, so she grabbed one of my hands again to comfort me. "I'm fine now before you start getting upset. We obviously knew that this diagnosis would take priority over trying for a child. Together, we decided that we would remove both ovaries so we could be proactive. My mother passed away from cancer when I was young, so I didn't want to take any chances. It was a hard decision, but we knew we had other options. We started to do the paperwork for adoption, and in doing so, we started learning about the system and foster care. Once we realized how many kids were in the system, we knew that would be the route we would take. I wanted to be able to help families that were working to get their children back. I felt like that was my calling. I felt that if we found a child that could be adopted and the time was right, we would. We fostered about ten kids before we found Lincoln. I'm proud to say eight of those kids ended up reunified with their families."

"Liza, I'm so sorry you went through that. It sounds like God planned to give you something even better. I hope you realize what you did for those kids. What you did for Link."

"I do, and I hope you realize now just how special you are to us. How grateful we are to know you. You are the miracle for which we have prayed." I grabbed her and pulled her into me as the tears flowed. She pulled away once we both calmed down.

"A few years after we began fostering Lincoln, we realized his mother wouldn't be trying to get him back. She was awarded visitations but very rarely showed up for them. At that point, I knew he would be the child who got to stay with us. His mother hadn't contacted us in two years. We spent the next year trying to get her to sign the paperwork. She dragged it out until he was on the cusp of being eighteen years old. At that point, we sat Lincoln down and asked if he wanted us to continue with the adoption or use the money for his school-ing. As a unit, we chose college, which was more important because a piece of paper wouldn't change what we meant to each other; he is our son, with or without it. Our family was complete... well, until you, of course."

"I am so glad he found you," I said.

She leaned into me, "And I am so glad that both the men

in my life found you. I have never seen either one of them this happy. August has been so happy knowing he gets to work with and learn about you; we talk about what new things he learned about you every night." My stomach dropped a little. I feel bad that I am occupying their conversations.

"Lincoln has been a tough one to crack for most people." She gave me a knowing eye. "I love my son, but he had, and I'm sure still has, some serious hurt to work through, and I've never once judged him for how he chooses to do so. I always just hoped he was safe and made sure he knew we were here when he needed us. He's never looked at a woman the way he looks at you. Aubrey, you've shown him how to care. He's never shown that sort of emotion toward anyone...ever. I knew the minute I saw him look at you that something was different. He studies you. He finally saw someone that was worth changing for. I don't mean to put any pressure on you. I just wanted you to know I saw it."

My heart swelled with so much joy. Everything she said made me know that giving Link a chance was the right thing.

"Thank you. Thank you for welcoming me into your life with no questions asked. Thank you for letting me get to know you and sharing all this with me."

She pulled me into a hug again. Our moment was inter-rupted when I heard August speak from the hallway, and I pulled away to look at him.

"I'm grateful you spent the time and money to find me, and I'm even more grateful that you are taking the time to stay and get to know me. I know being here takes you away from everything you know, and I know how much courage it took for you to do it."

He placed his hands on my shoulders and lightly squeezed them as he looked down at me as if to reassure me.

"I will be forever grateful for the miracle of you, and I hope you know we love you."

Liza nodded her head in agreement with him, and she was sobbing even harder now.

"Meeting you guys gave me a lot of answers to questions I've had throughout my entire life," I said with tears streaming down my face. "We will forever be a family no matter what, I promise."

CHAPTER TWENTY-THREE

Lincoln

I heard the end of their conversation when I walked in the door. I felt my heart tugging as I stopped and listened for a moment. I couldn't explain this feeling, but Mom was right, something in me was changing, and it was all because of her. Last night was a new experience for me too. I've never shared my feelings like that. I've never cared about giving a woman pleasure. It has always just been getting it done, down and dirty, then kicking them out. I feel different with Aubrey like I can trust her with anything.

I've never trusted anyone, which I'm sure has everything to do with my biological mother and the scars she left me. The only people I have really ever trusted fully are Mom and Pops. I know I can trust them because they genuinely love me and have proven it to me time and time again, but even that took a few years for me to realize. I've never been able to fully trust most of my friends, either. I have a lot of them, but do I trust them? No, not really. I don't get close enough. I'm always super skeptical of people, but not her. I've never gotten the feeling that I couldn't trust Aubrey. It was just something that came instantly.

I walked into the kitchen, and everyone was crying; I knew why, of course, but I didn't say anything because I didn't want to get sucked into the cry fest. My heart was already doing weird flips and shit. Instead, I made everyone bagels and passed them out as they were ready.

"Thanks," Mom and Pops said simultaneously, then jinxed each other.

It was seriously sickening sometimes how perfect they were together.

I handed Aubrey hers and kissed her forehead. She looked up at me and smiled. Her eyes were so blue today that they looked like they were actually sparkling.

"Thank you, Link."

I leaned down again and whispered in her ear.

"You're welcome, Songbird."

She looked at my parents to see if they were looking and then pulled my face to hers and kissed my lips quickly. I chuckled against her lips. She turned away and blushed immediately when she saw that they did in fact notice.

After we ate, Aubrey and I went to shower, separately, unfortunately. Mom and Pops went out because they were meeting friends today while Aubrey and I worked at The Music Box.

I got out of the shower and sent a text telling her I was ready. A few minutes later I heard a knock at the door, so I opened it figuring it was her.

"Hey, Linky!"

My eyes went wide when I saw it was Kayla standing in front of me. "Um, hey." I rubbed the back of my neck to try to hold in my discomfort. "What's up? Is everything okay?"

She looked confused. "Yes, silly, everything's fine. I just

wanted to invite you to dinner with a few of the teachers tonight so we can talk about the play. We all wanted to start the week strong and have everything figured out before Monday."

I gave her a confused look. "Shouldn't that have been something I planned as the director?"

She looked shy and shrugged. "I don't know; I was just trying to help, I guess."

"Oh… I mean…thank you, I guess," I was still very confused. "I don't really need any help though honestly."

She gave me a pushy look.

"Since it's already planned, I'll have to check with Aubrey. I'm not sure what she's doing tonight."

"I think you should go; sounds important."

I didn't realize it, but Aubrey had walked up behind Kayla. Kayla turned to look at her. Aubrey gave me a genuine smile. I think she really meant it.

"It sounds like it will be fun; enjoy time out of school with everyone," Aubrey added.

Kayla sneered. "Oh, hi, Audrey. Are you okay? You look a bit tired."

Kayla meant it as an insult, but Aubrey didn't miss a beat. She rolled her eyes at Kayla and walked up next to me to put her arm around my waist. It was really sexy seeing her being territorial.

"It's Aubrey, and yeah, you could say that we are both a bit tired. We had a bit of a long night."

Kayla's eyes widened. Aubrey smiled up at me, and I couldn't help but chuckle when I looked down at her.

"You think I should go? What are you going to do tonight? Do you want to come with me? You will meet some of them when you come to the school anyway."

She thought about it then looked at Kayla and back at me. She put her hand on my chest.

"Thank you for checking with me first; that's really sweet but completely unnecessary. You go and have fun with your colleagues. I'm going to cook dinner tonight and meal prep a little bit. I want to be prepared when I help with the play; I need to stop eating so much crap. Just call me when you get back, and I'll come over." She smiled big, looked at Kayla, and then back at me, "Or maybe I'll just wait in your bed for you." My dick jumped at the possibility of her waiting in my bed naked.

"You're helping with the play? Why?" Kayla asked as if she was disgusted at the thought.

I got a little defensive. "I asked her to, and I'm the director."

"Oh. Um, well cool, I guess." Kayla said, sounding defeated.

Aubrey just smiled at her and didn't respond to her last statement. She pulled away from me and started walking towards the car, but she turned back towards us.

"Link, I'll be in the car; we need to leave in five minutes or so if we're going to open on time." Then her attention went to Kayla. "It was good to see you, Kayla. Next time, please call first, just in case we're busy. I'll see you at the school soon."

Before she turned around, I saw the satisfied look on her face.

God, that girl is feisty. "I'll only be a second," I called out to assure her.

I grabbed my keys, walked outside, and shut the door. "I'll be there, Kayla. What time?"

"Oh, I can pick you up if you want," she said hopefully.

"No, that's okay. I probably won't stay long so I can get back here to my girl." Then I winked to send the point home.

Kayla's hopeful face fell. "Oh, I'll text you the details, I guess."

"Great, thanks. I have to head out. I'm opening today, and I'm late, as you heard." I walked away and left her standing at my door.

AUBREY

It took everything in me not to act jealous, but I think I did okay.

"She's persistent," I said as Link pulled the car out of the driveway. He looked a bit uneasy. He probably thought I was mad, which I wasn't. It wasn't his fault she's a desperate idiot.

"Yeah, I'm sorry. I know that didn't look great, but I—"

I held up my hand to cut him off. "No need to apologize for her. You didn't know she was coming. I could tell that before I even got over to you guys. You don't owe me an explanation. Also, as I said, it was unnecessary for you to check with me. You don't owe me that either."

His shoulders relaxed like he had been nervous that I would be mad.

"I just wanted you to know I didn't ask her to come over... and I will check with you whether you want me to or not. I would much rather have plans with you." He gave me a handsome grin. I grabbed his hand intertwining our fingers and smiled back.

Once we got to the shop, the day flew by. Link and I snuck in some make-out sessions when we had moments of no customers. It was so damn hot being pushed up against the wall like that. It made me regret telling him to go out tonight. I couldn't wait to be lying in his arms again.

The more I thought about it, the more I realized that it really did bother me that Kayla just showed up like that.

"Is Kayla going to give up soon?" He turned towards me when I started to speak. "I mean, like I said, what happened today was whatever, but she can't just keep showing up. Even if I didn't exist, she shouldn't just show up randomly at your house, right?"

Link smiled, "I knew it was bothering you."

He walked up to me and put his hand on the back of my neck, then pushed his fingers into my hair. "I'll make sure it doesn't happen again." He leaned down and whispered. "Just so you know, you're very sexy when you're jealous."

I felt the blush travel up my neck. I pushed him back and turned away. "I'm not jealous. I was just saying. Don't you think showing up uninvited is rude?"

I started walking away, but he grabbed my hand and spun me toward him to pull me close. His hands captured both sides of my neck and face as he ran his thumbs over my cheeks. His face got more serious.

"You are jealous, and it is fucking sexy as hell, but I will make sure you don't have a reason to be anymore. I will tell her once again, to back off for good this time."

He pushed away the hair that was hanging around my face. "I'm grateful you do exist, by the way."

He leaned in to kiss me, but I pulled back and gave him a confused look.

"What?" I asked.

He chuckled. "You said even if you didn't exist, she shouldn't be coming over unannounced. I want you to know I'm glad you do."

My heart melted into a puddle, and butterflies filled my stomach. I leaned up and kissed him.

"Thank you, grumpy butt." I smiled against his mouth.

He rolled his eyes jokingly. "We're still doing that, are we?" he smiled playfully.

I looked at him with a smile. "You are still calling me Songbird, are you not?"

"Yup, never gonna stop," he said proudly. "But you like it."

"Good, I hope not, and you will grow to like your nick-name too." I paused and whispered in his ear. "Maybe I can make you like it more when I'm screaming it next time you fuck me." I winked and walked away to assist a customer.

I saw him close his eyes and physically shiver at the thought, and then I heard him whisper, "You are an evil woman."

I couldn't help but let out a chuckle.

Although things were going great with us since we talked and connected, I've got a weird feeling a few times when I've caught him writing something on a piece of paper. When I caught him, he would put it away really fast. After the third time catching him and him having that same weird reaction, I finally just asked.

"What are you writing over there?" I know I had abso-lutely no right to ask, but I did anyway.

He looked up at me from Pop's desk. "Nothing, just some stuff for work."

"You hide everything you write for work?"

"I'm not hiding it."

I started thinking about how amazing last night was. I really didn't want to cause a fight, so I let it go.

"Okay." I began walking back out front when I heard the wheels on the desk chair move so I turned around just as he was walking up to me.

"Don't do that," he said calmly.

"Do what?"

"Don't downplay when something is bothering you."

This man… "Link, I really am fine. If you say it's nothing, then it's nothing. Right?"

He pulled me into a hug and kissed the top of my head. "Yeah, right."

I looked up at him and kissed his lips fleetingly before I walked back out front. I am trying my best to work on my trust issues with him, and maybe this is just the first step.

I told Link I would walk home so he could go right to dinner. I gave him a quick hug and kiss to say goodbye. After I walked away, Link quickly came up behind me putting his chin on my shoulder and put his arms around me before I even made it out the door.

"We're good right?" he asked

"We are fine, don't think anything of it."

"Are you sure you can't come with me?" He started kissing my neck trying to persuade me.

"I'll miss you too," I said with a giggle.

His mouth felt so good on my neck. I was thinking about telling him to just come home with me, but I knew he had to do this for work.

My next sentence came out more unsure. "You will have fun, and I will be there when you get home."

"Promise?" he asked.

"I promise." I turned toward him and put my arms around his neck to look up at him. He looked nervous, but I could tell he had something to say.

"So, can I tell them you're my girlfriend?"

He had the cutest damn nervous smile on his face. Could this man be any more perfect?

I blushed because the question surprised me a little. "Am I your girlfriend, Lincoln Matthew? I don't recall being asked."

"God, I hope so," he blurted out as he grabbed my ass with both hands. "I don't want anyone else ever getting to kiss and touch you like I do. I want you to be mine." He leaned in and gave me a deep, passionate, mind-blowing kiss.

His directness turned me on.

I put my lips to his ear, "Then I'm yours."

He smiled and kissed me again to say goodbye.

A boyfriend. I have a boyfriend! I texted my friends in a group chat, including Brie, and they were ecstatic. Callie said she made a bet with Nick that it would happen, so although he was happy for me, he was pissed. Now he owes her fifty dollars because he didn't believe I would actually start dating anyone, let alone someone from another state.

After talking with them for a while, I texted my parents to say hello. I omitted the boyfriend thing, even though Brie would probably tell them when she called them to check in. She's got a big mouth, but I don't feel like giving a million details or answering questions about anything, especially about going home.

I was sitting on my bed. My anxiety was kicking in a little bit just thinking about how this place was starting to feel more and more like home every day. Although it felt good and I felt carefree here, I was really starting to miss my friends and family back home. Luckily, it's only a few days until Brielle comes. She moved her flight to Friday night so we could have an extra night together. After this trip, I most likely won't see her until my birthday weekend in March. I'm not sure what she and I will do while she's here but, knowing her, she will want to hang out at home, watch some movies, probably check out the bookstore, and spend time bonding which I'm one hundred percent okay with.

I started to play some random notes on my guitar, trying to busy my mind. I'm pretty nervous about everyone coming here, but I'm also very excited for them all to finally meet—especially Link and my parents. My parents have been asking lately when I might start dating again. That's the main reason I'm waiting to tell them.

At one point, they even thought I was hiding someone because I was staying at Callie's so often. They thought I was actually staying with a boy and just didn't want to admit I was seeing someone. Then I reminded them that we didn't hide things from each other.

I guess I was wrong about that, wasn't I? I wonder what else I was wrong about.

CHAPTER TWENTY-FOUR

Lincoln

I saw through the window of the restaurant that only Kayla and one other teacher were waiting at the table. I waved as I walked in, then went straight to the bar to get a drink but mostly to buy some time so I didn't have to be there with just the two of them. I didn't want to be here in the first place. I told the bartender to take his time. He saw the way I was looking over at them, and I think he understood what I was saying, thank God.

Once I got my drink and saw that two others from our teacher's group had finally arrived. I figured it was safe to head over to the table. We got right into the voting. The students voted last week. The top student choices were Grease, RENT, and Guys and Dolls. My vote would be for Grease because it's one of my favorite movies. Unfortunately, when we took the teacher vote, RENT won by a landslide, everyone but me.

I started going over who was doing what, and when the subject of Aubrey helping came up Kayla had a lot to say.

"Why would we have her help? We don't even really know what she's capable of. What if she sucks?"

Some of the other guys looked at me with dumb smiles, clearly trying hard not to make a joke about Aubrey sucking. Some of these guys still acted like complete tools a lot of the time... I guess I was one of them still because I wasn't sure whether to answer in a snarky way and be inappropriate or answer her actual question.

"She went to college and majored in music and voice in some capacity." I couldn't remember exactly what she told me, but I knew I was close. "She is a better choice to help us with this play than almost anyone in this room. She will play some of the songs for us on the guitar so they have more of an acoustic feel, and she will help the kids with some vocals, that's it."

Kayla didn't like that answer and went on.

"I don't understand why we wouldn't hire a professional. She shouldn't be able to help just because she's staying at your house, and it's convenient."

"Do you have a problem with her, Kayla? Do you know her or something?" Jack, one of the other teachers asked.

"No, not really. I just don't think it's appropriate for Link to bring his flavor of the week around the kids. It's weird."

That was the last straw for me.

"Enough, Kayla!" I said, probably way too loud because people not even at our table turned to look at me. "You are being inappropriate. Number one, Aubrey is a professional. I just told you that and explained how she would be of value to this production. Number two, She's not a flavor of the week. As much as you don't like it, Aubrey is my girlfriend and she is here to stay. Number three, really just reiterating number one, she would never be inappropriate near the kids... her job is to work with kids teaching guitar. I would appreciate it if you would stop judging her simply because we are dating. If you want to explain why you're so pressed about this, let's go outside because we both know your issue with her is purely personal. If anything, we can do this without you. You're only providing help with costumes. I can find anyone to help with that. My mother will be doing most of the hard stuff for it anyway. Let me know if you want to remove yourself from helping. It won't be an issue, I promise we will be ok without you."

Her eyes went wide with shock. She could only nod her head in agreement. Everyone else was just sipping their drinks, looking anywhere but at me. I think they were surprised that I responded that way. I'm usually a pretty laid back guy, especially at work, but I will not let anyone talk negatively about Aubrey. Ever.

"Ooookay! Since that's settled, let's move on to who's building the sets," Jessica said.

We ironed out all the details and planned for tryouts to be this week after school on Wednesday, Thursday, and Friday. Hopefully, Aubrey will be able to join because she will definitely be a big help with that.

I paid my portion of the bill and gathered my jacket to leave.

"See everyone tomorrow; drive safe." As I was leaving, Kayla stood up as well. I was hoping and praying she wasn't trying to follow me. Unfortunately, I wasn't that lucky.

"Link, you got a sec?"

"Not really, Kayla. I think you and I have said enough, don't you? I need to get home."

"I wanted to apologize. I'm sorry. I shouldn't have acted like that." I stopped walking because that surprised the shit out of me. I've never heard Kayla apologize for anything.

"Uh, thanks, I guess... I hope the third degree with Aubrey

will stop now. She doesn't deserve it. She's been nothing but nice to you and you can't even call her by her actual name. You keep acting like a jealous ex or something and, as far as I can remember, we only slept together once, a long time ago, and we were very drunk. I've tried to tell you time and time again that we are only friends, and you still try to make it into something more. I am sorry if you misunderstood or if I did something to confuse you. It was fine before because I thought you were just being flirty and funny. After all, you flirt with all of us. Just know it's no longer okay—"

"Link, I'm sorry." She cut me off. "I am jealous."

My eyes went wide. "Why?"

"I've been trying to get with you for years, and you just haven't seen me. No matter what I do, I'm stuck being your friend. You never see me differently. I even tried flirting with some of the guys to get you to care or maybe even get a little bit jealous, and it didn't even faze you. Then here she comes, little miss perfect, and you fall in love with her overnight, so I'm fucking jealous, okay!"

"I'm not in—" I breathed out. "Kayla, I'm sorry you feel that way. I don't have an explanation for you. I just know I want this to work with her. Having you show up uninvited and flirting with me every chance you get isn't okay."

I'm not quite sure why I cut myself off just now. *I couldn't really love her...could I? I mean we barely know enough about each other to feel that way... right?* I shook my head to clear my thoughts.

"Okay, I'll give it a rest. Again, I'm really sorry. I hope we can still be friends without it being weird between us," she said almost desperately.

"Let's see how this play goes, and we will go from there, okay?"

"Yeah. Have a good night, Link. Tell Aubrey I'm sorry too."

I felt like I couldn't drive away fast enough. I just needed to get home to Aubrey.

It was later than I had hoped. I didn't think I'd be there for four hours. I walked in and saw her shoes at the door. I didn't immediately see her, so I got excited that she stuck to her word and was probably naked in my bed. I went to my bedroom and there she was, snuggled in my bed with my shirt on. She had on some cheek-hugging panties that formed around her ass perfectly. Her hair was in a loose bun and she was sound asleep. She was clutching onto one of my pillows. Her mouth was open with the soft sound of quiet snores escaping. She looked stunning.

Seeing her like this made my heart do that weird flippy thing again. It was like I saw my life flashing before me. Everything I ever envisioned happening in my life now seemed to include her. I was just standing there staring at her. I don't understand how I could feel this way after such a short time. It's impossible. This shit isn't real. It doesn't actually happen this fast. Love like this isn't a real thing.

Dozens of questions were clouding my thoughts. Could I really love her? How did she consume me so quickly? How was this going to work? When is she going to get sick of this place and leave it? Leave me?

I didn't know the answer to anything I just asked myself, but I knew I would never feel this way about anyone else. She is it for me. I don't know how, and I don't know why it happened so quickly, but I do know it feels fucking amazing.

I tried my best not to disturb her when I climbed into bed. I replaced the pillow she was clutching with my body, and she barely stirred. It felt like I was truly home, here with her in my arms. I rubbed her forehead with one finger, lightly pushing the hair away from her face so I could press a gentle kiss to it.

I shut my eyes and just as I was drifting off to sleep I felt her fingers begin to trace the V below my stomach, leading into my sweatpants. My dick immediately sprung awake. Her hand started traveling into my waistband. I thought I was dreaming at first until my eyes flew open, and she was staring at me with those perfect eyes of hers. The moonlight was hitting them just perfectly through the blinds. Something serious passed between us, but it was quick, almost as if I imagined it.

My breath hitched, and my lips fell open as she moved her hand ever so slowly and stroked me. There was already a bead of moisture forming on my tip. She was so damn mesmerizing, I couldn't look away from her.

"I missed you," she whispered.

"I missed you more," I answered.

"How was your dinner?" she whispered as her fingers gripped me harder. It was seductive like she was trying to tease me into talking.

"It...It was...My God don't stop." I had to pause and breathe between words because she was so good at taking what she wanted. She began to stroke me faster, kissing my neck and then down to my collarbone.

Between the kisses and light bites, she asked me another question. "Did you have fun tonight?" Then another kiss. "Did you get your work done?"

I moaned and gripped the sheets. I did my best to answer her question. "Fuck, baby...Yes. Work done, but it was...eventful." Her hands cupped my balls making my hips lift off the bed as my body responded increasingly with every stroke.

"Wanna talk about it?" she asked.

"Fuck no!" I shook my head no.Because the last thing I wanted to do right now was talk about anything other than fucking her. Aubrey let go of me, and pulled my sweatpants further down. She climbed on top of me and placed herself over me so we were in the perfect position for her to grind on my erection. She bent her face down and began to kiss my body as she slowly circled her hips over mine, just a thin triangle of her underwear between us. She licked up my neck and kissed the sensitive spot on my collarbone.

"If you couldn't tell, I missed you a lot." I felt her smile against my neck.

"Fuck, baby—" she cut me off.

"Next time...I'll come with you. I hated the waiting. I hated missing you."

She stopped and sat back, interrupting the moment. "Am I being too possessive? Is that weird?"

I pulled her back to me. "Never stop being possessive over what's yours. I like the way you tell me you missed me. Maybe you should miss me more often."

She smiled as she stripped off her shirt.

"Fuck baby." My hands started to travel along her torso, feeling every perfect curve, cupping her full breasts in my hands so I could feel her skin on mine. I leaned up and took her perfect, pink, pebbled nipple into my mouth and she gasped. She held my head to her chest like she was scared I would pull away.

"You are supposed to sit back and let me take control," she said breathlessly. She pulled away and reached over to grab a condom. I blinked and she was already putting it on me. Aubrey lifted herself and spread her wetness with my tip. She slowly inched down onto me, moaning as I filled her. She started to ride me with no hesitation.

"Fuck, you are so sexy." I cried out. She put her hand over my mouth, and her thumb brushed my bottom lip, so I pulled her finger into my mouth. She must have liked it because she didn't pull her hand away, and she was moaning my name in seconds.

This was perfect; she is perfect. I moved my hand to grab her neck and give her the pressure I know she loves. We spent the next half hour enjoying each other and learning each other's bodies even better. This only solidified my earlier feelings. I love this woman, and I can't let her leave.

CHAPTER TWENTY-FIVE

Aubrey

God, I missed him. I was waiting to touch him all night. The sex we just had was better than the first time, and the second for that matter. Now I was laying on his chest, listening to his heartbeat as he ran his fingers methodically up and down my bare back. It was making me shudder. I looked up at him.

"I'm glad you had fun at dinner. What made tonight so interesting?"

He hesitated, like he wasn't sure he was going to tell me.

"Well... Kayla, actually."

I felt my eyes go wide. I sat up and pulled the blanket up over my chest. "Explain," I said calmly.

He sat up, leaned against the headboard, and held my hand as he went through exactly what was said. I was internally beaming that he'd stuck up for me like that, but I also felt a little bad that my helping with the production was causing issues, and they hadn't even started yet. I also felt even worse because I know what it's like not to be wanted, and it's hard to come to grips with, at least it was for me.

I laid back down on him and got quiet, and he nudged me so I would look at him.

"I meant it, you know, everything I said to them. I meant every word," he said.

I smiled at him adoringly, "I know you did. Thank you." I kissed him deeply. "I'm excited to come to work with you. RENT is one of my favorite movies. I hope I can do you guys justice, and I promise no inappropriateness." Then I licked his nipple playfully; he practically yelped and swiped me away.

He turned over and flipped himself on top of me. "Maybe you can get a little inappropriate," he said as he gave me a wink and a sly grin right before he began kissing me all over; his hands traveled down my body, and he slipped a finger, then another, into me, turning me on again. It's going to be a long night... and I am going to enjoy every fucking minute of it.

The following day when I woke up, I threw on my clothes and went to shower in the main house. I left Link a note that I wasn't going for a run today because of the rain, but I made sure I told him to come say goodbye before he went to work.

After my shower, I lit my candle to give my room a cozy vibe and got dressed. I texted Callie because I knew she would be up since she was working doubles at the diner. Something in my heart told me I needed to talk to her.

Me: Hey bestieeee, Good morning.

Callie: Hey stranger, what's up?

Me: How's Connecticut? Is it missing me yet?"

My phone rang.

"It's been missing you since you left, babe."

She said it jokingly, but I could hear the hurt in her voice. She and I had never been apart this long before, so I knew she was missing me just like I was her. "I've been missing you something fierce, Aubs. Like really fucking missing you. I should be so excited about planning this wedding, but something seems off since I got back."

"I miss you too, Cal. Do you think it's something serious? Do I need to come back now? Will that help you feel at ease?" I know she heard the slight panic in my voice.

"I don't know if I need you immediately, but I will soon. Nothing is normal about this, Aubs. Everything is different now, no?"

"I don't know Cal. Can we talk about everything good for now and not talk about that? I don't want to think about leaving here and going home just yet."

She huffed like she was getting annoyed with me. "You can't ignore it, Aubrey. You do this every time a difficult conversation comes up. It doesn't just go away because you don't talk about it. I know you have a whole other family there, and now the man you love is there. What are you going to do?"

I ignored what she said about love because I didn't want to have that conversation right now, either. She doesn't know anything about how I feel. She isn't even here. I love her, but I hate when she won't drop something. The thought of leaving August, Liza, and especially Link, hurt to think about.

"Callie, if you want to talk about something else or what's going on with you, I will, but if you only want to talk about me coming home, I'm going to go. I have to make breakfast anyway."

"Okay, I guess I'll talk to you later then." She hung up without letting me say goodbye.

"FUCK!" I yelled as I threw my phone onto the bed. I plopped face down onto the bed and screamed into the pillow. I felt myself starting to panic. At that moment, I realized I've had very few panic attacks since I've been here. I know the only reason I'm acting like this is because she's right and it's pissing me off.

I sat up and saw August standing in the doorway. He looked surprised and very concerned.

"You okay, sweetie?" he asked hesitantly.

I was so embarrassed. I sounded so silly, gasping for air. I held my hand to my chest and got out some words. "Yeah, I'm sorry if I woke you."

Weirdly, the site of him calmed me a little, almost like my brain was finally associating him with being safe.

"Do you need me to get you something? Leave you alone? Tell me what you need."

I put up one finger to signify I just needed a second. A few moments later, I was able to continue speaking.

"I didn't mean to yell like that. I'll have breakfast ready in a few. I just wanted to check in at home first, and it didn't go as planned." I sat there with my face in my hands.

"Oh, don't worry about that. We were both up already. As far as breakfast goes, we're all adults and can fend for ourselves. Do you want to call them back? Do you want to talk with me about it? I'm here to listen." He smiled sweetly.

I looked up at him and smiled. "I'd love to chat, actually."

He came in and sat next to me on the bed. "Lay it on me." He smiled to show he was trying to be carefree and funny, but my smile back was weak and didn't reach my eyes. I didn't know where to start. I didn't want to hurt him by talking about leaving and didn't exactly want to dump my feelings all over him, but that's what dads are for, right?

"I can't stop thinking about leaving," I said sadly.

"What do you mean? Do you want to leave today?" He leaned back suddenly, like he had been hit hard by my words.

"Well, no, not right now, but eventually I will have to. When everyone comes for my birthday, I think they expect me to go home. By then, it will be two months of being here. That's long enough, no?"

He looked pretty sad at my admission. "Well, I personally don't think any amount of time is long enough because I'm enjoying you being here." He placed his hand gently on my knee. "Working with you and getting to know you has become the best part of my days. I love our lunch talks."

I smiled. "Me too." I placed his hand in mine.

"But Aubrey, I'm not naive to the fact that this isn't where you plan to stay. I know you will go home, and then we will have to plan visits together." He paused. "I'm really excited about that, by the way. I can't wait to visit your home so you can show me some stuff up there."

I smiled but didn't respond right away. I looked down at my hands. "What if I don't know what I want anymore? I mean, I miss my friends and family, but... you guys are my family too. I feel like I'll never be able to make up for all the time we missed out on. I feel very cheated. Then there is the added complication of—" I cut myself off because I didn't want to admit what I was going to say.

"Are we talking about Lincoln now?" he said.

I nodded my head in conformation. "I think he's a bit of a factor, don't you? I know you didn't want anything to happen between us, but it did. We've been getting close, and things are going well, but it's only been a few weeks since we met and only days since we decided to try making it something more. I can't exactly call it serious, right?" I chuckled at myself and started tearing up a little. "How the hell do I even bring up leaving when we're just getting started? I've tried, and we agreed just to let things happen, but things are happening so fast, and my feelings are getting very invested. I think— I can't just leave without thinking of him, especially since our relationship could be a lot more serious by my birthday."

He gave me an understanding smile. "Sweetie, I know this isn't the answer you want, but you are the only person who can make these decisions. You love everyone that this decision affects." He leaned in, nudging my shoulder. "They love you too, you know."

"I know."

"Whatever decision you make is the right one, and we will all—" His voice cut off, and he froze. He was staring toward the corner of the room where I had all my music stuff in the chair. "Where did you get that?" He pointed to all my stuff.

"The chair? It was here when I—"

"No, the guitar." He said as he walked over to it.

"Actually, I got that in Nashville if you can believe it. I was here on a trip during my first year of college, and it was given to me by a complete stranger. I know that sounds strange, but I guess he was sick and wanted it to go to someone who would love it and use it like he did. I only use it for special occasions because I can tell it's old."

He approached it and was looking at something inside its body as I was talking.

"His name was David."

"I'm sorry, what?" My stomach lurched with nerves.

He cleared his throat. "David gave that to you."

He looked like he was going to be sick. He was rubbing the base of the guitar with one finger like he was memorizing it. I couldn't tell if he was asking me a question or making a statement. My heart started beating really fast. I thought I may have misheard him.

"How could you possibly know that? I mean, I don't know if you are right, but why would you think that? Who is David?"

"My best friend." He was looking at me now with tears in his eyes. "He died a few years ago. His wife and I looked everywhere for this. It was his most prized possession. We thought maybe he gave it to an auction or something toward the end. He knew he was sick and started donating things to various charities."

Then he pulled a picture from his wallet. When he showed it to me, I saw a younger version of him and my mystery guitar guy holding *my* guitar. He handed it to me.

"Wait, that's–" I looked at August. "That's the man who gave this to me. How–" I tried hard to swallow the huge lump that had formed in my throat.

He left the room without saying anything else. I was sitting there stunned. He came back with a little circle compact mirror. He walked over and placed the guitar flat on the ground. Then he placed the mirror inside the body, careful not to disturb the strings too much. I kneeled beside him.

"See that? I inscribed that when I made this." It said the words 'Cradle to Grave' with two sets of initials, one set being AF. August Foster. He removed the mirror and held the guitar in his hands, just staring at it in awe.

"You... you made it?" I was speechless for a few moments. "But how did you... how did you know by just looking at it?"

He smiled like he was recalling a thought. "Green was our favorite color." He wiped a stray tear from his eye. "I took an instrument-making workshop my father held when he first opened the shop, and this was what I made. The grains looked funny to me, which is why I chose them.

David was becoming more famous and about to go on tour, so I made it for him. Making instruments definitely wasn't a passion, but this one was perfect. Taking that class is what made me buy the music store from my dad."

I felt like I was paralyzed with shock. My mind finally cleared, and I needed to know more. "Tell me about him. About David."

We got up and sat back on the bed, and he began. "Our mothers were best friends, so we knew each other from birth and we were friends through everything. Him leaving to tour, me staying here, all of it. I even introduced him and his wife. We were best friends until the day he died."

My heart utterly shattered for him. I couldn't imagine losing Callie or Nick. I would be absolutely broken. "How did he die?" I asked.

"Heart attack, but he was really sick. He was diagnosed with MS and it progressed fast."

I hugged him snugly around the neck. "I'm so sorry for your loss, Dad. I couldn't imagine losing someone that important to me." My heart felt like the floodgates had opened.

He pushed back and looked at me, stunned, but he was smiling and started to cry. "You called me Dad."

I was crying now, too. "I sure did."

We sat there crying and embracing one another for a while, neither one of us wanting to let go. "I think David led you to me in a roundabout way. A true coincidence."

I can't even explain the feelings flowing through me. A few moments later, Link came up and found us crying. He realized they were happy tears and left to give us privacy.

CHAPTER TWENTY-SIX

Lincoln

I woke up to Aubrey's note and got dressed quickly; I was hoping to catch her in the shower and maybe get my hands on her before I had to leave. I went up the stairs two steps at a time trying to be quiet but I froze when I saw Pops sitting with her on the bed, crying. I was about to walk in until I realized they were smiling. I thought I should give them some time to finish whatever they were talking about.

Aubrey looked over at me. "I will be downstairs," I said as I walked away from the doorway. Since it seemed like a happy moment, I didn't want to ruin it. I walked down to the kitchen where Mom was cooking, but she didn't seem concerned, which eased my mind a little.

"Hey honey, good morning. Want some eggs?"

"Morning Momma. Sure! Are they okay up there?"

Mom didn't look at me when I spoke, but I saw her back tense up. Now I'm worried. "They are fine. Just some father-daughter bonding, I think. You can ask Aubrey about it later, I'm sure."

I paused, and my heart sank. "Why? Is Aubrey not okay?" I started to rethink leaving her room and I was about to turn my ass back around. Mom cleared her throat abruptly and turned towards me, holding a plate of food.

"Lincoln, sit down and eat. You're going to be late to work."

"Fuck work. If she's not okay, I need to go up there; that should be me consoling her, not Pops. She's my—"

"LINCOLN MATTHEW! WATCH YOUR MOUTH!"

My eyes widened in surprise. I've heard my mom raise her voice like that very few times in my life. I immediately sat down and didn't say another word. She placed my plate of food down and sat beside me.

"Some conversations don't require your presence or concern you. You guys could use some space, don't you think? You are getting quite hot and heavy quickly. Give her a minute to breathe." She didn't wait for me to answer her first question; she kept talking. "Now, please just sit and eat and then go to work."

I gave her a look like I wasn't going to let this go, and she knew me well enough to know I wouldn't sit here wondering, so she either had to tell me something, or I was going up there.

"I heard her on the phone this morning. It sounded somewhat heated, so I woke your dad up and had him go check on her. They have been up there for about half an hour, so I don't know how it's going. Just give them time, okay?"

I felt terrible for yelling like that at her. "I'm sorry I swore, but with all due respect, you don't know anything about what's happening with us... we barely do." She gave me a look, and I immediately felt like I was sixteen again.

"Lincoln, I know a lot more than you think, I always have, and I know you have never acted like this toward any other woman. I also know you care deeply for each other. I can see it when you two are together, but I think she might be a little confused."

Mom placed her hands on my cheeks. My heart did the weird flutter thing again. "She is struggling knowing she's leaving soon and needs time to figure it out."

"But—" I tried to speak, and she just raised her hand to stop me. She placed her hand on my arm and looked at me.

"I've already said too much. Just give Aubrey some time. She just needs her dad right now, okay? This is between them for now."

She got up and started cooking again for Aubrey and Pops. I went on eating without saying anything else.

A few minutes later, Aubrey came down dressed and ready for her day. Pops was trailing right behind her. She seemed okay. Seeing her gave me an instant sense of comfort.

It took everything in me not to stand up and take her into my arms. She must have read my mind because she bent down, from behind the chair, put her arms around my neck, and kissed my cheek.

"Good morning, sleepy head."

She began to walk away, and I reached over and grabbed her hips to pull her toward me. "Good morning, beautiful. Everything okay?"

I rubbed her lower back. I love how perceptive we are to each other's need for touch. Her touch is my new favorite drug. She massaged the back of my neck with one hand. Her nails grazed over my skin and turned me on. I could tell she knew by the radiating smile that was plastered on her face.

"Of course, just an interesting morning. I will tell you all about it later. How about I make you and me some dinner at your place so we can talk alone? I'll have it ready when you get home if you want to leave your key with me, so I don't have to steal the spare again."

She placed her open hand out for the key. She gave me a simple smile, but it didn't quite reach her eyes. I noticed the blue of her eyes wasn't as vibrant as it usually is. I reached into my pocket and handed it to her. I felt an almost painful loss when she walked out of my reach. She walked over to grab her food, and I looked at Pops. He gave nothing away. Without making direct eye contact with me he walked over and grabbed his plate of food.

"Link, how was your dinner last night? Did you and your coworkers get a lot done? What did you guys choose for the play?" Pops asked.

"Yeah, we figured out most of it, but we'll finish today after school and start auditions mid-week. RENT won the vote. It wasn't my top choice, but I'm still excited."

"I'm really excited; it's my absolute favorite!" Aubrey added.

He chuckled and looked at her. "That's great! We can't wait to see how it turns out, let me know what you need from us, and we will make it happen. If I need to cover some shifts for either of you, let me know." He barely looked at me while talking, but I didn't think it was intentional. I would look at her over me, too.

We ate in silence, except for the news playing in the background. I went to my house to grab my work stuff and then returned to say goodbye to everyone. I asked Aubrey to walk me out. I just wanted to hold her and kiss her before I left. When we got to the door, she wrapped her arms around me, hugging me and putting her head on my chest. My heart did that little flutter again. I feel like melting every time it happens. I couldn't help but kiss the top of her head. It felt like she was holding something back, but I didn't want to press her and ruin her day.

She looked up at me with those perfect eyes. I felt like I could see the world in her eyes. This is my favorite version of her, no makeup, nothing hiding her perfect skin and eyes. I leaned down and kissed her nose. I felt like I was going to drown in my feelings.

I finally pulled away and put my forehead to hers for a moment, then I started kissing her again and kissed down her neck a little. I picked her up so her legs would wrap around my waist.

"I missed waking up to you, Songbird," I whispered against her neck.

I felt her giggle then she made this beautiful, soft moaning sound that sent a wave of pulses straight to my dick. She pulled away to look at me as she intertwined her fingers into my hair.

"I missed it too, but I had to shower and check in with Callie. I didn't want to disturb you."

I leaned in to start kissing her neck again, but she stopped me by placing a finger across my lips. "I always want to be disturbed by you," I groaned, going in for another kiss. "Disturb me, baby."

She gave a seductive smile and whispered, "Don't start something you can't finish before you leave, big boy."

I gave her a groan. "I'll give you a big boy, don't tempt me, baby. I'll take you upstairs right now and bend you over the —" She covered my mouth and looked toward the kitchen. She chuckled and shushed me as her cheeks flashed a pretty shade of pink.

Then she leaned into my ear. "Later."

She gave me a final peck and wriggled out of my hold. She

started walking away, but I pulled her back toward me. I put my hand on her cheek and then lifted her chin with my thumb and finger.

"You're sure everything is okay? I don't mind being late. We can talk if you need to."

She kissed my lips fleetingly. "I'm positive. We will talk over dinner. Have a good day at work, okay?" Then she pulled out of my reach and went back into the kitchen. She paused to blow me a kiss. For some reason, that goodbye felt final, and I fucking hated it. I'm sure I'm just being paranoid, but I know deep down that this will continue bothering me all day.

AUBREY

My mind is still reeling from my dad's news of David and his guitar. How is it even possible? I always thought stuff like that happening, was fake. I always thought it was only in the books and movies and never actually thought that it could happen in real life. Especially my life.

Liza wrapped me in the tightest hug I've ever felt when I made my way into the kitchen. She had tears streaming down her face when she let go and looked at me.

"His wife will want to meet you...Well, she already wants to since August told her about you being his daughter but this...she will love this intimate connection even more." She sniffled a little. "I just can't believe this. You were meant to find us, and he knew it." I looked at my dad, and he just nodded.

I could only get out a few words. "I'd really love to meet her."

"She is away right now on a cruise, but I'll make the call while we are at work so she gets the message as soon as she returns." It sounded almost like he was asking if I was coming to work, so I took it as an opportunity.

"Do you mind if I stay home today? I have a lot to think about, and I really need to talk to my mom and dad." It felt weird saying that in front of him after our breakthrough, but my dad will always be my dad. Whether August and I get closer or not, they will both forever be important to me.

"Of course, honey, I got you covered." He kissed Liza and me on the cheek. Before he let me go, he whispered, "Take all the time you need."

Once I was back upstairs, I texted Callie again. I hate leaving things like that with her.

> Me: Asshole moment. Forgive me?

> Callie: You weren't an asshole. I shouldn't have been so harsh. I'm just dealing with my own shit and I'm mad you're not here, so I'm taking it out on you. I will always forgive you. Always.

That made me smile, but it also worried me that whatever

was going on with her was so bad, that she felt she couldn't tell me.

> Me: I'm sorry I'm not there. If you need me, I'll be there tonight. I'll book a flight, and you can pick me up.

> Callie: You drove there, dummy. What about your car?

> Me: You are more important. If you need me that much, I will leave. I can have Brie get a ride here and get it when she comes this weekend. You come first.

> Callie: No, I'm fine. Just promise me you are coming home at some point soon. I need my best friend. I can't do this without you. Nick is no help. He said he's not helping with the "girly stuff." Plus, you know he's not happy about this. He hates Jake.

> Me: I promise to help with your wedding planning and all the girly stuff. And I'm serious; the minute you really need me to be there, I will be, babe.

> Callie: I really miss you bitch!

> Me: I know. Stop before my baby bitch heart starts to cry. I have to call my parents. Call me later, okay?

> Callie: Always.

I closed out of our messages and sat on the bed letting the events of today process a little more. I know she's looking for a more solid answer, and she deserves one. Living in limbo was not only affecting me anymore. I picked up my phone and sent a text.

> Me: I'll be home the week after my birthday. I
> Promise. Our secret for now, okay?

She didn't answer, so I figured she had returned to work. I video-called my parents and told them about David and August's guitar. They were in utter shock. They thought I was making it up until I showed them the picture of August holding it. I also told my parents that August and I had a breakthrough and I called him Dad.

My dad was quiet for a few seconds but then spoke up. "So, since we're both your dad, does this mean I can get a cool nickname so you can differentiate us when referring to us?"

"Like what, Dad?" I was practically howling with laughter. He would try to make me feel better by making jokes. It is one of the things I love most about him.

"I don't know, pumpkin. Pick something rad."

I heard my mom laugh at him. "No one says rad anymore, dear; you are showing your age."

I cut in. "I think I may just call August 'Pops' like Link does. It will cause less confusion."

"Why does he get the cool name?" He sounded so offended.

"DAD!" I said with a loud laugh.

"All right, okay, boring old Dad it is," he chuckled.

Mom cut in. "You are anything but boring, dear. Now, let's let her get back to her day. I have a client, and you need to get to the hospital."

We finished the conversation, and I wasn't any better off because laughing with them again made me miss them even more. I feel like I'm choosing between families, and I don't know if I can do that.

I texted Liza and Pops to let them know the new plan for

leaving. I told them I would ask Link to try long-distance for a while, maybe even ask him to come with me eventually, depending on how the conversation went. I know moving might be too big of a step so soon, but I know I need to go home for Callie. I also know that I am falling in love with their son. It's not ideal, but I can do it for now, and we can figure out the rest as we go along.

They were thrilled that I was doing what was best for me, obviously a little sad, but they also said they would be hiring more people so they could spend time visiting me once I left. It made my heart swell that I wasn't the only one willing to make sacrifices for this new family dynamic to work.

CHAPTER TWENTY-SEVEN

Lincoln

I couldn't get Aubrey off my mind; not unusual lately, but I was more worried for obvious reasons. I thought maybe another opinion might help me calm down a little.

> Me: Hey, you busy?

> Elijah: Nah, not really. What's up?

> Me: Come to the school at one o'clock and help me. I need to talk to you.

> Elijah: Is this a trick? Is this really Link? You never ask for help.

He sent it with a laughing-crying emoji, so I know he was joking, but it still pissed me off. I rolled my eyes, but he was right. Although he's my closest friend, we're not really that close. It was probably the first time I'd ever asked him for something. His teasing wasn't worth it.

> Me: NVM, forget I even asked.

Elijah: I was joking, dickhead. I'll be there.
Need me to bring anything?

Me: Maybe some vodka.

Elijah: I can do that. I got you.

Me: Bro, I was kidding. I work at a school, for Christ's sake.

Elijah: Uh… yeah, I was kidding too.

I was finishing up with the teacher in the next room when I saw him walk into the hall. I held up my finger to signify I needed a second, and he nodded to acknowledge he saw me.

I walked into my classroom and he was sitting in one of the seats with his feet on the desk. "So, what's this secret mission you need help with?"

I grunted because I was already pissed off at his smugness. "I never said I had a secret mission. I just asked you to stop by."

"Yeah, yeah, yeah, cut the bullshit. What's up? What do you need?"

I wasn't quite sure how to start because, again, I never asked for help from anyone. It took me longer to get the words out than I'd like to admit. Elijah just kept staring at me, waiting for me to talk.

"Well, it's Aubrey." I sat down behind my desk, and he just stared some more. When I didn't keep going, he sat up and looked a little concerned.

"What about her? Is she okay?"

"She's okay…I think. She's just acting weird, and I feel like she's hiding something from me. My mom mentioned giving her space like she knows something I don't, and I don't know whether to leave her alone or keep bugging her about what's up."

The smugness returned to his face, and I knew he was about to break my balls.

"You think Aubrey is over you already? Moving on or something?"

"NO! Absolutely not," *At least, I hope not.* I got an awful feeling in my stomach, and there was a lump in my throat that I couldn't swallow.

He was giving me a pitiful look like he felt bad for me.

"What? Do you know something I don't?" I said it a little too loudly.

He put his hands up in defense. "Dude, chill. I've just never seen you spiral out like this. Are you ok? I've had one convo with the girl, which you were basically holding her during, by the way. How the hell would I know something you don't?" I didn't answer and just kept looking at him. "See, this is why I don't get involved with bitches."

My fists started to clench together, and I gave him a nasty look. "Aubrey is not a bi—"

He put his hands up again. "Women, I mean women, my bad."

"What do you mean anyway?" I asked through gritted teeth.

"I mean, you guys have been dating for all of a few days, and she's already fucking you up; this isn't you, bro. You don't get all torn up over girls. You need to fuck someone else and get over this chick."

"You aren't helping." I rolled my eyes at him. The thought of touching anyone but her turned my stomach.

"What exactly do you want me to say? I'm not the best

person for love advice, bro. It sounds like you won't be okay till you guys talk it out. Did she seem mad when you left?"

"No, she said we would talk later... She's making me dinner."

He looked at me like I was crazy. "So, what exactly is the issue if she's acting normal?"

He was making me more mad by the second, but realistically, I knew it was not his fault and, honestly, he was right. I'm just in a mood and can't articulate my feelings because this is all new.

"Just never mind. She's not acting normal; something is off, but you can't help."

"Sorry bro, I just don't get women. I don't think I ever will. Single for life over here." Then he laughed loudly.

That broke my grumpy mood a little. It made me laugh because Elijah is the typical single-for-life guy, and I can't believe I ever sounded like that.

We started chatting about my play and he offered to hook me up with a friend of his that does stage lights for the play, so at least he's good for something. Our guy retired last year so we need a new one. He set up a meeting for the guy to come by later this week to see if the play is something he can help with. He was heading toward the door to my office, but he turned and grabbed something from his jacket.

"Oh hey, can you give these to Aubrey? I told her I would get her VIP tickets for when we are in Connecticut in June. Let her know it also comes with a wristband that covers unlimited food and drinks; she will get the wristbands when they check in that day. I got her four tickets, but if she needs more, tell her to let me know. Oh, and tell her to bring her hot friends." He slapped my chest with the back of his hand.

I stared down at the tickets and then back up at him. I

didn't move. He started to pull them back, but then I grabbed them.

"Yeah, got it." I wish the thought of her being in Connecticut in June didn't bother me so much. "I'll walk out with you. I'm going to leave early so I can see my girl."

Then he laughed deep and loud. "You are so pussy whipped bro."

I smiled back and slapped his shoulder. "You are such a dick sometimes. At least I'm getting some."

He laughed. "Fuck you, dude."

I sat in my car for a while before heading home. I was tempted to rip the tickets up, simply because I didn't want to have this conversation, but I knew she would be seeing Elijah here and there, and I knew he would make sure to ask her if she had gotten them. I turned my phone on and I saw I had a message. The words in the text made my blood go cold. I placed the tickets on the seat next to me and drove away.

AUBREY

I went grocery shopping and settled on making Link pulled pork tacos. I prepped everything so it would be ready when Link texted to say he was on his way home. I worked on one of the songs for the play and then took a nap until he texted me. Which he never did.

I heard the door open. Link was home early. I checked my phone and had no missed calls or texts, so I was confused. I got up and walked into the kitchen. I'm sure he was looking around the kitchen and snooping to figure out what I was making. I leaned against the door frame and smiled.

"Hey, you were supposed to let me know you were on your way. You're early."

He looked at me and didn't say a word. He looked like he had a bad day. I rushed up and tried to hug him, but he stepped back, and my smile instantly fell.

"What? What's wrong? Are you okay? Did something happen?"

He gave me a stern look. "You could say that," he said. He took off his work clothes and changed into his sweats to be more comfortable. I was even more confused when he put his sneakers on.

"Where are you going?" I asked.

"I'm going for a run." He turned and looked at me. "Alone, preferably." He sounded so cold and distant. I know we don't know each other super well, but I've never seen him act like this, especially toward me.

"What hap—" Before I could finish speaking, he was out the door.

What the hell just happened? I couldn't wrap my head around how he looked at me or the way he talked to me. Maybe he just needed some space from a stressful day at work. I figured maybe dinner might help. Even though it was early, I started heating it up and setting the table. It couldn't take him that long, right?

Wrong. Two and a half hours later, Link came walking in. He looked startled to see me still sitting there. After the surprised look faded, the anger and coldness returned.

"I said I didn't want to talk. What are you not understanding?" he said coldly.

I still didn't know what was wrong, but now I'm angry at how he's treating me. I looked right at him and made sure he was looking me in the eye.

"Actually, no, you didn't. You acted like I had some kind of disease and pushed away from me, and you've barely said anything before just leaving. Are you going to tell me what's going on, or are you going to make me guess?" I thought using the words he used on me before would change the mood. I thought wrong.

He sat down and started eating the cold food with a shit-eating grin. "Oh, I'd love to see you guess." He gave an almost evil laugh; one I'd never heard.

"Link that was rhetorical. I'm not playing a guessing game. What is going on?"

He looked at me and kept shoving the cold, soggy food into his mouth. I almost didn't think he was going to answer me but he did.

"So, the week after your birthday, huh?"

"What about it?" I was racking my brain as to what he could be talking about, and then it hit me. Callie never answered me. I ran to my phone and saw that my last text meant for Callie went to him. "Shit," I said aloud. "Link, I'm sorry, I didn't mean—"

He put his hand up. "Save it. I don't want to hear your bullshit. Were you even going to tell me? Were you even going to leave a note for me? Anything?"

I looked at him in disbelief. "Are you being fucking serious right now?"

He just stared at me without saying a word, so I continued.

"Of course, I would have told you Link. I was going to talk to you tonight."

He gestured toward the plate in front of him. "So that's what this shitty dinner is? A goodbye dinner?"

My eyes went wide, in disbelief. I couldn't believe Link was talking to me like this. I definitely didn't care for this version of Link at all. I don't get mad easily, but I could feel myself becoming flushed from anger and embarrassment. I stood up in anger.

"Yeah, Link, I spent all morning and afternoon purposely making you a shitty ass dinner just to say goodbye. You caught me."

Now it was his eyes that went wide. I don't think he was expecting me to react that way.

"Well, you certainly weren't being honest with me, that's for sure."

"How could you say that? You didn't even give me five seconds to talk when you got home. And in case you missed the sarcasm, I'll help you out. No, this wasn't a goodbye dinner. My birthday isn't for almost another month and a half. I was trying to do something nice for my boyfriend. I never meant to text that to you. I would never tell you in that way. I wanted to talk to you about it over dinner. I was excited, but my excitement is long gone now, in case you were wondering."

I started to clean up but then I slammed the plate back down. "Link, this isn't a new development; you always knew I wasn't staying forever, and I never told you I was. I never lied to you. I have been so torn about starting this relationship with you because I knew this would happen. This is exactly what I was talking about. I have been so fucking torn between being here and going home, and I was partially staying because of you. I was giving us time to figure this out." I was becoming winded.

His voice seemed a little calmer now, but he looked down at his plate, moving his "shitty" food around.

"But you are leaving? And you will forget all about me."

"What the hell are you talking about?" I walked over and sat next to him and grabbed the hand that was pushing around his food. "What makes you think I would just leave and not look back?"

He looked at me with sad eyes. "Because everyone leaves. They never choose me."

He got up and started walking away, but I stood up and grabbed him to pull him towards me. I rubbed his cheeks and tried to make him look me in the eye. "Link, talk to me."

He pushed my hands away and looked me right in the eyes. "I made a mistake thinking you were any different. Thinking you would care enough to stay."

I felt like I was going to throw up. "Link, You can't expect me just not to return home, and you don't mean that. You never even let us have a real conversation about my staying or going. We are not a mistake; we are new, fun, and really exciting, and we are just getting started...at least, I thought we were."

"We are a fucking mistake. You are temporary, just like everyone else."

My stomach sank, and I stepped back so he could no longer reach for me even if he wanted to. His face fell a little, but he continued verbally tearing me down, and I just stood there, frozen, taking it for some reason. "I never should have let you in. I knew this would happen. That's on me, and you tried to warn me. I'm sorry I didn't listen. We can't be anything but friends. I see that now."

Tears were welling up in my eyes now. I wanted this conversation to be over so I could cry. I wanted to ask him what was happening. I am so confused, but I'm also so damn mad at him for how he's treating me. I honestly don't know what to say to him right now.

"Is this what you really want, Link?" He was silent, and no longer looking at me. This is not how I saw today going, it's the literal opposite actually. "If that's what you want, I'll leave this house right now. I will stay out of your way. I will leave and I will pretend this never happened, and you can go back to your life. I'll see you on holidays and maybe a vacation or two. I can do that for you if that's what you want."

"What do you mean what I want? This is your doing. You chose this, not me."

I thought silently for a moment. This is not my fault and I won't let another man tell me his actions are my fault. I kept my voice low so he would have to pay attention to what I was saying.

"I'm sorry you feel this is my fault, but I disagree. I'm sorry I came and uprooted your life and your feelings; that was not my intention, as I told you multiple times. I'm sorry that you are losing someone who would have cared for you unconditionally whether you were here, came with me to Connecticut, or even moved to Alaska."

He started to look hopeful and tried to speak, but I cut him off.

"I don't deserve to be treated this way by anyone, let alone someone I love. Goodbye, Lincoln." I stepped away and felt my heart breaking into a million pieces. I started to walk away, but he spoke anyway.

"Wait, you...you love me? You wanted me to stay with you?"

"That's a moot point now, don't you think?" He just kept staring at me. "Yes, Lincoln, I was going to ask you to continue dating me and we could figure out how to make the long distance work. We aren't sixteen-year-old children with no way of seeing each other. I would like to think that would have eventually turned into you moving to be with me or vice versa. I went back and forth with the decision because this was so new and I didn't want to scare you off, but my mom has always told me that when you know, you know. I always thought it was bullshit...until you. But I guess I was right, it is bullshit," I paused and took a breath. "Lincoln, I've lost the person I thought I loved more than anything before... I loved him even when he broke me down to nothing. I overcame him. This love was different, and I thought I was crazy for falling so fast and deeply for you. It all happened in such a short time. I guess that makes me the stupid one, but I will move on again no matter how much it kills me. I will never let another man make his insecurities my fault."

His eyes sparkled with unshed tears, and he seemed to inch a little closer to me. "You said you love me?"

He was missing the damn point, so I stepped back towards the door. "Goodbye, Lincoln. I'll see you around. I'll be there on Wednesday if you still need my help. Just text me and let me know if you would prefer someone else to help you."

"But Aubrey—"

I didn't stay to hear what else he had to say. Tears were falling, and I thanked God that Pops and Liza were out to dinner so I wouldn't have to answer any questions about why I was upset and crying.

CHAPTER TWENTY-EIGHT

Lincoln

incoln? She called me Lincoln again.

"Aubrey, wait!" After pausing for a moment, I tried to follow her, but before I could reach her door, she had already locked it, and I heard the shower running. I knocked anyway, but she didn't answer.

"Baby, please." Still no answer, I held my head against the door and whispered, "I love you too." I knew she didn't hear me and she wouldn't be opening this door, so I gave her some space and returned to my house.

What the fuck did I just do? I sat there in disbelief. *She told me she loved me.* I love her too, but I didn't say it yet because I thought I was going crazy. I sure as hell didn't think she was even close to loving me. I thought she was leaving me. I thought that the text I had received proved that.

I started thinking about the look on her face and how hurt she truly was. I am already regretting how I spoke to her. I can't believe I flipped out on her like that. I gave her zero chance to explain what it even meant. What was I thinking?

I punched the workout bag in my bedroom and realized I hit it harder than I intended to, when I saw my knuckles were cracked and bleeding. I slowly became more rational as I went over everything in my head. I heard my phone ding from my bag. I ran to it, hoping it was Aubrey.

Elijah- You fuck her and make it better yet?

I rolled my eyes.

Me: I fucked up, bro. I need to fix this, and I need to fix this now.

Elijah: Let me know how I can help. I'm in town till we leave for tour again.

Me: I'll take you up on that.

I took a shower to calm my nerves and then wrapped my knuckles. I took some time to sit and chill to give her some space. I need to talk to her again, so we can fix this. If she loves me, we will fix this, and I will make this work. I sent her a text asking her to come back over, but it went unanswered.

I saw Mom and Pops pull in and wanted to get ahead of this so we didn't have to explain anything to them, but when I walked in Mom was holding a note. All the blood rushed from my face, and I ran up the stairs.

She was gone. The only thing left was the music for the play. I sat down on her bed and put my head in my hands.

"What happened?" I didn't hear her come up, but Mom stood in the doorway.

"I fucked up, Mom."

She cleared her throat as a warning, and I'm sure she gave me a death stare because of the swear word, but she didn't comment further.

"I'm sorry," I added.

"It sounds like I'm not the one who needs an apology. Fix it, Lincoln. Your father is beside himself. He is blaming himself. For what, I have no idea. I told him to let me come up here because he looked like he was going to punch something, punch you. He is going to want you to explain this, you know." She handed me the note.

Dear Dad and Liza,

I know this may come as a shock since we had such a great morning, but I've decided to leave after everyone comes for my birthday in a few weeks, and I will be leaving alone. I need to go home and get back to life in Connecticut.

I'm going to stay at my friend Dan's for a few days. I need some quiet to finish something for the local high school at home. I've been neglecting it way too long because I'm having too much fun with you guys.

When Brie arrives, she and I will get a hotel for a few days so we can have some actual sister time alone; surprisingly, we never do that. I think I need a little space, and I've inconvenienced you guys enough. I want to give you a little break and one less mouth to feed.

Thank you so much for letting me stay. I will be back so you can meet Brie and me for dinner one night maybe, and I'll be back to stay once Brie leaves until I'm ready to go home, if that's okay. If not, I can grab a hotel for the remainder of my stay. The last thing I want to do is uproot anyone and hurt anyone else. I'll be at work every morning till two, and if Lincoln still needs my help, I will help him after that at the school, but I'd like to take the weekends off unless you absolutely need me. I'll be busy helping Callie with some plans over the phone. They are hoping for a fall wedding, but she needs everything planned right now.

I'm sure you will want things explained. Just know I didn't mean for any of this to happen, and I'm really sorry. I am sorry that I hurt Lincoln. Please know that was not my intention, and I will forever regret it. I am sure we will get over it soon. I promise everything will return to normal. I love you both so much, no matter what. See you in a few days.

With Love, Aubrey

"She called him Dad?" I asked, hoping she would explain. I looked at my mom and saw the hurt in her eyes.

"They had a pretty good morning. Aubrey discovered some cool things about her and your father's past that she was really excited to share with you. I'll let him give you all the details. What I want to know right now is what really happened, and why did she leave? Why aren't you running after her?"

I handed her my phone. "She sent me this by mistake, and my temper took over as soon as I saw her. I literally flipped and broke up with her the minute she tried to talk to me. I didn't even let her talk. The only fucking relationship I've ever had, ever cared about lasted two fucking days. What the hell is wrong with me?" I hung my head even lower. I was so embarrassed.

It surprised me when she didn't yell at me. She was weirdly calm for just finding out about Aubrey leaving. My eyes went wide in accusation.

"You knew? You knew she was going to leave me and you didn't bother to tell me...I'm your son." I started to get up because I knew if I stayed, I would say something I would regret, and I couldn't hurt another person I loved today.

"And she is our daughter, Lincoln," Pops spoke from the hallway. "She was going to ask you to date long distance. She even asked us how we would feel if she asked you to go with her. Guess you not only ruined that, but you pushed her away from us too."

"What? How would you know she wanted—"

Pops got a bit louder as he stepped into the room toward me. My mom rose and placed her hand on his chest so he would stop moving.

"I know, Lincoln, because she told us! She was telling us because you leaving affects us; she was being God damn considerate for the other people in this family! She obviously didn't know what your answer would be but just in case, she wanted us to know so we weren't blindsided by losing you and her simultaneously." He looked down and then back at me after taking a few breaths. "For the record, this is what I asked you NOT to do. I told you not to treat her like one of your throwaways, and you couldn't do it. Aubrey is a part of this family... What the fuck Lincoln?"

I put my hands over my face and sat back on the bed. "I'm a fucking dumbass idiot."

"Boys, the swearing," Mom said in a hushed voice.

Pops turned and walked back out the door. "I couldn't agree with you more. You said it, Link, not me."

Mom touched my shoulder, "Give her time, Lincoln. When she returns, talk to her. You are both important to us no matter what."

"I will, Mom. I'm sorry I raised my voice."

She nodded her head in acknowledgment and left without another word. Mom said to give her time, but I can't leave it like this. Maybe she will talk to me if I get her to help with the play.

> Me: I would love your help if you're still willing. I'm really sorry I acted that way. I hope you will forgive me.

The message went unanswered until the following day. I checked my messages when I woke up and found a short, concise response.

> Songbird: I'll be there at two on Wednesday for auditions, and no worries. It was a mistake anyway. Nothing happened.

Her words made my heart hurt. I was hoping for a glimpse of the girl I love, but I think she's gone, and it's all my fault.

CHAPTER TWENTY-NINE

Aubrey

I was sitting on Dan's bed, going through the story of what brought me here while he was painting my toenails. I wanted to go home and run into Lincoln's arms, but he made it very clear that he didn't want to continue this relationship. Even if he changed his mind and started to feel bad, I couldn't do this. It should never have happened in the first place. This is precisely what I was afraid of. He and I just won't work. We are too connected to other people, and it wouldn't end well. Every little fight would affect everyone around us. No matter how much I wish it didn't happen like this, I know in the end it is for the best.

Once I'm home in Connecticut, it will be better. Easier even. I can get back to everyday life and make plans to have Pops and Liza come visit me, and that will keep me free of Lincoln until Thanksgiving at least. I know I'll have to deal with seeing him eventually after I leave, but I will make it work. These feelings will fade, and the hurt will subside. For now, I will do my best only to see him when I have to.

On Tuesday and Wednesday morning, things with Pops and I were normal. He tried apologizing for Lincoln, and I told him not to even think about it. We talked a lot about me leaving and even about him visiting after I left and how we would make it work. It sounds like it will be pretty easy to figure out. He said he would hire more people, just so he could take time off to visit me. He didn't bring up Lincoln again or even ask what really happened, and for that I was thankful.

I couldn't get the flutters in my stomach to subside when I left work on Wednesday, to go help Lincoln with the play. I didn't really want to do this, but at the same time, I couldn't wait to be near him and see for myself that he was okay.

I walked into the auditorium, and Lincoln was the only one there. His back was to me, and I couldn't stop checking him out. I don't know if my heart can take this. I mentally kicked my own ass into gear and started walking toward him. He must have felt my presence because he turned around when I was only halfway down the aisle.

My breath hitched in my throat when he looked into my eyes, but I swallowed whatever lump was there. "Hey, I know I'm a bit early, but I wanted to get here before the kids. I hope that's okay."

He stared momentarily and then shook his head as if shaking off a thought. "Of course, it's fine. I got you a staff pass, so you don't need to do all that sign-in stuff every day." He handed it to me, and our fingers brushed, and my breath hitched once again. He let go of the staff pass, and his eyes lifted and met mine.

"I'm glad you're here. It's really good to see you." I smiled but didn't say anything back because I wanted to tell him just how much I loved him but knew I couldn't. He continued, "Do you, by chance, know this song on the guitar?" He handed me some sheet music. "We will audition for Mimi and Roger today, so all the kids have practiced it. If not—"

My eyes lit up. "Yes, I do. I love Light My Candle. It's my favorite."

"I was thinking you could play and then sing the other parts while the kids tried out if you're okay with that."

I nodded my head. "I can do that."

"Great, I set up a stool on stage. Feel free to get comfortable. Let me know if you need anything else.

"Just a second music stand if you have one."

The students were so good. Some of them are going to be famous one day, I just know it. As they were singing, I was trying my best to focus on them as well as trying to keep my voice from shaking when I sang. I was working hard not to look out to where Lincoln and his coworkers were sitting. One of the guys kept looking my way and smiling, but I don't think anyone else noticed.

After the auditions, I started to pack up. Lincoln called out to me and asked if I would mind staying for a bit to help them go through and choose the parts. He gave us all a ten-minute break before we convened for the decisions. I continued packing up my guitar on stage so I could bring it down to the chairs. Some of the other teachers came up to me, to thank me for my overall help with the auditions. I felt a little embarrassed because they were fawning over my playing and singing. Although their attention felt awkward, deep down It made me feel good.

We chose the two main characters and then I collected my

things off the chair beside me and said goodbye to everyone, but I was purposely avoiding Lincoln.

The man who wouldn't stop staring at me came over. "Hey, we're all going to dinner tonight. Want to join us? I'd love to hear about what you do in Connecticut." Lincoln made his way over to us, and he looked pretty pissed.

I touched the man's arm, and Lincoln stopped walking. "Oh, thanks for the invite, but I'm only temporarily here. I wouldn't want to take up any of your time." Then I smiled and walked away. Lincoln went ghostly white. I was hoping he realized I just threw his words to me right back at him. He followed me. He was basically running by the time he caught up to me outside.

"Aubrey, can I talk to you for a second?"

I answered while still walking away, "Just send me the song for tomorrow. I will learn it tonight if I don't know it. See you tomorrow Lincoln."

"That's not what I was—"

I shut the car door, cutting off his words, and drove away.

LINCOLN

I thought we would be able to get over this today, and I would have been able to get her to come home. It's only been a few days and I'm already a mess without her.

I can't get my mind to calm down. I needed to talk to her.

Me: I miss you!

The text went unanswered for about twenty minutes, and I was going stir-crazy the entire time. I told myself I would be chill about this, but I just couldn't be chill. I was over waiting, so I sent another text.

Me: I really need to talk to you. Can I call you
or come see you?

Songbird: A voice call is fine.

Me: I was going to Facetime you. I want to
see you.

Songbird: I can't see you more than I need
to, Lincoln. Let's just chat tomorrow, okay?
I'm going out.

I didn't bother answering. I called the bookstore to get Dan's number, and his dad gave it to me without question. There were perks of everyone knowing everyone, I guess. I texted Dan and asked where they were off to.

Dan: Why would I tell you that?

Me: I need to fix this dude. Please, just tell
me where you guys are going.

Dan: Just leave her alone. You have done
enough, don't you think?

Me: Dan, I love her. I overreacted, and I
know that. I've never had someone care
about me like she does. I've never loved
someone the way I love her. Please.

The text went unanswered for a few minutes. Then my phone finally beeped.

> Dan: I can't break the girl code and tell you. When I'm upset I like to go somewhere I can be myself and let loose. Sorry I couldn't be of more help.

I realized they were going to the karaoke bar.

> Me: THANK YOU! I owe you one dude.

> Dan: I didn't do anything.

I called Elijah and told him to bring the guys and meet me at the bar. I am getting her back, even if it kills me.

AUBREY

Dan told me we were going out, and honestly, I could use a drink. He chose the bar we went to before because we had so much fun. Although, I was sure the karaoke bar would make me think of Lincoln, I guess it would actually do me some good to think of him. No time like the present to try to let it go right?

Dan asked me to dance. He dragged me onto the dance floor, knowing I was not in the mood, but I tried my hardest to live in the moment.

The music slowed, and I started to let go of Dan so he

could dance with his boyfriend. When I turned around, I smacked right into someone's chest.

I was mortified. "Oh, I'm so sorry I—"

"May I have this dance?" Lincoln said.

"Lincoln! What are you doing here?"

"It's fate." he said as he grabbed my hand.

Dan smiled at me and mouthed 'wasn't me' and shrugged his shoulders as he walked away. I tried to back away, but he pulled me in and placed his hand on my back just like he did the first night we danced. The memories, his touch, it all gave me chills, and I felt as if I was frozen in place.

He leaned down, and I could feel him just basking in my warmth for a moment as he brushed our cheeks together; then he whispered, "I miss you, baby," and I felt his lips on my cheek inching toward mine.

My breath hitched, and a lump formed in my throat. I could feel my walls melting down just from those four simple words.

"Don't...I can't, Lincoln."

"You can't what baby?"

I was lost in my own thoughts and didn't answer him. He rubbed his nose on my earlobe. I felt the goosebumps run right through me. "Talk to me. Let me show you just how sorry I am." He pulled me in closer and began to kiss down my neck. I was trying so hard not to let my guard down. I can't. I can't let him do this to me with no consequence. I swallowed the knot in my throat and pulled away from his embrace to look up at him.

"You lost that privilege when you called me temporary." His smile fell.

He paused and smoothed his thumb over my lips, and the gesture made me close my eyes and hold my breath a little.

"Let me apologize to you properly, and I will apologize every single night and day until you are sick of me." He leaned in and pecked my lips. I felt my body betray me and shiver, and it felt like a fire was re-lit throughout my entire body. I looked away from him because I couldn't look him in the eye any longer. His voice caught in his throat. "I can't let you go, Aubrey; I can't lose you."

My heart broke, but I knew I had to make him understand me. I gained some courage and smirked as I lifted my head, looked him right in the eye, and leaned in toward his ear. I saw him visibly shutter as I got close.

"You already did." I walked away without another look back. I walked as fast as I could to my car. I texted Dan that I was leaving and he came out immediately. I sobbed all the way to bed.

CHAPTER THIRTY

Aubrey

The next two days of helping at the school went without much incident from Lincoln. I kept myself busy during the breaks and made sure I was never directly next to him or alone with him. This week was only auditions, and I can already tell that this show will be amazing; I'm pretty sad I won't be here for its entirety. Who knows, maybe I'll come to the show in May to support it.

It's finally Friday and today I get to see Brie. I just can't wait to hug her and fall apart in her arms. I haven't told my family or friends about what happened because I'm embarrassed, but I know I will have to tell them now that Brie will know.

As I'm waiting for Brie to walk out the airport doors, I can't help but prepare myself for her chatter. My sister is pretty quiet when it comes to most people, but when she gets around someone she's comfortable with, she doesn't shut up. She's going to have so much to tell me about her trip with her friends; I can already hear her excitement. I feel bad that I am going to ruin her time here with the news of my breakup.

Maybe I shouldn't tell her right away. It won't hurt to tell her tomorrow, right?

"AUBS!" she yelled as she threw her bags down.

"BEAN!" I yelled back.

She hugged me so tight I thought I would lose my breath. She is a strong little thing. She pulled back to look up at me with her pretty green eyes. She was crying happy tears, and at that moment, I noticed I was too. "How are you? How's August? How's Liza? How's Li—"

"Slow your roll, Bean." I couldn't help but laugh because, as I said, this was what I expected. "Let's get you in the car before we overwhelm each other with questions." I wrapped my arm around her shoulder, grabbed her bags, and put them in the trunk.

"Where's Link? I thought for sure you would be showing him off right away."

My stomach dropped. She wasted no time at all. "He's been working a lot." I felt terrible telling her a half-lie. Although he is working a lot, that's not why he's missing in action right now. "I got us a hotel room so we could have some alone sister time. So how was your trip?"

She looked suspicious but didn't comment about the hotel. "The trip was amazing. We saw so many different things. I have a ton of pictures to show you. I hope you don't have any plans tonight because we are looking at all of them. Oh, and I met a boy... he's from Maine, and we connected on one of the tours we did, so we swapped numbers, and we've been texting each other a little."

I was shocked and it showed. My mouth was gaping open like I was catching flies or something. "My baby sister met a boy!" I was screeching in excitement. "I need all the details right now."

She slapped me on the arm. "Chill. Just drive and try not to kill us," she laughed. "Plus, it's nothing serious, just friends, and we have a lot in common. We did kiss," she blushed and averted her eyes.

"Oh my god Bean, did you—"

She cut me off. "God, no. You know I wouldn't sleep with someone I just met. You know my history. Plus it made me really uncomfortable and I just wasn't ready. I'm waiting for that forever kind of thing."

She winked at me. She always knows how to make me smile, though when she said that it made me think of Lincoln. My smile faltered slightly.

She put her hand on my arm. "What happened?"

"What do you mean?" I asked.

She gave me a knowing look. "I saw the smile come and go when I said forever kind of thing. So what happened? And whose ass am I kicking?" She was joking about that last part, but her smile also fell, and her voice got softer. "Did he hurt you?"

"Bean, I'm fine. Let's talk about it when we get settled."

She let it go as I continued driving. We just sang and listened to music the rest of the way to the hotel.

"What do you mean you are overbooked?" I asked the hotel attendant. I was being rude unintentionally, but this is the only hotel in town. I have no other options.

"I'm sorry, ma'am. Whoever booked your room didn't realize we were doing maintenance on the third floor, so we overbooked. I'm really sorry. For the inconvenience we can give you credit for a free stay in the future. You can use it anywhere in the USA this year."

I was still confused. "So, you have no rooms available at all? Where am I supposed to stay?"

"Aubrey," I felt her nudge me out of my panic. "It's not a big deal. Let's go to your dad's."

"Yeah, but I—I wanted alone time with you."

This would happen when I was trying not to see him while she was here. She will know the minute she meets him that something is off.

"Aubrey, we are alone all the time. If it is that important, we can just stay in your room."

I looked at her, and she looked worried. I realized I was acting crazy, and I needed to chill out.

"Um, Yes. Yes, we can. Let's go."

I texted Pops on the way to his house to let him know I was coming back earlier than originally planned, and he was ecstatic. He told me they were out with a few friends, so they probably wouldn't see us until later tonight or in the morning, which was fine with me.

I was relieved that Lincoln's car wasn't there when I pulled up to the house. I got Brie all situated in my room. She immediately wanted to shower, so I went downstairs to grab something for us to eat, and that's when I heard a car door shut. Before I could move an inch, Lincoln was rushing through the door.

"Hey! You're home," he said breathlessly.

I bit my lip to keep my smile at bay because it was actually kind of cute.

"Hey. The hotel is overbooked, so I'm back."

"Where is Brielle?"

I pointed up the stairs. "Showering. I was making us some food. Do you want some?" I was proud of myself for holding a conversation without faltering much. I think I'm doing pretty well.

"Um, sure," He sat down and stared at me. I wasn't looking at him, but I could feel his gaze on my back.

"You look nice," he added when the silence took over.

I smiled but I couldn't let him see it, so I didn't turn around. "You saw me a few hours ago Lincoln."

"You looked good then too," he retorted.

My insides were twisting. I needed to gain some self-control before I turned around and tried to kiss his stupid face.

"She always looks good," I heard from the hallway.

I turned and saw Brie standing there smiling with my clothes on, and she was pulling the towel off her head letting her long dark hair fall to the sides. I never understood why she tried to wear my clothes. She's so little, and I'm so not. She literally swims in them.

"Brielle. You have an entire suitcase of clothes, and you're wearing mine?"

She looked down at herself and then back up at me, "Bitch I missed you, okay?" I just laughed at her and let it go.

Lincoln got up and introduced himself.

"Ah, so you're the infamous Lincoln, huh? You better be treating my sister right or I'll kick your ass."

I froze in place, but managed to turn back toward the food. I didn't want to have this conversation right now, not ever, really. I just wanted to eat and go upstairs.

"I will. Aubrey deserves the world. I'd love to give it to her if she will let me." I felt them both staring at my back, but I couldn't turn around. Hearing him say those words stung..

I never wanted the world...I just wanted him, and now I'll never have either one.

CHAPTER THIRTY-ONE

Lincoln

*L**ook at me... please.*

I don't want to make a scene in front of Brielle, but I wanted to talk to her so badly. Her sister seems sweet, but she just gave me a look when she talked about hurting her sister, and I don't ever want to see that look again. It doesn't seem like she knows anything about Aubrey and I not being together because she surely wouldn't have made that comment if she did. Maybe there is a sliver of hope to get Aubrey back, but first I need to get her to hear me out. There has got to be a reason she hasn't said anything to Brielle about us not being together. It's best for now if I act as if everything is fine, and then I'll talk to Aubrey when we can be alone.

Brielle was telling us about the trip she took with her friends and Aubrey was telling her something about Callie and Nick. It sounds like Callie and Nick fight like they're married, but who am I to judge? I hope to get a the chance to know them both better. I hope this thing with Aubrey and me will blow over soon, and we can be happy again.

"So, Lincoln, what is it that you do here in White Mountain? I heard you were quite the ladies' man before my sister stole your heart. I heard—"

"Brielle. Quit it," Aubrey mumbled.

Brielle gave Aubrey a sly look. "What, the way you talk about him, it's like you found your soulmate. I assume he feels the same way."

I looked over at Aubrey, and she was blushing. I could only see the side of her face, but I could swear I saw some shine in her eyes, which broke my heart.

I tried to remain calm as I spoke, "She did steal my heart," I smiled. "It's hers forever."

I thought hearing that would make her smile...Wrong.

"I can't do this," Aubrey admitted.

She started to walk away, so I stood up to go after her. "Aubrey, wait."

"Enough Lincoln. I don't wanna hear it."

I stopped and watched her go up the stairs.

Brielle was still staring at the stairs. I sat back down as I saw her fist clench around her fork, and then she looked right at me, a death stare worse than Aubrey's.

"Are you going to explain that before I do something stupid or am I going to have to google how to hide a body?"

AUBREY

I could hear Brielle yelling at Lincoln, but I couldn't hear exactly what she was saying. Honestly, I didn't care. I just needed to let out a good cry. It will be fine. I know it will. I just need some time. I took a shower, and while I was in there, I heard a light knock at the door.

"You okay Aubs?"

I swallowed down my cries and tried to sound as normal as possible. "I'm fine, Bean. I'll be out in a minute." I heard her feet shuffle away from the door, and I sighed in relief.

When I came out of the bathroom, my dinner was sitting on my bed, and it made me smile that she was always thinking of me and trying to take care of me.

"You didn't finish; thought you might want it."

"Thanks. So is Lincoln alive or dead in the backyard?" I tried to sound carefree like I was making a joke despite not smiling.

"He's alive...for now. He told me everything though." She looked pissed. "Or I guess his side of things. Why didn't you tell me instead of letting me go on and on like an idiot?"

I shrugged.

"You told him you love him?" she said hesitantly. It was definitely a question, not an accusation.

My breath caught a little. "Kind of. It's too fast, I know... I didn't mean to, but I meant it, so I guess in a way I did."

She continued without any judgment. "You asked him to come home with you?"

I started brushing my hair, and she motioned for me to sit in front of her so she could do it for me. I sat between her legs. "No, I didn't get to that part before he broke up with me... but I think I would have at least asked him to date me for a little while."

"Damn Aubs, that's serious. I didn't think you would ever talk about love like that again after Max."

I turned and gave her a look. "Are you trying to make me feel worse, Bean?"

She bopped me on top of my head with the brush softly. "Of course not."

She turned my head back around to start braiding my hair. I pushed her leg playfully but since she's so light she almost fell right off the side of the bed. She gripped my shoulder so she didn't fall, which made me laugh uncontrollably.

"Damn bitch, you tryna kill me!" she exclaimed.

"Maybe," I said jokingly.

We caught up a little while I ate my food and she unpacked. Then we watched a movie. I thought the previous conversation was over, but as we settled into bed, I heard her whisper.

"It sounds like he knows he really fucked up."

"I know," I whispered with my back to her.

"Are you gonna...forgive him?" I felt her shift, so I knew she was now looking at the back of my head. I turned toward her and just stared at her for a moment.

"I can't, not after everything he said to me. I can't let my heart break like that again. I shouldn't have crossed that line in the first place. I know that now."

"But—"

I sat up to change the subject.

"I'm going to get some water. Do you want any?" I just wanted her to go to sleep and leave this conversation alone. She shook her head, and I headed downstairs.

There was a light on in the kitchen. I looked out the front window and saw that Pops and Liza made it home. I sighed in relief that it was them and not Lincoln. I reached the kitchen and stopped in my tracks. Lincoln was sitting at the kitchen island with a bunch of papers spread out. He looked at me, surprised.

"Sorry. I didn't realize you were still in here." I turned and started to walk away.

"Songbird," he sounded desperate.

I stopped walking but didn't turn around. I could feel myself becoming nervous. I heard the chair scrape against the floor like he was getting up, and I flinched. I felt his warmth come up behind me, and then I felt his nose caress the spot right under my ear.

"Aubrey," he whispered. His breath on the back of my neck took my breath away. I was frozen where I stood. My brain was no longer controlling my legs. "Aubrey, please let me explain what happened that day."

I finally got the strength to move. I turned toward him and stepped back. "I'm aware of what happened, Lincoln. I was there when you tore me down."

He turned a dark shade of crimson. He stepped towards me and grabbed my shoulders. "Don't do this... don't give up on me." He moved his hands into the hair at the base of my neck.

"I didn't give up on you, Lincoln. You gave up on yourself by thinking no one else would ever care about how wonderful you are. You showed your true colors and made it crystal clear I was just a big mistake to begin with. You told me I was temporary; that was all I needed to hear." He was just staring at me, not saying a word.

"Can I just grab my water and go? I need to go to sleep." I tried to pull back, but he didn't let me go.

"No."

My eyes went wide when he said it. "Aubrey Lynn Miller, you are mine. I will spend every day proving that I am worthy of your love. Even if you walk away from me, I won't give up on us, no matter how long it takes. I will wait forever."

He leaned down and crashed his lips into mine before I knew what was happening. This kiss was desperate. I felt my resolve melting away. I could feel the passion behind this kiss, but I couldn't help hearing his words replaying in the back of my mind.

You are only temporary.

My lips parted, and Lincoln took my tongue into his mouth and continued kissing me like he couldn't breathe without me. My heart and brain are telling me two different things. My heart knows I want this; I want him. All of him, forever. But my brain is only replaying his harsh words and telling me to stay away and to be safe and guard my heart.

He picked me up, digging his fingers into my ass, instinctively making my legs wrap around him. He swiped his papers off the kitchen island and deposited me onto it. He started kissing down my neck, and he continued by sucking on my collarbone like he was trying to brand me.

"Why are you even in here?" I said breathlessly.

He had a look of lust in his eyes. "I was waiting for you, Songbird."

"This is the last time. This can't happen again. This is just to say goodbye since we didn't know our last time was going to be the last," I whispered into his ear.

He chuckled against my skin. "This is just the beginning, baby."

His hand slipped under my nightshirt, and he began massaging my breast, pinching my nipple between his fingers. I felt an instant jolt of arousal travel straight to my clit. He pulled back to lift my shirt over my head. His mouth went to my nipple, and he sucked on it. It caused me to release a loud moan. He used one of his hands to cover my lips. Then he looked me right in the eyes and whispered against my lips.

"I am the only one who gets to hear those moans baby."

I bit one of his fingers that was covering my mouth. He growled deeply then bent his face back down and nipped at my nipple softly, causing me to moan again. My hand went into his hair.

I felt him smile against my nipple. He took his hand away from my mouth and used it to travel up my shorts when he looked me in the eyes again.

"You are mine, and I'm never letting you go."

I was about to respond no, but my breath was taken away when his finger dipped inside my warm center. He only moved his finger in and out once before I froze when I heard my sister open the bedroom door.

"Aubs? Are you okay down there?"

Lincoln started to grin, and I thought he was going to answer for me. I covered his mouth. "Yeah, Bean, I just grabbed something else to eat. I'll be right up." He added another finger and started moving them inside me again. I held my breath. He was shaking his head no, but I ignored him.

"Okay, grab me some water too. I changed my mind," she added.

"Mmhmm...Okay."

I waited until I heard the door close again. Then I leaned forward and whispered in his ear. "You have two minutes to get me off, or I'm leaving."

He smirked and whispered back. "I only need one."

He lowered himself to his knees, taking my shorts down with him but leaving my thong on. He pushed the wet triangle of my thong aside and took my clit in his mouth and moved his fingers inside me. He brought me to an orgasm in one minute flat. I tried so hard not to, but I moaned his name in an almost whisper as he sent me over the edge. I held him there until I came down from the high.

I hopped down and corrected my clothing. I grabbed two glasses of water and looked at him. "Thank you, goodnight."

His facial expression was that of utter disbelief.

I smiled as I walked upstairs. As soon as I walked in, Brie stared at me with a knowing grin.

"Shut up. It was nothing."

She smirked. "Didn't sound like nothing."

"A goodbye orgasm then," I said.

"You are so dumb," she said as she rolled her eyes and laughed.

I laughed right back. "I know. I hate myself right now."

"No, you don't.... but you wish you did," she smirked.

Lincoln

The next morning, I lay in bed dumbfounded, and for a few reasons. One, she said fucking thank you and walked away and just left me there wanting more. Second, she finally let me touch her. It's been a long few days without touching her and tasting her. My dick was getting hard just thinking about it again.

All I want is for her to forgive me, and that was an excellent first step. I got dressed for a morning run and went into the house. Brielle was sitting there reading a book and drinking her coffee. She looked up at me but didn't say anything, just went back to reading.

"Good morning, Brie."

"It's Brielle," she said without even looking up.

"Got it, not my biggest fan." I went to the fridge to fill my water bottle.

"Not your fan at all," she added.

I heard the front door open. It was Aubrey. She looked like she had just finished her run. I looked at my watch. It wasn't even six.

"Hey, good morning." She directed it toward me, but then

she walked over and grabbed Brie's shoulder to acknowledge her. She went over to grab some coffee, and they carried on as if I wasn't standing right fucking there.

"Bean, why are you up so early? I was letting you sleep in." Brielle just shrugged, so she continued. "The bookstore I wanted to show you opens at nine if you want to go. I called Dan yesterday to let him know we would be stopping by and he is going to make sure he's there."

Brie raised her cup in acknowledgment without looking up. "Sounds good."

"Do you want to shower first, and I'll make breakfast? That run was exhilarating, but now I'm starving."

She smiled really big like the old Aubrey was back.

Brielle finally looked up at her. "You good if I go up now?"

She nudged her head towards me. She is not very subtle, but I also don't think she was trying to be. I can tell she is a good sister. Although I understood why she was asking her sister if it was okay to leave her alone with me, it honestly irked me a bit.

"Of course, I'll start breakfast."

Brie went on her way, and I didn't miss the dirty look she gave me.

Aubrey seemed to be kind of happy for the first time in a few days. It was so good to see her running and smiling again.

"Good run? Why didn't you wake me up? I would have gone with."

"Oh, not necessary. I'm just getting back into it, so I'm still on schedule when I go home. I've been slacking, but I'm all good now. Enjoy your run."

She was speaking to me without looking at me. I walked up to her and put my hand on her hip, and she jumped away and slapped my hand like I burned her or something.

"What are you doing?" She looked at me with disgust.

I looked her straight in the eyes. "Giving my girl a kiss before I leave."

She laughed like I'd never heard before. It almost sounded evil.

"Lincoln, I'm so sorry if you misunderstood what last night was, but I told you that was it, no more after that. It was a fun goodbye, right?" She turned back around and finished what she was doing.

I was shocked. "Who are you, and what have you done with Aubrey? My Aubrey doesn't talk like this. I—"

She turned back toward me and pointed the egg-covered spatula at me. "No. No, Lincoln, we're not doing this. I'm not "your Aubrey" anymore; actually, according to you, I never was. I'm just here temporarily, right? You lost that Aubrey a few days ago. We will go on as if nothing happened, except the fact that we share parents, but that's it."

She looked away like she had to prepare for what she was about to say. I saw the flash of hurt again for a second when she turned, but it faded back into anger rather quickly.

"We are nothing. Like I said, it was fun. It's over, but you're used to that, though, right? One and done, was it?"

She sounded so bitter I couldn't take it anymore. I turned and left without saying a word. My heart was genuinely breaking. I hadn't felt this type of hurt ever unless you count my biological mom tearing my heart out. Tears were burning my eyes, and I now know exactly how she felt when she left my house the other day... and it fucking blows.

AUBREY

I turned back to the food, only to realize how harsh I sounded. I turned around to apologize to him, but he was gone. I just proved that hurt people hurt people. I feel like crap. No matter what he did, he didn't deserve to be treated like that, just as I didn't deserve it either.

I finished making breakfast and headed upstairs. I realized that I hadn't introduced Liza and Pops to Brie yet, so once she was out of the shower, I took mine, and then we went downstairs and waited for them to wake up.

They fell in love with her instantly. She has that effect on people. They wanted to hear some stories about me. She chose to make them all embarrassing, of course. Seeing her with them made my heart happy. It gave me hope for when my parents visit. I know that conversation will be much more emotionally-filled, but it still gives me hope. I saw Lincoln returning to his cottage through the back window.

I excused myself and went to apologize. I knocked. Lincoln opened the door quickly, and I word-vomited my apology.

"I'm so sorry, Lincoln. I shouldn't have spoken to you that way."

He was hesitant but stepped back, giving me space to walk in. After looking at him, I realized his eyes were red, like he had been crying.

"Lincoln, I'm so sorry."

I started internally freaking out. My chest was becoming

tight. Lincoln realized immediately that something was wrong.

"How can I help?" he said nervously.

I couldn't talk, so I took my phone out and called Brie. I handed Lincoln the phone. She must not have picked up on the first ring because he hung up and called again.

"She's having a panic attack. What do I do?" he blurted out. "No, I can't wait for you to get dressed. Just tell me what to do."

He was listening intently as he sat me down on the couch. He knelt down beside me.

"Okay, yeah, I got it." He hung up and looked at me with fear in his eyes. I felt bad that I was scaring him so much.

"Aubrey, look around. What are five things you can see?"

I turned my head, taking in the room. "You, your T.V.," I said, gasping for air. "Video games, papers...the door."

"That's great. Now try four things you can..." He looked down at the phone. "Touch or feel."

I grabbed his hand as a silent thank you. "You, the couch," I leaned forward to put my hand on the coffee table and took a breath. "The table and this paper."

Speaking was definitely getting easier. My heart was warming that he was taking this so seriously.

"Great, good job." He rubbed his hand down my back and looked at the phone again. I realized then that Brie must have texted him what to say when they hung up.

"Okay, three things you hear?"

My heart was calming down a little. "Your voice, the wind, and I don't know, I don't hear...anything else."

"It's okay, close your eyes, try for me," Lincoln said softly.

I closed my eyes, and Lincoln started humming. It made

me smile. "You humming." I opened my eyes and bit my bottom lip.

He smiled back. "Okay, now two things you smell."

The door opened and I assumed it was Brie who walked in. He held his hand up to stop her. I didn't even look at her because I was staring at Lincoln.

"Your cologne and my perfume," I said with a gulp.

His smile grew bigger. "Okay, we are almost done, last one. Name one thing you can taste."

I took a deep breath before answering. I reached down and took a sip of the coffee he had on the table. "Coffee."

He looked at me, noticeably less scared. He gently stroked his thumb over my cheek and jaw. "Are you okay?"

"Yes. I'm sorry I scared you." I took another deep breath.

"Aubs, you okay?" Brie said from behind us. I turned to look at her. "Yeah, thank you for helping him."

She nodded, her eyes silently asking me if she should stay.

"You can go, thanks Bean."

She nodded her head again and walked out the door. I looked back at Lincoln.

"Aubrey, I'm so sorry. I'm sorry this conversation gave you that panic attack. All you did inside was repeat my words back to me, and they made me realize how much I really hurt you, so I'm really fucking sorry. I will forever regret what I said and how I acted. I hope one day you can forgive me."

I stared at him, and I think in that moment, I saw the Lincoln I was falling in love with. I saw the man who woke my soul, but we can't be that again. If we tried this again and broke up, it could be catastrophic...It almost was this time honestly.

I choked back tears. "I hope we get there too, but right now I think we need space to get over this. If we are fighting like this and hurting each other already I don't want to see what will happen long term. We can't keep hurting each other, and we can't take the chance of hurting Pops and Liza. If you want me to leave sooner, I will."

He stood me up and took my face in his hands and looked into my eyes. "I don't need space to get over you because I don't plan to. You were my chance at happiness, and I blew it. I don't want to find this with anyone else." He rubbed his thumb over my cheekbone, wiping some of my tears away.

"Please stay. You deserve to stay because this is your home too; they are your family now. Also, the kids doing the play love you. They deserve the best person to help them while we have her."

He tried to smile but it didn't quite reach his eyes.

"I'll be the one loving you from afar. I'll be the one you can call for anything, and I'll be there. I'll be the one who updates you on Pops' crazy endeavors." We both chuckled a little. "I'll be your pen pal, your confidant, whatever you need me to be, and most of all, I'll keep the promise we made before we even started all of this."

I thought back to our conversation that night before we had sex.

"Promise we will always be friends first."

"Lastly, Promise me that we will keep in touch no matter what. I want you in my life no matter what happens between us."

"I intend to keep those promises because I fully believe you are meant to be mine. This is the right person, the wrong time situation, and our chance will come when we have more time to figure this out. I will get help. I will prove I can be the man for you. It's not fair to drag you along while I deal with my healing so I will do my best to give you space." He placed something small in my hand. I opened it, and I found a necklace with his nickname for me on it.

"Lincoln," I whispered.

"I know. It was for Valentine's Day. I figured you should have it either way."

I was losing the battle with my tears again. "I'm sorry, Lincoln."

We were both quiet, just staring at each other. I had to break the silence... I hated this awkward feeling around him.

"I hope you are right about the right person, wrong time thing," I whispered.

He moved my face toward his. "Me too, baby." He kissed me one more time.

The final kiss.

The best kiss.

I went inside the house and started writing. Something Lincoln said gave me an idea for a song. I needed to start it now while it was fresh. Brie was still busy chatting with Liza, so I took some time to write and digest what had just happened.

About an hour had gone by, and I was well into writing the lyrics...it was like they were flowing out of me.

I heard a knock at the door. "You okay, Sweetie?"

It was Pops.

"Come in."

He opened the door; I smiled. "Yeah, I'm fine. I just had an idea for a song; I figured I'd start while the idea was there."

"Can I hear what you've got?" he asked.

"Of course. Come on in and have a seat."

CHAPTER THIRTY-THREE

Aubrey

Brie and I got to the bookstore as soon as it opened. We spent a while in there buying entirely too many books. After Dan got sick of us, we went around town so I could show her everything else.

She nudged my arm. "You really like it here, huh?"

"I do Bean. I really do. I love that I found them and that they accepted me so easily. That could have gone differently. The people in this town are great. It's like one of those hallmark movies we watch at Christmas where everyone knows everyone."

She laughed. "Yeah, it could have gone pretty bad, huh? I'm glad it went in your favor. They are lovely."

She looked like she thought about something sad, and her smile dropped a little. "Let's go out tonight. I want to sing and dance around with you."

I looked at Brie like she had five heads.

"What? I want to do something fun." She looked confused at why I was looking at her that way.

I chuckled. "Who are you, and what have you done with Brielle? You never want to go anywhere, let alone out to dance.

I've tried to get you to go out with me a million times; plus, there will be alcohol there."

"I never said I wanted to drink Aubrey. You know I don't do that. I want to have fun with my sister. Plus, they won't serve me anyway. I'm too young."

"You know that's not what I meant. What if—" She cut me off and gave me an annoyed look.

She rolled her eyes. "Aubrey, I'll be fine. You will be there."

"Yeah, but—"

She cut me off and grabbed my hands. "Aubrey...Let's just do something different. Well, maybe not for you, but for me it will be different."

I wasn't sure what to say. I never want to hurt my sister or put her in an environment that she will be uncomfortable in, and a bar with alcohol could turn into exactly that for her.

Brielle was sexually assaulted while drunk at a party when she was sixteen. She hasn't had a drink since. That party is the reason Brie became introverted. She won't admit that, but I know it was. I almost lost her when she was eighteen when she tried and failed thank God, at taking her own life.

"Okay, let's do it, but not tonight. I wanted to take you to Dan's tonight. He has some rare books that I wanted you to see. We can go out one day this week, and then we can do some dancing and karaoke?"

"Yes please!"

I worked on the song I had started earlier this morning when we got back to the house. The lyrics were pouring out of me again.

Brielle cooked dinner to thank them for letting her stay here with me. She made us one of the dishes she learned to make from a college friend. It was an intricate meal, chicken stuffed with ham and cheese. I don't know what it's called, but I know it's delicious.

Pops, Liza, Brie, and I were eating, and I heard a rough clearing of the throat. Lincoln walked in. I motioned over to the stove. "Hey, there's some food over there if you want it."

He looked at me with a weird grin. "Always taking care of me, Songbird."

I shrugged. "Just trying to be nice."

Everyone else at the table was giving me weird looks.

He sat down beside Brie, and she gave him the stink eye. I smacked her arm and she shrugged. I heard Pops chuckle, so I know he saw it.

I asked Lincoln if Brie could help with anything at the play. I saw a hopeful glint in his eye, but it was quick. I wouldn't have seen it if I wasn't already looking at him.

"She is really good at art, so maybe the sets could use her help." I suggested.

"Yeah, that's definitely a good idea," Lincoln said.

I smiled and went back to the conversation I was having with Pops. I could feel Lincoln's eyes on me the whole time...I didn't know whether it gave me comfort or if I hated it.

On Monday, Brie and I showed up to help with the play and I immediately started working with some students who would be singing solos and even some of the chorus kids because they were taking on the opening song, Seasons of Love.

After about an hour, I checked on Brie, and she looked like she was in her element. I haven't seen her smile like that in a long time. I haven't seen Brie paint in what feels like forever. She was even teaching some of the students how to draw. Some of them weren't even in the play; they were just there for work-study to get credit for graduation.

I was taking a break sitting in the audience, watching Lincoln work. You could tell he was really in his element up there. He really loves this place. I could never take him away from this. If things ever got serious I couldn't hurt him by asking him to come to Connecticut. I was starting to think our breakup was a good thing.

My thoughts were interrupted when I heard Kayla come up behind me. "Hey Aubrey, how are you?"

She called me by the correct name this time. I tried not to look so shocked. "Hey, I'm good. Just taking a break. How are you?"

"Well, I should be helping with the costumes, but I got pulled into a meeting with one of my student's parents, so I'm a bit late."

She pointed up at Brie. "Who's the new girl?"

"That's my sister, Brielle. She will be helping with the sets. Only for a few more days, unfortunately. Then she'll be going home."

"Did she paint all that by herself? She's amazing...She's pretty hot too." She was gesturing to the cardboard buildings that Brie was working on.

I was caught off guard by the hot comment but again, everyone thinks so, so it was nothing new.

"Mostly, yeah. She's great, but she doesn't paint a lot anymore, unfortunately."

"Why?" she asked.

I shrugged. "Not sure, but I'm glad she's doing it again."

"Well, she should keep doing it because she is great. Better than anything I would have done." She laughed. "All right, It was good talking to you. I'm going to head up there. I'll see you later." She started to walk away.

"Oh, Aubrey, I hope Link told you how sorry I am. I don't know what had gotten into me. I was just super jealous and didn't know how to handle it. I've never been turned down before if you could believe that."

I smiled at her. "I believe that wholeheartedly, Kayla. Thank you for apologizing, and I forgive you. Let's pretend it never happened." It seems like I'm doing a lot of pretending things didn't happen lately.

My brain finally registered the conversation that just took place once she walked away. I couldn't believe I just had a civil conversation with Kayla, of all people.

"Is that the hot redhead that was trying to get with Link?" Brie asked as she came off the stage, wiping paint on MY leggings that she stole.

"Yep, that's her, and she thinks you're hot." I chuckled.

She thought for a moment. "Well, she is fucking gorgeous, but she was mean to you so that makes her off-limits. Need me to kick her ass?" Brie raised her brow.

I laughed loudly. Some kids looked at me like I was crazy, but they moved on quickly, talking about some girl dating some guy.

"Brie, I love you, but she would break you in half. I don't need you to kick her ass. She apologized again, and we had a civilized conversation. It was nice for a change." She didn't look convinced but she let it go.

I gave Brie the keys and told her I would walk or get a ride home with Lincoln after I helped him clean up. She left without saying anything else.

"You were great up there, ya know," I said to Lincoln, motioning to the stage. "With the kids, they love you."

He looked over and smiled at me. "Thanks, Songbird. You are pretty great yourself."

I helped Link carry a few things to his house after rehearsal. I lingered at the door before walking in.

"Thanks for today," he said in a hushed tone. I almost didn't hear him.

"Anytime Lincoln." I turned to leave, but he spoke again.

"Hey, Aubrey...are you sure about all this?" He gestured his hand between us.

I shrugged, "I have to be."

He looked away. "If you say so."

CHAPTER THIRTY-FOUR

Aubrey

The first thing I saw when I walked into the karaoke bar was Elijah talking to the bartender, and I prayed that Lincoln wasn't with him. I didn't see him, but I was nervous because he was Lincoln's friend. Right about now, he's probably going to text him to tell him I'm here. When he spotted me, he smiled and started walking over to me. He placed his arm around my shoulder.

"Looking good, girl." Then he looked at Brie with a shit-eating grin. He looked her up and down. He stood up straight, taking his arm off me. "Who's your cute friend?"

"My baby sister." I poked him in his ribs. "So, hands off, Casanova."

He raised his hands in defense with a smirk and gave the loudest, most resounding laugh I think I've ever heard. "Yes, mom... I apologize...now let me buy your drinks."

She stuck out her hand for him to shake. "The name is Brielle. Please call me Brie, and I'll take a coke."

"No alcohol... I can dig it. I love a woman who knows what she wants." He grabbed Brie's hand and kissed the back of it.

"My name is Elijah. You can call me Eli."

I slapped his chest with the back of my hand. "Why was I never told to call you Eli? Wait... Lincoln doesn't even call you Eli."

"It's reserved for special ladies." He raised his brows.

I poked him in the ribs again. "Ok, Casanova, we get it... She's twenty, and I'll have a margarita."

"Coming right up, ladies... Aubrey, go join everyone over there."

He bowed as he walked away. What is with these Tennessee boys and their bowing?

Brie nudged me. "He's definitely a player...too bad, he's so fucking hot."

I laughed, "Yes, he's very handsome, but he is way too old for you, so don't even think about it. He's Lincoln's best friend, if you can even call him that. He's in that band I was telling you about that I want to see in June."

"Don't worry about it. I am not dating anyone anytime soon." Brie said.

I looked over where Elijah had gestured and saw Lincoln with a beautiful brunette whispering in his ear. She has that beautiful nerdy thing going on like Brie. He looked like he was laughing and having fun; the last thing I wanted to do was change that.

I waited for Elijah to return with our drinks and told him we would sit near the stage. He nodded without commenting. I'm sure he knew why.

"See you around, Brie. I hope," He said as he moved away from us.

She laughed. "See ya, Eli."

I asked Elijah if he could not mention that I was there, and he agreed, but true to bros before hoes, I saw him gesture toward us as soon as he went over there.

Lincoln looked over, and I saw the smile leave his face when he saw me. He waved. I waved back. He gestured for me to come over, but I waved him off, mouthing, "It's okay; enjoy your night."

"Please," he mouthed.

I looked over at Brie and asked if she wanted to go over, and of course, she said yes. She likes making me uncomfortable. I introduced everyone to Brie. They became immediately obsessed like everyone she meets. Everyone was asking her all kinds of questions, and most of them were hitting on her. Story of my life, honestly, but it was good to see her socializing. She doesn't do it much.

I saw Elijah move to the seat next to her, and he put his arm around the back of it. I pointed and gave him the evil eye; he removed it and gave that contagious laugh again.

I was about to go over and talk to Lincoln, but I felt a hand on my arm.

"So sorry to hear about you and Linky."

Ugh! Fucking Kayla.

I should have seen this coming. Kayla was too friendly earlier, and I'm sure it was all fake. Someone must have told her about Lincoln and me, and now she thinks she's got an in again.

I rolled my eyes, not bothering to hide it. "I'm sure you are, Kayla. Thanks for your concern, but I'm fine," I said in a condescending tone. The only saving grace in this conversation is that I know he wants nothing to do with her whether we are together or not.

She walked away, swaying her hips, and sat in the chair next to him where I was headed. About a second later, he got up to come over to me. I couldn't help but snicker and cover my lips with my hand to cover the smile. I know she saw me.

Her face turned a very bright shade of red. I'm not sure if it was embarrassment or anger, maybe both. Either way, I don't give a shit.

Lincoln hugged me. His cologne's scent was so intoxicating. "Hey you. I'm glad you came over. You don't have to avoid me. We will never make it through this if you ignore me. Plus, you said we were good, remember? It was just a few hours ago."

"I wasn't. I didn't want to make you feel awkward. It looked like you were having fun. Didn't want to be the annoying sister in the way."

He winced. "Yeah, I am still not calling you that," he chuckled a little.

I winced right back, "Yeah, that was a bad choice of words."

We were both laughing now, "My bad."

The night went on, and we acted like old friends. I tried not to stare when he wasn't with me, but I couldn't help it. I would tense a little whenever I felt him brush against me or when I smelled his cologne.

Surprisingly Elijah got Brie to get up and sing with him. It was pretty comical because she's horrible. It made me smile to see her having fun again. I know this was a big step for her.

I excused myself to the bathroom when I saw that brunette approaching Lincoln again. I removed myself from the situation before the awkwardness came.

"I'll be right back. Brie, are you good?"

She gave me the thumbs up while she was talking with someone about some book being made into a movie.

I spent some extra time in there trying to talk to myself in the mirror, giving myself a pep talk to get my ass back out there and just get over it. Lincoln was leaning on the wall waiting for me when I opened the door. He gestured outside to the back. I followed him.

"What's up? You good?" I asked.

He looked down at the ground. "You didn't have to do that. She's no one that should make you feel awkward, just a friend of one of the guys in the band."

I put my hand on his forearm and instantly felt his muscles tense up.

"You don't owe me an explanation Lincoln. You're single. You can do whatever you want with whomever you want." I tried to smile, hoping it looked genuine and not strained.

He looked like he was getting angry with me. "God Aubrey, I'm not— I don't wanna be— Fuck!"

His loudness surprised me, but I realized he wasn't going to finish his statement. He wasn't looking at me. He was looking at the gravel on the ground, kicking a piece away.

"Lincoln, look at me."

He looked up but didn't say anything. My stomach fluttered when his eyes hit mine, and I lost my thoughts momentarily. I shook it off and continued.

"You owe me nothing. We will get through it, I promise. It's just weird right now and hurts more than normal, like a fresh wound."

He sighed. "Do you really think so, Aubrey? You really think this is just going to blow over?"

"I hope so." I know I sounded uncertain, but I was trying.

He was quiet and kept looking down like he was afraid to look at me.

"Lincoln, let's go inside and—"

He looked at me with those dark blue eyes. "How are we going to get through it, Aubrey? All I want to do is grab you and throw you against this wall and make love to you until you say you're mine."

That made my body quiver, and I know he saw it. "Lincoln."

He reached for me and grabbed the top of my arms. "Baby, this is stupid. I want you...You want me...Why are we doing this? I know I'm the one that fucked this up, but it's been a few days, and I'm fucking dying, Aubrey. I can't fucking do this. Not being with you is making me go crazy."

I looked down and bit my lip. He used his thumb and pointer finger to lift my chin up so I was looking at him. He rubbed his thumb over my bottom lip. "Tell me you honestly don't want this."

His face was so close to mine that I had to close my eyes to relieve my racing heart. It was beating so fast that I thought I might pass out.

He pushed me up against the wall and grabbed the sides of my neck, pushing his fingers into the hair at the base of my neck.

"Tell me you are mine. I already told you I can't get over you, and I fucking mean it. I know I said I would stay away, but I don't think I can."

I finally opened my eyes.

"Lincoln, we will just hurt each other again, or worse, blow up this family. We couldn't even last a week without fighting. I'm not doing this again."

He looked so defeated. "Aubrey, this," he gestured

between us, "is hurting us. Being apart hurts us, and we haven't even really been apart yet. What happens when you leave here without me, and you meet someone else? What if you want to bring him home for Christmas? Am I supposed to be okay with that?"

I tried to push away, but his hold on me was solid. "Lincoln, please," I didn't know how to stop the tears from falling this time. I was starting to panic a little. "This isn't healthy... I can't do this right now. I need to go back to Brie."

He let go and stepped back, giving me some room. "This isn't over. We will have this conversation a million times until you take me back."

"No, Lincoln. No, we won't."

He leaned forward, kissed my forehead, and walked inside.

I sank to the ground against the wall and put my head between my knees. This was too much. I'm so scared of us hurting each other, but mostly I'm scared of us hurting everyone around us. It's like we can't be apart but we can't be together either. I don't know what to do. I need to leave.

> Me: Bean, I'm not feeling great; I'm going for a walk to get some air. My keys are in your purse. See you when I get back. Make sure Lincoln has a ride home, please.

> Bean: Wait by the car. I will drive you. I'll be right there.

> Me: No. Please stay and have some fun. I just need some fresh air.

> Bean: No, I don't wanna stay if you are not here.

> Me: Okay I get it. But I'm still going to walk as long as you are good.

> Bean: Yeah I'll be okay. I will meet you back at the house. Please call Nick or Callie to talk to you while you walk.

> Me: I will.

I called Nick. I felt like we hadn't spoken in forever. The minute he picked up, I let go of everything that had been happening. I knew I called him and not Callie because he wouldn't try to give me advice; he just listened. He knows what it's like to not be with the person you love. I wish he would tell Callie how he feels, but I guess it doesn't matter now, and he would be blowing up everything for something that can't happen, so I get it.

After I finished speaking and catching my breath, I sat down on a bench. I appreciated that he didn't ask any further questions about what I said. He simply listened and moved on to talking about himself and what was happening at home.

I brought my notebook in my purse so while he talked, I listened and wrote. He said he met someone, a new teacher at the high school. He said she looked like Callie, which was no surprise...the man definitely has a type, but I could already tell he wasn't as interested as he was letting on.

We talked for over an hour; I let him keep talking, interjecting when necessary. I was writing a few letters, but Connecticut was an hour ahead, so my ten o'clock was his eleven o'clock, so he needed to get to bed.

"Check on Cal for me, Nick. She seemed sad when I called her."

"Always, Aubs, I'll always protect you both."

"I know. I'll see you soon."

I walked the rest of the way home, and Lincoln was sitting on the front porch when I arrived. I could tell this conversation was not going to go well. He looked like he hadn't calmed down at all since I left him at the bar.

Lord, help me.

CHAPTER THIRTY-FIVE

Lincoln

"Where were you?" I said it without looking up at her. I was trying hard not to blow up. I just kept wringing my hands together.

"Why? Are you my keeper now?"

I looked up at her, "Aubrey."

She huffed. "I went for a walk so I could clear my head."

"Alone? At night? You left the bar over an hour ago." I looked at her accusingly. She stared at me like she thought I was joking or something.

"Not that it's your business, but I called Nick on the way home and I sat and talked to him on a bench; I wanted to relax outside and get some space, okay? Goodnight, Lincoln."

She tried to walk by me, but I grabbed her wrist. "Wait, please."

My demeanor changed immediately. My anger had resolved a little just from my hand touching her. She looked at me, and the moon was illuminating her features perfectly, but I saw tear streaks from when she was crying. Her makeup had run, but she was still so beautiful.

She is perfect.

She looked annoyed with me, but I didn't care. "Lincoln, can we do this when we don't have alcohol in our systems?" She pleaded with me. I don't know why she won't just talk to me about this.

"Stay with me tonight." I declared.

She looked stunned. "Lincoln... we are not having sex. That won't solve anything."

She rolled her eyes at me, and I pulled her towards me.

"I didn't ask you to have sex with me... I asked you to stay with me." I bent my lips down to her ear. "Please."

I felt her shudder in my hands. "Lincoln, I can't."

I hung my head and placed my forehead on her shoulder. We were quiet for about thirty seconds, but I couldn't stand it.

"Spend the night with me and I won't ask you for anything else. I will let this go."

I heard her breath hitch, and she leaned her head into mine. She seemed to think about it for a second, then I felt her pull away a little and thought she would walk away, but instead she laced her fingers into mine and then whispered, "Okay."

"Okay?" I repeated.

"Okay. I'll stay with you."

I couldn't help the big ass smile that formed on my lips. We walked hand in hand to my house in the back. She paused at the door, and my heart stopped because I thought she was changing her mind. She told me she wanted to go inside and change, but I knew she wouldn't come back out if she went inside. I pulled her toward me and stroked her cheek.

"Let me give you a shirt. Let me be with you. You know as well as I do that if you get up there and see Brie, you won't come back out." She looked at me, not saying a word, and walked inside.

She headed straight to my dresser and grabbed a shirt. She disappeared into the bathroom as I got ready for bed and sat on the couch. My breath stopped when I saw her. Seeing her always made my breath stop.

Her hair was down. She wore my Reckless Riders shirt, which hit the top of her thighs just below where I could no longer see her underwear. It accentuated her curves quite well. It was one of the first shirts I ever got from Elijah's band, so it was a little faded. She bent down a little, and I saw that she had on a light blue thong that hugged her ass. I felt my cock stir.

She sat down on the other side of the couch. She curled her legs into herself and looked over at me. "What are we watching?"

She pulled her hair to one side and braided it, and then she looked at me like this was a completely normal thing we do.

"Whatever you want."

"How about a movie? You pick, no love stories." She smirked.

She picked up her phone and sent a text, and I can only assume she was letting Brielle know she was okay and had made it home safely.

We didn't speak the entire movie. Neither one of us moved, not even glancing at each other. She got up silently when the movie ended and got into bed. I watched her perfect ass bend over my bed to pull the covers down. I shut all the lights off and followed suit. At first, I wasn't sure if I should say anything or just be quiet. Her back was to me, and I could see the bottom of her ass cheeks peeking out when I moved the comforter to get into bed. I wanted to trace my fingers over her curves so badly. I was praying my cock would stop throbbing, but thinking about it only made it worse. I started tracing the band's name on the back of the shirt, and I felt her shiver.

"Songbird?" I said in a hesitant whisper.

"Yeah?" she whispered back.

"Thank you."

She was silent, and for a second, I thought she had fallen asleep mid-conversation. Finally she spoke. "For what?"

I was quiet, so she turned to me and saw I was still awake and looking at her. There was so much I was thanking her for, but all I could manage to do was stare into her eyes and say, "Everything."

She smiled and touched my cheek. I hoped she would lean in and kiss me, but she didn't. She just turned back over without saying anything else.

I traced the words I love you on her back. I hope one day I can say them to her face.

I woke up around three in the morning having a nightmare. I must have been thrashing or talking out loud because she was shaking me, and I heard her talking to me telling me to calm down.

"Lincoln, it's okay. Wake up, Lincoln, I'm here."

I finally opened my eyes and saw the worry in hers. I pulled her close and kissed her on her soft lips. She didn't pull away immediately, so I deepened the kiss for a moment. I realized I had to pull away because I told her I just wanted to be with her and wanted to stick to it.

She laid her head down on my shoulder, and I kissed the top of her head as she snuggled down into me. I felt at peace with her here. At some point, I drifted back to sleep...I could swear I was dreaming about her. I heard her voice whisper, "I hope someday you find someone who makes you happy, Lincoln." All I could think was, *I already did.* Then I drifted to sleep.

I woke up slowly when I heard my blaring alarm, reaching over to where Aubrey had been, but she wasn't there. My shirt was folded on the bed. I checked my phone and found a text from her.

> Songbird: I'm sorry. I hope you forgive me.
> We will be okay one day...I promise.

My mind was racing, and I didn't know what that could have meant. I started to get dressed, and that's when I saw it. A letter was folded in half on my counter, and my name was written on it in perfect cursive writing. I didn't know anyone still wrote in cursive. *Well, I guess now I do.*

I was afraid to open it because I knew what it said before I even read it, but I knew not opening it wouldn't change the fact that she was gone.

Dear Lincoln,

I'm writing this as I sit on a bench in town. I just left you at the karaoke bar, and it broke my heart to do so because I know what I'm about to do. If you're reading this, I'm gone. Brie and I are driving back together, so I'm not alone. I texted Brie and asked her to pack my stuff because I knew I wouldn't have had the heart to do it. I don't want to leave you, Lincoln, but I have to.

At this point, we're bad for each other and our family, and it won't get better unless we give ourselves space. We are so consumed by each other that we're not thinking clearly.

I'm going home so we can have some space to think and hopefully get over this. I wrote letters for Liza and Pops too, just letting them know I'll be back for my birthday in a few weeks when my parents are coming down to meet them. I hope you're here too.

I know I'm leaving early, and I know I'm prob-ably leaving you in the lurch with the play, but this is something I have to do, not only for me but for us. I'm sorry. Me being around does not give you or me the time that we need to move on. You shouldn't feel uncomfortable in your own space.

I'm leaving the rest of the music you need on my bed. I hope you can forgive me. I genuinely believe you are the right person at the wrong time. I don't know how this will ever work with us being so far away, but I do know that if it's meant to be, we will make it happen. I can't wait to hear how your healing journey *is going next time I see you. Take care of Pops and Liza for me. See you soon.*

P.S. Don't cut your hair just yet. I'll do it when I see you next.

With Love,

Songbird.

I ran inside to see if I could catch her before she left because I didn't know when she left the note for me, but Pops sat at the kitchen table with his coffee almost gone and a letter of his own.

"She left." I meant to ask it as a question, but it came out as more of a statement.

He looked at me, and I was expecting him to be upset with me, but he wasn't. "She will be back. Fate has a way of making things happen at the perfect time."

"I...I love her."

He gave me a look of sympathy. "I know... so what will we do about it?"

I was taken aback by what he said. "We? You're going to help me?"

"Don't I always? Plus, I want to be able to visit you both and see a wedding and some grandbabies before I die." Then he flashed me a grin, telling me we were thinking the same thing.

"I am going to get some help."

"And then?"

"I'm moving to Connecticut!"

He stood up and smacked my back. "You're moving to Connecticut!"

CHAPTER THIRTY-SIX

Aubrey

Brie and I are about an hour into our drive, and neither of us has said a word. I let Brie choose the music, and of course, she chose some instrumental shit so she could read. I was always jealous that she could read in the car. If I look at my phone for more than five minutes, I'm nauseated the entire ride. It was pretty calming though. After our first stop, she finally put her book down and turned to me.

"Do you wanna talk about it?" she said without a hint of judgment.

I smiled. "Not really, but I know you'll make me."

"If you really don't want to talk about it, I won't force you to, but I really do want to know what happened. Are you okay?"

I shrugged, trying to seem unbothered. "I will be. I need to get home and get things back to normal. Things will blow over with Lincoln. They have to. Crazy circumstances brought us together and tore us apart at basically the same time, but I'm hoping they will keep us together somehow. If not, we can move forward as friends. That's all I want."

She was silent for the next few minutes.

"He is perfect for you; in case you didn't realize it."

I didn't really believe that, but it made me happy to hear her say it. I cried a few times on the way home, but I have a feeling I'll be doing a lot of that in the near future.

We chose to try to drive all the way through since we left early. With both of us driving, we would be home in no time. I drove most of the way, and Brie drove the last three hours.

I stopped in to see my parents before driving the rest of the way home; they were waiting for us even though it was late. Things were weird when I left, but being home now, everything felt right, like everything would be okay. I really missed them. As mad as I was at them, I couldn't help but think that this happened for a reason. Maybe I was supposed to wait to find my biological dad so that I would know Lincoln. If I had found him sooner, he might not have taken Lincoln in; he probably wouldn't even exist in his life. I'm now a firm believer in what's meant to be will be.

We chatted a little about my time there, but it was late, so I needed to get home. I hugged them goodbye and headed to my house. I was excited to see Callie, but I figured I'd show up to a quiet house because of the time. The lights popped on when I walked in and Callie and Nick stood there with balloons and one of those annoying popper things.

I'm going to kill Brielle.

She must have told them I was coming home today, and they stayed up to see me. This is why they are my best friends. They are there for me even when I haven't asked. I grabbed them both and started sobbing. We all made our way to my room and Nick brought the wine.

"Where is Jake?" I asked.

Callie just shrugged so I let it go. I had to fill her in on everything I had told Nick over the phone. She was pissed that I called him instead of her, but she'll get over it. We talked all night about literally everything. I even shared a little about Brie coming out of her shell. They were just as surprised as I was. Now she'll be stuck going out with us forever.

Callie said Brielle texted her this morning to let them know we were coming home. Callie called a few of my clients to let them know I would be back in commission starting the following Monday if they wanted to schedule appointments. I'm so grateful for her that she was giving me some time to get back into being home, but she also wasn't going to let me sulk and waste away.

The one thing I didn't tell my friends was that I started writing a song. I need to spend more time on it because it's only been a few hours of writing, but this song will be epic.

It felt good to be home. It felt even better to hug my friends. It felt good to lay in my own bed, but then again it felt like part of me was missing. I left part of me with Lincoln, and I think he'll have it forever.

A few days later, I called Pops to check-in. They were doing well. They said they were planning a party for me at their house the day after we arrive back in Tennessee. Hearing their voices made me happy. I secretly hoped to hear Lincoln. Sadly it was Friday, so he probably wasn't even home. I realized I have Pops laugh too. He had me dying about some customer in his shop that we constantly gossiped about. I was doing that I can't-breathe kind of laugh.

I asked them to invite David's wife since she and I hadn't met before I left. I really can't wait to meet her. I told them I would bring my guitar so she could see it, and maybe we could jam around a fire pit or something. I want to learn all about David.

When we hung up, I clicked on Lincoln's name in my texts... I was typing "hey" when I saw those three little bubbles pop up... then they disappeared. I deleted mine and put my phone down, hoping a text would come through, but it didn't.

I was just lying in bed, staring at the ceiling and saw my phone screen light up from the corner of my eye. Very few people would text me this late, but I prayed it was him.

Mr. Grumpy Butt: Hi.

Me: Hey.

Mr. Grumpy Butt: How are you?

Me: I'm good. I missed my family a lot, and I'm glad to be home. I'm writing a song… it was inspired by one of our conversations actually.

Mr. Grumpy Butt: Wow, that's great. I can't wait to hear it. I bet it's beautiful...everything you do is beautiful.

Both of us stopped typing for a moment, and then I saw the text bubbles pop up, and he sent another one.

Mr. Grumpy Butt: You're beautiful. I miss you, Songbird.

I wanted to say I miss you too. Tears started forming in my eyes. If I start crying now, I will spiral. I know saying I miss you would add insult to injury, so I just said what I thought I was supposed to say.

Me: I'll see you for my birthday, right?

Mr. Grumpy Butt: Yeah, I'll be here. I can't wait to be near you again.

Neither one of us sent another text.

The following day I was sitting in my room, working on the song when Brielle walked in.

"Hey, Callie let me in. Hope that's okay."

I looked at her like she was being stupid because she was. "Bean, you have a key... of course it's okay," I laughed.

She sat on the edge of my bed and held what looked like a card in her hand. She was tapping the edge of it on her palm.

I pointed to it. "Is it for me?"

She looked down at it and then back at me. "Yup, Callie asked me to bring it up. She was leaving when I got here."

I stared at her for a second, trying to figure out why she was being so weird. "Are you going to give it to me or what?"

"I haven't decided yet?"

"Brielle." I waved my fingers in a give-it-to-me motion, and when she still wouldn't fork it over, I grabbed it.

"If it's mine, you have to—" I was staring at my address, and I knew the handwriting immediately. I swallowed the hardened lump that was now in my throat. I looked up at her. "Lincoln sent this?"

She shrugged. "That's what the return address says. It came by overnight mail by the looks of it."

I took a few deep breaths to calm my heart because it was palpating so fast. I don't think this is something I want to open in front of anyone else, so I placed it on the bed. I realized I didn't know why she was here yet.

"Forget this for a second. What are you doing here?"

"I just wanted to make sure you were okay. I decided to stay in the dorms this semester so I won't be home." She paused, "I don't know. I just wanted to make sure you were good, I guess."

I love how protective she is of me even though she's my younger sister. She is the perfect sister. I grabbed her hand and squeezed it. "I love you, Bean. I'm good, I promise."

"Good. Then can I give you the bad news, and you promise you won't get mad at me?" I looked at her worriedly but didn't say anything so she would continue. "I won't be able to come to your party in Tennessee. I have a super important group test on the Monday after that trip, so I'll need to be home to study and be here for my group. God forbid the flight gets canceled or something. I can't miss it. I'm sorry."

I let out the breath I was holding. "God, Brielle, don't do that. I thought it was something horrible. That's not bad news; it's okay. It might be better with fewer people there anyway, with everything happening. You and I will celebrate with each other after school is done. Don't sweat it." Her birthday is only 13 days after mine so we normally celebrate together.

Now that I think about it, I should tell Callie and Nick to

stay behind too. They would be driving since Nick is terrified of flying, and I was already feeling bad about it and considering driving with them. It's just a long weekend, and I can celebrate with them when I get back. I sent them both a text as well as one to Liza so she knew not to plan for so many people.

Brie left a few minutes later, and I wanted to open the letter immediately. I held my breath and ripped the seal. A few folded pieces of paper fell out when I opened it, but one was labeled "read first".

Dear Songbird,

I hope you're doing okay. I miss you like crazy. You haven't even been gone for twelve hours while I'm writing this, but I figured I would start my promise to you immediately. I promised to be a penpal. I know one of your dreams is to have letters and love notes written to you, so I figured I would start now... technically I started when you first told me that during one of our very first conversations about our families. I wrote you one for every time we did something I wanted to commemorate. I didn't send them all, but I sent you the first one. I wanted you to know my initial thoughts about you; we were just friends if you can call it that. It was after our night at the bar where we danced for the first time. I want this to be the beginning of the perfect love story Aubrey, and I hope we get to keep writing it forever.

With Love,
Mr. Grumpy Butt

324

I almost couldn't read through my tear filled eyes, but I wiped them away and read the others.

Love letters.

He wrote me love letters.

CHAPTER THIRTY-SEVEN

Lincoln

I started pacing back and forth. "Wait, what? She's not coming for her birthday. How could she not come to her own damn party? What the—"

"LINCOLN MATTHEW!"

Shit, I didn't mean to freak like that out loud. My stomach felt like it was going to drop out of my ass. I started getting nervous that my letter was the reason. Maybe I shouldn't have written to her or even texted her.

"Lincoln. You didn't even listen to what I said. I said her sister and her friends wouldn't be coming. You need to chill out." Mom gave me a crazy look.

"Sorry, Momma."

I was so embarrassed because I realized how much I just sounded like a little bitch throwing a fit. I would have died if I was the reason she wasn't coming. I don't even know if she read the letters yet. I went back to my house to watch some T.V. and tried to get my mind to relax. I was dozing off because I hadn't been sleeping all too well. I thought I heard my phone ding in my sleepy haze, but I figured it was a dream.

I woke up on the couch the following day. I never set my alarm, so I was late getting to the school for the weekend rehearsal. I was rushing around and never even looked at my phone until about an hour into work.

The students still ask about Aubrey even though she's been gone for a while now. A pit formed in my stomach every time I heard Aubrey's name mentioned, but I tried my hardest not to show how much it hurt. I checked my phone on the first break and saw her name on my screen.

> Songbird: I love them; thank you for these. I'll cherish them forever.

I wasn't sure if I should answer her because I wanted to say so much, but this was not the place to get into it, so I sent a simple **"You're Welcome."** I saw the text bubbles pop up and disappear. I don't know if that was a good thing or a bad thing.

After rehearsal ended, I texted Elijah to see if he wanted to go out for a beer, but he said he was packing for the tour and told me I could go over to his house if I wanted to, so I did. I don't want to admit it, but I will miss the shit out of him when he leaves, but I don't need tickets for his shows since I have a VIP

All Access Pass, so I can visit him while he's on tour whenever and wherever I want. I'm pretty sure it's just something that Elijah made up for me.

I stopped and grabbed a six-pack at the store to drown my sorrows while he packed. I think he could tell I wanted to talk, but he didn't push me. I sat on his couch for about twenty minutes, watching a basketball game that I didn't even care about. I didn't say a word, and he just kept packing.

He finally looked at me and said something I never expected him to say. "I talked to Aubrey yesterday."

I was bringing my beer to my mouth and paused before turning to look at him. "Excuse me? You what?"

"Aubrey called me yesterday." He said it like it was no big deal.

I sat up a little straighter and put my beer down. "For what?" I felt a pang of jealousy, even though I knew there was nothing weird going on between them, because he would never do that to me and neither would she for that matter.

"She asked me not to tell you."

I stared at him because he was obviously going to tell me. Otherwise, he wouldn't have said anything at all.

"She wants the band to sing a song she's writing." I know I visibly relaxed because he chuckled a little. "She played it for me and it's really fucking good. She's not even done with it yet."

I contemplated what to say next. "Are you going to do it?"

"I'm not sure. If she finishes it before our Connecticut show, maybe we could debut it there. If all the guys like it, of course. It's not just up to me."

I looked away and went back to the game. "They will like it... she's amazing."

He went back to packing, but he kept looking up at me. "I

actually had a better idea if you want to hear it. You'll hate it, but I think it might just be what you need to make her see you are meant to be together."

I gave him a confused look. "You want to help me? Why?"

He gave me an annoyed look and threw a pair of jeans at my head. "Are you serious, bro? Of course, I want to help you. You're my best friend, asshole."

I smiled but didn't want this conversation to get too sappy, so I moved on. "Okay, best friend, what's the idea?"

He smirked. "You're going to fucking hate it. It has to do with me teaching you how to play guitar better."

I didn't even have to think about it. I was all in. "If it's for her, I'll do anything."

AUBREY

March 1st

Meeting day is finally here. We are about thirty minutes away from Tennessee, and my parents are about to meet. Technically, I guess Mom and Pops are meeting *again*. I just hope it goes well. I started to get a bit anxious but Mom gave me some water and helped me breathe through it. I've had quite a few anxiety attacks leading up to this trip. Hopefully, they will get better once this meeting is over.

Mom and Dad thought it would be more appropriate if we

stayed at the hotel and rented a car so we didn't disrupt anyone. It was probably better and would be less awkward anyway.

We went down the escalator to grab the car as soon as we landed, and there they were. All three of them were holding big signs for us and had huge smiles on their faces. I felt a bunch of anxiety lift off my shoulders. *This is a great start.*

My dads shook hands, and Mom and Liza hugged for what seemed like forever. Pops and Mom looked at each other for a moment. They finally embraced and cried together, almost in unison. They were both saying "I'm sorry," repeatedly. Then Lincoln came up next to me.

"Hey, beautiful. Let me grab those."

I turned to Lincoln and wrapped him in a massive hug before he could grab my bags. He looked surprised but recovered quickly by picking me up and spinning me around in his arms.

"This is the best hello ever. I missed you too, Songbird," he said as he chuckled. I turned my head towards my mom because I saw her eyebrows go up out of the corner of my eye, so she must have heard him. I never did tell them what really happened.

I looked back at Lincoln. He was still holding onto me. "Uh, Hey, yeah, I guess I missed you too." I blushed and couldn't get any other words out. I was just glad it wasn't awkward. It felt so good to have his arms around me again.

After all the hellos, they grabbed our luggage and helped us outside to the rental car area.

"Head right to our house. We have both rooms set up for you guys to stay with us." Pops said nervously.

My mom looked at him shyly. "Oh no, that won't be necessary, We would never want to impose. We have already booked the hotel for the stay."

Pops gave an embarrassed look as he grabbed Liza's hand. "I know for a fact I overstepped, but I canceled your reservation."

My insides immediately twisted like I was going to hurl up the cookies that I had eaten on the plane.

No, no, no

This can't happen. I was going to have a somewhat easy time this trip being able to just go back to the hotel to get some space from Lincoln. We cannot stay there. Under no circumstances can I let this happen. I looked over at my dad, hoping he was going to insist we stay elsewhere, but Liza added the winning blow.

"We thought it would be nice for all of us to wake up with Aubrey on her birthday since it will be our first." This woman was good.

My mom and dad gave each other a look. Not even two seconds later both of them looked at me.

Mom touched my arm softly. "As long as you are okay with that, sweetie, then I think it is a great idea."

Shit.

I looked around. They were all watching me with hopeful smiles. How the hell could I say no to them now? I tried to speak in my most enthusiastic tone. "Sure, great idea."

As we were loading the car Lincoln leaned in. "It will be okay." He smiled when I looked at him.

"I hope so," I whispered back.

The first few minutes of the ride were quiet but Mom broke the silence as soon as I put the signal on to take the first turn.

"So are you sure you're okay with staying there?"

"Of course, why wouldn't I be?" I was grateful for being the driver at this moment so I had an excuse not to look at her. I could feel her eyes boring into me.

"So you don't want to talk about what happened between you and Lincoln in there?"

"Not particularly," I said through gritted teeth.

My dad chuckled and Mom gave me a smirk but, thankfully, she let it go.

There was an entire spread of food for us when we arrived. It looked like Liza had prepared to be hosting twenty people. I glanced around and saw Lincoln wasn't there anymore, but I also saw a woman I didn't recognize. She stood when we walked in, and her skin went pale. I looked at Pops because the way she was staring was making me increasingly uncomfortable. She looked like she was going to throw up or something.

Liza began to introduce us. "Aubrey, this is Patty, David's wife. She wanted to—"

"You're the girl... the girl in the picture!" Patty choked out, cutting Liza off.

We all looked at each other, and then I realized she was talking to me.

"I'm sorry?" I asked.

She went to a bag she had on the table. It looked like a bunch of photo albums and items that I can only assume belonged to David. She pulled out a picture and handed it to me.

It was me.

It was a picture of me laughing and playing David's, or I guess *my* guitar. It was a candid picture, and I don't think I've ever seen myself look so happy. My head was thrown back in laughter. It looked like a picture from a magazine.

I stared at it. "Where did you get this?"

She looked at me with tears welling in her eyes and put her hand on mine.

"It was David's. I found it in one of his photo albums after he died. I didn't know who you were, but I knew you were important because you had his guitar in your hand. I kept it in there because it obviously meant something; I just didn't know what...until now."

"What...He...He took this? He...He kept this?" I finally managed to get out after stuttering through it.

"I guess so. He wrote the date on the back with a little saying, which is what prompted me to keep it the most."

I turned it over. Sure enough, it was marked with the day I met him. It had chicken scratch writing on the back, "Fate Will Bring You Home." My heart felt like it was going to fall out of my ass.

"I had no idea what it meant, but because you had his guitar in the picture, I knew you meant something to him. He never let anyone touch that thing. He barely even let me touch it." Patty laughed. Her laugh was quiet and small.

I looked at Pops, he was speechless with tears in my eyes. I handed him the picture.

"I've never seen this. How...Why would he have a picture of you? Are you sure you didn't know about it?"

He looked at Patty and me, clearly just as confused as we were.

"August, you know he always said he felt auras, spirits, etc. He felt that she belonged. He knew she was important, so he gave her the guitar and kept this picture in our family album. He knew Auggie. He knew she was family. He knew she would find you."

I looked around, and everyone was in tears. This was the most beautiful moment in my life, and I will remember it forever.

Only one thing could make it better.

Lincoln.

All the excitement finally died down and Patty left for the night. Pops took my mom into Lincoln's place so they could talk just the two of them. They needed to have a bit more in-depth conversation, which I totally understood. It was definitely something that should be more private.

I kept looking into the backyard at Lincoln's cottage. Liza put her hand on my forearm to get my attention.

"He will be home later. He had to head to rehearsal."

I smiled and placed my hand on hers. It was a silent thank you, and she knew it. Seeing my parents talking brought up all kinds of feelings. I was a little overwhelmed but in a good way. I took a moment and brought my bags and guitar up to my room. I excused myself to take a shower, and when I got up there, I froze when I saw Lincoln's t-shirt, the one I had worn the night I left. It was folded on my bed with a note.

Looks better on you. You should keep it.
With love,
Mr. Grumpy Butt

I knew I had the goofiest grin on my face, and I was happy no one else was here to see it. I took a shower and put on the shirt with some pajama shorts. I spent about an hour up there just writing. I was so lost in playing my guitar that I had my eyes closed when I heard a knock at the door.

"Come in."

I smiled really big when I saw it was Lincoln. I put the guitar down and moved to the edge of my bed.

"I was right," he said.

He looked so handsome leaning against the doorframe in his flannel with the arms rolled up a quarter of the way, and dark ripped jeans. He had black paint smeared on his cheek. He looked like a lumberjack without the big burly beard.

"Right about what?"

He nudged his head toward me. "Looks better on you." He gave me a shy grin, and I rolled my eyes but couldn't help that goofy grin coming back to my face.

We talked for a few minutes about what has been happening around here since I left. Nothing spectacular. When he was walking out the door, I couldn't help but ask.

"Will you be at dinner?"

"Of course I will. It's for you... I would do anything for you."

He turned and smiled as he walked down the stairs.

Dinner was great. We went to IHOP, which is my favorite. Weird, I know, but I never even look at the menu anymore. I always get an American cheese omelet with pancakes, strawberry syrup, and a giant glass of chocolate milk. I tried to get fruit instead of pancakes once, and it completely ruined the entire experience.

It was probably a coincidence, but Pops got an omelet too. It was so fun seeing both sides of my family getting along so well. I'm glad we came without everyone else. It was good for my parents to talk and get to know each other. They never had that chance, and now they will.

I overheard their conversation once they returned to the kitchen to bring in Liza and my dad a little bit earlier. There were a lot of stern words given to my Mom and Dad for the fact that they didn't continue looking. There was a lot of crying. It seems to have ended okay because there was no animosity on either side and they were all sitting here getting along. I am sure the conversation isn't completely over, but hopefully, everything stays civil.

I chose to walk home. I missed running around here. Lincoln came along for the walk. I stopped and turned toward him. "You walking too?" He just smiled and kept looking straight ahead. I smiled and started walking again. "Thanks, Lincoln."

"Anytime."

Once we got home, we were about to go our separate ways when he spoke up. "Wanna cut my hair?"

I was surprised by the question. "Now? Um...sure. Come up to my room."

I went into the bathroom and changed out of my jeans into comfy clothes. I set the chair on some towels to save myself from cleaning. I wet his hair and started cutting. I didn't even ask him how he wanted it cut; I also had absolutely no idea what I was doing.

"This is not going to look good." I laughed.

"I will just buzz it if it sucks."

"Really," I paused and looked at him. He just smiled. "Don't buzz it."

He smirked, "Then don't make it suck."

I jokingly pushed his shoulder. "I'll do my best, I promise."

After another moment, he gently clutched my wrist and sincerely stared into my eyes. "Thanks for this."

I nodded my head and pulled my arm away and went on cutting.

When I was done, he checked himself out in my mirror and kissed my cheek.

"It looks great, Songbird. Thanks again."

I smirked at him, knowing he was trying to make me feel like I did a good job...Which I didn't.

"I thought we didn't lie to each other, Lincoln?"

"What?" He looked back at the mirror. "It looks great, no?"

"If you say so," I shrugged.

He stood there momentarily, and I thought he was going to ask to stay, but he just helped me clean up the towels. He opened my door to leave as I was walking into the bathroom but then he turned around.

"Hey, Aubrey?" It sounded like a question, so I looked over at him.

"Yeah?"

"Nothing, I just wanted to look at your beautiful face again." I felt my cheeks flush as he walked out the door without another word.

I couldn't help but lay in bed and smile about how incredible today was. How normal it all felt. Even seeing Lincoln again, it felt like we would really be okay. I felt my eyes drifting closed, and I got a great night's sleep.

CHAPTER THIRTY-EIGHT

Aubrey

I walked outside the following day, my birthday, and Lincoln was leaning on his car waiting to go running.

"Happy birthday, beautiful."

He scooped me up into a big bear hug. His hand grazed my ass, and a tingle went through my body. His touch always does that to me. I slapped his shoulder.

"Put me down, crazy."

My cheeks hurt from smiling. He slowly put me down then he took off running to try to get ahead of me.

After our run, I went upstairs and put the finishing touches on the song so I could show Elijah when he came for my birthday celebration. Lincoln invited him and a few others I grew semi-close to while I was here. Elijah just happened to be on a break for a few days.

About an hour later, I went down to help Liza prepare the house for all the guests. She wouldn't let me do much, but I tried. It seems like this will be a lot bigger than I thought.

Liza and my mom talked about my childhood and some of the crazy things I've gotten myself into. My mom and dad brought all kinds of pictures, which made me super embarrassed, but at the same time, I was so happy that I honestly didn't care.

The house was packed with friendly faces once four o'clock hit. It was good to see some of the people I've met here. Even Miss Mabel was here. Elijah and the rest of the band came by. I got him to sneak away with me to play what I had for him. He loved it and said they would consider it. I just had to send him a demo. He told me that if they chose to use it, they would be able to debut it at the Connecticut show.

He handed me the tickets I asked for. "I gave these to Link to give you, but he never got the chance to, so he gave them back to me, but they are yours if you want them. Do you need more than this?"

"Four is perfect. I'll bring my sister and friends."

"Fuck yes, please bring your sister. Tell her I'll give her a VIP tour of the bus if she wants one." He laughed that big laugh I've come to know.

I slapped him on his shoulder. "You better not corrupt my perfect little sister."

He held up one hand and put the other one down on the sheet music like he was swearing on a bible. "I plead the fifth."

I chuckled and rolled my eyes.

We went downstairs as soon as we were finished and found the party had moved into the backyard. Pops lit the fire pit and gave everyone sticks for marshmallows. Elijah brought his guitar, so he and some friends played some songs. Then he asked me if I wanted to play with him. Of course I did. We played a few songs that we both knew, like *Better Together by Jack Johnson* and *Wonderwall by Oasis*.

Elijah continued to play a little bit longer once I stopped. I was sitting with my mom and she leaned over and gave me a side hug.

"Tennessee looks good on you, ya know."

I smiled at her. "I love it here."

"I can tell... it fits you." She thought for a moment. "Or maybe it's the company. Maybe he is the one that fits you."

She smiled this time, making it more genuine, nodding toward Lincoln.

Lincoln was pretty quiet all day, and he chose not to sit near me outside. I don't think it was on purpose, but he kept giving me a grin here and there, anytime I would catch him staring. I missed that smile. I missed *everything* about him.

Lincoln

God, she's beautiful. I can't stop stealing glances at her. She's like a drug.... and hearing her sing...God, I'm doing my best not to run up and drag her into my house. That hug this morning was everything; I needed to touch her...but now I need to keep my distance. I need to give her the space she asked for, continue to heal, and let her miss me so that when I make the ultimate move, it will actually mean something. Pops and Elijah have been helping me plan for the ultimate romantic gesture to show her I'm all in.

I got up to go inside to her room. I have a few letters I want to give her, but I will put them in her luggage so she will get them when she gets home. I put them in the zipper on the front of her bag. She's mentioned before that she never remembers to check that pocket when she unpacks. For now, I need to love her from a distance.

She was in the kitchen when I made my way back downstairs.

"Hey you."

"Hey. What are you doing inside?" she asked.

"Just needed to warm up a bit."

She looked down at her feet and bit her lip like she wanted to say something else but stopped herself. She looked back at me, and I felt like her eyes were seeing right through me.

"Lincoln. Are you okay?"

I paused for a second. I wasn't sure if I was going to lie or tell her the truth, so I went with a little bit of both.

"I will be. I am talking to someone about my trauma. It's getting better every day, I think."

She looked back down. She almost looked sad at my answer. "Good…Good, I'm glad."

I want to pick her up and kiss her and let her know that it will all be okay, but we aren't there yet. "Are you? Okay, I mean."

She paused for a beat. "Me? Yeah, don't worry about me. I'll be fine. Today's been amazing. I missed it here."

"It missed you too."

I smiled at her, and she smiled back. She knew I was talking about myself missing her, but she didn't comment on it.

"Okay, I'll see you back outside, I guess."

She turned around, and I couldn't help but reach for her hand.

"Aubrey," She turned toward me. "I'm happy I got to see you. I hope you enjoyed today. I know I did."

She leaned up and kissed my cheek. Then she whispered

in my ear. "I had an amazing birthday." She moved away and smiled. "I'm happy I got to see you too."

I couldn't help but smile back. "Good, I just wanted you to know in case we don't get to talk before you leave tomorrow."

"Thanks, but I will make sure I come say goodbye. I can't leave without a hug from my favorite person." She paused for a second but it was short-lived. "Pops gives the best hugs." She laughed and winked before walking out the door.

CHAPTER THIRTY-NINE

Aubrey

It's been a few days since I've been back in Connecticut. I finally unpacked last night and found some of Lincoln's letters wrapped up as a present. It was such a sweet gesture, but the letters were even more beautiful. My favorite was after we made love for the first time. It was sweet and simple but meaningful as hell. I definitely didn't think he had this kind of sweetness in him.

Dear Songbird,

I'm writing this the day after we made love for the first time. It was beautiful. You are beautiful. I loved hearing your sexy sounds and having you in my arms. I hope I get to have you in my arms for the foreseeable future. You are perfect. I hope you know that.

Thank you for being so open with me about your past. Thank you for trusting me. I hope I can prove that I can be the man you deserve.

You just caught me writing this at work and I think you are having some weird feelings and are afraid to tell me. I hope you know you can tell me anything. Like I told you last night in our conversation, I can see this going somewhere. I don't exactly know what makes this situation different or why I suddenly want more than a fling, but I do know that last night was the best day of my life thus far, and I can't wait for the next one.

P.S. I'll keep those panties safe; I promise.

With love,

Mr. Grumpy Butt

This man... I love him. I'm starting to think I made the wrong decision coming back. I can't stop thinking about him. I can't stop loving him. The last trip was strictly platonic, and I couldn't stop my brain from pining for him. He said it was getting better for him. I can't ruin that by telling him I made a mistake. I need to just let him heal.

My attraction for him is only getting more intense. The dream I had on my birthday... hot damn, what that man was doing with his mouth. Good Lord, I woke up sweating. I felt myself getting a little hot and bothered, but then a text from Callie ripped me from those thoughts. We are meeting a few towns over in about an hour at a bridal shop so she can look at dresses. But first, coffee.

As always, I walked into my favorite coffee shop. There was a line, but it was not horrible. So I waited.

"Can I buy you a drink?"

I froze at that voice because I knew who it was before I

even turned around. I swallowed the lump in my throat and turned.

"Max? What are you doing here?" I tried to keep my voice level and unbothered, but I knew I was failing miserably.

"I'm just home seeing my parents. My dad had a heart attack a few days ago, and I took off work to spend time with him so my mom could get a break. I'm just grabbing Mom a coffee before heading to the hospital so she can go home."

My defenses fell, and I placed my hand on his arm. "Wow, Max, I'm so sorry. Is everything okay?"

He smiled. "Other than him bitching about having to eat better, everything's great," he laughed. "You know him."

"I do," I replied. We both broke into laughter.

His laugh was still the same, and it made me smile for a moment.

"So, can I buy you a coffee? We can sit and catch up for a few?" he asked.

I didn't answer, but I think he saw how hesitant I was.

"Just a few minutes, Aubrey. I think we have a few things to discuss, don't you?"

After a few moments, I agreed.

"Why the hell not? Throw in a muffin, and you have yourself a deal."

He smiled and I went to sit down while he ordered. *I can do this.* We were both relatively quiet at first, so I broke the silence. "So, how is everything other than the stuff with your dad?"

He looked a little nervous. "Things are okay. I broke up with Stacey not too long ago because I caught her sleeping with one of my teammates."

I couldn't help the shock that covered my face. "Max, I'm so sorry."

He shook his head and smiled. "No, please don't do that. You do not feel sorry for me. I hurt you and got exactly what I deserved. Karma really got my ass."

I couldn't help but smile a little because he was right, but no one deserves this. "No, you didn't deserve that, Max. No one deserves to feel the way I did. So I'm sorry she hurt you like that."

"I appreciate it, but as I said, I don't deserve your sympathy. I don't even deserve to have this coffee with you." He sipped his coffee and continued. "How are things for you?"

I went on to tell him about the changes in my life over the last few months. I told him about Pops and Liza and even Lincoln. I told him about the turmoil between Lincoln and I.

"Wow, sounds like you have a lot of stuff happening." Then he looked me in the eyes. "It also sounds like he really loves you."

I blushed a little because I didn't expect him to respond that way, and now I don't really know how to respond back. It was weird talking to him like this. We didn't even talk like this when we were together.

I began telling him how I was battling with all the feelings of coming home, and he looked at me kind of funny... surprised almost.

"What is that look for?" I asked.

"Really Aubrey? When I was talking about going to the NHL, you were willing to figure it out and let's be honest, we thought we loved each other, but we were just comfortable. We weren't really in love."

I gave him a surprised look. He held up his hand. "Let me rephrase that. I was in love, which I didn't realize until you finally left me. You on the other hand were not. You just thought you were, but you just wanted to fix me. I was so scared to love you that I fucked it up on purpose. You and him have real love, Aubs."

My eyebrows went up in surprise. "Wow, Max, I um… I don't really know what to say to that."

He looked at me with what looked like pity or maybe concern. "Give him a chance Aubs. It sounds like he royally fucked up and he knows it… it's not his fault I hurt you, and I'm the one who gave you all the insecurities. Don't take that out on one mistake he made. He deserves a chance. You deserve to be happy finally, don't you think?"

I looked down and sipped my coffee. This conversation was getting a little deeper than I was expecting. I spoke without looking at him. "How do you know I haven't been happy?"

When I looked up at him, he smiled at me with a sad smile. "I have my ways." He looked a lot more serious now. "I never stopped worrying about you, and I missed you since the moment you left that day. I knew it was the biggest mistake of my life."

"You didn't try to fix things," I said matter-of-factly.

"You were better than me. You would have taken me back to make me feel better and not think about yourself at all." He smiled again. I'm sure he was trying to break the tension. "I've kept up with my internet stalking skills a bit to check on you."

I laughed and changed the subject and asked about him because I have not kept up with my stalking skills and know nothing about what he's been up to.

"I'm moving to Boston next season to play for the Bruins."

"Max, that's great. That's always been your dream, right?"

He looked surprised. "Yes. I'm flattered that you remember." He looked at his watch. "Crap, I need to get to the hospital to relieve my mom, but I'll see you around, okay?"

"Sure, and please let me know if your mom or dad need anything if you're not here. I loved them so much. I would love to see them when your dad is back home."

"They loved you too, Aubs. More than me, I think. You wouldn't believe the shit I got when we broke up."

"I can imagine." I smiled at him.

He grabbed my hand as we were saying goodbye and gave it a light squeeze.

"Be happy, beautiful girl."

He kissed my cheek and walked out the door. I needed that closure more than I knew.

CHAPTER FORTY

Lincoln

May

It's been about two and a half months since I saw Aubrey. We've messaged a little here and there, but I haven't let her in on my plans yet. I'm hoping no one involved ruins the surprise.

I hoped she would come today, but I haven't heard from her in a few days. I'm guessing she forgot. I'm really trying hard not to think about it because this show needs my focus. It's going to be awesome. These kids have been working their tails off for this production, and today is the last day. It will also be my last as their teacher. I've resigned since I'm going to be doing some traveling soon.

Watching these kids perform makes me realize how much I love what I do and that, when I eventually settle, I want to continue helping young minds find their passion for acting and music. The curtain is about to go up, and I keep scanning the crowd for her, but no luck. I will not give up on her, even if she gives up on me.

I clapped my hands to get everyone's attention backstage. "Break a leg, everyone. Let's make it the best."

The first act went amazingly. I feel like every show is better than the last. These kids impress the hell out of me every time they open their mouths. At intermission, I was in the back, just taking a moment alone. I heard the door to my office open, and there she was. She was standing there with her hair down, in her pretty sundress and flip-flops.

I ran up to her and lifted her off her feet.

"You're here...but I didn't see you in the audience. Why didn't you tell me you were coming? I could have picked you up or something."

"It was supposed to be a surprise, dummy. I asked someone else for help."

I looked back at the door and Pops was standing there smiling. I put her down.

Pops nodded. "I will give you guys some time to talk."

I looked back at her.

"You think I would miss your play Lincoln? I know how hard you have worked on it. Friends show up for each other."

My stomach dropped a little at the thought of her just being my friend.

"Yeah, of course." I tried my best not to show how crappy that made me feel. Hopefully, it worked. "Aubrey, you have to stay for the cast party. The kids would love to see you."

"I planned on it as long as it was okay. I'm flying out early tomorrow, so this is a quick trip thanks to Pops. I told him he didn't have to pay, but I knew I was going to find a way to get here to support you."

"You never have to ask," I told her

She smiled really big. I love that smile.

After the play, the kids presented me with a photo album

of my time as their teacher... some of them I've had for over six years because I first taught at the middle school, then moved into the high school. They mentioned me leaving in their speech, and I saw the surprised look on Aubrey's face, but I can't tell her yet what's going on. It will ruin my master plan, and it's not ready. She seemed to let the wondering look dissipate rather quickly, but now I'm hoping she won't ask me questions.

AUBREY

After the cast party Lincoln invited me to his place to catch up. We talked briefly about Callie and how crazy she was driving me with all the wedding stuff and Brie, who is doing amazing in school. Brie took up painting again after leaving here. Helping with the play showed her how much she missed being creative. She said something about changing her major back to art which made me really happy. I missed the old Brie. It was good to see her genuinely happy again. He was busying himself with straightening up his kitchen, which had some dishes in the sink. I thought it was a bit odd because he never ate in here, let alone cooked.

"You cook now? Or did you have a guest?" I looked at him with a curious smile. I wasn't sure if I even wanted to know the answer. I definitely didn't have the right to ask.

He turned and gave me that grin that made my insides go wild. The butterflies immediately kicked up inside me. "No guests since you unless you count Elijah. I've just been teaching myself to cook simple stuff. Gotta prepare to be on my own."

"Oh right, you're leaving soon. You didn't mention it last time we talked. Are you staying in White Mountain?"

He gave a scared look like he was hiding something.

"I'm not sure yet. Elijah's band needs a summer tour manager. The guy they hired got arrested for drug possession. I'm taking over for the summer, so for now I will live on the road. The tour ends in November, so I may stay on until then or leave at the end of summer. We will see. I honestly have no idea what it entails other than keeping them organized, but we have gotten closer over the past few months. He helped me through some of the hard stuff, so I owe him. When he asked, I delivered. I start next week. I have a substitute covering my last few weeks of classes."

Hearing him talk about moving hurt my heart a little. It made me think back to when I was thinking about him moving for me. If only things had gone down differently. Suppose I hadn't sent that message to him by mistake, or even if he just responded differently.

He turned toward me because I got quiet. I was so deep in thought.

"You okay, Songbird?"

"Oh. Um, yeah, I was just thinking." I smiled to ease his mind. "Are you excited about meeting some groupies? I'm sure that would be fun for you."

His face got somber. *Why the fuck did I just say that?* What is wrong with me? I guess the awkwardness isn't going anywhere now.

He turned back to what he was doing. "No, I haven't even thought about it. That's not me anymore."

I felt like such an ass. "I'm sorry I shouldn't have said—"

He turned and looked at me, cutting me off. "Don't worry about it; I get it."

I was making this more awkward by the second, so I needed to go. "I should go. I have an early flight. I'll see you next time I come down."

I stood up, and he walked over and hugged me. I felt my body react to his touch. He held me a little longer than expected for just being a friendly hug. We stood in each other's embrace, and neither of us was really ready to let go. I felt his lips on top of my head.

"I'm thrilled you came, Songbird. You don't know what it meant to me to have you here. I miss you more than you could possibly understand."

I pulled away just enough to look at him. "I would do anything for you, Lincoln." Then I hugged him again. This hug was quick and final. "I'll see you soon."

He nodded and walked me to the door. I was about ten steps out of his door when he called out to me. "Are you happy?"

I turned and chose to be fully honest for once. "No, but I'll get there."

I turned and walked inside. I heard my phone go off the moment my head hit the pillow.

Mr. Grumpy Butt: I'll see you soon, Songbird.

I couldn't respond. I just hugged my phone and drifted off to sleep.

Lincoln

Today I leave for a tour with the Reckless Riders. I was only a little truthful in telling Aubrey I was touring with them. I am helping out but don't plan on staying on tour. The actual The actual plan is even better, but I couldn't ruin it. It's going to be perfect.

The show she attends will be my last with them, barring any unforeseen complications with their new manager. They do have one, but he's still under contract with someone else until the beginning of July, so they have me until then. I don't mind because it gives me time to relax and look for a place to live. It doesn't feel like home here without her anymore, so it's time for a new home that will hopefully eventually have her in it.

Staying with Mom and Pops in their cottage has saved me a ton of money, so I should be good with money for quite some time, maybe even a year. I essentially had no bills other than my phone and a few other small things, plus the band was paying me way too much to do basically nothing. So I can take my time finding the perfect job.

"You ready, man?"

Hunter, the drummer, was picking me up so I could leave my car for my mom if she needed it. He and I were going to meet everyone else on the bus. Hunter was way too excited to get going. I'm pretty sure he's running from someone or something, but I don't know the guy well enough to judge, so I don't bother asking questions.

"I'll meet you in the car; I just need to say goodbye to Mom and Pops. Give me ten minutes, and I'll be out."

He didn't say anything but gave me a nod like he understood. I walked in and found Mom crying, of course. She's probably the sappiest person I know.

I wrapped her in a giant bear hug. "Mom, stop. I'm not going away forever, just for now, and I'll be back occasionally."

She smiled, or she tried her best to.

"I need you to promise me you will be safe. No being stupid on the road. We will see you at the Connecticut show. We will surprise Aubrey and get to see you both."

Pops smiled at me from the table, both of us knowing what the real surprise would be at that show. My mom kept speaking.

"Lincoln, do you have a plan? Where will you live? Who's going to cook for you? What if you are alone and something happens to you?"

"Momma, relax. If things go as planned, I'll never be alone again, God willing. I have a plan. It just has layers that I haven't quite figured out yet. Pops will fill you in on everything, okay?"

Mom looked at him, worried like she had just now realized we were hiding something. I kissed her head, and then Pops came up and took my mom out of my arms, probably because he knew she wasn't going to let me leave if he didn't. I hugged Pops as well and said my goodbyes.

"Lincoln, you call me if you need anything, you got it? I will get you anything you need to make this happen, son."

"I know, Pops; I love you guys. I'll see you soon."

I got in the car and had an overwhelming feeling of excitement. This is going to be the craziest thing I've ever done in my life, but I need to make it happen.

I took a selfie and sent it to Aubrey.

Me: I'm off to tour. Wish me luck trying to keep these dumbasses in line for the next few months. I hope you're doing well.

Her response came about ten minutes later, and she sent me a selfie back. She was wearing my Reckless shirt and shorts. Her hair was in a bun falling off one side of her head. So, fucking cute.

Songbird: Aw, look at you doing big boy things, lol. I'm proud of you for doing something out of your comfort zone. You're going to do great, and I'm doing good. I hope you are too. Callie and Brie say hey.

I took that picture and saved it as my screensaver. I can't wait to see her and make her mine.

AUBREY

"What are you smiling like a five-year-old with a giant stick of cotton candy at?" Callie inquired.

I looked up at Callie, and I got defensive. "I am not smiling like a five-year-old."

She just stared at me like, "Come on, girl. We both know you were." I looked at Nick, and he just shrugged. I rolled my eyes at her and huffed.

"It was Link, okay? He sent me a pic of himself leaving for tour."

"Oh, we are calling him 'Link' again, are we?" Callie asked.

Only in my head, not to his face, I thought. I ignored her.

A look passed between Nick and Callie, and they were both smiling at each other.

"Did I miss the joke? What are you two looking at each other like that for?"

"Nothing, she's just admiring my beauty," Nick joked.

"Ew! Yeah, right!" Callie exclaimed.

Nick laughed so hard he had tears forming in his eyes.

I let it go, but only because we were busy putting the final touches on some of the costumes for Nick's play next week.

We kept working for about an hour, but Callie was getting increasingly upset and looking at her phone every ten minutes. When I asked what was wrong, she told me Jake should have been here an hour ago. Apparently, his location was off. She said it was because he never set it up when he got a new phone last week, but I thought that was a bit weird. Jake was always the one who insisted they share their locations. It was cute at first because we were in college, so it was nice knowing that her man knew where we were if we ever needed a ride or anything, and he seemed like he was just worried about her.

Lately, though, she said he's been really on top of wanting

to know where she was, like when she would go to a store or somewhere else before coming home; he was asking her why and with whom, and things like that. She brushed it off as pre-wedding jitters, but they had been fighting more than usual. It's hard not to hear when they are right down the hall.

"I'm sure he is fine, Cal. Maybe he just got caught up at a job? He will be here soon."

As soon as I said that, her phone rang with a text.

"Guess he's not coming. He said he went home to change, got tired, and fell asleep. He's sorry he can't make it."

"It's four in the afternoon, Callie. Why would he be sleeping?"

I looked at her, and she knew I was really asking her if she believed him. We have this unspoken way of talking to each other sometimes; it's weird.

She just looked back at me and reassured me it was fine. I looked at Nick, and he just shrugged. Nick and I have had the occasional conversation with Callie about how Jake is a bit dismissive lately. She doesn't seem to mind, and who are we to judge her relationship while neither of us has one?

I changed the subject to something more fun. "Are you guys still coming with me to the concert in a few weeks?"

"God, yes. Free VIP tickets? I wouldn't miss it." Nick said.

"I'll ask Jake," Callie replied.

"Well, let me know if he's coming; I'll need to get more tickets. I only have four. You, Nick, Brie, and me."

She just nodded her head.

I headed for home once we finished. Callie, on the other hand, went to get us some dinner. I saw a woman I didn't recognize getting into a car in front of our house when I pulled up. I walked in and Jake was sitting at the counter eating cereal. His spoon paused on its way up to his mouth, and he looked a little thrown off that I was home.

"Hey," I said curtly.

"Hey, where's Cal?" His voice was a bit shaky.

"The store." I was still standing in the doorway, deciding if I was going to ask or not... I was. "Who was that woman?"

"What woman?" His face lost most of its color.

"Are you being serious right now?" He was looking at me like I was the stupid one. I hitched my thumb and pointed to the door. "The one getting in her car in front of our house."

"I have no idea what you're talking about, Aubrey. I was asleep, and when Callie texted me, I got up, showered, and just came downstairs about five minutes ago."

I paused before talking because he could be telling the truth, but I needed to know for sure.

"So, if I go check my camera I put up I won't see her leaving here through the back door?"

He sat up a little straighter. "We don't have a camera at the backdoor. Only the Ring doorbell out front."

Got him. "So, the correct answer would have been, no, you won't because she wasn't here. And then maybe asking when we got a camera in the back."

His eyes went wide. "Aubrey."

I threw everything I was holding down on the ground. "Are you fucking serious, Jake? You're fucking cheating on her. How could—"

I heard the door open and stopped talking mid-sentence when Callie walked in. "Hey, what's—what's wrong?"

"Do we have a camera in the back?" Jake blurted out.

"Not that I know of... should we?" she asked suspiciously.

Jake looked at me, and I smiled. "You tell her, or I will." And then I left and went to Nick's house because if I didn't leave, I would put my fist through Jake's stupid fucking face.

Nick was just as pissed as me, and it took everything in him not to beat the shit out of Jake, but I sent Callie a text to call me, so we waited. She seemed okay when she showed up at Nick's a few hours later.

"Hey, are you okay? How did it go?" I was expecting her to be broken and distraught, so something didn't happen as I thought.

"Fine; he explained that he was having a client come and pick up paperwork."

My mouth dropped open. I know he is lying to her. I saw the look on his face when he thought I had caught him on camera. "Really, Cal? You believe that he had a client pick up paperwork at our home while he was wearing nothing but a towel, and he had her come through the back door, and you don't see anything wrong with that?"

"No, he said you misunderstood him."

"What is there to misunderstand, Callie? He told me he fell asleep, got up, showered, and came downstairs. Not once did he mention a woman coming over to pick up paperwork. Not until I called him out for cheating, and only because he thought I had a camera in the back. He wasn't going to tell you about her. Why do you think that is?"

She huffed like she was mad at me. "He said he didn't want me to think anything of it, so he had her come in the back door so I wouldn't even have to ask questions."

"And you believe that?" Nick asked.

"I do. I trust him. He would never cheat on me," Callie said confidently.

I had to walk away from her. I might say something I don't mean, and she's too vulnerable right now. I know she doesn't really believe what she is telling me. She can't. She's not this dumb. I couldn't hold my tongue.

I turned back toward her. "I can't fucking believe you are serious, Callie. There is no way you are this stupid."

She didn't say anything, she just stared. I realized that she wasn't going to respond so I left. I didn't know what else to do; I needed to blow off steam. The next thing I knew, I was clicking on Link's number on my phone.

> Me: Hey, can you call me? I need to vent, and I can't call anyone around here because it's not my business to spread, but I need to talk to someone.

My phone rang immediately, and Mr. Grumpy Butt appeared on the screen. I couldn't help but smile.

"Hey, beautiful. What's up?"

CHAPTER FORTY-TWO

Lincoln

June

I can't keep my excitement at bay. It's only two days until I get to see her. Until I make her mine. Today we are in Boston, and the next stop is Hartford, Connecticut. My parents are meeting us at the concert, as are her friends and family. I told them I wanted them all to be there when I told her I was staying. I wasn't sure where or how I would get a job, but when I reached out to Brie, she gave me Nick's number. Nick told me they were looking for a second drama teacher to teach some classes part-time, he said once I interview he could almost guarantee the job on the spot since he was one of my interviewers. It was just a formality.

I can't believe I used to be a little jealous of him and how Aubrey talked about him, but I can genuinely tell that he loves her like a sister and would do anything for her. She needs more people like that.

The only thing that could ruin this plan is if she finds out beforehand and doesn't show or completely turns me down. I'm hoping that doesn't happen. I'm just asking her to give us a shot. It's not like I'm proposing. At least not yet. I want her to give us a shot when we both aren't thinking about how it will work or who's living where. I will make it an easy choice; I will be wherever she is. I know she wants this just as much as I do. Now I have to make it happen.

Here goes nothing.

AUBREY

Concert Day

Link texted that we were welcome to arrive early if we wanted to take advantage of the VIP lounge a little longer, so we made our way to Hartford as soon as everyone was ready.

I saw Elijah first, and he gave me the biggest hug and then shook Brie's hand and then kissed the top of it. Brie blushed a little. She tried to hide it, but I think she's got a bit of a crush. She would never act on it since she is so closed off from guys, but seeing her blush is cute.

I was talking to a few of the guys when I was scooped up from behind, and for a moment I freaked, but then I saw everyone else smiling, so I knew it was Link.

"Songbird! You made it!"

I laughed hysterically when my feet touched the ground again, and I turned and hugged him tightly.

"Of course we made it. I've missed you." My body froze as soon as it came out of my mouth, and I felt a nervous flutter in my lower belly. But he hugged me a little bit tighter.

"I missed you so much. You have no idea."

He kissed the top of my head and I looked up at him, and his eyes met mine.

"I have a little idea. You look good, Link." He smiled, and I turned back around, but he stayed standing behind me with his arm around my neck.

He leaned down to whisper in my ear. "You called me Link again."

My face heated when he winked back at me. He looked away and started chatting with everyone else. It felt good to have him hold me again, even if it was only for a few minutes.

He introduced us to some of the road crew. He and Nick were getting chummy, but that didn't surprise me because they are alike in so many ways. It was weird though, and they were closer than I expected for a first-time conversation.

It was finally show time, so we took our seats, and I could see Link on stage right. His smile was shining super white in the dark area behind the curtain. Their opener was the bomb. He was a country singer who was discovered on social media. I followed him immediately.

Once the opener was done, we had about ten minutes or so until Reckless Riders went on stage, so I went to get a drink in the VIP lounge. When I returned to my seat, I was surprised to see my mom and dad standing with Brie.

I ran up to them and gave them all a hug. I haven't seen

them in over a week because of work. I'm trying my hardest to leave the house with Callie and Jake. I know they will implode soon and I don't want to be there when it happens.

"What are you doing here? I asked.

"We wanted to see the band. Link invited us."

"He did?"

"He invited us too," I heard Liza's voice from behind me.

"Oh my God! Hey!"

We all hugged, and Reckless Riders started their first song before I could even ask what was happening. I kept looking behind the stage but didn't see Link anymore. He was probably dealing with band stuff, I'm sure.

I was getting nervous because Elijah told me he would be debuting the song I wrote. Then it clicked. Link invited everyone to hear my song. That man is something else.

I finally saw Link waiting in the wings again and he blew me a kiss. My cheeks instantly heated, and I felt flutters erupt in my stomach. The feeling caught me a little off guard. I knew I was still a little nervous around him, and I fucking miss him like crazy, but that feeling... I want that again.

Elijah got on the microphone and asked me to come up on stage. I was mortified. I was doing everything I could not to go up there, but my oh-so-supportive and loving family practically dragged me up there.

I walked up there with my hands covering my face, then he asked me to sit on the stool. He told everyone a little about me.

"Everyone make sure to have those cameras out to catch this new song that isn't even released yet. This song is called Right Person, Wrong Time."

The applause began to die down when I heard someone start playing it on an acoustic guitar. It was supposed to be an entire band arrangement, so I was a bit confused. I started looking around, then I saw him. Link was playing my song... the one I wrote about him. I looked at Elijah.

"Everyone, please welcome my best friend, Lincoln Marx. He will be performing this amazing song for you all today."

Elijah looked over at me and smirked. I looked out at my family and friends but could barely see them through the tears that were forming. I thought I was the one surprising Link tonight but he was the one who surprised me. He walked up next to me, never taking his eyes off me.

"Hey Songbird," he said with a smile.

I was sobbing uncontrollably. It felt like I was in a dream. My mind was racing. He began singing my song...*our song*. He told me he wasn't any good at singing or playing but his confidence is saying otherwise. His voice was sultry and smooth.

He continued to stare into my eyes and I felt my heart swelling with every note he played. After he finished playing I stood up trying to reach for him. Instead of letting me, he held me at arm's length and started speaking to the crowd.

"If I could just have everyone's attention. I'm going to hijack this concert for a moment. I hope everyone doesn't mind."

A string of applause and other cheers erupted. Just as it began to dissipate, he turned to me and pulled out a letter.

"Aubrey, I promised I would write you letters so we would always be connected in some way. I thought what I had to share today should be written in a letter and we could keep it forever." Then he took a breath and began to read.

"A little less than six months ago, you walked into my life like a tornado and changed everything I thought I knew about myself. You took over my thoughts. You took over my life, and most of all, you took over my heart. You showed me what love was. You showed me how it felt to not only love someone but have that same kind of love reciprocated."

I didn't think I could sob more than I already was, but here I am, barely breathing.

"We tried to make it work, but I failed you rather quickly. I didn't listen to my heart, and I let you get away because of my stupid ego. I wasn't ready to talk about the sacrifices or I should say changes–because nothing is a sacrifice when it comes to you. I wasn't ready to talk about what this relationship becoming something more would take. I pushed you away before you could leave me, and I was stupid."

He paused and took a breath.

"I got the help I needed, and I don't need any more time to figure this out. I don't need to give this any more time to blow over. You are my best friend."

Elijah gasped jokingly, like he was offended, and the whole place started laughing, but Link continued.

"I know what I want, and what I want is you. I made all the changes necessary to make this work. I am ready to be the man you deserve now and forever. I have spent the last few months closing all the loose ends in Tennessee so I can be all in and be wherever you are. Now we can both live here and visit Tennessee together."

He pulled me closer and put his hand on my cheek while he ran his thumb across my bottom lip.

"Songbird, I'm yours forever. I am moving here and getting a job in Connecticut, so we don't need to worry about distance. Nick is letting me stay with him until I find somewhere to live. I honestly haven't looked much because I'm waiting to find somewhere with you. I never want to be without you."

My heart was blowing up. I can't believe this man is mine.

"I know what it's like to breathe your air. I know what it's like to kiss those lips, and I know what it feels like to wake up next to you and what it feels like looking into your beautiful eyes. It feels like home. Sometimes home isn't the four walls where you live. Sometimes it is the two eyes you look into and the heartbeat that fuels your soul. You are my home, baby."

He paused again to clear his throat. His eyes were shining with unshed tears.

"I love you, Aubrey Lynn Miller. If you will have me, I'm yours. Now, forever, and always."

The entire venue was quiet.

I took a breath so I could calm down. I put my hands into his and looked him right in his eyes.

"Lincoln Matthew Marx. I cannot wait to love you forever, no matter where we are. I am yours, and you are mine."

The crowd erupted into applause and awe. There were all kinds of whistling and hollering. I jumped into his arms for a kiss, and it felt like fireworks, it was just like the first time all over again.

The band started playing again, which was our sign to move out of the way. Once we finally walked off stage, he took me to the green room. I turned to him the moment the door shut.

"How...How did you get everyone to keep this from me?"

He smirked. "They all knew how important this was. Not only to me but to you."

I walked up to him and kissed him again. I looked up at him in disbelief. "You practiced the guitar... you learned how to play the song... I can't believe—" More tears started to fall, so I looked down because I couldn't even get the rest of my words out.

He lifted my chin to look me in the eyes.

"I'll do anything and everything for the rest of my life to ensure you know how much I love you. I love you so much, Songbird."

I put my arms around his neck. "I don't know how a proposal will ever top this."

He chuckled. I leaned in to kiss him. "I love you more, Grumpy Butt."

EPILOGUE

Six Months Later

December

It's been almost a year since I learned about Pops, and my life changed forever. Link and I visited them for a long weekend once so far. We are closer than ever, despite being so far apart.

It's been amazing living with Link. We found a place just for us rather quickly. As much as I love Callie, and will always be there for her, I couldn't handle her Jake drama. Sadly though, they broke up and moved out soon after I did, so it was the right move.

Link and I found the most perfect three-bedroom house just a few towns away from my parents, Callie, and Nick. We made one of the rooms into a music room. I now run my own business teaching music, and he got a job at the local high school. He is the new drama teacher there. He was planning on working with Nick part-time, but when this full-time job opened up, he had to take it.

We still run together all the time, although getting out of bed is a bit harder now because I much prefer morning sex to running. One thing that hasn't changed is that he still writes me letters all the time. He leaves them on my pillow every week. He says that the letters will never get boring, and so far, he's right.

Everyone is here. Mom and Dad, of course. Pops and Liza are staying until the New Year, so we have some extra time to spend with them. They are staying in my old room at my parents' house. The four of them are like best friends. It's the cutest thing ever. I think they are going on a cruise together or something next year.

Brielle is home from college. Nick and Callie are here of course. They have something weird going on between them and haven't shared exactly what. Callie's mom is here. She is being super helpful with the food as always. We even invited Elijah and the band since the band's last show of the year was just a few days ago in Philly. He was going to be alone on Christmas, and we couldn't have that.

I was standing in the kitchen doing a few things when I heard Link's sexy ass voice.

"Need any help, Songbird?" He kissed right below my ear in my favorite spot and hugged me around the waist from behind. His hands scaled up my body trying to feel me up like he always does.

I hummed from his warmth. "No, baby." I turned in his arms so we were facing each other "As good as you are at most things, you suck at cooking, and I don't want to poison our guests." He pulled me in and tickled my side as he pinched my butt.

"Are you talking shit, Songbird?" Then he kissed me and

whispered on my lips, "If you're talking shit, I'm going to have to punish you later."

I leaned into him and whispered back. "I can't wait." I kissed his nose and pushed him away followed by a wink. "Now go entertain everyone so I can finish."

He whined. "But they like you better."

"Everyone in there loves you, so hush it and suck it up." I laughed as he walked out.

After dinner, we moved to the living room to give our Secret Santa gifts. I got Link a watch because I broke his when I knocked it off the nightstand in the middle of one of our sexcapades. He told me not to worry about it but I felt absolutely horrible since it was his favorite. He said I could break anything I wanted as long as I always screamed like that when he made me cum.

Callie was leaning against the counter while I was cleaning up some dishes after almost everyone left. She was looking into the living room, and I could tell her head was spinning. She has gone through a lot lately, and I think she's still processing everything. Callie and Nick are acting weird, but I am trying not to pry. They have been getting along amazingly since he helped her after her breakup with Jake. There has even been a new development in their relationship.

They haven't said anything was wrong, but they are acting like strangers today.

I put the dishrag down and leaned in beside her. I nudged her shoulder to get her to look at me. "You gonna tell me what's up willingly, or are you going to make me pull it out of you?"

"What? What do you mean?" She looked genuinely confused.

I got quieter so no one else would hear us. "Cal, you look

sad. And you look especially sad while looking at Nick. What happened? You guys barely spoke today. The last time I saw you guys, you were announcing your relationship to people, the way you are acting today was a complete one-eighty."

"I'm not sad, Aubs; I just wish things were a bit different. We are going through some stuff and I don't know if it will ever get better."

I know the answer already, but I'm going to ask anyway. "Wanna talk about it?"

She turned and smiled at me. "Not today, no." Then she leaned closer and whispered. "I am so happy for you, Aubrey. If anyone deserves this amazing life, it's you, babe. You guys are so happy and put together, all in such a short amount of time."

I hugged her. "We are the furthest thing from put together," we both laughed loudly, attracting the attention of the boys in the living room. "I love you, Cal. It will all work out. You can tell me anything. Never forget that, okay."

"I hope so. Now let's get this cleaned up."

Callie and Nick left about an hour later. Link didn't even wait for them to pull out of the driveway before he bent me over the back of the couch and fucked me senseless. I went into the shower to clean up before bed and we had the best shower sex I think we've ever had.

After getting into bed I flipped on the TV in order to distract myself from the urge to jump his bones again because he said he had another present for me. I swear to God, if this man proposes in this bed with me looking like a sex addict with my hair all crazy, I will marry him and then kill his ass for not letting me get cute engagement photos.

When he walked in he hit the power button on the TV and smiled.

"Hey, I was watching that."

I was kidding, but he knows that. He looked at me with absolute desire in his eyes and started teasing me.

"It's time for your punishment that I spoke of earlier."

I shook my finger at him. "Oh no, you don't, Mr. Marx. You already got your dick wet twice tonight." I put my feet up to block him from coming any closer. "You have a gift to give me. Open first, then more fun."

He stopped trying to tickle and grope me. "We can wait."

He began to pull away to get comfortable, so I pulled him back towards me. He is a big guy and I am definitely not strong enough to pull him anywhere, but he let me anyway. "Oh no you don't mister."

He laughed as he grabbed a letter and handed it to me.

I opened it like an excited little girl.

> Dear Songbird,
> You are the most beautiful human I have ever met. Not just on the outside but on the inside too. The amount of love you have for the people around you is something I've never seen before in my life. I thank you for your willingness to love me. I hope you know you make me a better man just by breathing my air. I would still be lost and lonely if fate hadn't made our paths cross.

I know you have spent a lot of your life feeling lost and not knowing why. I feel like that is just one more thing we have in common. Two lost souls who were destined to find each other. I know you missed out on so much time with Pops, and you even missed out on really knowing who you were and struggled with your identity in this world. I want to make sure you always know who you are and where you come from.

P.S. Don't freak out. I'm not proposing. I know you would kill me if we didn't get pictures.

With Love,

Mr. Grumpy Butt.

I looked up at him with tears in my eyes. I kissed him deeply. "I love you." I looked back at the letter. "I love this note, but what does it mean?"

I laughed because I was a little confused. He smiled. I saw that his eyes were glossy too. He reached into his nightstand and pulled out another piece of paper.

"Another one?"

He nodded.

I opened it hesitantly. I was reading through it, still very confused. It looked like legal paperwork. Then I saw it. At the very bottom…

New Legal Name- Lincoln Matthew Foster

My breath caught in my throat. I was struggling to

swallow the lump that had formed. My eyes failed to hold in my tears, and they started flowing.

"They adopted you?" I choked out.

"No."

Okay, now I was really confused. "What? Then why did you change your name?"

He picked me up and put me onto his lap so I was straddling him.

"Songbird, you have always been a Foster. Now you always will be."

"What—" I was struggling to talk. "I thought you weren't proposing."

"Not yet, but when I do you will take my name and you will have the name you were always meant to have." He pulled me closer and started kissing me. "Fate brought you home baby. Now we will both have the name we were supposed to have and we will both have our forever home with each other."

I couldn't help the emotions pouring out of me. I can't believe this man is mine. I wanted to go tell everyone how fucking sweet my man is but since it was almost midnight, he made me promise to wait until the morning.

We settled into bed, and I was lying on his chest tracing the V peeking out of his pants, humming our song. He was mindlessly rubbing a circle on my lower back. It was turning me on, but I didn't want to ruin the perfect moment. Then I saw his erection growing and knew he was just as turned on as I was.

"What are you thinking, Mr. Foster?" I asked as I looked up and kissed him.

"I can't wait to surprise you with the perfect engagement." He pulled me on top of him and started to grind into me.

Intense pleasure ran down my spine as my heart swelled with excitement. I can't wait to be his wife. I kissed his lips softly as he flipped himself on top of me. He whispered against my lips. "I also can't wait for you to have my babies."

I chuckled as he pulled my thong down my legs. He spread the wetness that had formed between my legs and pressed his thumb to my clit. I moaned.

I managed to get out a few words before he slid himself inside me for the third time tonight.

"One thing at a time, baby. One thing at a time."

Right Person, Wrong Time

We met at a time when I was lost
You showed me love, no matter the cost
We had a chemistry that was undeniable
But the timing was never on our side; it was unreliable

You are my right person at the wrong time
Our love was a victim of circumstance; it's a crime
We had something special, but it couldn't be
Right person, wrong time, it's our destiny

We tried to make it work, but it was tough
We were both in different places; it was rough
Our hearts were willing, but the timing was wrong
We couldn't fight fate; it was too strong

Right person, wrong time
Our love was a victim of circumstance; it's a crime
We had something special, but it couldn't be

Right person, wrong time, it's our destiny

Maybe in another life, we'll find each other again
When the timing is right, we'll make it to the end
For now, we have to let go and move on
With memories of what could've been and what's gone

Right person, wrong time
Our love was a victim of circumstance; it's a crime
We had something special, but it couldn't be
Right person, wrong time, it's our destiny

Right person, wrong time, it's bittersweet
Our love was real, but we couldn't compete
We'll always have the memories, and that's okay
Right person, wrong time, but we'll find our way.

Acknowledgments

Dave, thank you for being my rock during this process. Thank you for taking on the brunt of parenting when needed while also working full-time. You will never know how much I appreciate you.

Cooper and Carson, I love you more than the air I breathe. Thank you for letting Mommy chase her dreams and find herself again. I would give my identity up one hundred times over for you both, but I am very happy to find it again. You are the best kids a girl could ask for.

I want to thank my parents for always instilling in my sister and me that we can do anything we set our minds to. I love you both so much.

To my Alpha and Beta readers who helped this book become what it is.

Jahiara, thank you for being my sounding board. Thank you for never letting me give up on myself. Thank you for enriching not only my book but also my life in more ways than one. You are the best friend someone could ask for. Your edits helped make this book what it is today.

Jenn (AKA Bean), I love you so much. I am so grateful to have had you cheering me on and helping me edit this book. It couldn't have come to fruition without you.

Angel, you are a godsend. I am so blessed that TikTok brought you into my life. I can't wait to see where our friendship takes us. Thank you for being my book recommendation library.

Lora, thank you for being the friend I needed at this point in my life. I appreciate you so much for helping me make this book what it is. I love you, and I am blessed to have met you.

Jessica, Thank you for being my A1Day1, sitting with me night after night through my writing process, and helping me stay calm through all my "I don't know how to do this" moments.

Bec, Ris, and Alex, you ladies helped me at the most crucial time and helped me make this book even better. I love you ladies so much. I am so blessed to have met you.

Arthur Avalos, I did it boo, but not without your help. I wouldn't have been able to get through this without you and everything you did for me. Going on this writing journey with you has been nothing but amazing. I cannot wait for you to publish your book *Something Happened* so I can brag about my bestie to everyone.

To my ARC Team. Thank you for taking the chance on me and sharing your honest reviews. No matter what they are, they are helping me become a better writer. I can't wait for you to see what is coming next.

To my amazing editor Emarie...I AM OBSESSED WITH YOU. Thank you so much for helping me navigate this book. Thank you for helping me become a better writer. I don't know what I would do without you.

A massive thank you to Miss DJ Krimmer for saving me at the last minute and helping me bring my formatting to life. I don't know where I would be without you. I am so blessed to have found you and your *Hel's Ink* series. (If you haven't read DJ's books, you are missing out).

To my cover designer, Kristin, Thank you so much for this

beautiful cover. You made magic happen with the mess of ideas in my brain.

Thank you to every family member, friend, and stranger who has supported me throughout this journey. Especially my TikTok family. I couldn't have done it without the help of all of you cheering me on every day while I wrote. Special shoutout to the Bookies and Besties.

To my readers, thank you for taking a chance on this first-time author. I hope you all enjoyed Aubrey and Lincoln's story. I hope you stick around to see where Callie, Nick, Brielle, and Elijah's lives go.

About the Author

Danielle Lynn is a wife to her amazing husband David whom she met at the tender age of eighteen and they have been together ever since. She is a mother to two amazing boys, Cooper and Carson. She spends most of her days happily consumed by those two titles, and that is actually where this book came from. She gave up her career in data entry to take care of those perfect boys (willingly and happily of course) but lost who she was in the process. She was never a reader or writer until she needed something to help with her post-partum depression and anxiety. She found books and writing. She currently resides in Connecticut with everything and everyone she loves around her. She can always be found listening to music or reading. Fate Will Bring You Home is her debut novel. She can't wait to continue writing for you all.

Where to follow Danielle for updates on future projects.